WAR FOR IMMORTALITY

Also by Philip S Davies:

The *Destiny's Rebel* Trilogy:

Destiny's Rebel (2015)

Destiny's Revenge (2017)

Destiny's Ruin (2018)

The *Immortality* Series:

Cave of Immortality (2023)

War for Immortality

Book Two in the Immortality Series

Philip S. Davies

Dedicated to the amazing young people in the schools
where I am their Volunteer Resident Author:
North Oxfordshire Academy,
The Warriner School,
Wykham Park Academy,
Banbury and Bicester College.

Map of Albany Valley

Map of The Plains

CHAPTER ONE

Why did she agree to this?

Roza grumbled to herself as she trudged down the dusty path from the plateau towards town.

Because you can help people, she answered herself at once. You are Rozabella the Warlock now, and you have an incredible gift that can change people's lives. The people of Albany – and in fact the citizens of the whole Sapien Empire – are clamouring for as much of your gift as you can give.

Roza sighed. It was right. However much she wanted to hide in her cave on the plateau and learn all she could about magic, it was selfish to keep her unique ability to herself.

The power to Rejuvenate, to make people physically younger. It sounded simple and straight-forward, and yet it had already transformed her life beyond recognition and saved Albany valley from destruction. How long was it since she'd negotiated with the Dragon Emperor to cancel three centuries of Albany's debts in return for making him younger? A few weeks? It felt like months ago.

And so, she'd announced her Rejuvenate gift to the world. Instead of keeping it private and quiet until ready to deal with its consequences, her ability could hardly be less secret.

No doubt the news of her power had spread with lightning speed, and soon the Empire's people on the Plains would join the queue for her life-prolonging touch. Come along, everyone, she thought grimly to herself, come along, and get your practical immortality here. It was all too much for everyone to expect of a plain, seventeen-year-old girl from an ordinary town.

Roza reached the bottom of the route down from the plateau, where the dry rock and dust gave way to a green and bushy hillside with a beaten earth path, and turned right along the farm track towards town.

To manage the throngs wanting her rejuvenation, she'd agreed with the Town Committee to spend alternate days in the marketplace. In between, she could stay up on her beautiful plateau, undisturbed by visitors, and teach herself magic. But today was a marketplace day. Maybe today would be quiet, civilised, organised and calm, she mused.

No chance.

As her farm track approached the warlock gate through the south side of Albany's stockade, she saw the burgeoning crowds beyond. The harassed town guards were struggling to restrain the masses from forcing their way through the barricade across the road.

Roza drew a deep breath as she stepped towards the gate. The hubbub from the waiting people rose as those in front saw her, cried out, and passed their excitement back through the ranks behind.

Only one factor redeemed the scene for Roza. A boy stood outside the gate to meet her.

Jorxy.

Her best friend. Her childhood playmate from the town's schoolroom. Her comrade-in-arms during the hours and years of throwing stones into the town's stinking rubbish ditch. He wasn't anything to look at: skinny, tattered clothes, messy red-brown hair, and a lop-sided, if not ugly, face. But never mind about his face. He was a friend, and therefore what Roza needed the most.

"I'm not late, am I?" she asked him.

Jorxy grinned. "It don't matter what time you get here, there's always folk waiting. I reckon as warlock you get to set your own time for everything anyway."

"Too right. Make them wait for me, eh?"

"Definitely." He dropped his voice. "But tread careful with our Rufus. He's not in his best frame of mind. Been spitting teeth about needing to guard your warlock gate, he has."

Roza nodded. Jorxy's older brother Rufus was one of those charged with guarding this gate to prevent disturbance of her studies on the plateau. So, keeping on the right side of the town guards here was a worthwhile thing to do.

Before passing through the gate, therefore, she stepped across to where the guards stood ready to admit her. "Guys," she called. "I'm sorry for the hassle of guarding my gate. You're doing a brilliant job and I'm very grateful. If there's ever any magic I can do for you in return, just let me know." She beamed at them with what she hoped looked a genuine, winning smile.

Rufus turned to face her. He was black-haired and beefy, the opposite in build from his younger brother. Roza was glad Jorxy had warned her about the discontent and challenge in his eyes.

"Yeah, Miss Warlock. Since you mention it, there is something magical you can do for us. How about you multiply our rations?"

The other guards grinned at this, but Roza frowned. "Hmm, I don't know how to do that yet. It would be an enlarging or multiplying spell on foodstuff. That would be incredibly useful, so leave this with me, and I'll look up how to do it. I promise that once I've figured it out, you guys will be the first to benefit. Deal?"

"You're on, Miss Roza," Rufus replied, and the guards slapped each other's backs at the prospect of extra rations. He turned to face the crowds beyond the gate. "Make way now," he bellowed. "Clear a path, or our precious warlock won't even get into town."

His voice held enough menace for the throngs to part, but only reluctantly. As usual, Jorxy led the way before her, swinging his stick at anyone who threatened to jostle her. Even so, hands reached out towards her, hoping to catch even a little of her magic from a brush of her clothing. Her stomach always clenched with how demanding and stifling this felt. She'd learned to keep her eyes on her scuffed leather boots as she went, to avoid being overwhelmed by everyone watching her.

Jorxy swung his stick, rapping the wrists and forearms of those who stretched too close to her, so those lining the way to the marketplace edged backwards.

The market square was packed. But Roza noticed one small thing to be relieved about. For the first time a tent had been erected for her. Today, instead of being in the sun all day, she could work in the shade and administer her magic to her visitors privately.

Another thing impressed her as she neared the tent. The town guards had marshalled the waiting crowds into a queue, an orderly line that snaked back and forth following the lines of the flagstones. With a wry smile, Roza conceded she should have expected this. The Captain of the Guards couldn't abide a lack of order or control, such as the disorderly rabble and crush on her previous visits to town. Trust him to sort this out, and she made a mental note to thank him.

She reached the tent, Jorxy lifted the flap for her, and she went in to sit on a plain wooden stool inside. The tent wasn't large, but tall enough to stand up and walk around in. She tied up her light brown hair, rolled up the sleeves of her tunic, and got to work.

Her first visitors were her usual sort of customers. Some with an aging body part that didn't work properly, such as a deaf ear, a curved spine, or crippled joints. Roza knew how to treat them now, reaching for her spark of magic deep within her belly or gut and fanning it into flame. Then letting that power flow out through her fingers into whatever needed rejuvenating: the ear, spine, or joints.

Others were the elderly, wanting to turn back the years of their lives and enjoy a few more decades. These took more energy from Roza, administering her transforming power to their whole body, but her supply of magic seemed inexhaustible, so she didn't mind. In fact, the more she used her magic, the stronger it seemed to become.

All her customers were inexpressibly grateful. They marvelled in wonder at what Roza had done, restoring their youth, strength and vigour, transformations that no one had believed possible.

But there were always one or two visitors Roza had to disappoint. These came in with something missing – an eye or a finger – hoping their warlock could regrow it for them. She explained that her power was to Rejuvenate, making people and body parts younger, not restoring something that wasn't there. These people left her tent crushed with despair after their hopes had been raised, and Roza could only ache in her heart for them.

Each time this happened she resolved to manage it better. Someone should go along the queue and ask people what they wanted rejuvenating. Those she couldn't help could be sent away without further waiting or needing the explanation. They would still be heart-broken, but the process for the others would be quicker and more efficient.

Then there was the question of money. As a poor boy, Jorxy couldn't resist the prospect of a source of fabulous income and thought they should charge everyone for the benefits she could give them.

Roza countered that those who needed her help the most were often the least able to pay – the elderly poor. Was her gift for the benefit of the rich alone? No, she refused to operate that way, and decided her power would be freely available for everyone, irrespective of their wealth.

Jorxy called her impossibly idealistic and naive. Her rejuvenation benefits were so incredible – extra decades of life, renewed youth, health, and strength – that many would give away their entire fortunes for it.

Exactly, Roza responded. The rewards of rejuvenation were so immeasurable that no one could put a figure on how valuable they were. Her power was literally priceless.

But the rich should definitely contribute towards her

upkeep and costs, Jorxy argued back. And who would assess who was rich or not, Roza demanded? She refused to judge anyone's financial affairs.

In the end, they compromised that her rejuvenation would be offered for free, but those willing and able to give a donation could do so. Her donations bag lay in the corner of her tent, and she pointedly didn't watch whether, or how much, her customers put in. But each evening, Jorxy's eyes popped at all the coins, gems, and jewellery they carried back up to their plateau and cave. Roza felt vindicated about being generous with her gift, since the consciences of her customers prompted them to respond as lavishly as they could. Maybe human nature had a streak of goodness in it after all.

An elderly couple sat on the stools in Roza's tent now, and she began to rejuvenate the woman, when shouting from outside disturbed her. The town square always had calls and cries – greetings, vendors advertising their wares, haggling over prices, occasional arguments – but today's shouts were angry. On previous days, people had pushed into the queue, elbowed others aside and fought to see her first, but the town guards were meant to deal with that. Roza tried to ignore it and concentrate on helping the old woman before her.

But it was no good. The shouts got nearer, louder, and angrier. Roza opened her eyes as the couple before her became increasingly frightened and agitated. Her flow of rejuvenation magic dwindled and stopped, because it sounded like a fight was going on right outside her tent, with the voices of Jorxy and the guards joining in the uproar.

The tent flap was thrown back, and a muscular man barged in. The elderly couple stumbled to their feet, but Roza was determined to remain seated. The newcomer was tall, heavily built, wearing armour, and holding a sword. Two armed henchmen followed him into the tent, one of them holding Jorxy in a neck lock. Behind them, more of the man's retinue were keeping the town guards at bay.

"Get out," the newcomer barked at the elderly couple, and they scurried to obey.

"Stay where you are," Roza countermanded, and the couple halted. "I haven't rejuvenated you yet, and I object to being disturbed in the middle of it."

The man waved his sword at her. "You can object all you like, Miss Warlock," he sneered, "but now I'm first in the queue and I don't like waiting."

The elderly couple were too terrified to stay and hurried out past the man's henchmen. Roza couldn't blame them and would have vacated the tent herself if she reasonably could. But she had to stay and face this man, however much she shook inside. She stood up at last, in a measured and controlled way, glad she was tall enough to look this intruder straight in the eye.

"Who are you to barge your way in here and disrupt my important work?" She hoped he couldn't hear the tremble in her voice.

"Wicksteed is my name," he replied, "and I'm Thain of Heismith Castle in the mountains to the south. I heard tales of your supposedly miraculous powers and thought I'd come and obtain some of my former youthful vigour."

Roza looked him up and down. "You're only middle-aged. The others outside deserve my help more than you do."

"More deserving?" he scoffed, fingering the edge of his sword. "It's not about who deserves what, but who has the power to take what they want."

Jorxy made a bid to escape his captor, but it earned him a punch and a kick from a henchman.

Roza's fury burned. "Stop it," she shouted. "Don't you know who I am? That I have magical power to use against you? No one forces me to do anything, and it will be the worse for anyone who tries it."

She immediately realised how empty her threats were.

She was a warlock with only one spell – Rejuvenate – and had little idea about any other magic. She knew no spells to defend herself or avoid unwanted advances, an omission she resolved to rectify as soon as she returned to her plateau.

Unfortunately, Wicksteed chose to call her bluff. "Go on, then," he taunted. "Let's see some of your magic, Missy Warlock. Then I might believe you can actually make me younger."

Roza was thinking fast. If she couldn't use magic against him, what options did she have? The Captain of the Guards could be marshalling his forces to restore order in the marketplace. They might be on their way. If so, she could play for time, keeping this Wicksteed man talking until they got here.

She made a show of rolling her eyes at him, folding her arms and starting a slow pacing back and forth across the tent. "Suppose I agree to rejuvenate you," she mused. "You'll have heard that I expect donations from those who benefit from my priceless gift of restored youth. So, what will you give me, because a Thain of a castle can afford to be generous."

Wicksteed laughed. "A generous gift? You must be joking. I'm not giving you anything until I see proof you can do it."

"In which case, no, I won't do it. Get out of my tent and make way for those who believe in my powers."

Wicksteed stepped closer until they were almost nose to nose. Roza forced herself not to flinch or quail in the slightest. "Be careful, little girl," he murmured. "I can make it my business to find out how much pain you can endure." He glanced sideways, towards Jorxy's red and choking face. "Or maybe you don't mind pain, so you could watch your ugly friend here suffer instead. How much pain can he take, do you think?"

Roza raised her eyebrows at him, as though daring him to try it. But help hadn't arrived, and she needed to keep him talking. What else could she ask? Or make it look as though he'd beaten her?

She unfolded her arms, relaxed her stance, and resumed pacing the tent. "So, Thain Wicksteed from a castle in the south, how old are you now? What age would you like to be? How many years would you like to lose?"

He also stepped back, looking delighted that he'd cowed this warlock girl into submission.

That was when they all heard the sound of running feet.

CHAPTER TWO

Roza was sure to hold Thain Wicksteed's gaze as she smiled and watched his triumph turn to fury. She'd tricked him into talking until help came for her, and he knew it.

"Lower your weapons," came the command from outside the tent in the unmistakeable tones of the Captain of the Guard. "The tent is surrounded, and we have archers trained on you. Come out slowly if you want to live."

Roza couldn't stop herself from raising her eyebrows at the troublesome Thain of Heismith Castle … but thought it better to say nothing.

Wicksteed took a menacing step towards her and hissed, "This is not the last you will see of me, Missy Warlock of Albany."

Roza kept her smile in place but didn't trust herself to reply in case her voice shook with her mingled fear and relief.

"Come on, boys," Wicksteed raised his voice. "We're wasting our time here. This warlock girl hasn't got magical powers at all. Let's go home." He sheathed his sword and swept out of the tent. His henchmen released Jorxy and followed their master out.

Roza rushed to where Jorxy had collapsed onto the ground, gasping for breath. She knelt beside him and helped him to sit up as he massaged his neck and heaved the air into his lungs. "I'm sorry you ended up on the wrong side of Thain Wicksteed and his brutes," she said.

Jorxy nodded and gasped, "I'd heard of him … but not met him before."

She decided he needed cheering up and knew what would do it. "Well, you've earned today's pay as my assistant and bodyguard. You get first pick of anything from today's donations."

The boy's face lit up and he scrambled to his feet, all discomfort forgotten. "Really? Can I look in your bag for what you've got so far?"

Roza wagged a finger at him. "Patience, my friend. There isn't much yet, but there's plenty of time for further earnings if we feel up to carrying on today."

"Yep, I'm up for it," Jorxy declared and bounded back to the tent flap.

The Captain of the Guard was standing outside the tent restoring order to the marketplace queue. Thain Wicksteed's arrival and barging through the lines had thrown everything into chaos, and now arguments had broken out over who had been where before the interruption.

"Warlock Rozabella," the Captain said, frowning. "I apologise that you had to endure that intrusion. It seems we have sufficient guards to marshal a queue but not to resist an armed gang. I shall see what can be done, both here and at the town's east gate, to prevent any further disturbances."

Roza laid a reassuring hand on the Captain's arm. "We may not be able to stop those bent on causing trouble, but I'm grateful for your efforts to maintain order and keep me safe. This morning has taught me one good thing: that I should learn to defend myself with my magic. But I fear such attempts to reach me by force or exploit my powers will only continue or get worse."

The Captain grunted. "In that case, I'll talk to the Reeve, and the Town Committee should discuss extra security."

"I leave that with you. And thank you for the tent, and for organising the crowds into a proper line."

The Captain smiled, then marched away. Roza turned back to Jorxy. "Now, I want a minute to refocus myself, then send in that elderly couple I was helping before Wicksteed barged in."

Jorxy nodded and walked over to the front of the queue, still rubbing his sore neck.

Roza re-entered the tent and savoured the stillness and solitude inside. So much for that good streak in people, she mused. Was she too naïve to pretend that kindness and generosity could win over those obsessed with wealth, power and violence? She shrugged and sat down on her wooden stool. Maybe it was beyond her to fathom the mysteries of human nature, and she should leave that to Reeves, Lords and Emperors. Instead, she could focus on helping the person in front of her, and with that in mind, she prepared to rejuvenate the elderly couple when they came in.

The rest of the day passed uneventfully. Or rather, without further drama or crisis for Roza, although the lives of those who came to see her were transformed. She suppressed a smile that for her this was simply another afternoon's work, while to those who received her magical touch, it was a life-changing return to youth, health, and strength.

By late afternoon, Roza was tired. The queue in the marketplace was not finished, but then, it never was. There were always more people waiting to see her than she could ever rejuvenate, even if she worked all day and all night for all seven days of the week. She passed the message to Jorxy to call a halt for the day, and heard him and the Captain of the Guard dismissing the crowd, followed by the moans of the people when they heard they needed to return two days later.

Roza stood, stretched and picked up the heavy bag of donations. Jorxy would be pleased to pick over the generous haul of gold and jewels for the day. She went outside and drew deep breaths of the cool autumn evening, avoiding the disappointed gaze of those who waited nearby in the hope that she would still help them. She handed her bag to Jorxy, and they set off from the marketplace.

As she walked, head down, towards warlock gate, a sadness and heaviness gathered inside Roza. The world had simply too much illness, old age and death for her to stem that invincible tide. Was it a fruitless, pointless endeavour to try to help a few, when there were so many others that she would never be able to help? And by making rejuvenation available in this way, did that invite the inevitable troublemakers, the power-hungry and violent exploiters to take advantage of her?

This was exhausting her. Not only was she giving out in compassion and magical power all day, but now she needed to learn and train in her magic too. She'd promised the guards at the gate that she'd try to multiply their rations, and she urgently needed to learn some defensive spells too. What she longed for was a brief period of a quiet life, to recover her strength and come to terms with all that had happened to her.

"Rozabella."

She looked up. It wasn't Jorxy walking beside her who had spoken, but a girl's voice.

"Roza." The call came again, not loud, but urgent.

She stopped and scanned the faces of the people in the street who were all watching her. A girl at the entrance to an alley raised a hand to gain her attention in a wave, and Roza recognised her at once.

"Amber-Jane," she said, and stepped towards her. Roza saw how distraught the girl was, wringing her hands and tear-tracks glistening down her dark cheeks.

Amber-Jane was a couple of years older than her and Jorxy, and had been the schoolroom's prettiest girl, with her wide dark eyes and long wavy black hair. But Roza liked her because Amber-Jane didn't seem to know that she was beautiful, and because she'd always been thoughtful and caring towards the younger children.

"What's the matter?" Roza asked, as she and Jorxy stopped in front of their school friend.

"Um … I'm really sorry to bother you, Rozabella, because I know how busy and important you are now, and how tired you must be…" Amber-Jane stopped, because she didn't seem to know how to go on.

"Amber-Jane, don't be silly," Roza encouraged her. "We're your friends from the schoolroom and of course we'll help you if we can. What is it?"

The girl gave a nervous, relieved laugh that turned into a sob. "Oh, I wasn't sure you'd remember me." She swallowed hard. "It's just that … I know you don't do house visits, but my grandma's too frail to make it to the marketplace. And she's dying." This last came out as a whisper, and the tears leaked over her lashes again.

By instinct, Roza reached and enfolded Amber-Jane in her arms and squeezed her tight, as the older girl sobbed on her shoulder.

"Where is she?" Roza asked. "Take me to her."

Amber-Jane grabbed her hand and led her in as desperate a hurry as she could manage into the alley. Roza heard Jorxy say her name in a tone of weary protest, but she stalled him with a look.

She knew where Amber-Jane lived but had never been inside her house, because the older, prettier girl had always been too far above her to be a possible friend. As the three of them mounted the stone steps to the ornate front door, it was clear that Amber-Jane's family were significantly wealthier than Roza's, and especially Jorxy's. The poor boy's jaw dropped as they were welcomed into a spacious hall.

It was a household already in mourning, with everyone dressed in black, all conversations held in whispers, and the tip-toeing around so that no heavy footfall disturbed the dying woman. The relief and hope that Roza had come to see them was like a ray of sunlight piercing the deathly gloom.

"Rozabella our Warlock, you've come, you've come," Amber-Jane's mother exclaimed, forgetting to whisper. "She's come, she's come," she repeated to anyone who would listen.

"Where is she?" Roza asked again. "And just Amber-Jane and Jorxy to come with me, please." She was afraid that a host of concerned and despairing family huddled around a deathbed would distract her concentration.

Amber-Jane guided them through a panelled door into what looked like a study or library and closed the door behind them. A bed had been positioned between the bookcases and desks, and the gentle glow of oil lamps showed a frail and shrivelled figure lying under a sheet. Some chairs were arranged around the bed, and the three of them sat down.

At first glance, Roza thought the old woman had already died. Amber-Jane's grandma had hardly any flesh under her wafer-thin and waxy skin, pulled taut like dark brown parchment across her bony skull and skeleton. The breaths, when they came, were rattling and irregular, and Roza feared she'd arrived here when Death could come for this old lady at any moment.

Wasting no time, she took the skeletal hand in hers, reached inside for her spark and flame of magic, and began to send the power of her gift into the dying woman. But something was different this time. The magical flow wasn't being received; there was a blockage.

Roza paused and opened her eyes. "Amber-Jane, my rejuvenation power only works when someone wants to be younger. Hasn't your grandma got anything left to live for?"

Amber-Jane sighed and wiped her face as she gazed at her grandmother. "Grandma Lily has accepted her death. She's wise enough to know that we all pass away and is reconciled that this is her time. But we all hoped she'd still be with us for my wedding in the spring." The girl looked up, and Roza saw a depth of love and sadness in her pretty dark eyes. "If she was well enough, we hoped she'd conduct my wedding, because she is an Officiant for Marriages. But what makes her the proudest is that she's the oldest woman in Albany."

Roza smiled, and Amber-Jane managed a tear-stained one in return. Roza closed her eyes again, squeezed the old woman's hand, started the magical rejuvenation flow, and began to speak.

"Grandma Lily, you may not know me, but I'm Rozabella, Amber-Jane's friend from the schoolroom. I'm Albany's warlock now, and I've got the unique power of Rejuvenate, to make people physically younger. I'm here to give you more years of life, if you want them. You could attend Amber-Jane's wedding in the spring, or even conduct it for her. But if you can hear me, and if I were you, I'd make sure no one beats me to being the oldest woman in town. Would you like to retain that title?"

Roza felt an unmistakeable squeeze of her fingers in return. The magic began to flow, and was received, and she got to work on every part of the grandmother's body – heart, lungs, skin, flesh, muscles, and everything else she could think of. It was a harder task than she'd tried before, because she'd never touched a body so close to death, and it felt as though Death himself wrestled with her over the fate of this soul. But little by little she drew the dying woman back from her end. How much younger to make her? Roza didn't know but guessed that a decade or two would suffice. She'd still want to be a venerable lady and could always come back for more rejuvenation later if she wished.

When she finished, Roza re-opened her eyes and laid the warmer hand back on the sheet. The old lady looked vastly improved, with flesh on her bones and blood in her cheeks, more asleep than dying. Roza looked up, and saw Amber-Jane's open mouth, round eyes and tears trickling down her cheeks again. "Your grandma will be all right now," she said simply.

Amber-Jane jumped to her feet, stifling a shriek, not worrying about disturbing the sleeping patient. She rushed around the bed, hugged and kissed Roza, and then to Jorxy's obvious delight, did the same to him as well. Only in his dreams had the boy ever been hugged or kissed by anyone so attractive. "I must tell the others," Amber-Jane panted, and rushed from the room.

"Are you this Rozabella, then, Amber-Jane's friend?" came a croaking voice from the bed, and the two of them jumped. The old woman was not just living, but awake, aroused from her rest by the commotion around her deathbed. And Roza saw at once from whom Amber-Jane had inherited her deep dark eyes.

"Um, yes, that's right, and this is our friend Jorxy. I'm Warlock of Albany now, and I hope it's all right that I've used my Rejuvenate power to give you extra years of life. You seemed willing to accept them…" She trailed off, not knowing what more to say.

The old woman stared at her. "You hope it's all right that you've saved my life? Well, I should certainly say that it is. Especially since you're cheeky enough to tease me about staying the oldest woman in town." She gave Roza a wink and they all laughed.

Amber-Jane's family started entering the room and exclaimed in amazement about the friendly conversation going on where there should have been only the silence of death.

Grandma Lily cut across the excited chatter to say, "Now, has anyone invited the two of you to stay with us for dinner?"

Roza and Jorxy exchanged a look, and while she wished for the solitude of the plateau, she'd still need to eat once she got there, so she said, "That would be lovely, thank you."

When the previously dying woman called for her clothes, and the family responded with "Are you sure you're up to it?" and "Are you feeling well enough?", she banished them from the study so she could get up and change.

The dinner that evening was the best Roza and Jorxy had enjoyed since the Town Hall banquet on the day she'd defeated the Dragon. As she gazed around the table at the smiling, laughing, celebrating family, the upset with Thain Wicksteed that morning seemed a long time ago. Yes, this was the point of her powerful, remarkable gift. She might not save everyone in the world from death, but she could rescue one person at a time and transform the lives and relationships of all who knew them. This family had been in the grip of fear and mourning, and she'd delivered them from it all. She was their saviour, the bringer of joy, relief, reunions, and even life itself. This was something worth doing, worth spending her life for.

At the end of the meal, Grandma Lily tapped her glass and silence fell around the table. "Rozabella the Warlock, my family and I owe you an enormous debt of gratitude. I understand from our Amber-Jane that you refuse to charge for what you do but are willing to accept donations. Now, nothing we possess could repay you for our extra years of life together, but if there's something here you like, anything at all, please name it and you can have it."

Roza didn't know how to answer that and looked around the dining room to see polished display cabinets full of valuable treasures. She'd already had her reward for her day's work, in having her faith in human kindness restored, so she said, "Thank you, but I don't know what to ask for. I hope that Jorxy and I can be your friends, because in the schoolroom, your Amber-Jane was older and more beautiful than either of us, so we never hoped to be her friend." Everyone laughed at this and Roza blushed. "But if you insist we have something, I ask for something for Jorxy. He had an unfortunate experience this morning, and in return I promised him the pick of today's donations, so have you anything suitable for him?"

Jorxy's spoon stopped halfway to his mouth with his second helpings of dessert, his face turning bright red. "I – I'm only a poor boy," he stuttered, "and we never had nothing fancy in our house. I – I wouldn't know what to ask for."

"In which case," Grandma Lily replied, "it's only proper that we offer you the most valuable thing our family possesses. Amber-Jane, would you be kind enough to fetch my husband's chain of office and give it to Jorxy, please?"

Roza heard sharp intakes of breath from the family as the girl rose from her chair, but no one dared to object to what the grandmother had offered. When Amber-Jane came around the table to put the family heirloom around Jorxy's neck, Roza saw at once why none of them wanted to give this away.

"My husband was Reeve of Albany for many years," Grandma Lily was saying, "and when he retired, the Town Committee presented him with his chain of office in gratitude for his years of service." She glanced around the table, seeming to sense the family's unease. "I inherited it from my husband and gladly give it now to this young man to be his for ever. Let no one around this table grumble or regret my generosity, for it is mine to bestow as I wish. No kind or generous deed should go unrewarded, and what this young warlock has freely given me is beyond price." She now addressed Jorxy. "The chain links are of gold and silver, studded with various gems, but as you can see, the centrepiece is a ruby of unrivalled size, beauty, and value. Treasure it well."

Once Amber-Jane had fixed the clasp of the chain around Jorxy's neck, she kissed him again on the cheek. Roza couldn't be sure whether the blush on his face was from the kiss or the reflected glow of the candlelight in the ruby. Apart from a mumbled, "Thank you, lady," Jorxy was silent for the rest of the evening.

Roza noticed later that Jorxy was careful to hide the chain and its ruby under his jacket when they passed his brother Rufus and the fellow guards at the warlock gate, and that his fingers kept straying to touch the priceless jewel all their way back up the dusty path to the plateau.

CHAPTER THREE

Halfway up the track, their eyes accustomed to the darkness, Roza and Jorxy passed two further guards, posted to prevent stray visitors from disturbing the warlock on her plateau. The moon was nearing its full as the two of them reached the summit of the path and breathed the cool, fresh air of the plateau. Roza always enjoyed walking on the level grass again, and among the trees of her orchard, after the exertions of the climb up the hillside. The moonlight gave the plateau a bright, silvery wash, punctuated by the black shadows of the trees.

They neared the cave, and a warm glow of lamplight welcomed them home. Unlike when Roza had first awoken in this cave as a prisoner of the previous warlock, Philoe, the place was now clean and tidy, with most of the rubbish and paraphernalia either thrown away or put in its proper place. Jorxy slept on a mat in this outer cave, while Roza had her own bedchamber further in.

"Standley, we're back," Roza called, as she and Jorxy deposited the bag of donations on the large kitchen table.

From the passageway deeper into the hillside came Standley the enchanted coat stand, clattering towards them on his four polished wooden feet. Roza was constantly amazed by this magical piece of furniture that she had inherited from Philoe, whose pole and hooks were flexible enough to milk their cow and collect eggs from the chickens, while also being so tough and strong.

Although Standley couldn't speak (he had no mouth), he understood everything they said and responded 'Yes' or 'No' by nodding or shaking his top hooks. He also had two knots in the dark, polished wood near his top that looked remarkably like eyes, and Roza was getting better at reading his expressions: a frown if he was displeased, a shrug if he didn't know or the crinkling of the lines around his knot eyes when he smiled.

"Sorry we're back later than we expected," Roza went on, "but we made a house-call to a schoolroom friend of ours, Amber-Jane. Her Grandma Lily was dying, so I saved her from death and gave her some extra years of life." She chuckled to herself. "Listen to me, Standley, wittering on about life and death, when what you really need to know is that we don't need any food tonight because the family were so grateful they fed us both a slap-up meal."

Her coat stand was smiling, listening to her, and Roza loved the way he would patiently listen to all that she said without interruption or complaint.

Jorxy was rubbing his extended belly. "Oh, yeah, Standley, you should've seen it, a real feast. And look what Amber-Jane's Grandma Lily gave me as a thank you present." He held out the former Reeve's chain of office with its marvellous embedded ruby. Standley touched, held and inspected the wonderful gift, like a close friend would, as Jorxy lowered his voice. "And what's more, that Amber-Jane is only the prettiest girl in the whole of Albany and this evening she actually kissed me – twice. I reckon she must fancy me and I'm in with a chance there, mate."

Standley nodded his encouragement, but Roza could only laugh. "Erm, Jorxy, did you miss that bit about Amber-Jane wanting her grandma to attend her wedding in the spring? I think you might be a little late in stealing her affections."

Jorxy's face fell. "Oh, yeah, I forgot about that." He shrugged and beamed again. "Anyway, it don't stop a boy enjoying being kissed by her, does it?"

"No, I suppose not. Now, Standley, I want your help with finding a new book to study. I need to move on from those Basics of Magic for Beginners, and Fundamentals of Magical Theory books, and start learning some defensive spells. I needed to defend myself today and didn't know a single spell to do so. Where should I start?"

Roza and her coat stand turned to survey the large bookcase that filled one wall of the cave from floor to ceiling. Standley shuffled forward, scanning the shelves, and then hooked out two of the books. Roza flicked through them both and decided to start with one entitled, 'Defend Yourself – First Steps in Self-Protection for the Young Warlock'. It was the slimmer of the two volumes and looked to have shorter chapters.

She was desperate enough to learn some self-defence that she sat down on a stool and read at the kitchen table. Jorxy busied himself with emptying the day's bag of donations, counting the coins, and then stowing them away in a locked chest hidden in a cluttered storeroom far back in the cave.

In her book, Roza found the 'Barrier' spell that Philoe had used to keep her trapped inside this cave and thought that might be useful. But the day's exhaustion caught up with her, and she wasn't taking much in, so when Jorxy lay down on his mat, Roza also went off to her bedchamber.

Before she got to sleep, two conflicting thoughts chased each other round her mind. The first was the glow from celebrating with Amber-Jane's family that Grandma Lily's life had been prolonged, all thanks to her wonderful gift. The second was the sneering disdain from Thain Wicksteed who doubted she could perform any magic at all. Roza refused to prove herself to anyone, but it niggled at her self-confidence that anyone considered the new Warlock of Albany an imposter and a fraud.

Roza woke suddenly in the dark midnight to the sound of shouting. Jorxy was arguing with someone, and there were several harsh, male voices in the outer cave. She leapt up, trembling, and fumbled her way towards the flickering torchlight that filtered along the cave passage.

Jorxy was standing by his sleeping mat, facing off against eight armed men crowding around him, two of whom held flaming torches. "Get out," he was yelling. "She ain't here. You've come to the wrong place."

With a chilling dread, Roza recognised the answering voice as that of the previous morning: Thain Wicksteed of Heismith Castle. "You're lying. You're the ugly whelp who was with her yesterday, so she must be around here somewhere. Where is she?"

Roza hesitated for only a moment. She couldn't hide and hope that Jorxy convinced them to leave, because the Thain and his henchmen were sure to search the whole cave before they left. And whatever else they found they'd probably beat up the poor boy for good measure. She glanced at Standley standing motionless in front of the bookshelves and then stepped forward into view.

"Leave him alone," she called. "Yes, I'm here. What do you want and how did you get up here?"

Wicksteed and his followers whirled around. Two of them restrained Jorxy while the other six approached her. The Thain wore the same look of smug triumph that Roza had hated before.

"Aha, so the pathetic girl pretending to be Warlock of Albany is here after all. Excellent. After your rude insults and trickery yesterday, I decided you needed teaching a lesson. So, we've nipped across the town walls, fields and hills towards your little track up here. Those guards on the way up didn't need much persuading to let us through, did they, lads?" The henchmen grinned.

Roza was trying to think. This time there was no help on the way to rescue them, no Captain of the Guards or soldiers. So, there was no point in stalling for time and the sooner they got this over with, the better.

"Okay, fine," she said, moving forwards. "You want some rejuvenation, let's get on with it. How much younger do you want to be?"

"Not so fast, young lady," Wicksteed said, with a sly smile that froze Roza's blood. "I said you needed teaching a lesson, and I'm the one who's going to do it. I saw those crowds in Albany's marketplace yesterday and thought here's an opportunity I can't resist. You tried to get one over on me earlier, and that's one thing I won't allow. I'm getting my revenge on you, and you've no one to rescue you now."

Roza folded her arms and tensed her muscles to hide how much she was shaking. If only she had an array of defensive magic already at her disposal, to blast these ruffians out of her cave. But she didn't. And she couldn't see how to bluff her way out of this one either. "What do you mean?" she asked quietly. "What are you going to do?"

Thain Wicksteed looked around the cave. "First of all, I'll take a look at that bag of donations you collected yesterday. We deserve some financial recompense for all the trouble you've put us through, don't we, boys? There it is," he said pointing to where Jorxy had left the bag lying on the table. A henchman went across to it, peered inside and tipped it up. "So, it's empty now. Where have you put the treasure?"

Roza tried a defiant tone but wasn't sure whether it worked. "Those are our well-deserved expenses for the hard work we put into improving the lives of others. And we're not stupid enough to leave them lying about where just anyone can find them." She hoped that Jorxy had stuffed his ruby chain of office well under his sleeping mat.

Wicksteed stepped so close to her that the red lines stood out in his bloodshot eyeballs. "No, I don't think you're that stupid, young girlie warlock, but you're still going to tell me where that treasure is. Either right now, or after a great deal of pain. Which is it to be?"

Roza didn't answer him. Instead, to buy herself some thinking time, she looked across to where Jorxy was held prisoner by the pair of henchmen.

"Don't tell them nothing," he spat, which earned him a punch in the stomach, and he doubled over.

She looked away, and her gaze landed on Standley in

front of the bookcases. Her coat stand looked poised, watching her, as though waiting for a signal from her before moving even an inch.

Wicksteed was losing patience. "Let me make this clear. Once you've given me your treasure, you're coming back with me to Heismith Castle. I reckon having someone as popular and famous as you in my dungeons will be good for business. So, what you decide now will determine how pain-filled or tolerable your stay with me will be."

No! Roza swallowed hard. How could she avoid this man abducting her and leaving her to rot in his castle? Or even worse, abusing her and exploiting her gift for his own selfish gain? Could she, Jorxy and Standley hope to put up a fight and resist this band of armed men?

She remembered one time when Philoe's coat stand had restrained her, and how strong and quick he was then. Was Standley the one piece of magic she could use now?

"Um, Standley, would you come over here, please." Roza watched the reaction of the men as the familiar sound of wooden feet scraped across the cave floor. None of them had expected this coat stand to move, let alone respond to her bidding. Their jaws dropped, their eyes stared, and they backed away at this uncanny display of magic.

But not Thain Wicksteed. He glared at the approaching piece of furniture. "What is this?"

Roza forced a confident, menacing smile onto her lips. "This is Standley, my enchanted coat stand. You weren't stupid enough to think I have no magical defences, were you? I should warn you that he's strong, fast, tough, and somewhat protective of me. You anger him and me at your peril." This was the best bluff she could think of, because she had little idea of Standley's strengths or weaknesses if this should come to a fight.

"Stop that thing," Wicksteed ordered, as the tottering coat stand was clearly unnerving him.

One of the henchmen was brave enough to step

forwards, reach out his arms and grab Standley's polished wooden pole. The coat stand glanced up at Roza, who said to him, "Feel free to defend yourself, Standley, and to help us get these unwelcome men out of our cave."

As though finally getting permission to act, Standley sprang to life. He flexed in the middle enough to sink his top and middle hooks into the flesh of the henchman holding him. The man screamed, let go, and recoiled backwards as far from the coat stand as he could.

"All of you on it at once," Wicksteed bellowed, and Roza noted the Thain kept clear of the coat stand himself. The henchmen surged forwards, and Standley toppled backwards under the combined weight of the four men. Roza braced herself for the terrible sound of breaking wood.

But it never came.

Instead, Standley was gouging, scratching, kicking, and clawing each of the henchmen in turn, as they successively yelled in pain and leapt away from the polished wooden beast. Soon, an unscratched Standley emerged, bending his feet to lever himself back to upright again.

One of the henchmen roared with rage, drew his sabre, and lunged towards the coat stand. He swung the blade with all his might, and Roza stared in horror for Standley to be chopped in half in a splintering of hacked up wood.

But it was the sabre that bounced back from the impact, jarring the man's arm as he yelped and dropped the blade.

There was a moment of stunned silence as the five injured henchmen backed away towards the cave entrance, and the two holding Jorxy wondered whether they should stay there, fight or flee.

But Thain Wicksteed was still standing in front of Roza. He whipped out a knife, grabbed her, and held the blade to her throat. "Stop right there, you evil thing," he commanded, "or I will kill her."

It was the wrong thing to say, and almost the last mistake he ever made. As though the threat to his mistress's life was the one thing he couldn't allow, Standley crossed the distance between them faster than Roza's eye could follow him. Before Wicksteed knew what was happening, the coat stand's hooks had clawed both his arm and the knife away from Roza's neck.

And then Standley was onto the Thain of Heismith Castle, sinking his hooks into any part of the man's skin and flesh he could reach. Wicksteed's screams echoed in the cave as he collapsed, and his blood spilled onto the floor.

"Standley, stop," Roza yelled, and the coat stand froze, pivoting back upright, then stepping away.

The bleeding, ragged bully crawled away across the cave floor to where his nervous henchmen hesitated at the exit.

"Release my friend," Roza commanded, and the last two unhurt henchmen released Jorxy and shuffled across to join their fellows. "I warned you not to anger him or me," Roza said. "Now, don't come back, or cross my path again."

And with that, Thain Wicksteed and his men of Heismith Castle turned and disappeared into the night.

Roza and Jorxy stared at each other, and then at Standley, stunned and trembling for a moment. Then they burst out laughing. The coat stand looked between them, as though wondering what was so funny.

"Wow, Standley," Roza managed at last. "You are amazing. I never imagined you'd see off Thain Wicksteed and all his men."

The coat stand bent into a modest bow and then seemed to shrug.

"Are we glad we've got you on our side, mate," said Jorxy, giving his hooks a timid pat. "How d'you manage all that?"

Roza tilted her head to regard Standley. "We know you're strong and surprisingly fast-moving for a piece of furniture." Jorxy grinned at this. "But you're also really tough and flexible, so that when four men land on you, you bend rather than crack or break." The coat stand was nodding. "And what about that sabre stroke? Let me have a look."

She leaned closer and examined the polished wooden pole where the blade had struck it. There was no scratch or dent, not even a mark.

"Could any blade or axe damage you, Standley?" she murmured. And then was even more incredulous when he shook his hooks.

Roza rested her hands on Jorxy's shoulder and Standley's top. "Well, it looks like we've got ourselves an indestructible bodyguard. Thank you, Standley, and if you're willing, we'll be sure to look after you for as long as you can manage to look after us. Agreed?"

Standley nodded, and then stuck out two of his middle hooks as though they should shake on it, and they both laughed as they did so.

"Now then, I'm going back to sleep," said Roza, "but if you wish to, most noble bodyguard, feel free to go outside and check that Wicksteed and his men have left the plateau."

The coat stand flexed his hooks and scuttled off into the darkness. Roza and Jorxy grinned at each other, shook their heads in disbelief, and made for their respective beds.

CHAPTER FOUR

The next morning was a studying magic day, and Roza was determined to master at least one defensive spell by the end of it. The slim book she'd flicked through the night before included Philoe's Barrier spell but recommended that young warlocks learn one called 'Repulser' first. It used similar techniques but was considered easier to master.

Over a breakfast of scrambled eggs cooked by Jorxy, Roza studied the method. Repulser promised to use the magical energy inside her to shove someone away from her. It was a basic spell in a field known as Telekinesis, using forces and energy to move objects around the warlock. Roza was both excited and daunted at the challenge of her first magic that wasn't Rejuvenate.

The book assumed that young warlocks would learn these spells in a group together, as a class of novices, and so instructed them to pair up to practise on each other. When Roza read this out, Jorxy volunteered at once to be her partner, but then added, "It won't hurt, will it?"

Roza shrugged. "No idea. You'll need to tell me."

They cleared away breakfast and stood facing each other several feet apart in an empty space in the cave. The first hour or two was extremely boring for Jorxy, as he stood there, arms folded, not feeling anything.

Roza knew how to summon the magical energy from a spark into a flame in her belly, but with Rejuvenate this was channelled through physical touch into someone else's body. Her first task was to launch this energy out of her and into the air. This sounded much easier than it proved to be.

The book taught her the hand and arm movements to accomplish the spell. She started with both hands resting on her belly and moved them up to her chest as though cradling the magic within them. Thrusting her hands away from her then sent the energy against her intended target. Roza's arm muscles became very tired long before Jorxy reported feeling any magic at all.

By late morning, Roza had worked out her problem. She was sending the magic out of her well enough, but in too wide and diffused an arc. She needed to focus and aim the power into a more direct and definite beam. The biggest celebration before they made a brief stop for lunch was when Roza's Repulser spell managed to ruffle Jorxy's hair.

After a hasty lunch of bread, ham, cheese and fruit, they returned to it. Now that Roza was mastering each stage of what was required, her progress came quickly. First, her spell made Jorxy take an involuntary step back. Then she sent the force into his feet so that he almost fell forward. The trick was to focus her magical energy just enough to shove the target's whole body backwards.

At last, she did it. Without lifting him off his feet, Roza's spell slid him nearly a foot backwards across the smooth cave floor. They whooped and hugged, and Roza was exhilarated enough to want to keep doing it again and again.

Jorxy became steadily less keen on 'practising on each other' when he began to be lifted off the floor and land backwards on the hard stone. He insisted they move outside, but even among the trees of the orchard, being repeatedly thrown onto the grass was not a pleasant experience. His anger was mounting. "It ain't the magic that hurts, it's the landing on the ground at the end of it."

It was Standley who saved their argument from worsening. The coat stand edged between them, pointed for Jorxy to go, and beckoned with his hooks for Roza to Repulse him.

Jorxy stomped off. "Brilliant. Why didn't we think of it earlier? Send the indestructible coat stand flying through the air instead. Who cares if he lands on his back a hundred times in a row, 'cause he don't feel it, does he?" He was still muttering and grumbling as he went, but Roza noticed he stopped at the cave entrance to watch.

Roza took a few tries to adjust to Standley's thinner and lighter frame, but soon she was sending her coat stand catapulting and cartwheeling across the grass. In complete contrast with Jorxy, Standley seemed to find this whole experience wonderfully entertaining and enjoyable. He leapt up from each landing and hurried back for more Repulsing. Roza was sure that the grain lines around his eye knots were scrunched up in laughter and delight.

Later in the afternoon, Roza was sending him flying through the trees. It became a game to see whether she could get him to land in the branches. At first, Roza thought Standley might have been pushing himself backwards, jumping away with his clawed feet, just to encourage her. But it didn't seem to be so. In fact, towards the end she insisted that he anchor himself into the earth, holding on with his claws and leaning forwards to resist the spell, but she still managed to uproot him and send him flying.

The sun was lowering when Roza's arm muscles were too aching to continue. She hadn't realised how much physical strength and fitness might be required for her warlock's life. Maybe Philoe had become so adept and proficient in his magic by the end that he'd sent out his spells with no more than a flick of his finger. But Roza found herself almost wishing that Thain Wicksteed or one of his henchmen might return that night, just so she could try her new Repulser spell on them.

The next day was a marketplace day again, but before she finished today's magical studies, she read what was required for the Barrier spell. The principle was the same of sending out her magical energy, but this time in an even circle around her. This created an impenetrable ring of defence, and she noted with a wry smile that the young warlock should spin on the spot with arms outstretched to achieve it. But she knew she wasn't a dancer and was more likely to topple over with dizziness than master it.

Sunset colours were bathing the cave in warm light, and Roza and Jorxy were eating their evening meal when there came a call of "Hello?" from outside.

They stood up and went to the entrance, to see a young man walking towards them through the trees. Roza hadn't seen him for a few weeks and was struck again by how annoyingly gorgeous he was.

Kerenzi. The immortal spirit lord. He'd been captured alongside her at the beginning of all this, for their body parts to be used in Philoe's longevity potion. The old warlock's discovery of Roza's Rejuvenate gift had spared their lives, and so this powerful magical being was in her debt, or at least well-disposed towards her.

Although as a spirit lord Kerenzi could be invisible in spirit form, he appeared today as he always had done, as a muscular young man with wavy shoulder-length auburn hair, and bare arms, legs, and feet. His tunic often matched the colour of where he was, so today it was light blue from flying across a clear sky. For Kerenzi had translucent rainbow-coloured wings, although his left one bore a jagged scar where the bottom of it had been hacked off – a lasting reminder of his mistreatment by warlock Philoe. Kerenzi had wreaked his revenge by killing Philoe when he had the chance, reminding Roza to beware of this friend's power and temper.

Today, though, the spirit lord was all smiles, and his eyes – whose colour matched his mood – were a fetching, playful purple. It was awkward for Roza, however, because she hadn't told Jorxy the full truth of their unfortunate history with warlock Philoe, or anything about Kerenzi either.

"Ah, my dear Rozabella," the spirit lord called, "Albany's new young warlock. How are you today? And you, young sir, must be her schoolroom friend, Jorxy, is that right?"

Jorxy glared at the handsome newcomer and didn't take the outstretched hand. "Who the hell are you?"

"Oh, Jorxy," Roza intervened quickly, "this is Kerenzi, a spirit lord. I met him a few weeks ago, while we were both here with warlock Philoe." She threw Kerenzi a desperate look, trying to communicate to him not to say too much about their painful time with Philoe.

The spirit lord's eyes flicked between Roza and Jorxy, and then he beamed. "Yes, that's right, but we don't need to talk about that, do we? And I'm not surprised if Roza hasn't told you much about me, because I'm a little hard to explain, aren't I?" He laughed, and Roza gave a nervous, relieved laugh too. Kerenzi made a point of taking Jorxy's hand and shaking it, whether the boy wanted to or not.

"A spirit lord?" Jorxy looked sceptical. "What's one of them? And what was the name?"

"Kerenzi, and maybe it's easiest if Roza explains everything to you later. I need to have a chat with your warlock friend here for a few minutes if I may borrow her from you?" The spirit lord gestured for Roza to accompany him away from the cave, and Jorxy looked affronted by that idea.

"It's okay, Jorxy," she tried to placate him. "We can trust Kerenzi, he's on our side. We won't be long." She could almost feel Jorxy's gaze on their backs as they walked off through the sunset colours between the trees. While it was touching that the boy looked jealous of the spirit lord, Roza knew she'd have lots of reassuring to do later.

Roza headed for one of her favourite spots, a large boulder by the cliff edge of the plateau that looked out over the whole town and valley of Albany. It was beside the top of the waterfall where the stream, Torrence, toppled over the cliff in a fine mist of rainbow sprays.

As they walked, Kerenzi said, "You haven't told the boy the full story of what happened with warlock Philoe."

Roza sighed. "No, I haven't. It seemed kinder to Jorxy and my parents not to worry them with tales of my kidnap, imprisonment, and threatened execution. There seemed no purpose in poisoning everyone's memory of the old warlock when we were all celebrating being saved from the Dragon."

"But it was the truth," Kerenzi protested. "Those dear to you deserve to know what really happened."

"I care for them and worry what they'll think. I don't want to upset or scare them about my new world of magic. And remember that my silence also hides that you're the one who murdered warlock Philoe."

"Not murdered," Kerenzi corrected. "I merely carried out the punishment that was justly due to him after all he'd done to us."

They reached the boulder and Roza clambered up to sit cross-legged on the top. To her surprise, Kerenzi climbed up too and sat next to her. It was intoxicating to be almost touching this bewitchingly attractive young man. She had to admit, it was more attraction than she'd ever felt towards Jorxy.

"Anyway." She wanted to change the subject from their past. "You wanted a chat with me?"

"Yes." He turned and smiled at her, and Roza had to ignore that his lips were easily within kissing distance. "How are you, Roza? How are you adjusting to being a world-famous warlock?"

She rolled her eyes. "I don't like being world-famous. And I guess you know what I've been doing, because you follow me around invisibly, spying on me."

The corner of his mouth twitched upwards. "No, I haven't. Not recently anyway. I've been away. Which is why I'm asking you."

She told him about her thrice-weekly stalls offering rejuvenation in Albany marketplace, about not charging but accepting donations, and about the queues and chaos there. And then how Thain Wicksteed had accosted her there and at the cave, and about learning the Repulser spell. She finished up with how she'd saved the life of Amber-Jane's Grandma Lily.

Kerenzi listened without interrupting and nodded throughout. "You have been busy. I admire your generosity in rejuvenating as many as possible for free. I won't criticise your kindness but must point out an unfortunate consequence of it. The word has spread, and is galloping daily further afield, that eternal youth is freely available in Albany. If you wanted to start a stampede of everyone in the Empire, you could hardly have done a better job."

"Yes, I know," Roza sighed. "But it still feels the right thing to do. The Universe has given me this unique, life-changing gift, and I won't hide away, keep it to myself, or refuse to share it with everyone."

"I take your point, but I'm sorry to report, Miss Roza, that your problems here are only going to get worse."

"Yes, I fear as much. You say you've been away, so where have you been?"

"Mainly in Gorge City, do you know it?"

Roza shook her head. "I've heard of it, of course, but never been there."

He stared at her. "You've lived here all your life and never been to Gorge City?"

"No, I've never left the valley. I've been as far as the cleft through the mountains, where the highway dips down onto the plains, but it's all dry and dusty as far as you can see. What's the point of an arduous trip to somewhere else when Albany has all I want?"

Kerenzi shook his head. "It's not that far to Gorge City. It's the capital of this part of the Empire, and home to Lord Vallance, Earl of the Plains. I trust you've heard of him."

"Yes, of course I have. I'm not that ignorant."

"Good, because Lord Vallance is currently on his way here to see you."

Roza almost fell off the boulder in shock. "*What?* The Earl of the Plains is coming here? And wants to see me? What does that mean?"

"I eavesdropped invisibly on some of Lord Vallance's

conversations. The public line is that he's coming to negotiate the best way to manage your remarkable gift to benefit the maximum number of people. But privately he's determined that you go back with him to Gorge City, even if it means abducting you by force."

Roza swallowed. "I guess he'll come with more followers than the half dozen who came with Thain Wicksteed."

"Indeed he does. He's riding here with a sizeable force, to invade and conquer the town of Albany if he must, if they choose to defend you. The Reeve would be mad to try that, of course, and is much more likely to hand you over at the Earl's first request."

Roza's fingers were gripping the rock. "What should I do, Kerenzi? Should I go with him?"

"Um, no, Roza, I wouldn't go with him if I were you. Lord Vallance has a certain public charisma, but he's a fundamentally self-centred man. He acts purely for his own benefit, aiming to free himself from the authority of the Dragon Emperor, whom you so conveniently weakened. He seeks independence, ruling the plains as he wishes, not answering to anyone. You are his first step to achieving that, to be his ally, puppet or figurehead in a civil war against the Emperor. If you're unwilling, he'll still tell everyone you're on his side anyway."

Roza's mind was reeling. How had it come to this? How had her ability to make people younger thrust her into the middle of the Empire's civil war? She didn't want power or authority over people, just as she didn't need great riches. Couldn't she remain a simple, straight-forward girl, helping those in need through what she could do for them? Why did the world make everything so complicated for her?

She turned back to the spirit lord who watched her closely. "I have no idea which way to turn. So, I ask you again, what do you think I should do?"

He gave a chuckle. "Oh, if I were you, I wouldn't follow the advice of a jaded, cynical immortal like me. After all, I'm a bitter, vengeful murderer, aren't I?" The playful, teasing look on his face made Roza roll her eyes again. "But more seriously," he went on, "if I were you, I'd trust your own instincts rather than anyone else's. I was impressed with you when we first met, and I'm increasingly impressed as time has gone on. You have a strong sense of the right thing to do, and that's usually kind and generous, so you should go with that rather than anything I might say."

Roza became aware that her mouth had fallen open at these compliments, and she gazed at him, enjoying the closeness of his face. "You really mean that? Those nice things you just said? You're not saying them to toy with my feelings?"

He tried to look affronted, but she knew he was only pretending. "Me? Toy with anyone's feelings? I would never do that. I'm an open, honest, genuine young man, I am." But his wide grin made it impossible for Roza to trust anything he said.

She decided to move the topic back onto the approaching Lord Vallance. "So anyway, here I am, a young and inexperienced warlock, with two spells in my repertoire – Rejuvenate and Repulser. An army is marching here to take me away, and you don't have any suggestions for me?"

Kerenzi shook his head. "Not about the best thing for you to do. But I do have a word of encouragement if you'd like to hear it." She nodded vigorously. He paused for a moment as though deciding how best to say this. "Did Philoe explain to you where magic comes from?"

"Yes, he told me it flows from beauty, so we talked about that a bit."

"Excellent. Well, I think you've always had a basic aptitude for magic, but all warlocks – as novices, apprentices and throughout their lives – take time to grow their magical strength. It's like exercising a muscle, or practising and training to master a skill, in that it takes time to grow. As a spirit lord, I'm pretty good at assessing the spirits of those I meet, and in your case, I'd say you might have been a warlock for many years, not just a few weeks."

Roza frowned. "What do you mean? Why do you say that?"

"Remember that magic flows from beauty, so I'd conclude that you're well versed in beauty."

She scoffed. "I hope you're not pretending that I'm beautiful, because I know I'm not."

He tilted his head and regarded her. "I'm not talking about physical attractiveness, because that's a matter of opinion. No, I'm talking about you doing beautiful things – rejuvenating people free of charge, saving their lives, improving their health, being kind, generous – those sorts of thing. Each time you do them you boost your inner beauty, and so also your resources of magical strength. I've never known anyone grow in magical power so quickly, and that must be because of what you're doing. If you'd like to hear me say that you're beautiful, then yes, Miss Rozabella the Warlock, you are supremely beautiful, and in the way that really matters."

Roza was speechless to that. Kerenzi leaned in and kissed her cheek, grinned, and jumped down from the boulder. The daylight was fading fast, and the first stars were coming out overhead. "I'll go now and leave you to explain to your boyfriend in the cave who the hell I am. Goodbye for now, Roza." And with that he vanished into invisibility and was gone.

Roza sat on the boulder for a while, gazing across the valley as the stars came out above her. She didn't know what to make of Kerenzi and his flirting, or what she was supposed to do as warlock, so she just sat there and enjoyed the last light of the sun darkening into night, the lamps coming on across Albany, the fresh smell of the air and the endless gush of the waterfall beside her.

And the fact that the most attractive and magically powerful young man she would ever meet had just told her she was supremely beautiful in the way that really matters.

The evening breeze became chill on her arms, so she climbed down from the boulder, said goodnight to the valley and walked back through her orchard to the cave.

As she appeared, Jorxy folded his arms and demanded, "So, go on then, who is he, your magical boyfriend?"

Roza thought it curious that both Kerenzi and Jorxy had referred to the other as her boyfriend, when it wasn't true for either of them. Could they both be jealous of the other, of the relationship they each had with her?

She smiled at him. "No, Kerenzi isn't my boyfriend, and I'm sorry I didn't tell you about him before. To be honest, I wasn't sure I'd ever see him again. We were both here with old warlock Philoe, but he left before I met up with you. By then, we were preoccupied with finding each other again, with me being the new warlock, with facing the Dragon Emperor and saving Albany from destruction, so Kerenzi didn't seem that important."

Jorxy looked a little reassured, but said, "Go on then, tell me about *spirit lords*." He gave a sarcastic emphasis to the last two words.

Roza shrugged. "Well, they're immortal spirit beings, and can appear in human form or remain invisible. They have wings and can fly, have strong magical powers, and their eyes and clothes change colour depending on where they are and what mood they're in. So, if I'd described him without you having seen him, would you have believed me?" She tried a tentative smile.

His frown melted into a grin. "No, suppose not. But I've seen him, so I have to believe in him, right? Come on, it's late, and it's a marketplace day tomorrow."

Roza nodded and wondered again what she should do about everything. But no answer to that question came before sleep soothed away her cares.

CHAPTER FIVE

When Roza and Jorxy arrived at the warlock gate the following morning, she realised she hadn't learned a spell to multiply the guards' rations. She'd been distracted by Thain Wicksteed and mastering the Repulser spell and so hadn't looked up about increasing food.

She apologised to Rufus and his fellow guards and promised them that the next time she came down they would each have more than enough to eat. With grumbles, they insisted on holding her to that promise.

Next, outside her marketplace tent, the Captain of the Guards informed Roza that she was required at a Town Committee meeting that morning. She needed to suspend her rejuvenation work to attend a discussion in the Town Hall about her security and the management of the crowds.

Roza groaned and longed already for the solitude of her plateau and sitting to watch the sunset and the stars. But she attended dutifully to those who came to be rejuvenated, and at her request, Jorxy checked among those in the queue that their ailments could be treated by Roza's gift.

With each person or family who came in, she recalled Kerenzi's words that acts of kindness and generosity were beautiful things, boosting her magical power. It was no longer any effort to summon the energy to perform her spells each time, so had her magical spirit really grown as quickly as the spirit lord had said?

At mid-morning, the Captain of the Guards interrupted the queue – to loud complaints from those at the front – to conduct their warlock to the Committee meeting. As usual, Roza kept her eyes down as she passed through the crowded marketplace and appreciated the calm quietness inside the Town Hall.

They didn't keep her waiting, for she was ushered at once

into the dim and dark-panelled Committee Chamber. Around twenty members were present, seated around a large square of tables, with the Reeve presiding in the middle of one side, his thinning silver-grey hair glinting in the lamplight. Roza was shown to an empty chair facing him, noting how the padded velvet upholstery in here was so much better than the plain wooden stools in her tent.

She didn't know many of the Committee members. Beside the Reeve and the Captain of the Guards, there were the town's Judge, Secretary, Treasurer, and representatives of the town guilds – merchants, bankers, innkeepers, market traders, blacksmiths, taverners, and so on. Notably fewer smiles came her way than a few weeks ago when she'd been officially congratulated and thanked for saving the town from the Dragon.

The Reeve welcomed her. "Ah, Warlock Rozabella, thank you for interrupting your magical rejuvenation efforts to join our discussions. We trust your work is going well?"

As she opened her mouth, Roza caught the impression the Reeve had only asked out of politeness, so she kept her answer short. "It's going wonderfully, thank you, and making a real life-changing difference to so many families."

"Excellent, well done," said the Reeve, although his smile didn't reach his eyes. "Now, you'll be aware that news of you saving our town from the … er … Emperor has spread far and wide, and that many across the Plains are keen to meet the young woman who performed such a miracle." The Albany townsfolk refused to say the word 'Dragon' in superstitious fear that mentioning the name served to summon the beast against them.

Roza decided to get her apologies and thanks in early before anyone complained about the crowds. "Yes, I'm sorry if my fame is causing any trouble, and I'm very grateful to the town guards for their excellent work in manning the gates and keeping order in the marketplace." She smiled at the Captain of the Guards, who inclined his head in return.

"Thank you, Miss Rozabella," the Reeve continued, "and we're gratified that our efforts behind the scenes enable your excellent work to go on. However, …"

Here we go, thought Roza, here come the complaints.

"… already we're needing to employ extra guards. We're using reservists, the newly retired, those in training, and anyone else suitable to fill the necessary posts. Which raises the issue of how these extra guards are to be paid for. Are we correct in hearing that you refuse to charge a fee for your rejuvenation, but merely accept donations instead?"

"Yes, that is correct. I insist that my unique ability, which came to me as a free gift, should be available to everyone who needs it, irrespective of their ability to pay. It mustn't be for the rich alone, as those most in need of it are often the elderly poor."

"I see," said the Reeve, although he clearly didn't agree with her. "A noble sentiment, I'm sure. What about these donations you receive, then? Would it be fair for you to contribute a portion of these to cover the reasonable expenses of enabling your valuable work to go ahead?"

Roza didn't like the sound of this. She had a vision of the town Treasurer helping himself to her donations bag each evening and taking most, if not all, of the coins and gems to fill his bottomless coffers.

"I can't agree," she countered. "Most of the donations are not large or valuable, and they barely cover my living expenses and the requirements for studying magic. They wouldn't make a significant difference to your finances." This wasn't strictly true, but Roza refused to allow her generosity with her gift to be exploited by the town treasury.

"I suppose we have to take your word for that," said the Reeve, and Roza sensed that few around the tables believed her either. "And so, Miss Warlock, we return to how you suggest we meet the expenses of the extra guards?"

"Well, I don't know," Roza replied. "I'm not on the Committee, or Reeve, or Treasurer. I'm just a seventeen-year-old girl who finds herself with an amazing and life-enhancing gift. How do you normally raise the money for your expenses? What about the inns and taverns and other traders in the town? Isn't their business booming? Couldn't you levy a little extra from each of them out of their unusually high profits?"

As soon as she said it, Roza knew this was a big mistake. The guild representatives of the innkeepers, taverners, merchants and others erupted into a tirade about how impossible their jobs were at present, unable to house or feed those visiting the town, needing to employ more staff than they could find, and so on, and so on.

When the Reeve finally managed to calm the outrage of his Committee, reassuring them that there was categorically no question of any extra levy on them, he turned back to Roza, his voice dripping with sarcasm. "Any more helpful suggestions from you, Miss Warlock?"

She hated to suggest this, because it undermined her desire to offer her gift for free, but it was all she could think of. "How about if I rejuvenate the good people of Albany without charge, but that you make a small levy on those coming through the cleft in the mountains, up the highway and through the east gate? Wouldn't that cover some of your costs from those coming here from the plains?"

The Captain of the Guards responded immediately. "There is no way that my guards, as well as keeping order, checking visitors for weapons, catching criminals and all our other peace-keeping duties, can now become tax collectors as well. My men can't do this."

The Treasurer chimed in too. "We don't have enough revenue officials to administer that. It would mean an extra security cordon, entrance levy booths, employing the staff to man them, etc., etc. It's the same problem as paying for the additional guards all over again."

Roza had had enough of this. It wouldn't advance the discussion, but she wanted to make her point. "You know what? It sounds like you're all wishing I didn't have my gift of Rejuvenate or hadn't discovered it. Or I'd kept quiet about it, or not used it, and certainly not to weaken someone like the Dragon Emperor. But then I wouldn't have saved the town from destruction, would I? But at least then you wouldn't have these annoying crowd, or security or revenue problems, and you could be the Town Committee of an Albany reduced to ashes and ruins by Dragon-fire."

There was stunned silence after this, until the Reeve answered smoothly, "We're sorry you think us ungrateful for you saving us from the Emperor, because we appreciate what you did immensely. However, our task now is to manage our town for the benefit of our residents and to respond to changed circumstances as they occur. Which brings us to the next matter we need to discuss with you."

Roza gulped that they had yet more complaints to bring against her. The Reeve glanced left and right and received affirmative Committee nods to proceed. "Miss Rozabella, a delegation is on its way here from Gorge City to discuss with you whether it might be more convenient to conduct your rejuvenation efforts from there."

The blood drained from her cheeks as she tried to process what the Reeve had said. A delegation from Gorge City. More convenient to work from there. Roza remembered Kerenzi's news of yesterday about Lord Vallance, Earl of the Plains, marching to Albany with an army to abduct her back to Gorge City, by force if necessary.

The Committee were waiting for a response from her, so Roza played for some thinking time. "I'm sorry, but I don't understand you. A delegation from Gorge City wants to ask whether I could work from there? Away from my parents, my friends, my home on the plateau, my hometown? Why would I want to do that?"

"Miss Rozabella," the Reeve answered, "we're trying to improve the current situation, for you, for our Albany townsfolk, and the citizens of the plains. Our small town is being overwhelmed by people coming to see you. We don't have the accommodation, food, security or finances to manage such an important operation on behalf of the whole Empire. A place like Gorge City has ample resources for your needs, and for those coming to see you as well. Isn't that a more convenient arrangement all round?"

"But I've never been to Gorge City," Roza protested. "I don't know anyone there. I've never even left this valley before. What if I don't want to go there?"

"We understand that you're young and haven't travelled far. But our Sapien Empire is in new and momentous circumstances, and you, young lady, are central to all that is changing. You can't hide away here any longer, in a small town in a valley up in the mountains. You should find your place in Gorge City, the capital of the plains, and one of the great cities of the world. The time has come for you to grow up and leave home, my dear."

Roza sensed the Reeve was desperate to persuade her, but she was equally determined to refuse. "But what about my studies of magic? In my cave on the plateau, I have a library of books that I need to study for my warlock training. I can't see this delegation transporting my books all the way to Gorge City. And besides, you won't understand this, but advancing as a warlock includes living in a beautiful place – such as my plateau – because magic flows from beauty, and that's what I need more than anything else."

The Reeve held up his hands to stop her. "The details of transporting books and living in a beautiful place are precisely what the delegation from Gorge City will discuss with you. We are sure they can satisfy all your hesitations about agreeing to accompany them there."

Roza decided to dig in her heels and see what they said. "No, I don't want to go. I refuse. I want to stay here on my plateau overlooking my home valley, with my parents and friends, to learn and practise my magic here." She stuck out her chin and glared at the Reeve across the tables.

The Reeve sighed and glanced at the others around the tables. "Please be reasonable, Miss Rozabella. We are trying to find a compromise for exercising your magic without overwhelming our small town. We are all on the same side here, to protect you and enable your work, to agree on a consensus going forward."

She thought for a moment and there was silence in the room. Perhaps the Committee members hoped she was reconsidering, coming to her senses and about to agree with them. Not a chance. Now was the time to challenge them.

"All on the same side, are we? This delegation from Gorge City – are they on your side, or on mine? Because you fail to mention that this 'delegation' includes Lord Vallance himself, Earl of the Plains, and that he rides here with an army, ready to abduct me back to Gorge City by force if necessary. Do you admit the truth of that, or not?"

The Committee all stared at her in shock, and the Reeve looked stricken. Was their alarm because they hadn't known about Vallance and his army, or did they know and were shocked that she knew it too?

"But ... but, Miss Rozabella," the Reeve stammered. "How could you possibly know about that?"

"So, it's true, but you chose not to tell me?"

The Reeve nodded.

"How do I know these things? You forget, Mister Reeve, that I am a warlock, and I have magical ways of acquiring information." She glanced at the Committee members. "I have other powers and protections that you know nothing about. Don't you dare underestimate me again."

"No, no, Miss Warlock," the Reeve began, "we won't–"

"Shut up, Reeve," Roza snapped, "I haven't finished." And that felt good. "Now, when will Lord Vallance and his army get here, and what will happen when he arrives?"

The Reeve indicated for the Captain of the Guards to answer. "Our scouts report that the Earl and his army are three or four days away from Albany. When he arrives, we have no strength to resist him. This is why, Miss Rozabella, we all very much hope you will accompany him willingly, rather than any force being used. Your hometown of Albany will be damaged or destroyed if he needs to assault or besiege us to capture you. I urge you please, young lady, to consider these things before you decide on your response."

Roza had greater respect and gratitude for the Captain of the Guards than towards the Reeve or the Committee, so she nodded. "For your sake, Captain, I will bear that in mind as I think this over in the next few days. Now, is there anything further you need to discuss with me, or can I return to my rejuvenation?"

"No, nothing more," said the Reeve, and he forced out a smile.

Roza pushed back her chair and marched out of the Committee Room in complete silence. As soon as the door closed behind her, she heard the voices of the members erupt into frenzied argument.

She stopped in the Town Hall entrance to draw some deep breaths and calm herself. Her limbs were trembling, her mind was whirling, and she doubted she could focus on spells for the afternoon. But she had to. Queues of people waited for her, and she needed to shove the Committee and her future out of her mind and concentrate on her gift.

Roza walked out of the Town Hall doors and collided with Amber-Jane, her schoolroom friend.

"Hello, Rozabella, how lovely to see you again," she enthused. "And thank you so much for what you did for my Grandma Lily, because we're all thrilled that she's back to bossing us around like before."

She laughed, but when Roza could only force out a smile in return, her face fell into concern. "Oh, Roza, what's the matter, is everything okay?"

Roza wondered how much to say and chose the truth. "No. I've had the dubious pleasure of a Town Committee meeting, and their long list of complaints about everything, so they've upset and annoyed me. But I must get back to my queue of people to rejuvenate. I'm glad that your Grandma Lily is so much better, and please give my best wishes to your family." She turned away, leaving Amber-Jane standing on the Town Hall steps.

Jorxy was also grinning as she approached her tent. "And how was your very important Town Committee meeting, Miss high and mighty Rozabella the Warlock?"

"Don't," Roza snapped at him. "They've annoyed and upset me. I'll tell you later. Give me a few minutes and then send the next people in."

She threw open the tent flap and slumped onto her wooden stool. No plush or padded velvet upholstery in here. No, she mustn't think about the Committee. Or Lord Vallance and his army. Think of something beautiful.

She chose the moment last night, as the colours of sunset faded behind the mountains and the stars began to twinkle, when a handsome young spirit lord sat beside her on a boulder overlooking a waterfall and told her she was beautiful in the way that really matters.

With the morning's interruption, the queue had waited longer than usual to see her, so Roza worked quickly and diligently through the afternoon. A few hours of drawing on her magical power and directing it carefully where it was needed, with life-changing benefits, enabled her to forget her worries for a while.

But when she and Jorxy finally stopped for the day, her gloom and bad mood returned. She kept her eyes down as usual all the way from her tent to the warlock gate but stopped short because of someone directly in her path. For a fleeting instant she was annoyed at Jorxy for not having beaten everyone out of their way with his stick, but as soon as she looked up, she saw why.

It was Amber-Jane. And there was no way the blushing Jorxy would have swung his stick anywhere near the girl.

"Oh, hello, Amber-Jane, are you all right?" And then

Roza noticed that Amber-Jane was wringing her hands and had tears in her eyes.

Without a word, Amber-Jane flung her arms around Roza's shoulders and squeezed her tight. At first, Roza couldn't understand why, or what was going on, but after a moment it was so nice to be held, and feel Amber-Jane stroking her back, the warmth of her body, the perfume of her hair, that she stopped wondering and just enjoyed it.

Then Amber-Jane whispered in her ear. "I can't bear it that anyone has annoyed or upset you, Rozabella. You've done so much for this town and my family that we can never thank you enough. You're so generous and kind, and so brave and wonderful, that you mustn't listen to a single word from anyone who says otherwise."

With a last squeeze, Amber-Jane leaned back far enough to see Roza's face. "Okay?"

Roza was embarrassed to wipe the tears off her cheeks but then saw that Amber-Jane's face was wet too. She nodded because she didn't know what to say.

"I wanted to say that to you," Amber-Jane added, "because when I saw you earlier, it looked like you needed it."

"Yes, thank you," Roza mumbled. "I did need it. And I do need it. Thank you, Amber-Jane. Can I do anything for you?"

She looked blank. "No, I don't need anything. I waited here to catch you on your way up to your plateau just to say that."

Roza stared at her. "You've been waiting here just to say that to me?"

Amber-Jane nodded. "Yes, it seemed important to me to say it."

Roza pulled Amber-Jane back into a hug but then she heard Jorxy clear his throat. "Um, I'm feeling a bit left out of all the hugging here."

The two girls laughed and broke apart, and Amber-Jane

gave Jorxy a brief hug, but then came back to Roza.

Her dark eyes looked straight into Roza's, and she said, "Remember, dear Roza, that you are brilliant and the best thing that has ever happened to this town. We love you and would do anything for you. Understand?"

"If you say so," Roza mumbled. "And thank you, Amber-Jane. I really did need to hear all that. I'll try to keep what you've said in my heart."

They squeezed hands, and then Roza and Jorxy passed through the warlock gate and along the farm track and path up to the plateau.

CHAPTER SIX

The two of them walked in silence all the way up to the plateau as darkness fell. Roza felt bad that Jorxy must have a thousand questions, and she was making him wait before answering them. But she didn't know what to think, say or do herself.

As they passed along the grass path through the orchard, Roza noticed that the edges of the leaves were turning yellow. Autumn was marching on, and the days were becoming shorter and colder.

In the cave, Standley had some food ready for them, and they plonked themselves on stools at the kitchen table and munched opposite each other. Normally Jorxy would be keen to examine their takings in the donations bag, but this evening it lay untouched on the table.

At last, Roza broke the silence. "Sorry I snapped at you earlier at the tent. The Committee upset me, and I had to tell you either the whole thing or nothing at all. We didn't have time for the whole story then, but I can tell you now, if you like."

Jorxy's face brightened a little, but he still looked uncertain whether she'd apologised enough for keeping him in the dark. "Yeah, I wondered when you'd let me in on all your big secrets. I'm happy to help how I can, but I need to know what's going on, even the stuff that goes over my head."

"Well, I'll start with the Committee today, but it connects with something Kerenzi the spirit lord told me yesterday." Jorxy's eyebrows rose. "The Reeve started off chuntering about paying for all the extra guards they need. He wants to help himself to our donations bag and take as much as he likes for the town coffers." Jorxy started to protest at this so Roza held up a hand. "Don't worry, I squashed that idea straight away."

"Good. They're not getting their grubby little hands on any of your hard-earned donations."

"They asked me for suggestions on how to pay for it all, so I said to tax the booming profits of the inns and taverns, or collect a levy at the eastern gate, but those hit the floor like lead weights. Then I began to lose my temper a bit."

Jorxy's mouth twitched with a smile, as though he'd like what was coming. "Go on, what did you say?"

Roza had been annoyed at the time, but looking back, she almost smiled too. "I said they must wish I never discovered my gift, or hadn't used it, and certainly not on the Dragon Emperor. That way, they could be free of all these hassles and be the Committee of a town reduced to ashes and ruins by Dragon-fire."

He grinned. "Too right. They should definitely be more grateful for you having saved everyone."

"Yeah, you should have seen their faces when I said that." Her smile faded. "But then they went on to what worried and upset me." She drew a deep breath. "A delegation from Gorge City is coming to negotiate with me about moving my rejuvenation work to there."

Jorxy stared at her. "What? You're supposed to go to Gorge City and see all these crowds of people there, and not here?"

"Yep. The Reeve said our small town is being overwhelmed by all these people, whereas Gorge City has the space and resources to cope with it all."

"And what did you say?"

Roza shrugged. "I said no. I don't want to go. And they didn't like that."

"So, what happens now, when these Gorge City people get here?"

She sighed. "Now we come to what Kerenzi told me. He knew about this delegation but said it's headed up by none other than Lord Vallance, the Earl of the Plains himself."

Jorxy's mouth fell open. "Lord Vallance is coming here to speak with you?"

"Yep. And that's not all. He's got an army with him."

His face creased into a worried frown. "What's he bringing an army for? To make sure you agree to everything he wants?"

"Something like that."

They were both quiet until Jorxy asked, "Did the Reeve and the Committee know about the Earl and the army?"

"Yeah, they did, but they weren't going to tell me until I challenged them about it."

Jorxy thumped his fist on the table. "I'm glad you lost your temper. When will the army get here?"

"Three or four days." She turned and looked out through the cave entrance at the gathering night, almost as though expecting to hear marching feet in the distance. But all was quiet on the plateau and across the valley.

"Roza, what are you going to do?"

She looked down at the table and traced her finger along the grain in the wood. Her voice was small and quiet. "I don't know. I'm starting to feel unsafe and unwelcome here. I can't even get my head around what my options might be."

Immediately, Jorxy was business-like. "All right, let's talk about your choices. Option One, you could agree and go with Lord Vallance to Gorge City."

Roza pulled a face. "That's the last thing I want to do. I don't want to leave my parents and friends, my hometown, this plateau, and go off to some unknown city full of strangers. And Kerenzi said this Lord Vallance is not a nice man, but selfish, greedy and ambitious. He's starting a civil war against the weakened Dragon Emperor to set himself up as an independent ruler of the plains. Apparently, I'm supposed to be his puppet and figurehead since I tricked and weakened the Emperor in the first place."

Jorxy was nodding. "Forget Option One then. Number Two, continue to say no, and see what happens when the

Earl and his army get here."

She shook her head. "I couldn't do that to Albany. Lord Vallance has brought his army so he can besiege and assault our town and take me away by force if necessary. The town guards will be slaughtered if they resist or oppose what the Earl wants to do. I couldn't live with the thought of anyone dying to defend me."

"So, cross out that option too. What other choices are there?"

"I can't think of anything else. What would you do in my position?"

He sucked in a breath through his teeth. "What would I do if someone is coming to get me? Like town guards wanting to arrest me? First rule: don't be where they expect you to be."

"You mean don't be at home or the rubbish ditch?"

"Exactly. That's the first place they'll look. Which means when the Earl arrives, don't be on the plateau."

"What, hide somewhere in town, or elsewhere in the valley? But Lord Vallance's army will tear the whole valley apart until they find me."

"Yes, they will." Jorxy was staring at her. "Which means … don't be in the valley."

Roza stared back. "What? You mean … leave Albany altogether?"

"Yeah." Jorxy leaned forward. "The idea of hiding is a good one, and it isn't safe for anyone to know where you are. Your problem right now is everyone knows where to find you."

"That's right. Make your way to Albany, and three times a week I'm in the marketplace and the rest of the time I'm on my plateau. So, the crowds gather here from across the Empire to receive my gift, and anyone who seeks to control or exploit me can also march here with all their strength to make sure I agree and submit. What if no one knows where I am any more?"

"Then the crowds and the armies wouldn't know where to go. They'd search and hunt for you, but over a much wider area. Where would you go?"

She shrugged. "I've no idea. I don't know what's out there. But your idea of being away from here feels like my best option."

Jorxy was animated now. "We should probably keep moving, not stay in one place for long. That will be harder for anyone to follow us, to track us down and find us."

She looked at his keen, enthusiastic face. "We? Us? I can't ask you to do this too. It's not fair on you. It's not you they're after. It's me. I'm the one with a price on my head and a target on my back. I don't expect you to exile yourself from your home and family for my sake."

He glared at her, his anger building, then suddenly burst out laughing.

"What's so funny?" Roza complained. "I can't see anything to laugh about."

Jorxy controlled his laughter, but he was still smiling. "Remember before all this happened? We sat above the town's rubbish ditch and threw stones at the refuse below. You moaned about looking after your sick parents, and I moaned about being poor. We said we should run away together, leave it all behind and make new lives for ourselves somewhere else."

Roza couldn't help smiling now. "Yeah, I remember that. But I never thought it'd be like this. Running away from danger. Fleeing for our lives and our freedom. It doesn't sound so much of an adventure, does it?"

"Oh, I dunno. It could still be an adventure once we make our escape from the danger here."

They were quiet for a while until Roza became aware that Standley was nearby and seemed to have listened to everything they said. She looked at Jorxy and held his gaze. "Are you sure about this? We should sleep on it and see how we feel in the morning."

He grinned. "Yeah, I'm pretty sure, but we might come up with other bright ideas. I always thought I'd end up running away with you, so I can't believe it's really come to this. I've nothing to leave behind here, only a poor family who won't miss me when I'm gone. A life on the run with the world-famous Warlock of Albany sounds a better deal to me."

Roza rolled her eyes and stood up. "Good night, Jorx. We'll decide what to do in the morning."

It took a while for Roza to fall asleep, because the thoughts about running away kept chasing each other around her mind. But when she woke to daylight filtering through the cave entrance to her bedroom, she'd slept soundly after all. Perhaps the decision to do something about her situation was a deeper comfort.

Jorxy was busy in the kitchen when she appeared, and he was beaming to himself as though the prospect of running away with her was the best thing that had ever happened to him. "Great morning," he chimed, nodding towards the bright sunlight streaming in through the cave entrance. "Standley is out milking Dairy the cow. Sleep well?"

"It took me a while to drop off. Too much to think about. But yeah, I slept well eventually. You?"

"I was almost too excited to sleep, but yep, best night I've had in years."

Roza snorted. "I take it you've changed your mind then and decided to stay here and welcome Lord Vallance with open arms."

Jorxy chuckled. "Yeah, right. Let me think now." He tapped his chin. "Carted off to some remote prison cell for the rest of my days, or off on an exciting adventure with my best friend in the world. It's a tough choice." He brought a platter of bread, butter, cold meat, cheese, and fruit to the table and sat down opposite her. "What about you? You still want to go?"

Roza reached for the loaf and knife and cut some slices before answering. "Yeah, I still think leaving here is my only sensible option, but I'm not calling it an exciting adventure."

"Ah, that depends on how you look at things. A positive attitude, that's what you need."

"Jorx," she said, buttering the bread for them both. "Was it a mistake to offer my rejuvenation to everyone? To keep using it to help people after what I did to the Dragon? Because that only confirmed my power, and advertised it to the whole Empire, leading to the crowds and difficulties now. I could have tried harder to keep it secret and hidden, and avoided all this mess."

"No, I'm not gonna say you should've hidden your power, because think of all the good you've done. Like Amber-Jane's Grandma Lily, and all those others you help each day in the marketplace, changing their lives for the better. You've done so much good, you have, and you shouldn't regret it."

"But if we're going away, moving around and hiding, then I won't rejuvenate anyone, will I? It'll be just us, and all those aging and elderly people will keep getting older and die. I could have helped them, but I didn't."

"Now, stop that," Jorxy chided. "Don't blame yourself. It's not your fault we need to go on the run. The ones to blame are that lot out there." He waved a lump of cheese towards the cave entrance. "Thain Wicksteed, and the Reeve and Committee, and Lord Vallance, and all those selfish, greedy, impatient ones who want your power before anyone else. If everyone waited their turn, doing things in a calm, ordered way, letting you rejuvenate them when you got the chance, then you could carry on here fine. It's them what's spoiled it all and made it impossible for you to keep helping them."

"I suppose so. But once things settle down, I need to think how I can keep doing it. Rejuvenate is my gift, and it's unique and meant to be shared, so there must be some way to do it."

Standley tottered into the cave, carrying a bucket of milk in his hooks. Roza marvelled again at how strong and supple, how dextrous and careful her enchanted coat stand was. Jorxy jumped up and dipped two cups into the bucket, bringing the still-warm milk back to the table for them. "Thanks, mate," he called, and the coat stand inclined his top as he put the bucket down.

"Standley," Roza said, and he came towards them. "Were you listening to what Jorxy and I discussed last night? About the threat to my safety and Lord Vallance wanting to take me off to Gorge City?"

He nodded his hooks and seemed to be listening carefully.

"We're thinking about going away from here to prevent that, so do you think that's a good idea?" Standley nodded. "Or what about if we don't go away? You fought so well against Thain Wicksteed and his men, could you keep me safe from Lord Vallance and his army?"

The coat stand seemed to think for a moment and then shook his hooks.

"In which case, if Jorxy and I leave here, will you stay here and look after the plateau, or come with us?"

Standley immediately pointed his hooks at Roza and Jorxy.

"Excellent," Roza beamed. "The two of us have just become three, and we'll appreciate the extra strength and protection on the way."

Jorxy was nodding. "Great. But if Standley comes with us, what happens to the plateau and the animals, the pigs, chickens, sheep and the cow?"

"Hm, they'll need looking after. What about your sister, Joidi? She looked after my parents' animals, didn't she?"

"So, we ask her to come up here and look after them once we've gone?"

Roza tried to think. "No, it won't be safe for anyone to

be up here when Lord Vallance and his army arrive. Especially not a young woman like Joidi. They don't know what I look like and won't believe her when she protests she's not the warlock. They might abduct her to Gorge City in case she really is me, and we can't risk that."

Jorxy looked horrified. "No, you're right, we can't risk that happening to our Joidi. She'd need to move the animals away from here. Oh, this is getting complicated."

"And I'm worried about anyone knowing we're going away. We can't risk that news spreading until we're well on our way. Maybe we could leave a message with your brother Rufus about what to do with Joidi and the animals if anything should happen to us, or if we ever need to go away. Would that work?"

Jorxy blew his breath from his cheeks. "That's probably the best we could manage if we really want to go in secret. But how soon are we going?"

"Lord Vallance could be here in two or three days. If I don't appear at my marketplace tent in the morning, the alarm will be raised at once. I think I should do my rejuvenating as usual tomorrow and then we leave tomorrow night. That should give us a day or two's head start until anyone notices we've gone from the plateau."

Jorxy was staring at her. "Tomorrow night?" Then he shook himself. "Yes, we can do that. What else do we need to get ready? Food and drink, warm clothes, I can look after the packing of those, as much as we can carry."

Looking around her cave home, Roza saw something that made her heart stop. And then sink. "Oh no," she cried. "My books. I need to take all my books with me, but I can't, can I?"

"Er, no. We can't take a whole library on the run with us."

Roza jumped up and walked over to the bookshelves filled with all the tomes on magic that old Philoe had bequeathed to her. "But these contain all I need to know about becoming a better warlock, to learn lots of new spells. How will I grow and improve without these?"

Jorxy could only shrug. "Well, you've got today to learn what you can."

Roza gave him a withering look. As though one day was enough time to learn all the magic they needed to stay safe and alive on their travels. Then she remembered something. "I promised your brother Rufus and the guards about enlarging or multiplying their rations. I could learn that today, share it with them in the morning, and then use it to multiply our food and drink in the days to come."

Jorxy clapped in delight. "Excellent. I was wondering how much we could take, or where to get more once we leave. But you can multiply our stocks of everything along the way."

Roza didn't feel as enthusiastic as Jorxy did, because the imminent loss of her magic books troubled her deeply. "Okay, Standley," she called. "A book with a spell to increase or multiply food and drink, please?"

The coat stand came forward, surveying the shelves before him. Then he hooked out a book high up and Roza reached and took it. "Basic Survival Spells for the Adventurous Warlock," she read. "That sounds about right. There must be so much in here that would be useful, if only we could take this and all the other books with us."

She returned to her kitchen stool and began to flick through the pages. Standley came with her and watched over her shoulder. There was a spell called Enflame which she could use for lighting fires.

At last, she came to a page entitled Maximise, and Standley leaned forward and tapped the paper. She read through the spell, and it sounded just what she needed: a way to enlarge what you already had of something. "Okay, thank you, Standley," she said and prepared to learn what was written there.

But the coat stand didn't move away as she expected.

Instead Standley nudged her shoulder with a hook. She looked up, puzzled. "What is it?" she asked, but of course, he couldn't tell her. He pointed at the book and did a motion with a hook like turning over a page.

Roza looked at the book, up at Standley, then back at the book. She turned over the page and saw written there the counter-spell to Maximise, entitled Minimise. She skim-read through it then looked up at the coat stand's knots, frowning. "A spell to reduce what we already have of something. I can't see what use that will be. We don't want to reduce how much food or drink we have."

But Standley pointed at the page, turned towards the bookcase and indicated the books. Roza picked up the book and carried it over to where Standley stood. She frowned at him. "A spell to reduce the number of books we have?"

He shook his hooks, pointed at the book, and then made a motion of bringing his hooks closer together.

And the brilliance of her coat stand's idea landed. "A spell to reduce the size of the books we have?" she asked in wonder. Standley nodded vigorously, and Roza was so excited that she jumped up and down and hugged him.

"Jorxy," she yelled. He was only across the cave, and had been listening to it all, but he still came over. "Listen to this. Our brilliant coat stand has solved my book problem. There's this spell Minimise which I can use to reduce the size of the books. I can make them as small as I like, can I?" Standley seemed to shrug, then nod. "So, I can make this whole bookcase of books take up no more room than a small box and take them all with me."

Jorxy still looked puzzled. "But what use will that be? The books will then be so small there's no way you could read even a single word."

Roza smacked his shoulder and turned back the page of her Survival Spells book. "When I want to read one of them, Mister Jorx, I take the tiny little book out of the box and use this counter-spell on it, which is called Maximise. This one will restore the book to its former size, and I can read it as normal. Isn't that brilliant?"

The light was dawning across Jorxy's face. "So today you Minimise all these books and place them in a box to take with us. Then whenever you want one, you take it out, enlarge it, read it, reduce it again and you've got all your magic books with you forever."

He smiled, but didn't look nearly as relieved and pleased as Roza felt inside about still being able to learn magic and advance as a warlock. This leaving Albany and going on the run might work after all.

CHAPTER SEVEN

While Jorxy busied himself with what backpacks, clothes and food they needed for their travels, Roza's first job was to learn these Maximise and Minimise spells. As with the Repulser spell, the principle was to channel her magical energy into the object to be transformed. Before she risked any of her books, she started by trying to enlarge a small, square piece of wood.

This time, Roza mastered more quickly the technique of directing her magic into the wood, and practised the necessary hand movements, concentrating on her desire to enlarge it. For Maximise, she tapped the bottom left of the object, and then above the top right at the new size she wanted.

At first, the piece of wood wouldn't change at all. Roza became excited when the wood finally began to stretch, but it was an uneven growth, ending up with a lopsided block. She continued to practise until she made the wood enlarge evenly into a larger version of the original.

She showed Jorxy and Standley her enlarged block of wood, but they didn't seem excited enough for the effort she'd put into this. So, she went back and worked on the Minimise spell, reducing the wood to its original size. These hand movements were reversed, tapping top right and then bottom left. Her success came more quickly, but it required concentration to enlarge and reduce the objects properly.

By the time they stopped for lunch, Roza was proficient at a regular and smooth Maximise and Minimise of the wood and decided to see how this went with foodstuffs. She spent the mealtime growing and reducing a slice of apple up to dinner plate size, and then down to no larger than her fingernail. She made Jorxy eat the larger and smaller apple slices to ensure there was no damage to the taste.

"What about drinks?" Jorxy demanded, so Roza set to enlarging and reducing a cup full of water. They discovered that in this case both the cup and the water grew and diminished alongside each other.

"Hold on," Jorxy interrupted, "this ain't gonna work. Suppose we're on top of a mountain with half a bottle of water. You enlarge the bottle and great, we've got twice as much water. But we can't walk around with ever larger bottles to drink out of. When you reduce the bottle back to normal size, we lose all the extra water."

"Oh, yeah," Roza replied, "I hadn't thought of that. The issue is enlarging both the substance and the container at the same time, and I don't know how to do that separately."

As though he'd been listening to them, Standley came forward, holding a jug in his hooks. He gave it to Jorxy, who looked at Roza, back at Standley, and then down at the jug.

"Is this another brilliant Standley idea?" he asked. "Because I don't get it."

Their coat stand began to mime with his hooks, which was extremely comical to behold. Roza and Jorxy were giggling too much to grasp his meaning but eventually gathered something about enlarging and pouring.

"Ah, I've got it," Roza said at last. "The answer is to separate the substance from the container. I enlarge the half-full bottle. We take this jug along with us, and tip all the water out of the bottle into the jug. I reduce the size of the bottle and then refill it to the top with all our lovely extra water from the jug. Would that work?"

She looked up at her coat stand, who nodded and seemed to smile. "Thank you, Standley, because I need to avoid making the magic any more complicated than necessary." She rubbed her forehead and temples. "I wonder how many of these things we'll need to work out as we go along."

"Cheer up," Jorxy patted her arm, beaming. "This is what makes the whole thing more of an adventure."

She rolled her eyes at him and decided it was time to try

her spells on a book. For their plan to work, she had a lot of them to reduce and needed to know she could do it well.

Roza picked a small, old book off a top shelf that looked like it hadn't been read for years, 'A Warlock's Guide to Seaside Plants'. She'd heard there were stretches of water in the world called 'the sea', but they weren't anywhere near Albany. This was a good test, because she didn't mind if she never knew about seaside plants. She flicked through it and saw coloured pictures of flowers and grasses and closed it again.

She tried Maximising it first, to know if she could restore whatever she did, concentrating hard on her hand movements and channelling the magic. It expanded by about a half; she opened it and gasped. The pictures and text were all larger, but some of them had shifted or become blurred. Unlike with the wooden block, the slice of apple or the cup of water, the crucial factor with the books was not the overall size but keeping all the fine detail inside.

It was a blow, but Roza was determined to correct this. Taking all her beloved books on their journey depended on this, and they needed to stay crystal clear for reading.

She considered what she did for rejuvenation. She didn't know all the workings of the human heart, eye, muscles, bones, or whatever, and simply trusted the magic to know what needed to be done and to do it. Maybe this was what had gone wrong here. Was she trying too hard to direct and control what the magic did, rather than trusting it and letting it flow?

She drew in some long breaths to help her to relax and focused on the seaside plants book to Minimise it back to its original size. She performed the hand tapping and allowed her energy to work on each page, diagram and writing as it thought fit. With trembling hand, she re-opened the cover and saw with relief that all was sharp and clear again for reading.

Trust the magic, she told herself, it knows what it's

doing. Next time she Minimised the book down to the size of her palm, too small to read, and then enlarged it again, and all remained clear. As a final test, she reduced it to the length of her little finger, and back again, and all was fine.

"I've got it at last," she announced to Jorxy and Standley. "I can start Minimising the books for our journey. Can you find a suitable box for them to go in?" Standley disappeared off to the storerooms deeper in the cave and came back with various boxes for Roza to choose from.

She collected a neat pile of tiny books next to her on the kitchen table, while Jorxy lifted the full-size books down from the shelves.

Suddenly he stopped. "Look at this."

"What is it?" Roza asked and read the title of the book he was holding. "Maps of the World, by Warlock Philoe of Albany". She stared at the cover, up at Jorxy, then back at the book again.

"Is this the old warlock who was here before you?"

Roza nodded. "Maybe my old mentor was something of a traveller in his youth."

Jorxy flicked through the pages. "Wow, this is great. Look at these, hand-drawn maps of all sorts of places I've never heard of. And see here, because he's from Albany, the whole book starts with a map of our valley and the routes around here. And here are maps of our Heismith mountains, with all the tracks, best places to shelter, the different passes and valleys. I'll look at this and decide which way to go before you Minimise it."

"Yes, please," said Roza, and Standley took over lifting down the books for her to reduce and pack.

By early evening, Roza finally finished Minimising the whole bookcase of books into one box that could fit into the bottom of a pack. Jorxy and Standley then brought out from the back of the cave the locked chest full of donated treasures. Rather than leaving them here for the Reeve, Committee or Lord Vallance to find, Roza decided to

Minimise both the chest and the contents to go into a backpack too.

Standley watched while she did this, and helped them lift the smaller, but still heavy, chest into the bottom of another pack. Roza wondered whether Jorxy was thinking that if she could enlarge silver, gold, gems, and jewellery as well as other things, then she was a source of limitless wealth. Roza shoved the implications of that aside because it didn't bear thinking about.

Standley chose only one small item as his entire luggage, the bottle of Gymbo's Furniture Polish, which he tucked into a corner of his pack.

At last, they surveyed their cave by evening candlelight, and it looked forlorn with its empty bookshelves and so much else tidied away. They'd decided to make it appear deserted, as though they'd left for good and weren't simply hiding away somewhere else in the valley. They wanted their pursuers – Lord Vallance and the Gorge City army – to give up on searching Albany as quickly as possible, so the townsfolk could go back to their normal lives.

As she lay down to sleep, Roza wondered whether this might be her last ever night of sleeping in this cave. And when would she next get to sleep in a bed? For all Jorxy's excitement about the coming adventure, she found it more daunting than anything else.

They woke early the next morning, and over breakfast Roza voiced to Jorxy a regret she had. "I wish I could see my mum and dad again before I leave. I don't have time to visit their Meadow Cottage today, and if I did, they'd wonder why I'd gone up specially to see them. No, I suppose we can't risk raising suspicions that we're up to something."

Jorxy looked thoughtful. "I'll see Rufus at the warlock gate but can't say I'll miss seeing the rest of my family. I wonder how long it'll take them to notice I'm gone."

They took their normal clothes and equipment down the

path to town – Jorxy's trusty stick to rap any over-enthusiastic members of the crowd, and the donations bag – to make their last day look as normal as possible.

When they approached the warlock gate, Roza called out to Rufus and the town guards there, "Good morning, and it's time to fulfil my promise about enlarging your rations."

The excited guards gathered around, and Rufus said, "You should know there are bets going over whether you can do this. Some of us," he looked around his circle of colleagues, "have doubts about your magical powers."

Roza raised her eyebrows. "Oh, really? In which case, I should confound my biggest doubter first. Come on, step up with your rations bag whoever feels this is beyond me."

The biggest and burliest of them stepped forward and handed her his small bag of ration biscuits. Roza picked out a medium-sized biscuit and placed it to fit comfortably within his palm.

"Better have your other hand ready to catch it once I've finished," she warned. The guard gave her his most disbelieving smile.

Roza reached down inside her for her spark of magical energy and fanned it into flame. She focused the power into the biscuit, tapped the bottom left and top right with her finger and commanded it to Maximise. The biscuit expanded smoothly to the length of a loaf of bread, and the guard almost dropped it. As Roza had warned, he brought his other hand up just in time to catch it.

The circle of guards gasped, cheered, marvelled at the huge biscuit, and the burliest stood there looking sheepish. He turned it over, poked it, examined it, smelled it.

"Go on, take a bite," Roza goaded him. "You need to know it still tastes good before you pay out on those bets."

The guard took a hesitant bite, chewed, and then had to nod. The other guards cheered again and clapped him on the back.

"Now, repeat after me," Roza said to him. "Thank you,

Warlock Roza, for enlarging my rations, and I will never doubt your magic again."

The guard mumbled the words back to her while his colleagues roared with laughter.

"Shall I enlarge the rest of your biscuits, then?" Roza asked, and when he nodded, she set the bag down on the ground. To save time, she enlarged the whole bag and contents together and then handed the man a sack now bulging with loaf-sized biscuits. "It takes a brave man to admit you're wrong, so learn well from this. Now, line up your bags, the rest of you, and I'll enlarge them all in turn."

After a few minutes, the guards had laid out their precious food supplies, and Roza had enlarged them all into sacks of over-sized ration biscuits. While she did this, Jorxy was chatting with Rufus, and she hoped the reputations of the two brothers would rise among the other guards.

As she finished, she noticed one guard still holding a couple of the smaller biscuits in his hand. "What's the matter with those?" she asked. "Don't you want me to enlarge them?"

"Oh, you don't need to worry about these," he replied. "They're old and stale so I took them out of my bag."

Roza had an idea and supposed it couldn't hurt to try it. "Luckily for you," she said to the guard, "I'm a bit of an expert with things that are old and past it. You know my gift is Rejuvenate, to make things physically younger, so shall I try to refresh your old biscuits as well as enlarge them?"

She caught Jorxy's eye as she said this and raised her eyebrows at him. He tilted his head, and she wondered if he was thinking the same as she was: this would be immensely useful on their journeys.

The guard nodded and held an old, stale biscuit on his palm. Roza decided on one spell after the other, rather than both at the same time, as safer for a first attempt.

She reached for her magic, touched the corner of the biscuit, and channelled a trickle of her power through her

Rejuvenate gift as she normally did with people. She made the substance younger by a few days, and then proceeded to Maximise it by tapping at the opposite corners. At once, the aroma of freshly baked biscuit filled the air, and the guards reacted with wonder and delight.

The guard pressed his fingers into the soft, warm biscuit and took a bite. His eyes widened. "It's like it's just come out the oven," he marvelled, with his mouth full.

As the guards breathed in the delicious fragrance and clapped again, Roza gave them all an exaggerated bow. But when they asked her to make their large biscuits freshly baked too, she laughed and shook her head. "Sorry, boys. I have people waiting for my rejuvenation in the marketplace, so enjoy your huge biscuits as they are."

They left the guards, passed through warlock gate, and started towards the centre of town. Close beside her, Jorxy whispered excitedly in her ear. "This is wonderful. You can refresh our milk and bread and fruit, as well as enlarge it, so we'll never run out of fresh food."

"I know." Roza was equally thrilled. "I wasn't sure I could do it, but this seemed a good time to try. I was so delighted when it smelled that fresh."

"You're amazing." He looked sideways at her. "And you seem in a really good mood this morning."

"Yes, I am." She wondered whether to say this, and then thought, why not? She leaned closer and whispered, "I must be happy because rumour has it that tonight I'm running away on an exciting adventure with my best friend in the whole wide world."

A grin of the utmost delight plastered itself across Jorxy's face.

When they arrived at her marketplace tent, Roza spoke with the Captain of the Guards. She wanted to calm everyone's nerves and sound as though she was considering negotiating with Lord Vallance about her future.

"Captain," she said quietly, "is there any news on when

our friends, the delegation from Gorge City, might arrive?"

"Yes, Miss Rozabella. The latest report from my scouts places them as due to reach our cleft in the mountains late tomorrow."

"Thank you. Tomorrow is my day on the plateau, so can you inform the Reeve and Committee that I'll meet the delegation in the Town Hall the day after, when I'm due here in the marketplace anyway? They can see my work at first hand if they'd like. I've decided it can't hurt to listen to what they propose." She gave him what she hoped was a reassuring smile, and if this plan gave her a night, a day and another night's head-start on Lord Vallance's pursuit, that was the best she could hope for.

"I am mightily relieved to hear you say that, Warlock Roza. I will pass on your message to the Committee at once, who are also most anxious to avoid any … unpleasantness."

Roza rested a hand on his arm. "I'll always be grateful for everything you and your men have done for me, and I couldn't bear the thought of anything unpleasant happening to Albany."

As the Captain of the Guards hurried off towards the Town Hall, Roza entered her tent and set to work rejuvenating the first of the people waiting in line to see her. She tried not to think that this would be the last time she would sit here doing this, because the thought threatened to distract and upset her.

The day passed uneventfully until the late afternoon when a middle-aged couple came in through her tent flaps. Roza jumped up at once. "Mum, Dad," she cried. "What are you doing here, are you all right?"

"Ah, Roza dear," her dad, Arthur, replied, "we're both fine, and we hope we're still allowed to come and see our own daughter."

"Of course you are," Roza said, hugging them each in turn. "Did you have to jump the queue?"

Her mum, Helena, pulled an apologetic face. "Yes, I'm

afraid we did. Some of those waiting didn't look pleased, but that nice boy Jorxy explained to everyone who we are, and that the warlock would be taking only a very short break to see us. Is this all right with you?"

"It's lovely to see you both, especially looking so well, with no blind eyes or weak heart between you. Are you down here in town for something else?"

Arthur and Helena exchanged a glance. "We'll be honest with you," her dad said. "This morning a guard from the town's west gate ran up to our Meadow Cottage. He'd heard from a guard at the warlock gate that your friend Jorxy told his brother Rufus that at breakfast today you mentioned about seeing us sometime." He looked at his wife. "Did I get that … thread … of messages right?"

Roza and her mum groaned at the weaving reference and then laughed. "Yes, that'll be right," Roza said. "I must thank Jorxy and Rufus when I see them."

"So of course," and Arthur winked at her, "we took that as a definite invitation, hopped on the cart and here we are. You can't expect any parents to miss out on their chance to see their favourite daughter."

"Only daughter, Dad," Roza corrected him.

"Only and favourite," Arthur insisted.

Roza realised that here were two people whose advice she trusted, so she asked, "Um … how much do you know about Lord Vallance and Gorge City?"

They looked at each other. Arthur replied, "Well, we've been to Gorge City and met the Earl of the Plains. Why?"

Roza chewed her lip. "With all the crowds here, the Town Committee have asked if I could move there to do my rejuvenating."

They stared at her. "You've never left the valley, have you?" Helena said. "Or met the Earl?"

"Gorge City's a very impressive place," Arthur said. "The vast canyon, huge towers, the Earl's Palace, the Sapien Bridge. Built by the Sapiens themselves many ages ago, or so it's said. But teeming with people, and too crowded for our taste."

"And I know how Lord Vallance has risen to become Earl of the Plains," Helena went on. "He has a way with words, making them sound smooth and agreeable when underneath there's sharp-edged steel. I wouldn't trust him for one minute."

Roza nodded. "That's roughly what I've heard."

"Please ask if you want to know more," Helena added. "But we won't keep you from your patient customers, so we'll be on our way. We're so proud of you and your excellent work, dear. We know you'll make the right decisions, so take good care of yourself."

They turned and left the tent with a farewell wave. Roza followed them out, caught Jorxy's eye, mouthed the words "Thank you," and beamed at him.

At last, it was time to finish work for the day. Roza's heart ached that the queue waiting to see her still stretched halfway across the marketplace, and the guards were telling people to return in two days when the warlock would be back.

No, I won't, Roza thought, and these people had probably missed their chance of being rejuvenated at all. She remembered Jorxy's words that this sad truth was not her fault, but had to be blamed on the selfish, greedy, power-hungry people like Lord Vallance.

The two of them walked from the marketplace to the warlock gate, with Roza saying mental goodbyes to the town schoolroom, and the streets of Albany. Rufus was still on duty at the gate, so they went over to him.

"Hey, thanks for sending a message to my parents about coming to see me, and they popped into my tent this afternoon. My life seems too busy to get myself up to Meadow Cottage these days."

"No problem," Rufus said. "The least we can do for a warlock who keeps us so well fed."

Roza smiled, and with a glance at Jorxy, she went on, "We've been meaning to say that if we ever need to go away for a while, would you and your sister Joidi keep an eye on the plateau and our animals for us? Joidi could bring our sheep, cow, pigs, and chickens down nearer to town if that would be easier for her."

Rufus's brow had furrowed into a frown. "Are there things going on I don't know about?"

Roza glanced at Jorxy again, stepped closer and lowered her voice. "This isn't to go beyond the three of us, but the Town Committee tell me there's a delegation from Gorge City due here tomorrow. They want to meet me and discuss moving my rejuvenation work to there because Albany is getting swamped with visitors. So, nothing's definite or decided yet, but we mention this in case we want to visit Gorge City soon and see what it's like there."

Rufus gazed at them as though thinking and then nodded. "Of course. I'll mention this to Joidi and I'm sure she'll be delighted because of how much she loves animals."

"Thanks," Roza said, and she and Jorxy passed through the warlock gate.

As soon as they were out of earshot, Jorxy muttered, "All the town guards will know about that by morning. Rufus is the worst person ever for keeping a secret. He just can't keep his mouth shut."

Roza looked at him. "Really? Oh well, I don't suppose it matters since the guards will know all about the arrivals from the plains later tomorrow."

They trudged to the end of the farm track and turned left onto the path up to the plateau. At the top, they found that Standley had got their backpacks and the last of the food supplies ready for them.

Roza took a goodbye stroll through the fruit trees of her orchard to the cliff edge that overlooked the valley. The surrounding mountain peaks thrust skywards against the last colours of the day, giving way to star-strewn blackness in the east. Lamps twinkled through the windows of homes and cottages down in Albany – and then she noticed something that washed a chill over her skin.

In front of the town's east gate, where the highway from the plains passed through Albany's protective stone wall, a line of horsemen carrying torches was riding up through the cleft in the mountains. Raising her eyes, Roza saw torches stretching further down the highway into the distance.

It could mean only one thing.

Lord Vallance, Earl of the Plains, had force-marched his troops and arrived at Albany a day earlier than expected.

And he had come here with a single purpose: to find, capture and abduct the Warlock of Albany.

CHAPTER EIGHT

Roza shook herself out of her horror and panic at what she could see below and sprinted back to the cave. So much for a night, a day and another night's head-start on the Earl and his men. How long would it take him to ride from the east gate up here to the plateau? She had less than an hour before he could be here. Don't underestimate Lord Vallance again, she chided herself. He's a man who likes to be one step ahead of whatever his enemies expect.

She skidded to a halt in the cave entrance. "We need to leave. Now," she shouted.

Jorxy was adding a few things to an evening meal laid out on the kitchen table. "But we need to eat before we go," he protested. "I thought you wanted–"

"We've no time," Roza yelled. "Lord Vallance is down there at Albany's east gate right now. How long will it take him to ride up here?"

"Um … he's on horseback?"

"Yes! An army of cavalry with torches has arrived up the highway and is coming to capture and abduct me. And you want to sit and eat dinner first?"

At last, Jorxy began to display the animation Roza felt. "No, no," he said, looking at the table. "I'll throw all this in a bag and be with you in ten seconds. We can eat later, whenever you feel it's safe."

It took longer than ten seconds, but Roza helped him to pack it all up, stoppering bottles and filling a sack with the food. They could sort it all out later.

She and Jorxy threw cloaks around their shoulders and loaded up their packs, Jorxy with the food and drink, and Roza with her library of Minimised magic books in a box at the bottom of hers. If they hadn't been in such a blinding hurry, Roza would have enjoyed the comical sight of

Standley also levering a pack onto his hooks, awarding himself the heaviest load, the bag with the Minimised chest of coins, gems, and jewellery.

"Goodbye, cave," Roza breathed, as she took one last glance around. Was there anything she'd forgotten? She didn't think so, and she'd no time to think further or check.

They turned left out of the cave entrance, hurrying along the grass path towards the waterfall, the pool, and the stone bridge over the stream. Goodbye, Torrence, and to you too, chickens, pigs, cow, and sheep, she thought, as they passed the animal pens and into the plateau's darkened grain fields.

At the far side of the fields, the path divided. To the right led up onto a great spur of the mountains that overlooked the valley and bordered the plateau to the west. The left fork climbed steeply in a zig-zag fashion up the cliff face that marked the southern edge of the warlock's home. Jorxy's studies of Philoe's maps had told them this latter path was the one they should take, so they picked their way upwards under the last daylight above the distant peaks on their right.

Her leg muscles soon complained at the effort, but an extreme urgency to get away pressed upon Roza. What would Lord Vallance do at the east gate? Demand to know from the guards where the warlock was? It was no secret that she lived on the plateau, and many people had seen her heading this way this evening.

So much for thinking the Earl and his men would arrive tomorrow, camp and rest for a night, and be content with a civilised meeting in the Town Hall the day after. No, the Lord of Gorge City was determined to complete his business here quickly, to catch this young warlock unawares and whisk her away from her home before she knew what was happening or could object.

After forcing her legs and feet to make each upward step, Roza needed a moment to catch her breath. Behind her, Jorxy was similarly labouring for air into his lungs. She'd wondered how her enchanted coat stand would manage to scramble up steep or rocky paths on his polished clawed feet, but she needn't have worried. Standley was climbing the easiest of the three of them – on level ground, scuttling along on his flexible feet, but where it was steeper, leaning forward and crawling upwards on his top hooks and feet. His heavy pack with the donation chest bounced around his wooden pole as he went, but there was no danger of it falling or sliding off him. Before long she conceded that their progress was limited not by the relative length of their legs, but by their reserves of strength and stamina, where Standley outstripped them by an infinite amount.

Roza glanced down towards the plateau but saw no signs of light or movement there. But she wasn't reassured, because from this angle she couldn't see if Lord Vallance's men were already riding up the path from the town.

The daylight was gone, and their eyes accustomed to the starlight. The full moon would rise soon, but the Heismith Range between them and the plains would shadow them from its light. Roza and Jorxy took a mouthful of water each, then heaved their breaths and pressed on.

She lost all sense of how long they'd been climbing, for an hour, or two or three, because she kept her focus on the mountain ridge above them. They settled into a steady and sustainable pace, matching the regularity of their breathing with the flexing of their hips and knees and the crunch of their boots on the stones.

At last, Roza crested the ridge and prepared to collapse for a rest on the tufty grass there. She turned to watch Jorxy and Standley make the last ascent … and let out a cry.

From where she stood, the mountainside descended in a long, steep slope to her plateau now far below them.

And there was fire.

She stared in disbelief, for these were not the isolated pinpricks of soldiers with torches moving over the grass. Parts of her plateau were ablaze. She tried to work out what she could see, and it looked as though fires had been set in her grain fields, spreading steadily and joining together. But as she watched, far worse was that tree after tree in her orchard erupted into flame.

"No!" she cried again. "What are they doing? Why are they destroying that beautiful place?"

Standley and Jorxy joined her, also gazing at the blaze below. "Lord Vallance is venting his fury that you're not there," Jorxy muttered.

"Or making sure I can't return to live there again so I need to find somewhere else. What about the animals, can you see anything?"

Jorxy shook his head. "It's too dark and far away, and I can't work out what's where with all that smoke. So much for asking Rufus and Joidi to keep an eye on the place and take the animals down into town."

Roza grunted in disgust. "There's nothing we can do now, but Lord Vallance is going to pay for this. One day, and somehow, I will get my revenge on him for burning my plateau." She turned away and walked further onto the mountain shoulder so that the curve of the cliff edge blocked her sight of the devastation below.

They sat and ate their evening meal in the silent darkness. There was much they needed to talk about, but Roza's seething anger meant she couldn't face any of it. Jorxy picked up her mood enough not to try to comfort or distract her.

Moonlight began to bathe the mountain slopes to their right, and without a word to the others, Roza decided to press on further for a while. The way was less steep, but still climbing, so they made a better pace, and it felt easier on their aching leg muscles.

At length Jorxy called out that he could go no further. Roza agreed to stopping for a sleep, because they'd been up all day and then climbed for half the night. They needed the rest now to keep going during the coming daylight. Up here there were scattered conifer trees with slopes of bracken, so they left the path and found a place to sleep among these.

As she tried to relax for sleep among the bracken, Roza consoled herself with one good thing: she and Jorxy didn't need to keep watch. Standley had nodded vigorously that yes, he would do that for them, and no, he didn't need any sleep. They asked their coat stand to wake them if he saw or heard anything, or at the first signs of daylight.

The first grey light of dawn was spreading into the high clouds when Standley nudged them awake. All was quiet on the mountainside, but Roza discovered she'd been lying across an ant highway through the bracken and needed Jorxy's help to brush them off her clothes and pick them from her hair. At least she'd been exhausted enough to sleep through being irritated by them.

They decided to go on further while they were freshly rested before stopping for breakfast. They found a stream tumbling down beside their path and took the chance to wash the sweat off their arms, faces and necks.

They'd only just started off from the stream when Jorxy said, "Wait, can you hear that?"

Roza stopped too and tilted her head against the breeze. It was faint and distant, but unmistakeable. "Dogs barking?"

He nodded. "That's what I thought too. Which means we're being tracked."

"Can we keep ahead of them, or find some way to lose them?"

Jorxy pulled a face. "That would be difficult. They'll be highly trained and can follow a recent scent even in the air. There was enough of our smell in and around the plateau cave for Lord Vallance's dogs to identify our trail easily enough."

"But we need to shake them off," Roza insisted, "or at least force them to stop following us. Should we halt and face them down?"

Jorxy's eyebrows rose. "Normally I wouldn't suggest that, because we don't know how many dog handlers are with them, and their scouts and trackers can be vicious sorts. But we've our own surprises for them with our bodyguard coat stand and your magic, so that might be our best bet."

"Agreed. We should find a good place for our showdown."

They pressed on, and soon their path rounded a spur in the mountainside where a sheer cliff rose above them on their left and fell away in a steep precipice on the right. Here the way narrowed to a stretch where they couldn't be outflanked or have anyone come at them from behind.

They stopped at the far end of this open space, hiding their packs further around the corner. They waited for the dogs and trackers to reach them, and had as much of a breakfast as they could stomach. Roza peered over the precipice at the drop below in case she needed to use her one and only defensive spell – Repulser – to throw a tracker or two over the edge. The slope was not vertical and ended with bushes and trees some distance down, so a push and tumble from her might not prove fatal. She hoped it wouldn't come to that.

At last, two dogs and four trackers came into sight, and they slowed on seeing Roza and Jorxy waiting, arms crossed, blocking the path. As agreed, Standley waited around the corner behind them to reveal himself only if needed. The men walked into the open space, holding the leashes of the dogs who were now barking their heads off. Two of the men had bows, and all of them had blades of some sort sheathed at their waists. By contrast, Jorxy was leaning on his stick and Roza was unarmed.

"Can we help you?" Roza called.

The men snapped at their dogs to quieten them, and a bald-headed one stepped nearer. "Yeah, you can help us, young Missy, by coming quietly with us back down to Albany."

"No, I don't want to come with you. And I don't like you following me, so clear off back there or you might regret it."

"Oh ho," jeered the bald tracker. "Did you hear that, boys? We might regret tangling with this girl and her ugly boyfriend. What do you make of that?" The other three laughed.

Roza waited until they finished and then said, "Are you aware who you're tracking? I should warn you that I have magic powers to defend us."

The bald man pretended to be terrified. "Oh no, oh no, lads, magic powers," he mocked. "We're done for. How can we survive this? We'd better run for our lives back to town." They all guffawed again.

Roza noticed they'd been edging closer. "Stay where you are," she ordered.

"Or what? We hear you've got the power to make people younger. So, are you going to turn us into babies?" More laughter.

"I think you'll find I've got one or two more powers than that." But Roza admitted to herself it was only one or two. And only one that was useful here, unless she threatened them with smaller rations. "So, will you go away and leave us alone, or do we have to deal with you?"

"Oh, deal with us, deal with us, please," he taunted. "Me first, me first."

Roza had had more than enough of this loathsome man. "Standley," she called over her shoulder, and her coat stand tottered into view.

The trackers stared in amazement and then roared with laughter even more. "What is this? A walking stick man?" The dogs were growling.

"No, you stupid man," Roza retorted, "he is an enchanted coat stand by the name of Standley."

The man put on a posh voice. "Oh, my word, an enchanted coat stand, is he now? Come here then, whatever your name is, and I'll chop you up for firewood." He drew his sword.

Standley glanced at Roza for permission, so she said,

"Go ahead, see them off."

He charged forward with astonishing speed, and the bald man barely drew back his sword in time. He swung at Standley's pole with full force, and as in the plateau cave, the blade rebounded, jarring the man's arm, and leaving no mark. Before he could recover, Standley was on him, gripping, gouging, and kicking him with his hooks and clawed feet.

"Argh! Help, get it off me," the man screamed, and the other trackers piled in. The dogs kept their distance, barking wildly. Standley was caught in a mass of arms, legs, and bodies, which all received bleeding gashes and gouges.

"Throw it over the edge," the bald man yelled, and the four trackers lifted Standley off the path. The coat stand lost his anchor for his hooks and claws but still tore at the flesh of those holding him. But one tracker managed to launch Standley away from him, and Roza watched in dismay as her coat stand sailed through the air and disappeared over the cliff edge.

She trusted his invulnerability in landing, but her anger burned that these bullies had escaped his clutches that way. She turned her gaze back to where the trackers were helping each other up, wiping blood off their hands and arms and rubbing their wounds.

"Ha!" the bald man crowed. "So much for your stick man. It's no more than broken sticks at the bottom of the cliff now. But you're gonna pay for the hurt it's caused us."

Roza shook her head. "The fall won't hurt him in the slightest, and he'll be back up here in a minute. But you shouldn't have done that."

"Why? Don't tell me young ugly here has tricks up his sleeve."

Jorxy raised his stick and started forward, but Roza held him back. "No," she breathed. "Allow me."

She was already reaching inside for her magic and igniting the flame as the two dogs and four trackers came for her. She brought her hands up and away from her, directing the Repulser spell over them all.

The force was intended to stop them, to keep them away from her, but Roza's anger was hot, and all four men fell backwards. The dogs turned tail and fled back down the open space. The trackers picked themselves up, looking around. "What was that?"

"That, you horrible creatures, was magic. That was a mere flick of my fingers. I have much more to offer if you'd like to follow my coat stand over the precipice. But I doubt you'll fare as well as him in your landing at the bottom." She forced a smile their way.

The trackers were looking at each other, until the bald man shouted, "Shoot her."

The two men with bows were readying arrows from their quivers, and Roza needed to be quick. The arrows flew and she flung up her hands, focusing her spell on them both and Repulsed them in mid-air. It looked like the missiles bounced off an invisible wall, and they ricocheted harmlessly over the edge.

"I've had enough of this," Roza bellowed, and Repulsed the four men again. This time she struck them harder, and they flew backwards to land further down the path. One landed perilously close to the edge and scrabbled at the grass not to fall.

Roza stepped towards them now. "Leave us alone. Go back to Albany and your master. Tell him you couldn't find me. Or I magically erased my tracks. Because if I see any of you following me again, I won't give you any warning before I throw you off a cliff."

She'd stalked close enough to see the fear in the whites of their eyes. But the bald-headed man gave a snarl and lunged for her. Roza reacted with instinct and her magical energy burned white hot. With a shove of her hand, the spell catapulted the man high off the mountainside, and his scream faded away high and long into the early morning air.

Roza didn't watch to see where the tracker leader landed, or whether he crashed into a tree or bushes to break his fall. But his three companions followed his arching flight with their eyes. When their terrified gaze returned to her, Roza held her hands ready and said, "If you want to live, go."

The three remaining men scrambled away from her, fleeing back down the mountain path, their dogs barking and bounding ahead of them.

Roza drew in a deep breath to calm herself and turned to face Jorxy.

He stepped up to her, staring. "You are one scary girl. That was awesome."

She let out a shaky laugh and hugged him to hide how much she was trembling.

A moment later they heard Standley's hooks clawing at the cliff edge to pull himself back over. They both ran to help him back onto his feet.

At last, Roza laughed with relief that they'd seen off their trackers, and she laid a hand on Standley's bloodied hooks and Jorxy's shoulder. "In the end, we did pretty well with our indestructible bodyguard and my one defensive spell, didn't we?"

CHAPTER NINE

Standley kept rotating his top to look back down the path, and Roza sensed he wanted to make sure the trackers and their dogs had really gone. "Go ahead and check they've fled from us, if you like. We'll stop here for a proper breakfast."

The coat stand scuttled back the way they'd come and disappeared from sight as Roza and Jorxy went to get their packs. The two of them leaned against a rock wall in a patch where the rising sun warmed them. Jorxy laid out all their food and drink so they could have a proper rest and feast, because it felt too long since they'd had one.

In contrast to the relief and freedom Roza felt, Jorxy looked more miserable than usual. "Are you all right? What's the matter?"

He didn't say anything at first but chewed his crusty loaf while staring down at the grass. Without looking up, he said, "A few times now we've ended up in a fight. Twice against Thain Wicksteed – at the tent and in the cave – and now against these trackers. And every time I've been completely useless. I haven't got magic like you, or Standley's strength and toughness. I want to help, but instead I'm rubbish."

Roza saw his point but wasn't going to say it. "It isn't all about the fighting, you know. I wish we didn't have to. There are more important things going on than that."

He looked up. "Yeah, and what important things can I do to help? Carry and look after the food and drink, like I'm the chief cook?"

"Um … I don't know what else there is to do. You had a look at those maps and helped us with the way to go. I appreciate you knowing where we are and which way all the tracks lead, so I don't need to think about that."

He shrugged. "I could keep following the maps, I

suppose. I'm feeling a bit useless, that's all."

Roza saw how his initial excitement of adventure had faded. What could she say to encourage him, to let him know she appreciated his company? "To me, you get to be the most important thing in the world right now. Do you know what that is?"

He shook his head.

"A friend. I haven't got many of those in the world, and up here, you're it. Can you imagine what it'd be like if I was up here on my own, with only a wordless coat stand for company?"

Jorxy's glum expression began to crack into a smile. "You mean, I get to do more than nod or shake my head in answer to yes or no questions?"

Roza chuckled. "Don't get me wrong, because Standley is great as a bodyguard, but he's not much for conversation, is he? And here we are: the whole world wants me, and you get me all to yourself. And I get you all to myself. Running away on our adventure together like we always dreamed."

He was smiling more now. "Yeah, that's right. But what are we going to do? Where will we go, and how will we live, and what's going to happen to us?"

She pointed a lump of cheese at him. "That, my only and faithful friend, is why I need you to help us find the answers to all of that."

Jorxy nodded. "So, if I'm following the maps, it would help to know where we're heading, if we know."

Roza shrugged. "No, we don't know. How about if we make this all up as we go along?"

He smiled. "Sounds good to me. Can you get the book of maps out then, and I'll have a look before Standley comes back?"

"Yes, of course." As she reached for her pack, Roza thought of something else. "Don't forget, you're the one who had the bright idea of leaving the valley before Lord Vallance arrived. And that worked well, because here we are, safe and free. So, if you can think up more brilliant ideas of what we should do and where we should go, that'd be great." She beamed at him.

Jorxy grinned back. "No pressure, then. Just keep us both safe and free."

Roza laughed. "Yes, please, Mister Ideas Man. Our lives are in your hands."

He chuckled. "Mister Ideas Man, I like that."

"The thing is," Roza said, more seriously, "as we go along, I need to learn as many new magic spells as I can. It feels as though that will be enough to make my brain explode, so if you can think about everything else for us, you might save that from happening."

Jorxy frowned a little. "No, don't explode your brain. And don't you worry about anything else, because I'll do some thinking for us."

She fished from the bottom of her pack the box of Minimised magic books and found Philoe's Maps of the World. She Maximised it back to normal size and handed it to Jorxy, relieved that he now looked less miserable.

He showed her the diagrams and pages to locate where they were, the local landmarks, and where their current path led. The Heismith Ranges south of Albany were a maze of criss-crossing tracks and routes, scaling passes, following valleys and streams, heading in all directions. For now, Roza was glad he'd identified where they were, and they agreed to worry about ultimate destinations later.

They put the map book away when Standley came back. Through a series of yes or no questions they learned he'd found the trackers a bit further down the mountainside, resting and bandaging their wounds. They'd been unnerved to see him again and taken off back towards Albany at once. He'd chased them for a little way but then returned, sure they wouldn't now be followed.

Once Roza and Jorxy were full of breakfast, they loaded up their packs and went on. The morning took them up to the summit of a pass, where a ridge between two mountains left them exposed to a cold wind. The view at the top was breathtaking, but they soon set off down the southward side to be out of the chilly breeze. After so much climbing since Albany and the plateau, it was a delight to use different muscles to descend.

They stopped before dark, because Roza and Jorxy both needed a full night's sleep, and a blanket of clouds hid the light of moon and stars. They found a grassy dell with a stream and Standley kept watch again.

Their blankets were damp in the morning from a nighttime shower, and during breakfast, Jorxy asked Roza to Rejuvenate their two-day-old milk and bread. As with the guards' biscuits at the warlock gate, she touched the loaf and dipped her finger in the milk, sending her magic through her Rejuvenate gift. They were both delighted to have fresh-tasting milk, and soft, warm bread again.

As they ate and drank, Jorxy asked, "How do you know how much to rejuvenate something? I mean, with people, you give them years of life, but with biscuits, milk or bread, it's only days. How do you control what you're doing?"

Roza frowned and then shrugged. "I don't know, but it feels like instinct. I do what feels right, or else the magic itself knows what to do. It depends on the lifecycle of the object or person as well. While days or years are vastly different to us, they're not when compared with the lifetimes of the bread or the person. Bread might last a week, so going back a few days is about half its lifetime. A person might live for seventy years, so going back thirty-five years is again about half their expected span. Does that make any sense?"

Jorxy's eyes looked glazed, his mind a bit boggled, but he nodded as though he understood, keen to fulfil his role as her valuable friend. "What will happen then," he asked, "if you rejuvenate the bread back beyond being freshly baked? Will it revert to being dough, and then back to the ingredients?"

Roza's eyebrows rose. "I haven't thought about trying that. Shall we do the experiment?"

Jorxy's excitement was back, and he laid out a cloth with a hunk of stale bread on it. Standley turned to watch what they were doing, and Roza sat cross-legged in front of the bread. She laid her hands on it and rejuvenated it as before.

When the portion of loaf reached freshly baked, there came a slight resistance from the magic, as though indicating that the bread was already young enough. But Roza pressed on, guiding the magical energy to submit to her will, and it obeyed. The loaf became sticky under her fingers as it reverted to dough, and then shrank as the rise of the yeast was reversed. The flour and water came apart, making a pile of damp paste on the cloth. Finally, the water soaked into the fabric and the flour clumped together to become a small mound of wheat grains before them.

Roza stopped the flow of magic and removed her hands, wiping them on her trousers. She looked at Jorxy and smiled.

"Wow, did you see that?" Jorxy stared at the cloth. "That was amazing. The whole lifecycle of making bread, but in reverse. But what about the wheat grains, they're seeds, aren't they? What do they go back to become?"

Roza picked up a single grain and placed it on her palm. Touching it with her finger, she rejuvenated it further, but all it did was shrink smaller and smaller until it disappeared completely. "I guess a seed reverses to before it even began, to being nothing at all inside a growing stalk of wheat."

Jorxy was looking at her sideways, and then at the pile of wheat grains, and Roza guessed he had another experiment to suggest. "You know those other spells, your Maximise and Minimise, they're the opposites of each other, right? So, is there an opposite to Rejuvenate? Like if we found some unripe blackberries, or some other fruit, you could age them for us to make them edible?"

"Um … I don't know," Roza replied. "No one's asked me to age anything before. I could have a go with these wheat grains and see if I can turn them back into bread."

"Yeah, go on," Jorxy enthused. "Let's see what happens, shall we?"

She frowned. "Hmm, I don't know how to do this. It will be a sort of backwards rejuvenation, won't it? I'll see if I can instruct the magic to make these wheat seeds go forwards in their lifecycle, instead of becoming younger. Here goes."

Roza placed her hands over the wheat grains, lit up her magic and sent it into the seeds. The energy was resisting her again, like when she'd reverted the bread from freshly baked back to ingredients. And she needed to flip her Rejuvenate gift backwards, or upside down, or inside out, or something, and it all felt awkward and wrong.

But she persisted and commanded the magic to move these wheat seeds forward, to make them expand and grow, like with her Maximise spell. And it began to work, for the magic was flowing, and she began to feel the individual grains sprout into life under her fingers. They were growing stalks and leaves, and soon she held a sheaf of wheat plants in her hands, complete with heads and kernels of grain.

Then something changed.

The wheat plants were full grown, but now they were aging beyond their prime. They were past their best, fading, withering, shrivelling. Roza felt the difference, but didn't know how to stop it. The magic was still flowing, but it was moving in reverse, flowing *from* the wheat and *into* her. She was taking away the magic of the plants, stealing their beauty, robbing them of their life. And then they were dead, lifeless husks of decaying vegetation crumbling to dust in her fingers.

She let out a cry of anguish, threw the last of the dead stalks and leaves away from her and leapt to her feet. "No, no," she cried, "stop, stop," and Jorxy jumped up to console her. But Roza was shaking with horror, trying to brush the last of the dust and ashes of death from her fingers.

She rounded on him. "Why did you make me do that? That was horrible. I'm never doing that again."

"I'm sorry, I'm sorry," Jorxy defended himself. "We didn't know what would happen, did we?"

She shook him off and stomped away to the edge of the grassy dell, shivering and revolted with herself. She washed her hands in the stream, rubbing and rinsing them to get the ugliness and death out of them, but she could still feel it inside. She paced up and down, unable to stay still. What she'd just done horrified and terrified her.

It took her a long time to calm down, and she saw Standley and Jorxy watching her with concern. She supposed she should try to explain what she felt, why it upset her so much. Eventually she wiped her face, walked back, and plonked herself beside the damp cloth with the dust and ashes of the dead wheat plants.

Jorxy sat down next to her and asked, "What happened? Why didn't we get our bread back?"

She swallowed and tried to think. "Um, well, I guess it's about the lifecycle, you see. The bread rejuvenated to dough, then flour, then wheat grains. So, if you start with seeds of wheat, they grow in the lifecycle of the wheat plant, as you saw. But then the magic doesn't replicate milling the grains into flour, or kneading with yeast, or baking in an oven, because those are not the natural lifecycle of wheat, but human interventions to make bread."

"Oh, I see," he said, and then was quiet for a while. "Why did it upset you so much?" he asked at last.

"It was horrible," she sobbed, as the terror and revulsion at what she'd done returned. "I was stealing the beauty from the plant. I was robbing the life and magic from it, until all it had left was death. Don't you understand, I was killing it. Do you see what this means? Suppose I use this reverse power on a person, what then?"

"Er …," he hesitated, "they will age, and get old, and

then … die?"

"Exactly! This is the power to kill people. It is magic at its worst – ugly and evil and death. I can't believe I have the power within me to do this, to make anything wither and shrivel and end up as nothing more than ashes and dust. It's terrible and horrible and I wish I'd never discovered it."

"I'm sorry," he said again. "But from what I saw, it worked for a while, didn't it? You made the seeds sprout into plants and grow into heads of grain, so that was good, wasn't it? If you stopped then, that was healthy and fruitful. It was just going further that destroyed them."

Roza reflected for a moment. "Yes, I suppose so," she answered quietly. "But that's the whole thing with this magic and rejuvenation and spells and power – I don't know what I'm doing. I have no experience, and no one to teach me, so I experiment with things, with some disastrous results. Like yesterday morning, I threw the leader of those trackers over a cliff with barely a push of my hand. That's a terrifying power to have."

Jorxy snorted. "That arrogant and vicious man deserved what you gave him, so don't you lose sleep over him." He shuffled closer to her. "But listen to me. You're a good person. You're kind and thoughtful and generous. You won't use your power to bully or abuse anyone. You use it to help people, or as a last resort in self-defence. Think of Amber-Jane and her Grandma Lily and the lifesaving help you gave them."

Roza nodded but still had doubts about her reverse rejuvenation power. "Philoe mentioned about warlocks who use their powers for selfish ends, which is why we train with mentors in the safe use of magic. I don't have that, so I'm a danger and a menace to everyone around me."

Jorxy shook his head. "Roza, you're the last person I think of as a danger or menace to anyone. Awesome and scary, yes, but only to those who deserve putting in their place. What you're doing is learning to use your magic as you go along. Yes, you'll do experiments that go wrong, and that's how you learn from them. Now you know not to push an aging process too far."

"Thanks for trying to help, but it's hard to explain. Right now, magic feels like a wild and untameable beast, rampaging around, out of my control. I thought I had an instinct for it, knowing how much to use, and when to stop, but maybe I don't know as much as I thought."

"Listen, I remember something. You told me when you Rejuvenate someone, they need to want to become younger. So, it'll be the same with the reverse process, they must want to age too. No one wants to wither or shrivel or die, do they? So, your reverse power won't work, and will stop if you try to go further than they want, won't it?"

Roza had had enough of talking about this and stood up. "Yes, you're probably right. Anyway, let's get ready for our day's walking." But as they packed up their bags, Roza couldn't help thinking, what if she grew in her magic and gift that she could use it on people without their consent or desire? Wouldn't that make her the most dangerous person in the world?

CHAPTER TEN

Their day's walking took them gently downhill into a valley in the midst of the mountains. But the gathering clouds began to spot with rain and then became a steady downpour. By mid-afternoon they were soaked to their skins and freezing and looking for somewhere to shelter for the night. The only cover was under the branches of a forest that carpeted the valley floor.

Before it got dark, they sheltered under the leaves of a huge sycamore tree, which kept off the steady rain but dripped large drops onto them. They agreed their priority was a fire, but most of the wood was too damp. Roza remembered seeing a fire spell in her Warlock Survival book, so she searched in her pack for that, while Jorxy and Standley gathered the driest kindling they could find.

Once she found the book, her fingers were almost shivering too much to perform the Maximise spell, but she managed to enlarge it enough to read it. The fire spell was entitled 'Enflame', and she hunched over the volume to protect it from the drips and tried to learn it through bleary eyes. Her brain felt too frozen to take it in, but at last she thought she'd mastered the technique.

The hand movement required was to click her fingers over the kindling, so she and Jorxy had to rub some warmth into her hands before she could do it adequately. By this time, Roza was so desperate for a fire that she put forth all her summoned magical power into producing a flame, and the click of her fingers dropped a fireball.

The small mound of kindling exploded into flame, singeing her front and throwing her backwards. If her clothes hadn't been sodden, they would have ignited too. Jorxy and Standley were standing far enough back not to be burned and rushed to make sure she was all right.

"I'm fine, I'm fine," she gasped. "Just keep that fire going, will you?"

Jorxy and Standley hurried to pile on branches, fallen logs, conifer cones, and whatever else would burn, and their fire hissed and cracked as it dried out all the damp fuel.

But they had a fire, so Roza and Jorxy stripped off their soaked outer clothes and hung them on branches to dry. They rotated themselves, warming and drying their underclothes and bodies as they steamed in the dark. Standley found this whole process highly entertaining, as his polished wooden pole took no notice of rain or cold.

At length, they stopped shivering and enjoyed the merry light of the flames, feeding in fuel against the continuing drips from above. When the rain finally abandoned its persecution of them and the drips from the sycamore leaves lessened, they dressed again, and prepared to eat, drink and dry the rest of their belongings.

They were in the middle of their meal when a call of "Hello?" startled them. They jumped to their feet, peering into the darkness, and Standley moved forward to defend them.

"It's only me, Kerenzi," the voice went on, and they relaxed. The spirit lord came strolling through the trees, wearing a dark silver tunic of moonlight through clouds. "A lively blaze you have there. But if you're hoping to remain secret, you should know it can be seen throughout the valley."

They started in alarm. "Is anyone out there?" Jorxy asked. "Anyone hunting or tracking us?"

Kerenzi tilted his face to the sky as though listening to check. "Not another human in the whole valley," he confirmed. "Although in future perhaps you should be more careful."

"I know," Roza sighed, "but we were soaked and frozen. We needed to warm up and dry off, so what else could we do?"

The spirit lord shrugged, as though bodily discomfort was of no interest to him. He sat by the fire, and Roza and Jorxy resumed their seats. Jorxy seemed relieved and pleased to be included in this conversation, rather than their visitor taking the warlock away for a private chat.

"Well, how are you all?" Kerenzi began. "Roza, Jorxy, Standley, what have you been doing since I saw you five evenings ago on the plateau?"

Roza gulped. Was it five days ago, when so much had happened since then? She remembered that after the spirit lord's visit she'd met the Town Committee and challenged them about Lord Vallance coming with his army. She told him about the plan to move her to Gorge City, and their subsequent decision to disappear from Albany and go on the run. She finished with recounting the burning of the plateau and seeing off the Plains trackers.

Kerenzi looked pleased with their going into hiding, and confronting their pursuers, but his brow furrowed at the destruction of the plateau orchard. "We can't expect you mortals to care about the trees as much as we forest spirits do, but I shall remember this if I ever get the chance to take revenge on Lord Vallance."

"Get in line," Roza muttered. "I have a few scores to settle with him as well. So, where have you been, and have you any news for us?"

The spirit lord's eyes flickered red in the firelight, and Roza wondered whether this was a reflection or his inner fire coming out. "I've been across the Plains again," Kerenzi answered slowly, "keeping track of what's taking place in this part of the Empire."

"So, what's happening then?" Jorxy demanded. "Apart from the Earl of Gorge City marching here with all his men to capture our Roza?"

The spirit lord regarded him. "Not all the Earl's men, no. It was a detachment of cavalry that came to Albany, led by Lord Vallance himself, but he left much of his force to defend his city. And it was well for him that he did."

"Why? What's happening at Gorge City?" asked Roza.

"The Dragon Emperor learned that Lord Vallance was away and took his chance to attack. Regiments of the Imperial Army marched on Gorge City to secure their continuing sovereignty over the Plains. The Earl was in Albany when he learned of this and rode back at full speed to intercept them. So, it seems that our quaint little town of Albany is free from being troubled by a world-famous warlock or a war-mongering Lord." Kerenzi gave Roza his most handsome smile.

"What happened at Gorge City, then?" Jorxy butted in. "Was there a battle?"

The spirit lord tilted his head. "I wouldn't call it a full-scale battle, no. There was a confrontation and a stand-off. Lord Vallance arrived in time to make the odds too even for either side to win a convincing victory. Neither the Earl nor the Emperor are willing to weaken their forces by risking a complete bloodbath. I'd call it an opening skirmish."

"So, what will happen now, do you think?" Roza asked.

"Seeing the Imperial Army at the gates of his city infuriated Lord Vallance. But the Dragon Emperor has played right into the Earl's hands. The Lord of Gorge City is calling the Emperor a bully and an invader, giving him the pretext to declare independence from the Empire. He has claimed the rule of the Plains to be his alone, with no overlordship by the Dragon Emperor."

"Does this mean civil war, then?" Roza asked in a small voice. "Just like you told me would happen. The Lords of the Empire rebelling against a weakened Dragon Emperor to seek power for themselves?"

Kerenzi nodded slowly. "Yes, my Roza, civil war is coming, but there haven't been bloody battles yet. The forces are mustering, alliances are being forged, the storm clouds of war are gathering, and the pieces are moving to their places on the board. It is only a matter of time before the great conflict of our time is unleashed."

Roza gazed into the crackling flames, which cast dancing shadows across the trunks and boughs around them. How strange it was to sit around this campfire, hearing tales of cities, lords, Empires and war, like stories of far away and long ago. "I'm very glad then," she said, "that we're well out of it, safe and hidden up here in the mountains, and we can leave them all to it. Let us know when it's all over, won't you, when it's safe to return to quiet little Albany again?"

Kerenzi let out a hollow laugh. "You think you're out of it, safe and hidden up here in the mountains? You may wish this were so, but it's far from the case. You won't remain safe and hidden if you keep lighting bonfires like this."

"All right," Jorxy snapped back. "We get the message about the fire. But why can't we hide away up here until the war is over?"

"You might be able to, young Jorxy," Kerenzi replied, "but I doubt Warlock Roza here will be so lucky."

"Why?" Roza demanded. "What's it all got to do with me?"

The spirit lord gazed at her for a moment. "What's it all got to do with you? You really don't know? Let me ask you this. When Lord Vallance returned to Gorge City and declared his independence from the Emperor, it was in a meeting of all his people in front of the Earl's Palace. What name do you think was on everyone's lips, that all the crowds were shouting?"

"Um … I've no idea," Roza replied, but a sinking dread had begun to form. "Lord Vallance's, I suppose."

Kerenzi gave a slow shake of his head. "The people of Gorge City were united in one voice, shouting, 'For Rozabella, Warlock of Albany!'".

The sinking dread crashed through the bottom of Roza's life, and she couldn't remain seated. She leapt up and started pacing around the fire. "You're kidding me. This is a joke, you're teasing me. There's no one in Gorge City who even knows me, let alone for them to shout my name."

Kerenzi was still shaking his head. "I would guess that everyone in Gorge City knows your name, or if they didn't already, they do now."

"But why?" Jorxy interrupted them. "Why is our Roza so famous in Gorge City? What's she ever done for them?"

"It's because I rejuvenated the Dragon, isn't it?" Roza answered him quietly.

Kerenzi nodded. "Lord Vallance has declared you a champion and hero of the city. According to him, you are their saviour and liberator, the one who provided their hope of freedom. You confronted and humbled the Dragon Emperor, their tyrant and oppressor. You weakened their mighty enemy, making him vulnerable, and so brought about their great deliverance. The people are being whipped up to worship and adore you."

"But that's not fair," Roza stamped her foot. "I didn't intend to do any of those things. I merely tried to save Albany from destruction, and it was you who made the Dragon's rejuvenation go further than he wanted."

"Nevertheless," Kerenzi went on, "this is what your gift has achieved for the people of Gorge City. And Lord Vallance has been kind enough to give you all the credit. It also means he can blame you for the subsequent deaths in their war for independence. It suits his purposes to share with you the responsibility for the consequences, however this turns out."

"So, now I understand why the Earl of the Plains was so keen to kidnap me from Albany. He wants me as a puppet and a scapegoat, to parade me around the city, a figurehead for his war. Well, no, I'm not going to do it, and I'm even more glad we escaped from his clutches."

"You don't understand," Kerenzi said. "What Lord Vallance has done is to raise the stakes. He has promised his people that you are coming to save them, that you're on your way to Gorge City to rescue them from the Emperor.

He needs you there more than ever. So, he has offered a handsome reward for information on your current location, or for escorting you to the city itself. He has put a price on you, Rozabella the Warlock, so everyone in the Plains is looking for you. And more to the point, every agent, spy, mercenary and bounty hunter is on their way here."

Roza and Jorxy looked at each other, and then at the surrounding trees, as though at any moment a host of trackers and kidnappers could burst out of the darkness. "Could you … could you check again whether there's anyone else in this valley?"

The spirit lord stood up and scanned the night with his fiery eyes, his head cocked for listening. "No, still all clear. A few bears and wolves, but no people. Although trust me on this, they're on their way."

Roza raised her arms in an appeal for help. "Kerenzi, what can I do? Someone is bound to catch up with us soon. I can't keep using Repulser spells to throw our hunters over the edges of cliffs. Should I hand myself in, and give myself up to Plains soldiers to escort me safely to Gorge City?"

The spirit lord shook his head again. "I'm sorry, dear Roza, but I won't risk giving you the wrong advice. However, I should pass on two more things. The first is that what Lord Vallance has done in putting a price on your head, the Dragon Emperor has also done. Both sides in this civil war desperately need you on their side, and while Gorge City hails you as their champion and saviour, the Emperor and his Army call you a traitor and enemy. If Lord Vallance would parade you as a puppet, the Dragon wants you to languish in his dungeons to show that he has finally vanquished the one who weakened him."

"Great," Roza said. "So, whichever side I pick in this civil war, I make an enemy of the other. I hope the other thing you need to tell me is better."

The spirit lord tilted his head and smiled at her, which only made Roza sure his next words would be even worse.

"I need to pass on what Lord Vallance has promised the good people of Gorge City. He calls you their saviour, liberator, their hope of freedom. He also promises his people that your arrival and their independence will usher in a new golden age of liberty and prosperity for the Plains. This new age to come – the age of Warlock Rozabella – will be marked by renewed health and youth and vigour for everyone. For our noble Earl of the Plains has explained about your gift of Rejuvenate, and that your coming will herald the dawn of eternal life for them all. No wonder the excited people of Gorge City are shouting your name in their streets, because when Rozabella the Warlock of Albany comes, they will be young again, and rich, and free, and they will live for ever."

Roza stopped pacing about the fire and stared at Kerenzi. "No, I won't, I won't do it. I'm not going to rejuvenate a single one of those wretched, deluded followers of Lord Vallance in Gorge City."

Kerenzi shrugged. "They're just people, Roza. Old people, young people, with hopes and dreams for a better life, to be free and healthy and better off. You can't blame them for that. How their political leaders manipulate and deceive them for their own ends is another matter. But in one sense, it's too late, the cork is already out of the bottle. The people of Gorge City aren't calling this their war for independence, they're calling it the war for immortality."

"The war for immortality?" Roza spluttered. "That's not fair. They're putting it all on me, as though this civil war is my fault, that I'm to decide who will win and lose, and then I'm the final prize and reward for whoever is victorious."

Kerenzi beamed at her. "My dear Rozabella, I think you've just expressed it all very clearly and succinctly."

In the silence that followed, Roza felt herself slump, and she came back to sit with the others by the fire. In time, she asked, "Who do you think is going to win this war then? Who's got the bigger army?"

"Well, the Emperor has the bigger army, but he's also got more territory to defend. He can't bring all his troops to the Plains because that would leave the rest of the Empire undefended. The armies attacking and defending Gorge City may be too evenly matched for either side to have a clear advantage. It might turn into a siege, a war of attrition, a long, drawn-out war of skirmishes and minor battles with a correspondingly large amount of suffering and loss of life."

Roza pulled a face. "That doesn't sound good. Not if I end up getting blamed for it all."

"But what about the Emperor?" Jorxy chimed in. He'd got up and was busy adding more wood to their fire. "He's a Dragon, isn't he? Can't he fly in and attack Gorge City himself, burning the city walls with his fiery breath, and reducing Lord Vallance's armies to charred corpses of cinders and ash?"

"Very colourfully put, young man," Kerenzi replied. "And yes, he could. Dragon-fire is a weapon the Imperial Army can use to their advantage, and previously the threat of that kept the entire Empire in check. No town or city dared to rebel against the Emperor for fear of him coming and reducing them all, as you say, to ashes and cinders. But not any more."

"What do you mean, not any more?" Jorxy protested. "He's still a Dragon and he still breathes fire, doesn't he, even if he is a bit smaller, younger and weaker now?"

"Yes, he still breathes fire, but now our Dragon Emperor is vulnerable in ways he never was before. Until recently, our Emperor could fly over any town or city knowing that his metal-hard scales were invulnerable to any arrow, dart or missile. His rejuvenated armour-plating is now softer and thinner, more vulnerable, so he won't risk being injured or killed by his enemies. While this civil war is raging, our brave Imperial Dragon hides away in his fortress in the northern mountains for his own protection."

"You mean that while his Imperial Army is fighting and dying for him," Jorxy said, aghast, "his Imperial Highness the fire-breathing Dragon won't even dare to stir from his treasure-filled lair to defend his own Empire?"

"Yep, that's about right," and Kerenzi smiled at them. "And while that remains the case, the battles around Gorge City will remain evenly matched. But of course, Lord Vallance still rushes to prepare his Dragon defences around his city."

"What sort of Dragon defences are there?" Roza asked. "I didn't realise there were such things."

Kerenzi tapped his chin, regarding her. "How much do you know about siege weapons? Particularly catapults."

Roza shrugged. "Almost nothing. Catapults hurl large rocks against city walls, don't they?"

Kerenzi nodded. "And I'm sure you know about shortbows, but have you heard of something called a crossbow?"

Roza shook her head, but Jorxy said, "Yes, I have. It's like a sideways shortbow, isn't it, but with a machine that stretches a wire to fire an arrow. I heard the weaponsmiths in Albany marketplace discussing them. Crossbows are supposed to fire over longer ranges, and be more accurate, more deadly."

"You are correct, Jorxy," Kerenzi replied. "And Lord Vallance has developed these crossbows into ones of giant size, as big as a normal catapult. It is called a ballista and can fire a metal arrow of four to six feet in length, which is a weapon that could injure or kill a Dragon. A well-aimed and well-timed missile from one of Lord Vallance's ballistae could bring our Dragon Emperor down, and both sides know this. So, Gorge City is ringed with ballistae and the Dragon is hiding away safe in his fortress."

Roza gazed into the flames in front of her. "This war business is too complicated for me. Why can't I just help people, rejuvenate them, and make their lives better? I'm a seventeen-year-old girl and should be pre-occupied with other things than this. Why is there so much violence, greed, and selfishness among power-hungry people to spoil it all?"

Kerenzi laid a warm hand on her shoulder. "I know, Roza, it doesn't seem right, does it? But I have great faith in your gift and abilities, and your sense of doing the right thing. I hope one day, once this is over, you'll get your wish and do lots of good across the Empire. In the meantime, I'll leave you to decide on your next move and return to my vigil over the affairs of the Plains. I promise I'll come and see you again soon. Good night and sleep well, Rozabella, Jorxy and Standley."

CHAPTER ELEVEN

Kerenzi walked off into the night with a cheery wave of his hand rather than vanishing into invisibility, and Roza was glad to have Jorxy's company to ease how alone she felt. There was too much responsibility, and too many hard decisions, being ladled into her young lap for her liking. They lay down to sleep by the embers of the fire, while Standley patrolled their forest on guard, but Roza had too much weighing on her mind to relax or sleep for a while.

She was woken by a gentle touch from Jorxy with a finger pressed to his lips. A pale light of pre-dawn was filtering under the trees and the air was cold.

"Standley saw someone else in the valley," he whispered. "The fire is out, but we wanted to make sure you didn't make any noise on waking."

Roza nodded and uncurled herself from her blanket. Jorxy was putting everything into his pack and Roza did the same in case they needed to flee. Once that was done, they crept towards the eaves of the forest where Standley stood in the shadows. He pointed with a hook, and Roza spotted a single cloaked figure walking along a track high up on the valley sides.

"Someone looking for us?" Roza breathed, and Standley nodded. As she watched, the figure kept scanning the valley, and checking the path for tracks, but she was relieved he was heading the way they'd come, back towards Albany. When they moved on today, they wouldn't be following him. And she was grateful that yesterday's rain might have washed away their boot-prints.

She and Jorxy tip-toed back to the ashes of the fire, leaving Standley to watch the figure out of sight, and held a whispered conversation.

"Given what Kerenzi told us last night," Roza began,

"what should we do? Where shall we go, Mister Ideas Man?"

Jorxy's face was grim. "That man walking past our forest confirms it. Soon there'll be too many people searching these mountains for us. If they know that Lord Vallance's trackers followed us south from Albany into this Heismith Range, then this part of the world is not a safe place. We need to be where they don't expect us."

"I agree. Let's look at Philoe's maps to decide on our best route away from here." Roza fished the tiny volume from the box at the bottom of her bag, Maximised it, and gave it to Jorxy to study.

He pored over it for a while before saying, "These mountain ranges extend northward, southward, and westward for a long way, and the routes look slow and difficult in all those directions. Westward, it looks like the mountains end in sheer cliffs down to an ocean – I didn't know that."

"Nor me. So, what about eastwards, but doesn't that take us back to the Plains?"

"Yes, it does. But I guess that's the last direction they'll expect us to take." His finger traced some lines in the map book for a minute or so. "Our most direct route out of the mountains is a path going southeast from this valley and over a mountain pass. It then descends steadily from the top, winding down to the Plains near Heismith Castle, Thain Wicksteed's territory. Old warlock Philoe has marked a cave near the top of the pass that we could use for shelter. It will be a long day's climb, but shall we head there for tonight?"

Roza nodded. "Let's set off as soon as it's clear and keep to the cover of these trees for as long as we can."

They crept back to Standley, who nodded that the cloaked figure had disappeared. Jorxy pointed out where they planned to go, and together they devised a route up and out of the valley keeping hidden as much as they could.

It was a long and tiring day's walking. It wasn't as easy to find their way through the trees as it had been following a path, and it was always upwards. But Roza preferred to be out of the reach of prying eyes for most of the time. Her most anxious minutes were when they crossed the line of the high track along the side of the valley, as she felt terribly exposed to view, and only relaxed again once the crest of a mountain shoulder obscured them from the view of the valley below.

They heard the bear before they saw it.

Jorxy was in front, with Standley and Roza following, each lost in their own thoughts among the trees. A low growl and breaking undergrowth snapped them to a halt.

Before they could react, a snuffling grunt meant the bear had caught their scent. It crashed into view between the trunks up the slope.

Standley sprang into action first, racing forwards to pass Jorxy and face the bear. The animal lifted onto its hind legs and roared at Standley, who seemed so thin and fragile before its massive bulk of black fur.

As the coat stand moved to attack, the bear swung its huge paw and swatted him aside. Standley flew away into the trees.

The bear dropped to its four paws and launched into a lolloping gallop. Jorxy readied his stick as Roza yelled at him, "Get out of the way!"

Her magic was igniting, but her first Repulser spell had to shove Jorxy aside from the bear's approach. She catapulted him into some bushes.

The bear was almost on her when Roza sent her next spell straight into its chest. The magical power would have sent a man flying, but it barely stopped the animal. It reared upwards, bellowing its anger at her.

Roza's terror made her magic hot and wild, but her flurry of Repulser spells became less controlled, achieving no more than making the beast sway and twist as it was pummelled with invisible blows. And its muscular forelegs flailed dangerously within claw-reach.

Roza stepped back and changed tactics.

Fire.

She clicked Enflame spells onto the ground in front of her, and the bear recoiled. She flicked a few more fireballs at it to give herself time to think and control her magic. She mustered her strongest Repulser yet and shoved its huge weight to one side. She didn't want to kill it, just move it away, and get it to leave them alone.

She repeated the Repulser to turn the roaring beast away from her, around her, and then off down the slope below. She added a few Enflame balls on the forest floor to convince the bear it would never reach this meat. And that alternative prey had to be easier down in the forested valley below.

At last, the bear seemed to admit defeat and lumbered away between the trees.

Roza heaved shaking breaths as Jorxy marched up to her.

"Landing in those bushes hurt, you know!"

"I'm sure it did, but what were you and your stick going to do against that bear?" Roza yelled back. "Get yourself killed, that's all. When I'm casting a spell, I need you out of my way, otherwise I'll Repulse you straight into that bear's belly."

"How should I know what magic spell you're casting? I'm not a mind-reader."

Standley reappeared between the trees and raced up to them. He placed a hook on Roza's and Jorxy's shoulders as though standing between their argument. Her coat stand's presence made her think better of yelling at Jorxy. She needed to make peace with her best friend.

She softened her voice. "Anyway, you standing there to face down that bear must be the bravest thing I've ever seen you do. And the stupidest."

"Yeah," Jorxy bragged, "I'd have seen it off. But your spells have done the trick, so no harm done."

They turned to their coat stand. "No scratches or damage

then, Standley?" Roza asked. When he shrugged and shook his hooks, she touched him and Jorxy's shoulder. "Well, then, a mountain bear's no sweat for the three of us, eh?"

At last, Jorxy smiled and nodded, and they could carry on climbing.

As they ascended, the conifer trees became sparser until they ended altogether, and they picked their way up mountainsides between patches of gorse and heather. Thinking that good firewood might be difficult to find around the cave, Jorxy suggested they collect up dry twigs to carry with them, reasoning that Roza could Maximise them into branches and logs when they got there. Standley was happy to be loaded up with kindling and brushwood.

A cold east wind over the top of the pass began to blow rain into their faces. As the clouds above them darkened, Jorxy reassured Roza that they were near the cave Philoe had marked. But it took some finding, as it lay concealed behind some large bushes at the foot of a sheer cliff face some way to the left of their route.

By the time they were dashing for the shelter, the rain in their faces had become sleet, and they were relieved to get out of the lashing wind. Standley motioned for the two of them to wait at the cave entrance while he checked that the whole place was empty. He soon returned, nodding, and pointed at a dip in the cave floor where ashes betrayed the remains of a previous fire. Jorxy prepared the firewood, asking Roza to Maximise some of it for later, and then she lit it with a more controlled Enflame spell.

The wind and sleet worsened into a true blizzard in the mountains, with flashes of lightning and rumbles of thunder. They were in the middle of eating, with Jorxy insisting on toasting bread on their fire, when Standley, on lookout near the cave entrance, rushed over to them, pointing to the outside.

"Is someone coming?" Roza hissed, and when their coat stand nodded, she and Jorxy jumped up. "We should hide further back," she ordered, and they grabbed their packs. But they couldn't conceal their crackling fire because she didn't have time to Maximise the water to douse it.

The three of them waited in the shadowed rear of the cave, peering over their fire at the darkness outside, when two people ran in to shelter from the storm. One was a blonde-haired young woman, her dark red cloak and hood soaked with the sleet, and the other a curly-haired boy who looked a few years younger than Roza and Jorxy. His green leather jacket was shiny and wet, and they shook the snow from their clothes and hair. As the woman shook out her cloak, there was chainmail and a sheathed sword beneath.

The two newcomers froze in the cave entrance, staring at the fire burning in the middle of the floor.

"Hey, Oxana," the boy started to say, "I thought I saw firelight coming–"

"Hush, Banno," the woman snapped, sweeping her sword from its sheath. "There's someone else here."

Roza held her breath and glanced sideways at Jorxy in the dark. He gave a shrug, and she realised they couldn't hope to hide back here now that their fire had given them away. And these two – Oxana and Banno, if those were their names – would search the cave and discover them at once. Roza motioned for Standley to stay where he was (for he would take a lot of explaining) and stepped forward to the edge of the firelight.

"Um … hello?" she said. "I hope you'll forgive us for hiding back here until we saw who you were." She turned and indicated for Jorxy to come out of the darkness too.

The four of them stared at each other for some moments across the dancing flames. The woman's sword tip was now pointing towards her, so Roza held out her arms and smiled. It seemed unreasonable to banish these two back out into the blizzard. "We're not armed and mean you no harm. You can shelter in here and share our fire if you like."

The boy, Banno, relaxed and grinned up at the woman,

but her blue eyes surveyed them both before she re-sheathed her sword. She was almost as tall as Roza but looked stronger and more muscular under her chainmail. "I am Oxana, and this is my brother, Banno," she said.

"Oh, my name is Jacey, and this is my school friend, Charly," Roza replied, with a meaningful look at Jorxy. If Rozabella the Warlock of Albany was so world-famous, they couldn't dare to use their real names.

"Hey, this is a great fire," Banno enthused, stepping closer to warm and dry himself. He looked at the twigs and Maximised branches and logs lying around it and frowned. "Did you carry all this wood up here yourselves?"

"No," Jorxy lied, coming nearer too, "only a little of it. Most of this was here in the cave already, thanks to whoever was here before us." He grinned in what Roza hoped was a convincing way. "Do you have your own food," he went on, "or do you want to share some of ours? I was trying to toast some bread on the fire."

Banno beamed at this suggestion and quickly joined Jorxy in kneeling by the fire. Oxana seemed more reserved and sat on the cave floor further away but still near enough for the fire to warm her. "Thank you, you are very generous," she said, "but we have our own food supplies."

"Hey, Oxana," Banno called out, "you've got to try their bread. It's much fresher and softer than ours."

Roza and Jorxy exchanged a glance, because she'd rejuvenated that loaf the day before, and this also risked giving her away. She needed to change the subject. "Where have you two come from and where are you travelling to?"

Oxana was about to answer when Banno jumped in. "We're from Gorge City and we're up here to find that Rozabella, the Warlock of Albany. Lord Vallance has offered a *huge* reward to anyone who finds the warlock or brings her to our city."

"Hush, Banno," Oxana cut him off before he said any more. "For all we know, these two kind people might also be up here looking for Albany's warlock." She smiled at them and Roza kept her face neutral and unconcerned.

Banno's eyes went wide. "Are you searching for her too?"

Roza shook her head. "No, Charly and I are from Heismith Castle and we're going back down there now."

Oxana nodded slowly. "So, have you seen or heard anything about Warlock Rozabella, any signs that she's up here? Did your journey take you as far as Albany, or have you met others searching for her?"

Roza wondered how long they could keep on lying before something gave them away. She looked at Jorxy and shrugged. "We've seen others in the distance on the mountain tracks, but we've only been as far as the valley below here on this trip. Did you know about this cave already, or did our firelight attract you to it?"

Oxana regarded her closely again. "Most people using this pass know about this cave as a shelter near the top. I thought everyone at Heismith Castle knew that."

Roza gave Oxana a sheepish smile, but the fighter woman got up, staring at something further back in the cave. Maybe her eyes had adjusted to the flickering gloom to see into the shadows at the rear.

"What's this?" Oxana asked. "There's something back here."

"Oh, that," Roza forced out a laugh. "Yeah, it looks like someone left an old coat stand in here." She willed Standley to stay motionless but dared not say any more.

A scrape on the cave floor made Roza jerk her head around to see that Oxana had picked Standley up. Holding him by the middle of his polished wooden pole, she brought him forward to examine him more closely in the firelight. Roza threw Jorxy an alarmed look but dared not betray any further reaction. Thankfully, Standley remained rigid and lifeless.

"This doesn't look old at all," Oxana said. "No cobwebs,

dust, or scratches. In fact, it looks brand new, highly polished, in excellent condition."

As Oxana scrutinised Standley, she held him increasingly close to the fire, and at last he reacted. He squirmed away from the flames and heat and flexed his hooks towards Oxana's arm that held him.

"Standley, no," Roza shouted, leaping to her feet. "Oxana, put him down, please. We don't want either of you to get hurt."

Jorxy and Banno jumped up too, and the boy cried out, "What is that?"

Oxana jerked her hand away, and Standley clattered to the cave floor beside the fire. In a moment he had twisted his clawed feet to lever himself back upright and stood tense and ready, the eye knots at his top fixed on Roza. Oxana's sword was out again, its tip towards the coat stand.

"It's all right," Roza tried to reassure them, "I can explain. This is Standley, and he's an enchanted coat stand. If you leave him alone, he won't cause you any trouble."

"An enchanted coat stand?" Banno asked, eyes wide. "Like … real magic?"

"I'll deal with this, thank you, Banno," Oxana said crisply. "Let me do the talking. And you're burning your bread in the fire."

The boy's bread was indeed smoking on the end of his stick, and Jorxy encouraged him to sit back down and concentrate on what they were doing.

"Standley, could you keep watch for us outside the cave entrance, please?" Roza asked, and her coat stand disappeared off into the stormy darkness.

"It understands you?" Banno asked, unable to restrain his questions.

"Yes, he does," Roza replied, and sat down by the fire as though this were perfectly normal. But she braced herself for how much had just been given away.

Oxana sheathed her sword and returned to her seat on

the cave floor. Roza felt the young woman watching her while she tried to gaze unconcerned into the fire.

"We find you here," Oxana began, "with a lovely fire burning, plenty of wood for fuel, and fresh, soft bread. With an enchanted coat stand as a servant or pet. I'm sure you'll forgive us for being curious. I get the impression you're not telling us the whole truth or are hiding something from us."

Roza didn't look up or meet Oxana's searching gaze, but the corner of her eye caught Banno looking between her and his sister.

"Wait a minute," the boy blurted out. "You're her, aren't you? That Warlock of Albany. We've found you and can collect that huge reward!"

"Silence, Banno," Oxana snapped.

Roza didn't dare to glance at Jorxy or lift her gaze from the flames. What could she say? She hated lying, and given the evidence against her, she couldn't make her denials convincing. Maybe her hesitating silence had already confirmed her identity. "Let me ask you something," she said. "Suppose you find this Rozabella, Warlock of Albany, what will you do?"

Oxana's voice was calm. "I understand what a difficult situation she's in, with everyone after her, so I'd want to help her. I can see why she's gone into hiding and would guess she needs people she can trust alongside her – friends, allies, protectors. I'd want to be one of those for her."

Roza looked up from the fire at last and met Oxana's clear, steady gaze. The young woman's face looked open and trustworthy, but Kerenzi's words of last night sounded warnings in Roza's mind: 'every agent, spy, mercenary and bounty hunter is on their way here'. Weren't agents and spies supposed to seem trustworthy to their victims?

Roza looked across at Jorxy, who gave the tiniest shake of his head to say, don't tell them the truth. But how else could she explain the evidence of magic here? Whatever she said to these two now, they'd probably keep following her.

And there were no plausible excuses for Standley.

Oxana spoke again. "I realise how hard it must be for Warlock Rozabella to trust anyone at present. Despite what my brother said just now, I'm not in this for the reward." She pointed to the silver clasp holding her dark red cloak together. "Do you know what this symbol means?"

Roza and Jorxy both peered forward to see the design of the ornate silver catch. Jorxy said, "Looks like a candle crossed with a sword. Never seen it before."

"The candle and sword emblem means I'm a paladin," Oxana explained. "Strength and skill with the sword, tempered by a candle, the light of honour and truth. Have you met a paladin before?"

Roza shook her head, but Jorxy added, "There's that saying, 'I wouldn't trust a paladin with that,' meaning you can't trust anyone."

Oxana smiled at him. "Or meaning a paladin might be the first or only person you can trust. Which brings us back to Warlock Rozabella, and that hers is the noblest adventure in the Empire these days. I'd love to be a part of it, to share in her story and choices, and in how this all turns out. To play my small part in shaping the destiny of the world."

Roza's eyebrows rose, and despite her reason and caution telling her to doubt this woman, her heart still wanted to trust. And besides, now these two suspected who she was, was it more dangerous to send them away than to keep them with her, so she knew where they were?

She sighed, and the silence around her felt increasingly awkward. "In which case," she said at last, "I guess you can call me Roza." She held out her hand, and Oxana took it, the young woman's face filled with genuine excitement.

Banno jumped up again. "I knew it!"

"Yes, young Banno, I'm the Warlock of Albany. We're sorry for the lies we've told you since you entered this cave, but I'm sure you understand why we needed to. This is my school friend from Albany, Jorxy."

"Can you show us some more magic?" Banno asked. "Like the coat stand?"

Before Oxana could scold him, Roza chuckled. "If you stick around, young sir, you will see more magic, but only when I need to use it for something, okay? And we must ask you both to promise to follow our lead and instructions over what we do, because Jorxy and I have more information about the wider situation than you do."

Oxana nodded. "Yes, I give you my word as a paladin that I and my sword are at your service. Banno, you must promise too."

The boy looked sulky, but muttered, "I promise."

"Well, Warlock Roza, what do you plan to do once this storm passes, and we can leave this cave?" Oxana asked.

Roza glanced at Jorxy, who looked furious that she'd given away her secret. "We guess there are many searching these mountains for me. So, we decided to leave here and escape to the Plains as soon as we can. We'll take the track east from this pass and come down near Heismith Castle."

Oxana nodded. "That's a good plan. But we saw others on that path before the storm hit, so the chances of meeting someone as we go down are high."

"Perhaps, Miss Warlock," said Jorxy through clenched teeth, his first words for a while, "there's something in your magic books to help us stay hidden. You know, to keep us safe from potentially unfriendly eyes." He jerked his head in an unsubtle way towards Oxana and Banno.

Roza ignored his sulky sarcasm, and if these two would travel with them, she could show them her Minimised magical library. "That's a good idea, thanks. So, if you two want to see some magic, let me show you these tiny books in the bottom of my bag."

CHAPTER TWELVE

Banno was all wonder and enthusiasm at anything Roza would show him of her magic. Oxana watched with what Roza reckoned might be wise and experienced eyes for someone of her young age.

Roza lifted her box of magic books from her bag and showed them her collection of volumes, each no larger than a finger. Picking the one she wanted – on Survival Skills – she showed Banno the unreadable, Minimised print. She Maximised it in stages until they could read it comfortably. Having demonstrated her portable library, she decided against saying she could do the same with food, drink and gold for fear of exciting him too much.

Roza found a spell called Camouflage, and while it was not true invisibility, it promised to hide her from all but stringent searches. This new one took some time to master the technique, because it involved directing her magical energy over herself, rather than outwards, and the correct arm movement was miming lifting a hood over her head. But at last, she concealed herself well against the shadowed cave wall and in front of the night-time blizzard outside.

However, the nearer she came to the fire, the Camouflage spell was less effective at hiding her. So Jorxy suggested they should travel at night now, not by daylight, which they agreed to, despite Banno's grumbles about enjoying his night's sleep. They decided to rest now and move on as soon as the storm abated.

So, they slept, and Standley kept watch outside, but daylight came, and the blizzard still raged. Roza took the time to master the Camouflage spell's next stage – to see if she could hide all five of them. This meant extending her spell energy beyond herself to someone standing next to her, then on both sides, and eventually as a small group. She needed a succession of patient volunteers to join in being Camouflaged, and others to say how well they were hidden, and Banno was always willing. In turn, Oxana, Jorxy and Standley also joined her, and in time Roza felt confident of concealing all five of them, provided they weren't in bright sunlight, or under close inspection.

By mid-afternoon, the wind and snow were lessening, and Roza was anxious to move on from the cave before any more searchers or hunters ventured out. The snow outside was waist deep, and Standley demonstrated his strength and cutting power by twirling his hooks to carve a route through it. Oxana's strong arms shoved the snow aside for others to follow behind, but there was no way of hiding their track.

In this way, they fought their way up to the top of the mountain pass, where the full force of the wind from the east blew the last of the snow in their faces. As they began their descent, the strength of the wind abated but the snow still lay as deep around them. The daylight was fading as they looked for somewhere off the path to rest for a short while from their labours against the snow.

They chose a shallow hollow below the path where they could hide under the shadow of some conifer trees, and huddled together for warmth because they dared not light a fire. The snow had ceased at last, and they passed around their food and drink in the gloom.

Soon they heard voices. Men were climbing up the mountainside towards their position, and Roza hurriedly cast the Camouflage spell over the five of them. They held their breath as three men appeared on the path above them, carrying flaming torches.

The men cried out to each other as they drew level with the Camouflaged figures. "Someone's ploughed a furrow through the snow here. A few people by the looks of it, the tracks are so wide and deep."

"Going up or down? Which way do the boot tracks face?"

"Coming down. So, they've come over the mountain pass and are heading for the Plains."

The flaming torches were lifted higher and towards the hiding figures. "The tracks leave the path here and head down into that hollow."

"But there's no one there now. Maybe they came here and then went back."

"Do you think they returned to that cave the other side of the top?"

"Yeah, maybe. Let's catch whoever they are before they head off anywhere else."

The torches, voices and the tramp of boots receded upwards, and the five Camouflaged figures breathed again.

Oxana spoke in a low voice. "At least we know that Camouflage spell works well, thank you, Roza."

Roza smiled but wasn't sure the others could see it in the half-light.

They decided not to linger over their meal, in case the three men came back, and were keen to descend to where the snow lay less thickly. The storm had blown through with ragged clouds trailing behind it, revealing stars in the east, but the moon was a few nights past the full and would not rise for an hour or two.

It was a slow and dark journey down the mountainside, and they walked in silence, but Roza's spirits had lifted knowing she could Camouflage them from sight. If they continued to travel by night, hunters would need to stand over them, or bump into them, to discover their prey.

The wind lessened, the snow reduced to under a foot deep, and the waning gibbous moon rose before them. Their downward path reached denser forest, and they all relaxed with even more cover around them. There was hardly any snow under the trees, and the trackers would need to be eagle-eyed to follow their boot-tracks through the pine-needled ground.

Then, in the distance, they heard the first wolf howl.

It was high on their left, so after a hurried discussion, they agreed to plunge deeper into the trees on their right. But the first howl was answered by others that seemed to echo around the valley.

They fought their way through the trees until they reached a small glade, where the roots of a massive fallen tree formed a sheltered hollow. But the calls of the wolves were growing nearer.

They agreed this was a defensible position if they needed to fight off the predators, so they offloaded their packs. Banno was the only one who couldn't fight, so he stayed at the back. Roza cast a Camouflage spell over them as they waited in the dark.

The approaching howls sent shivers down Roza's spine as she peered among the moonlit trees. On her left, Oxana stood tense, her sword at the ready. Standley waited on her right, next to Jorxy with his stick.

"Standley, make sure that Banno and Jorxy remain safe," Roza breathed.

He nodded, and she heard Oxana whisper, "Your coat stand can fight?"

"Oh, yes." Roza gave a grim smile. "He's fast, strong and indestructible, but let's hope it doesn't come to that."

Minutes later, the wolf howls were all around them.

"I don't think your Camouflage spell will help us this time," Oxana added. "Wolves have excellent night vision, and they've found us more by smell than sight. Know any spells to mask our scent?"

"Sorry, no. I could make a fire, but we hoped to remain hidden from searchers."

"Yeah, Roza, scare off these beasts with fire," Jorxy interrupted. "If anyone else on this mountainside sees it, the wolves can go after them instead of us."

"But we've no time to gather tinder or strike a flint," Oxana pointed out, for grey shapes were prowling through the trees.

"No problem." Roza flexed her fingers. "Allow me."

Her magic was already igniting, so she clicked her fingers and flicked a ball of Enflame onto the ground a few feet in front of her.

The sudden brightness of the flames seared their eyes and set off a chorus of howls from the wolves. Oxana raised her sword, and with a yell and a thud, Jorxy swung his stick at a wolf that had ventured too close.

The wolf eyes glowed bright in the flames, and with yapping and snarling the first ones leapt to attack. Oxana parried one with the flat of her sword. Roza Repulsed two leaping over her fire, Jorxy swung his stick with mad abandon, and Standley charged at any wolf within reach.

A cry on her left told Roza that a wolf had bitten Oxana's arm. "No more flat of the sword," the paladin cried. "Time to draw wolf blood." And her sword lunged and flashed in the firelight.

"More fire," Jorxy shouted, panting from the effort of keeping the circling wolves at bay.

Roza broke off from Repulsing any leaping grey shape she could see and started flicking fireballs into a wide semi-circle around them. The wolves howled even more but drew back from the flames.

Oxana and Jorxy roared in victory, seeing off any last brave beast. Standley scuttled between the fires, and the wolves could only growl at him before turning tail.

At last, the noises of the wolves receded, and they dared to relax their defensive stance. Oxana bound up her wounded arm with a cloth.

"That was awesome," Banno enthused behind them. "Fireballs and fighting, and your coat stand running around after them. And you throwing those wolves aside with your magic, Warlock Roza."

"Yes, it seems we can defend ourselves," Roza replied. "But I'd rather we didn't have to."

As Roza's fires died down, they saw the eastern horizon

begin to lighten with the first grey daylight filtering into their forest refuge. They ate a little and then cast themselves on the ground to sleep for the day.

Standley kept guard but didn't need to disturb them, although when they woke in the late afternoon, he nodded that he'd heard distant voices. Banno pleaded for hot food to warm himself up, and Jorxy promised not to let the fire smoke, so Roza obliged with an Enflame spell. Soon the boys were roasting cold pork and toasting slices of bread.

"How long have you adventured?" Roza asked Oxana, as they all chewed their hot meat and toast.

"A few years," Oxana answered. "I love the travelling, living outdoors, hunting for food, surviving on my wits. But earlier this year our father died, so I returned to Gorge City to look after Banno. We have an aunt and uncle in the city, but they have children of their own and are mostly too busy to be bothered with us. So, we're orphans, but I bring Banno away with me whenever his studies allow."

"Your studies?" Roza asked Banno. "What are you learning?"

"I'm training to be a treasure assistant," Banno replied, around a mouthful of half-chewed pork.

"What on earth is a treasure assistant?" interrupted Jorxy. "You mean a coin counter?"

This clearly hit a raw nerve. "I am *not* a coin counter," Banno protested, spitting bits of meat across the fire. "There's a lot more to being a treasure assistant than merely counting coins."

"Oh yeah," persisted Jorxy. "Like what?"

"You need to learn where coins come from, what they're made of, check their size and weight. Then there's the assessment of gems, the fashioning and valuing of jewellery, and lots more."

"And once you've checked all this about the coins, is that when you count them?" Jorxy teased.

Banno resented the joking at his expense and was

becoming annoyed. "Treasure is the most important thing in the world," he insisted. "Everyone needs it to buy things, and it determines your station in life – where you live, what you can do for a living and how much you own – so there."

"Can we drop this, please?" Oxana asked, and they fell silent and ate.

But when Banno wasn't looking, Roza caught Jorxy's eye, mouthed the words 'coin counter', and they both grinned.

When they were ready to go, Jorxy stamped out the fire and scattered the ashes. The dusk was deepening into twilight, and the wind had died, so it promised to be a fine night's walk, and all the better for being downhill. They found animal paths through the trees and made better progress as the mountainsides descended over ridges and shoulders into the hills of the eastern Heismith Range.

Jorxy came to walk beside Roza and indicated for them to lag a little so they could talk and not be overheard.

Roza spoke first. "So, you got to do some fighting at last, then?"

Jorxy twirled his stick. "Yeah, and nothing worse than a few nips and scratches. But why did you go and tell them who you are? It isn't safe that anyone knows where you are."

"It seemed the best option at the time. They'd guessed it already, especially when they saw Standley move. They wouldn't have believed our excuses."

"But to let them come with us? How long will they be tagging along?"

"I don't know. But again, it seemed better to know where they are than to let them go off and blab to anyone they meet. This way we can keep an eye on them."

"Or they can keep an eye on us, making sure we don't wander off, hide, change direction, or anything. And showing them all your magic – not just Standley, but your magic books and spells. That boy Banno will betray you for the reward, because he's mentioned it twice already."

"Oxana seems a wise and sensible young woman, and I like her. She'll keep her little brother in check."

They walked in silence until he spoke again. "To be honest, I'm a bit jealous of sharing your company with anyone. Whatever happened to having you all to myself, eh? I mean, Standley's all right, but two actual human people, that's different."

Roza laughed and looped her arm through his. "Ah, now I get it. You silly boy. Remember what our roles are here? Best friends. You are mine, and I am yours. That doesn't change with who else is here." She could see his face through the semi-darkness under the trees. "Don't tell me you're jealous that I'd prefer Banno's company to yours?"

He chuckled. "What, him? No, I don't reckon you could be interested in a greedy coin counter."

She punched his arm. "And what about you? Should I be jealous of your interest in that fit, strong, fighter-woman, Oxana?"

He pulled a face. "Nah, she's not my type. I prefer the more quiet, homely, girl-next-door, warlock-to-change-the-world sort of girl myself."

They laughed again and were quiet. Then he asked, "So, where will we go? I mean, there's nowhere safe, is there? Everyone's looking for you. Wherever we go, you'll be wanted and hunted and caught."

"Yes, you're right," she said quietly. "Which is why it's good to have friends and protectors when there are bears, wolves and hunters around. We need to find how to live and work with this gift of mine and get everyone to calm down and not go to war to control me. Who can we trust with the sense to stop this war for immortality and let me get on with helping people? Lord Vallance? The Dragon Emperor? I don't think so."

Jorxy nudged her arm and Roza saw that Standley, Oxana and Banno had stopped ahead and were waiting for them. When they caught up, they saw that their path had reached an outcrop of rock with an open view to the east. A hazy moon was rising behind wispy clouds to give a ghostly light to the panorama.

The hills of the Heismith Range were descending towards the Plains, and they stood at the head of a wide bay in the mountains. Below them on their right, a huge buttress of rock jutted out from the southern side of the bay, where stood a magnificent castle. Roza had never in her life seen such an impressive building, with its gatehouses, ramparts, battlements and towers.

"Heismith Castle," Oxana told them.

"Home of Thain Wicksteed," Roza added.

"What? You've heard of him?" asked Banno.

"Not just heard of him," Jorxy replied. "We've met the charming man himself, haven't we, Warlock Rozabella?"

"Indeed, we have," Roza said. "Not a happy memory. But we came out of that encounter a little better than he and his men, didn't we, Standley?"

If the coat stand could have chuckled, Roza was sure he would have done, but he merely turned and inclined his hooks to her, his eye knots crinkling.

Oxana and Banno were looking between the three of them in bewilderment. "Are you going to tell us this story, or not?" Oxana demanded.

Roza sighed. "The not-so-noble Thain of Heismith Castle came to Albany with his henchmen and tried to bully some rejuvenation out of me. When I refused, he came back later to my plateau, and we had to see them off with some force of our own. That's when we discovered how strong, flexible, and indestructible our bodyguard coat stand is."

"Yes, I saw that against the wolves," Oxana said. "What a useful coat stand you are, Standley, to be a bodyguard as well as a lookout. I'll be sure not to tread on your clawed feet, and I pray we'll always be on the same side in a fight." The coat stand bowed his top to her as well.

"How are we going to get past this castle?" Jorxy asked.

"It looks like it commands a view over the whole valley."

"Yes, it does," said Oxana. "All the paths down lead past its gates, and the soldiers check everyone on the road when they pay the toll."

"What, there's a toll?" demanded Jorxy. "Just for walking past his castle?"

"Of course there is," said Oxana, with a grim smile. "One small silver coin each. How else do you think Thain Wicksteed gathers the money to maintain his fine castle?"

"I'll pay it for all of us," said Roza. "Let me get to our treasure chest, Standley, and I'll get the correct coins ready."

"You have a treasure chest?" Banno asked at once, but the others ignored him.

"Do you think there's a special rate for coat stands?" Jorxy asked with a wicked grin. "Or on the basis of their previous encounter, will they let Standley pass for nothing?"

"That's a good point," said Roza. "We'll need to put him under a Camouflage spell to avoid arousing suspicion."

"Why don't you put us all under the Camouflage spell and avoid paying the toll at all?" asked Banno.

"That wouldn't be honest," Oxana chided him.

"And we can afford the coins, young man," Roza replied, fishing through her chest for the right ones. "And besides, we haven't tried the Camouflage spell on a moving subject yet. I'd rather we test that with just one of us rather than all five. We don't want to draw attention to ourselves by getting into a fight with the Thain's guards."

"And you should know that as a paladin, I won't lie to anyone," Oxana added.

Jorxy stared at her. "You can't tell lies?"

She shook her head. "So, when the soldiers ask our names and where we're from, I'll tell them the truth."

Jorxy rolled his eyes. "You can speak for you and your brother then, and I'll answer for Roza and me."

They left the outcrop and set off down the winding path towards the valley. It was a long way down, and the castle drew ever nearer until it loomed over their heads. On closer view, Roza saw that the walls had been constructed from cliff to cliff across the valley to make it impossible for anyone to climb from the Plains to the mountains without passing the Thain's tollbooth. It was still an hour or two before the first light of dawn and the walls looked deserted except for a solitary night shift guard at the gate.

Roza cast her Camouflage spell over Standley, and he disappeared from their view. She and Jorxy drew hoods over their faces, while Oxana and Banno stepped forward to the night guard with the coins for all four of them.

"Your names, where you're from, and where you're going," said the guard, yawning.

Oxana handed the four silver coins into his gloved hand. "Oxana and Banno from Gorge City. We came through here a few days ago and have been hunting in the mountains."

"And Charly and Jacey," Jorxy added. "We're heading for the inn at Thainsfoot."

As he spoke, Roza thought she heard the creak of Standley creeping past behind them.

The bored guard was too sleepy to notice and waved them through. They walked on, but Roza remained tense, waiting for the warning horns that the Warlock of Albany was escaping. But no alert came, and they disappeared away from Heismith Castle into the moonlit night.

But as she went, Roza couldn't shake the nagging suspicion that they were making a grave mistake. Leaving the bears, wolves and trackers in the mountains, they were now on the Plains with less cover to hide in, and many more people.

And all of them were looking for her.

CHAPTER THIRTEEN

"Will we stay at the Thainsfoot Inn, then?" Banno asked, once they were well out of earshot.

Jorxy shrugged. "Not necessarily. We hadn't discussed what we'll do, so I told the guard what he expected to hear."

"But why can't we stay at the inn?" Banno demanded. "Now we're down on the Plains, we can't camp in people's barns or fields or ditches all the time, can we?"

"He has a point," Oxana mused. "Sleeping rough makes us look like wanderers, outcasts, fugitives. We'd draw attention to ourselves every time someone kicks us off their land or moves us on. In the forests and mountains, we expect to camp. In civilised lands, legitimate travellers stay at inns in the towns and villages, so if we want to blend in, that's what we should do."

Banno had an eagerness in his voice. "And it's not as though we can't afford it, not with the treasure chest Warlock Roza has got."

"Hush," said Roza and the others together. "From now on, there's to be no mention of the word 'warlock' at all. And I'm not to be Roza either, but Jacey, like I told you up in the cave."

"And what about our Standley here?" Jorxy asked. "We can't exactly explain him away, can we?"

The coat stand and Roza turned to each other, and she thought he looked sad. "I'm sorry," she said, "but you will raise questions everywhere we go. What can we do? Would you be willing to hide away somewhere every time we enter a town or village?"

Standley nodded, and Roza appreciated how amenable he was to everything, as a tireless lookout, uncomplaining servant, and invincible bodyguard. She stepped closer to him and touched his top hooks. "You're very good to us, you know, Standley. We ask so much of you, and you never grumble or protest. We couldn't ask for a better friend, really."

He seemed to smile and gave her one of his awkward wooden hugs. The others laughed at the sight, but Roza patted him as they drew apart. "Good, we'll look for a good spot for you as we approach the village."

The track from the Heismith Castle tollbooth ran at an angle across the wide bay in the mountains, heading for the village of Thainsfoot which sat at its northern corner, where the last of the hills toppled over into the flat of the Plains. It was a prosperous collection of cottages, larger houses, and outlying farms, with the Inn being the largest and most imposing of the buildings.

The black of the eastern horizon was lightening to grey as they drew nearer to the village, and they looked for a place for Standley to hide. A line of bushes on their left formed a hedge in front of a hillside slope, and the coat stand tottered behind these and lay down. No one would find him unless they were conducting a detailed search of the whole countryside.

The village lay quiet as they walked into it, with only the sound of a distant cock crowing in an early morning farmyard. A few lamps showed behind curtained windows as labourers rose to milk their cows and the other chores of the day. Roza kept up the hood of her cloak but decided against casting magical concealment spells on them, so as not to confuse, intrigue, or otherwise distract the locals.

As agreed, Roza gave Oxana enough gold, and the paladin entered the inn alone to negotiate a couple of rooms for the four of them. This took longer than expected, and on returning she explained that the owners were too busy preparing breakfast for their existing guests. Furthermore, the inn was so full that they had only one room available, which was large enough for the four of them, but also the most expensive. She had taken this and had to pay upfront for the coming night.

Despite the indignation of Jorxy and Banno, Roza agreed to this, because she was tired from the night's walk, looking forward to sleeping in a bed, and becoming edgy about standing in the street for all to see in the growing daylight.

They entered the inn and were shown along a corridor to an impressive room containing six beds and its own washroom. It was on the ground floor at the side of the building with views from its windows towards Heismith Castle and the mountains. They unloaded their backpacks, took off their boots, decided not to trouble the owners further by ordering breakfast, and took it in turn to have a thorough wash. After eating some of their own food supplies, they collapsed into their beds and slept.

When Roza woke in the afternoon, she tried to remember how long it had been since she'd slept in a proper bed. That was in her bedroom in the warlock's cave on the plateau, which must have been about a week ago. She couldn't bear to think how that must look now, since Lord Vallance's men had searched and burned it. She gazed up at the inn's timbered ceiling and wondered when she'd last been in a proper building. Had that been Albany's Town Hall for the Committee meeting, or Amber-Jane's family home to rejuvenate her Grandma Lily?

How her life had changed, to be on the run, in hiding, a refugee. What had she done to deserve this? Nothing at all. She'd received a unique and remarkable gift, tried to help people with it, and then been hounded away from her home by selfish and greedy men who wanted to control and exploit her. It wasn't fair, but she had little idea what else to do about her situation now.

When the others all woke, they were hungry, and Banno insisted on a proper hot dinner from the inn. They all welcomed this idea, and Oxana went to ask the owners if they could have this served to their room. This request was flatly refused, as apparently all meals had to be served to, and eaten in, the common room, not bedrooms. After a brief discussion, they agreed to go to the common room, to avoid causing more trouble with the owners, to listen for whatever news they could overhear of the outside world, and otherwise keep their heads down and not say much. Roza hoped she wouldn't regret this.

The common room was a long, low-ceilinged room also on the ground floor, but on the other side of the building, and therefore looking out over the plains. In the centre of one wall stood a large hearth, opposite a long bar where food and drinks were ordered and served. Since it was still early evening, not many tables were occupied yet, so the four of them chose one in a corner and near a window with a good view. Roza wanted to watch the daylight fade over this part of the world she'd never seen before.

They ordered beef stew and dumplings for all four of them, with vegetables, bread, and jugs of ale. It felt good to sit and eat at a table like normal people, rather than munching cold bread and cheese on the ground in the dark. By the time their dinners arrived, the common room was filling up, and they received appraising glances from their fellow diners and drinkers.

The inn's owner was serving behind the bar, happy to hold conversations with all who would listen to him, and his voice was one that carried easily. He was clearly in an excellent mood, enthusing to everyone how good business was, with all his bedrooms full and a plentiful supply of customers for eating and drinking. His trade was booming because of everyone travelling from the Plains to Heismith Castle and up into the mountains.

At one point, he raised his tankard in a loud toast, "To the Warlock of Albany, and long may she bring her reward-seekers through my doors!"

Everyone laughed and raised their drinks in the toast. Roza and her friends exchanged nervous glances but kept their heads down over their food. Noticing this, a grey-haired man at a neighbouring table asked them, "What's the matter? You not toasting our saviour warlock?"

Oxana forced a smile back at him. "Oh, I'm sorry, we were too busy eating. Yes, of course, to the Warlock of Albany," she said, and they all raised their ale. The grey-haired man nodded and returned to his food and drink.

Meanwhile, the conversations with the owner at the bar had moved on to the affairs at Heismith Castle. It seemed that the nephew of one of the inn's regulars was a guard for Thain Wicksteed.

"The Thain hasn't been so well this last week, by all accounts," the guard's uncle was saying. "He got injured while on a trip away and the healers have been coming in to see him. And to see half a dozen of his men too, who are all bandaged up."

Roza and Jorxy exchanged a look and returned to their beef stew.

"And what's more," another man added, "I heard it was Albany he went to. So, what could he have gone there for, except to visit that warlock girl, eh?"

"Aye, that's what I heard too," said the first man. "He didn't come back with no rejuvenation neither. It seems our precious warlock has some fearsome beast with her to fight off anyone she doesn't like. Mind you, can't blame her for wanting some protection, given how all the world's beating a path to her door."

"Ah, but that's all stopped now, ain't it?" said another. "No point going to Albany any more, is there, seeing as how she's done a runner. By all accounts, Lord Vallance was right furious, he was, and burned the whole place down."

"What, burned up the whole of Albany?" said the first. "Nah, that can't be right. We'd have heard if he had. You can't burn a whole town anyway, not unless you've got Dragon-fire."

"Hush!" said lots of voices at the bar, and Roza noted that the superstition of not mentioning the word 'Dragon' applied here too.

The inn owner behind the bar was quick to cover up the mistake and raised his drink again, "To the good health and speedy recovery of our Thain Wicksteed."

Roza and her friends were sure to join in the toast this time and raised their ales, "To Thain Wicksteed, his good health," and hoped no one noticed their false enthusiasm for it. Roza reminded herself that the Thain had brought his injuries on himself and had thoroughly deserved them.

Their grey-haired neighbour seemed gratified that they'd partaken of the toast properly, but now unfortunately seemed inclined to start a conversation with them.

"So, welcome to Thainsfoot, you four youngsters," he said. "Where are you good people from?"

Roza noticed how everyone seemed to address their questions to Oxana, as she appeared the adult of their little group. She had to be a few years older than Roza, but only a few, so perhaps the paladin's emblem, red cloak, chainmail and sword gave her the look of authority.

"We're from Gorge City," Oxana replied.

"And what brings you over this way?" their nosey neighbour replied. "Not joining the hunt for the warlock, are you? Hoping to gain that handsome reward?"

Oxana forced out a laugh. "Oh no, we don't think we've much chance with that. No, we went hunting up in the mountains, but as you say, the hillsides and valleys up there were busy, which scares the wild animals away."

The neighbour accepted her answer, and the four of them exchanged glances, but now he went on. "And what's happening over at Gorge City? We hear war might be brewing between Earl Vallance and the Emperor."

Oxana shook her head. "I'm sorry, but we've no news for you about that. We left home a while ago, before Lord Vallance went to Albany, if that's what he did."

Their neighbour nodded, but then their conversation was interrupted by a newcomer into the common room. An older man was being welcomed back after a journey away.

"Here's someone who can tell us the news," called the inn's owner behind the bar. "Come on, Tom, tell us all about your trip to Albany."

Roza's heart sank. Would the conversation in this common room ever turn away from her and her affairs? It seemed not. If she'd doubted whether news of her gift had spread throughout the Empire, she couldn't doubt it now.

The newcomer, Tom, was ushered to a stool at the bar, and other conversations subsided to listen to him.

"But you don't look no younger to me, my old mate," one of his friends teased him. "Didn't that warlock girl's magic work on you?"

There was some friendly laughter at this, but Tom shook his head. "Nah, I never made it to the front of the queue to see her. But I can vouch for her magic, at any rate. Time and again, I saw elderly people shuffle into that tent of hers in Albany marketplace and stride out as younger men and women. Miraculous it was, every time."

The common room fell silent at this, and Roza felt the pangs in her heart. Yes, she'd done so much good to many people, but here was one who hadn't made it to the front of her queue. Part of her was willing to reveal her identity on the spot, offer to rejuvenate everyone who wanted it, as long as they kept quiet about it afterwards, and let the four of them go on their way in peace. But there was no chance of that happening.

"Are you sure it weren't that they just looked younger?" someone was quizzing Tom at the bar. "You know, they'd been tricked into thinking they were younger and so walked with a bit more confidence?"

Tom was shaking his head. "No, I'm not having that. Don't you think those of us in the queue asked them about it when they came out? I saw withered arms restored, blind eyes seeing, and then one old man, who had to be carried in, literally running and jumping about afterwards. It was miracle after miracle, I tell you."

Roza swallowed hard and remembered well her days of doing this hour after hour. It had been truly amazing, and she hardly believed she'd been able to do it. Now she busied herself with mopping up some of her beef stew gravy with a hunk of bread. But she felt Jorxy's, Oxana's and Banno's eyes on her.

"And then did Lord Vallance show up?" another was asking. "Did he burn all of Albany to the ground?"

Tom gave a visible shudder. "No, of course he didn't burn the town to the ground. Who told you that? But it was a nasty night, that was. Lots of shouting and galloping horses and angry voices. We all hid inside in fear for our lives. And then the warlock's plateau went up in flames. That's where she lived, up on the south side of the valley, and everyone could see the fires."

"But the warlock girl definitely survived and escaped, did she?" someone asked.

"Well, Lord Vallance didn't find her," Tom replied. "I heard trackers went into the mountains after her, and came back pretty smartish, tails between their legs. That's why everyone's combing the mountains west of here now, thinking that's where she must be."

The listening quiet in the common room was now so intense that everyone heard it when someone asked in an awed voice, "So, did you see her, then, this warlock girl? What does she look like?"

It was all Roza could do not to hide herself under the table as Tom replied, "Yes, I saw her, when she came and went from her tent. She's tall, young, light brown hair. Not much to look at, not all that slim."

She was determined not to react to this physical description of her, and forced her head to stay down, but the corner of her eye was aware of Tom looking around the common room.

She heard the unmistakeable sound of a bar stool being

scraped on the floor, as Tom stood up. "In fact," he said, "the best I can show you is that she's a bit like this young woman over here."

As much as Roza stared at her plate in growing horror, there was no doubt that Tom was walking towards her.

"Could you stand up for a minute, Miss, just to give everyone an idea of who I saw?"

Roza cast a desperate sideways look at Jorxy's anguished face, but what else could she do? It would cause more trouble to refuse. On shaking legs, she levered herself to her feet but kept her eyes fixedly downcast onto the table.

"Yes, there we go," Tom was saying. "Thank you, Miss. The Warlock of Albany is just about as tall as this young woman here, and has about the same colour of hair…" His voice trailed away, and Roza was terrified of what he might be thinking.

"You could be on to a winner here, Miss," someone called out. "You could go around pretending to be the Warlock of Albany and make yourself a fortune."

Everyone laughed at this and Roza felt she had to say something to distract all the attention. "Just so long as no one asks me to perform any magic, eh, or else I'd be in real trouble." They laughed again and Roza took the chance to sit down at the table.

But Tom was still standing there, gazing at her, and now he spoke again. "You're the spitting image of the girl I saw in Albany. And now I remember that outside the warlock's tent was an ugly boy letting people in to see her. A boy who looked very much like this young man sitting next to her."

The silence in the common room was broken by the scraping of chairs as others stood up to get a good look at Roza and Jorxy.

But Jorxy was on his feet. "Hey, who are you calling ugly, mister?"

Roza grabbed Jorxy's arm and pulled him back into his seat. "Leave it," she hissed. And then to Oxana and Banno,

"We need to get out of here."

Oxana stood up and raised her voice. "Hey, everyone, listen. Where is our famous Plains hospitality? Where are our manners? It's not our way to interrogate our guests or visitors, is it? Those who travel through our lands have a right to their privacy and to go about their lawful business."

While Oxana was saying this, Roza whispered to Jorxy, "We left our backpacks in the bedroom. If we need to leave in a hurry…"

"…I can cut back and get them," he nodded.

"They don't get no privacy if she's the Warlock of Albany!" someone shouted.

A clamour began and Roza wanted nothing more than to hide. Without thinking what she was doing, she cast a Camouflage spell over herself and Jorxy.

The common room gasped. "Where did they go?"

"Those two just disappeared right before my eyes."

But the grey-haired neighbour at the next table was peering their way and said, "What are you talking about? They're still here, can't you see them?"

And the spell was broken, since it was light enough, and he was near enough, to see them. Oxana tried to cover for them. "Well, that was weird, wasn't it? Did you see how the oil lamps flickered in this shadowy corner?"

Too late Roza realised they were sitting at the opposite end of the common room from the door to escape. She nudged Jorxy and whispered, "The window."

"That was magic, that was," someone was saying. "She must be the warlock."

As Jorxy fumbled with the window catches, Roza stood up and addressed the room. "Please calm down, everyone. There is a perfectly reasonable explanation for all of this."

But no one was listening, and several people were closing in on her. She did her best to control the force of her magic and gave a gentle Repulser shove in front of her. The four or five men closest to her stumbled backwards, colliding with chairs, tables, and other diners.

"What's going on here?" rose the inn owner's voice above the growing din.

From the corner of her eye, Roza saw Jorxy climbing out of the common room window into the night outside. "Listen, I don't want to use magic against any of you," she called, "but I really need you to let me go."

Jorxy was on the ground outside now. "Banno, out the window too," he called, and the boy scrambled over the sill.

Roza and Oxana stood side by side facing a swelling crowd of the inn's diners and drinkers, some amazed, some angry, all curious and desperate not to let her escape.

Oxana's sword swept from its sheath in a wide arc before her, causing the circle to gasp, fall back, and cry out. "You heard the young woman," Oxana cried. "She needs to be allowed to leave. Why won't you people let her go?"

"But she's the Warlock of Albany," someone shouted back. "Everyone's looking for her and there's a huge reward, and she's here in our village and inn."

"Let's grab her, all together," came a cry, and they surged forward.

Oxana's sword rose, but it never fell.

Roza had never mastered the Barrier spell, but she tried it now. It extended the Repulser into an arc around her, and she span on her heel to protect them both. But her desperation sent too much energy into the shove, and it was patchy. Those nearest to her went flying, crashing into those behind, landing on tables, turning over chairs.

Some were injured, and this was becoming a fight.

"Oxana, go," Roza cried, and the paladin dived to follow her brother through the window. "Stay back, please," Roza called. "I don't want to hurt anyone."

But the angry mob were picking themselves up to come at her again. What else could she do? She cast Enflame and clicked her fingers to drop a semi-circle of fires onto the common room floor. The crowded room shouted and screamed at her.

Roza cast one last Repulser into the lot of them and then leapt for the window.

She was larger than the others for getting through the opening, but before anyone grabbed her leg, she was caught by Oxana's strong arms as she fell onto the grass outside.

"Come on, this way," Oxana ordered, and as soon as Roza had picked herself up, she cast a hasty Camouflage over them both. They sped around the back of the building, away from the lights of the street. Already they could hear the uproar inside the inn spilling out into the village streets.

At the far corner of the inn, they saw Banno standing by a window. It was their bedroom, and Jorxy had broken in through the window and was handing their backpacks out to the boy. They reclaimed their bags, Jorxy climbed back out, and Roza repeated the Camouflage spell over the four of them. Only just in time.

The villagers from the inn spilled around the rear corners of the building. The darkness between the trees there saved them, as the four of them scrambled away through the night. No villager came close enough to penetrate their Camouflage spell in the gloom.

"Now we circle around behind the village," Oxana suggested, "keeping as quiet as we can. They'll be searching for hours, but no one will find us in this dark, so long as we don't make too much sound."

"And we make for that hedge where we left Standley," Roza added.

They hurried away like shadows, clambering over fences and gates where they needed to, keeping to bushes and trees as much as they could, edging around the skirts of the village until they reached the lane back towards Heismith Castle.

The streets and alleys of Thainsfoot were milling with villagers, those from the inn passing on to those roused from their cottages the news of all that had happened. The greediest and most adventurous were lighting flaming torches to begin the search for their reward at once.

A few times, Roza stopped them under the shadowed trees to repeat her Camouflage spell until the searching villagers had passed.

But eventually, they made it to the ditch behind the hedge where Standley lay, and they hid there until well after midnight. At long last, the clamour of Thainsfoot died down.

CHAPTER FOURTEEN

Roza rested her head on her arms in the dark and wondered whether the evening could have been any more disastrous.

Not only had everyone in the Thainsfoot Inn been talking about her, but someone – even from this small village – had been to Albany themselves and could now recognise her by sight. Was anywhere safe any more? Must she always wonder whether anyone she met recognised her?

But much worse was that her use of magic had confirmed her identity as a warlock, and broadcast to the Empire where she was. The news of the night's events would spread from Thainsfoot at lightning speed, and all those agents, spies, mercenaries, and bounty hunters would descend from the mountains as soon as they heard. By morning, it wouldn't be just the villagers, but also anyone else with a taste for Lord Vallance's reward, who would scour the plains for her.

And where could they hide on a flat and featureless plain? The mountains and forests had provided them with caves and clearings, but there would be no more of those. And how well would her Camouflage spell protect them in broad daylight?

As soon as she thought it safe to do so, Roza spoke in a low voice to the others lying in the dark behind the hedge. "By daybreak, we need to be as many miles away from here as possible. So, we have a few hours to find somewhere to hide during daylight. Any suggestions?"

"Does it matter which direction we go?" Oxana asked. "Our choices are north to the Plains, east to some distant hills and woods, or south to the Southern Wastes."

"We didn't have a plan beyond leaving the mountains," Roza replied. "None of those offer us much nearby cover, and after tonight, all ways will be searched."

"When I looked at old Philoe's maps," Jorxy whispered, "didn't I see a disused quarry near here?"

"Yes, that's right," Oxana said. "The old Heismith Quarry is some miles north of here along the edge of the hills and could provide us with somewhere to conceal ourselves."

"We make for that," Roza decided, "and then we'll need to plan what we do next. My Camouflage spell should hide us well at night, but we need to be as quiet as we can."

They rose behind the hedge and donned their packs. Roza Camouflaged them all and they edged out onto the lane, Standley following on tiptoe. There were still figures with flaming torches in the village, and along the ways to the Castle and over the Plains, so the five of them picked their way around the back of the village that abutted the hillside. It was slower to make their way around gardens and hedges, and to scramble across rocky slopes, but it was more secret.

Several times they had to freeze when they heard voices in a garden, through an open window or at the end of an alley, and creep past holding their breath. But the Camouflage spell held sure, and their passing was mistaken for no more than the scratchings of night animals or a rustle through the leaves.

They breathed easier once they'd left the village behind but still strained their ears for the sounds of voices or feet. A rough road headed north out of Thainsfoot, but they didn't dare to venture along this, keeping to the mountain side of it. More than once they halted in the shadows as lone travellers or groups of people went past.

As tiring as the night walk was, Roza wouldn't let them rest until they reached the quarry, for she feared that daylight would come before they got there. As the eastern horizon began to lighten, she panicked that they would be too easy to spot against a bare hillside in the rays of the rising sun.

Then they rounded a buttress of the hills and saw the old quarry a little way up the valley beyond. They hurried forward, anxious to get themselves out of sight of the main northward road before it got any lighter. The access way to the quarry was covered in gravel, and their boots sounded horribly loud as the crunching echoed up the narrow valley. Roza repeated her Camouflage spell on them all, and they sought the quietest places to lay their boots, but if anyone else was in the quarry, they must have heard them.

They were congratulating themselves on reaching the first pile of discarded rocks when a call of "Hello?" came from up ahead. They melted back into the shadows behind the rockpile and hoped that the half-light of early morning would still conceal them.

As they watched, two men came into view walking down from the heart of the quarry. They were hooded and cloaked, with leather armour underneath and quivers on their backs. They walked with arrows nocked to their bowstrings.

"Hello?" one called again. "Anyone there?" The two hunters slowed as they approached, their keen eyes scanning the sides of the valley and the rockpiles. "I definitely heard something, didn't you?"

"Yeah," the other replied. "Like boots on gravel."

Before Roza noticed what he was doing, Jorxy had bent down and picked up a handful of small stones. He launched one to land on the rockpile behind the hunters, where it caused a ripple of smaller stones to trickle down. The two men whirled around, bows bent, and waited as the sound died away. Jorxy sent another pebble in a different direction, and again the hunters turned to watch the small cascade down the rockpiles.

"What do you reckon, falling stones?" one hunter asked.

A shrug. "Perhaps. But I thought not."

Jorxy's next stone bounced off the top of a rockpile and disappeared behind it. This time a fox darted out from the shadows and bolted down the quarry access way. The hunters whirled, fired their arrows, but missed, and the fox scampered out of sight.

"So, a fox wearing his early morning boots, crunching his way up the gravel?" one called to the other as they chased their prey, nocking their next arrows. Soon the hunters were out of sound and sight.

The five of them breathed again, and Oxana whispered, "Good shooting, Jorxy."

He grinned. "I was lucky. I hoped they might think we were falling stones, but I didn't know that fox was there."

Roza silently thanked the fox for saving them from being discovered and prayed it might escape with its own life too.

The daylight was growing by the minute, so they hurried up into the quarry, discovering a campfire among the rockpiles where the hunters must have spent the night. They needed somewhere more hidden than that and found a gully behind a rubbish pile against a cliff wall. It smelled bad, and Banno wasn't shy in telling them so, but someone would have to climb or circle the dump to find them. Standley, with no apparent sense of smell, chose to keep a lookout by hiding himself among the other rubbish, which he did most effectively.

They were still full of the previous evening's cooked dinner, and the rubbish smell put them off, so they skipped breakfast and lay down to doze. Twice during the day, Standley clicked his hooks at them to warn of people coming, so Roza Camouflaged them again and they kept silent. Searchers roamed the quarry, calling to each other, and even looked behind the rubbish pile, but seemed to see nothing more than rubbish and a cliff wall.

The late afternoon was fading when they roused themselves and were hungry enough to overcome the smell of the rubbish and eat some food.

"Well, Roza," Oxana said, as they began to eat, "you said that when we got here, we'd plan what to do next."

Roza sighed. "Yes, I did. But the only conclusion I've come to is that we can't keep living like this. It's not fair on the rest of you and I can't say I like it much either. Scurrying along at night, hiding by day, sleeping by rubbish dumps, eating the same food all the time, occasional fights, and the constant fear of being caught."

The others seemed pleased to hear this, especially Banno.

"But what other options do we have?" Roza went on. "Any thoughts, Mister Ideas Man?" she added to Jorxy.

Jorxy frowned. "The main problem is that we stick out too much here on the Plains. Everyone we meet wants to ask who we are, what we're doing, where we're going, and so on. It will be even worse if we meet any bounty hunters, or any soldiers or agents of Lord Vallance or the Emperor. Your Camouflage spell will help us, Roza, but I don't think we want to get into a fight."

"I agree," said Oxana. "Apart from my sword, the only defences we have are magical ones, in Roza's spells and Standley. And the magic only confirms and advertises who you are."

"So, I ask again," said Roza, "what choices do we have? In your experience, Jorxy, what are the best ways to avoid being noticed?"

He gave her a sharp look, as though her question hinted that his 'experience' included thieving. She raised her eyebrows at him, and he volunteered, "It's no good sticking out at all if we want to avoid being noticed. Especially if people are looking for you. In that case, the best bet is to try to lose yourself in a crowd."

"Lose yourself in a crowd," Roza repeated. "But there aren't any crowds near here."

Jorxy was chewing his lip. "Unless … but you'll think I'm mad for suggesting it. The only crowds to lose ourselves in would be if we go to Gorge City."

"Brilliant," said Roza, rolling her eyes. "Let's go and hang out with the madman who burned up my plateau and tried to kidnap me."

"No, wait," Oxana interrupted. "Go on, Jorxy, say what you're thinking."

"Um … I've never been to Gorge City," Jorxy continued, "but I assume it's full of people. Would we be able to hide among the crowds?"

Oxana gave a small smile. "You're correct that Gorge City is crowded, but this would be a brave plan. We'd need to get ourselves there undetected, trick our way past the entry guards and find somewhere safe and secluded within the city to hide ourselves. And they'll be more watchful and suspicious than usual because of the threat of war and the spies of the Emperor. It's possible, but risky."

Banno stuck his hand in the air. "I vote for going home. No more sleeping in ditches or rubbish dumps. Proper food and beds and all of that."

Jorxy looked at Roza, who was tearing small hunks from her loaf and popping them in her mouth. "What do you think, Roza?"

After a moment, she shook her head. "I don't like it much. Out here we can see people coming, but in a city, everyone will be right on top of us. And the thought of trying to sneak into the lair of the one man who is hell bent on finding me gives me the creeps. But I did ask for your suggestions."

There was silence until Roza went on, "If there are no better options, then Gorge City is where we'll aim for. I'll get the maps out for you to look at how we'll get there."

She got out Philoe's map book and Maximised it, and then Jorxy and Oxana planned how to travel unnoticed from Heismith Quarry to Gorge City, avoiding all the main routes, and finding places to hide each day, a night's walk apart. Banno seemed simply delighted they were heading back towards civilisation and comfort.

As soon as they considered it dark enough, Standley dug himself out of the rubbish pile, and they donned their packs.

Roza cast Camouflage over them all, and they crept out from their hiding place and disappeared into the dusk. They waited in shadow until it was clear to dash across the main northward road from Thainsfoot and then set off over starlit open country.

Heading eastward away from the hills, the Plains became gradually flatter, which meant they could see or hear anyone coming from further away. Sometimes they were skirting cultivated fields, but at other times it was open grassland, interspersed with heather and peat bogs. At times they followed cart tracks or farm lanes but were always careful to steer clear of any buildings or any sign of lamp, torch, or fire. At the first light of dawn in the east, they sought somewhere to hide from the daylight, and that morning they huddled between bushes beside a stream that cut a slight channel through the land.

The daytime was uneventful apart from a rain that began and soaked them through, and the others had to overrule Banno by refusing to light a fire. The following night they pressed on until the rain stopped, and it took them a long time to dry out and warm up because the autumn nights were becoming colder. Their refuge the next day was an abandoned farm labourer's cottage, which had no roof or windows, but enabled them to hang up their sodden cloaks to dry while they slept under their blankets.

The night walks were long and cold, stumbling along across dreary landscapes, with little sense of direction. Sleeping by day was often nervous and fitful, in case they were discovered, when they could find no cover better than lying flat in a shallow dip in the ground.

But after one night of walking, Oxana was pleased with how far they'd come. She seemed able to recognise landmarks in what to the others was a featureless land. "We will near the edges of the Gorge City farmlands at the end of tonight's walk," she informed them. "So, we'll need to be careful about how and when we move, and where we choose to hide for the day. As we return to civilisation, the roads and people will increase, and so will the dangers."

Oxana's words were proved correct as they walked that night, and when the eastern sky began to pale, they could find no abandoned buildings or other good place to hide. As the daylight grew, the best they could manage was a barn at the edge of a cluster of farm buildings, but the farmhouse was clearly occupied. They scrambled up a ladder into a hayloft and tried to hide themselves among the straw. The wooden walls had ventilation slats which enabled Standley to keep a lookout in all directions as the farm workers and animals began their day.

Roza was drifting off to sleep when Standley clicked his hooks. Someone was moving in the barn below, and then a voice called, "Hello, you up there in the hayloft. There's no need to be worried, you're not in trouble or anything."

Yeah, not in trouble, Roza thought. I'm only about to be discovered. Again.

She freed her hands from the hay enough to cast Camouflage over them all, but that in itself made a rustle in the straw. And the sunlight streaming through the slatted walls made the hayloft bright.

The face of an old man appeared at the top of the ladder, squinting around. He blinked, peered at them all, and then said, "Ah, there you are. I couldn't see you for a moment. Why are you hiding up here? Haven't you heard about Plains hospitality? You don't need to sneak up here, but could have knocked on our front door, and we'd have given you food to eat and beds to sleep in."

Roza and Jorxy looked at each other in disbelief, while Oxana responded, "That's very hospitable of you, sir. We come from Gorge City and know of the traditions of welcoming travellers as guests, but sadly that kindness is often neglected of late. We didn't want to presume on your generosity or cause you any trouble."

"Nonsense," the man chuckled. "As the saying goes,

strangers are merely friends we haven't met yet. So, we welcome the chance to make new friends. Come on down into the house and let us make you some breakfast. What do you say?"

Banno was the first to clamber out of the straw and towards the ladder, while the others looked at each other, shrugged and agreed.

Then the man said, "And what's this? Is that a coat stand you've brought with you? It's not my place to enquire what sentimental value makes you carry a piece of furniture around with you, but you can bring that with you too if you've such a mind."

Standley had frozen rigid when the man appeared, so Roza picked him up by his pole to carry him with her. They processed down the ladder with their backpacks, picking bits of straw from their clothing and hair.

"My name is Enoch," the old man was saying, "and my wife is Celeste, but we won't ask nothing of your names and business any more than you're inclined to tell us yourselves." He looked them up and down. "Let's see now, two boys and two girls, very good."

"I'm Oxana and this is my brother, Banno," Oxana volunteered.

"And I'm Jacey, and this is my school friend, Charly," Roza added.

Old Enoch started. "Jacey and Charly, you say? Well, blow me if those aren't the names of two of our grandchildren. Anyway, welcome to Sunrise Farm, and come into the house." He led the way out of the barn and towards the farmyard.

Jorxy looked at Roza, frowning. "How on earth did you choose the names of two real people when you picked those for us?"

She shrugged and then grinned. "Who knows? Maybe magic had something to do with it. Perhaps the Universe wants to give us a sign that it's okay to trust these people."

Jorxy stared at her, as she followed the others towards the farmhouse.

"Celeste, dear," Enoch called, as they came in the door. "I was right, I did see someone moving in the hayloft. We have four guests for breakfast, and I'll show them their rooms."

"Righty oh," replied Celeste, a plump old woman, as she came bustling into the hall. "Get yourselves unloaded and washed upstairs, and we'll set something hot before you as soon as you're ready."

Banno was beaming from ear to ear, and Roza's wildest dreams hadn't imagined such a generous welcome. Or were this couple too good to be true? She couldn't sense anything other than genuine kindness from them.

Enoch led them up a wide staircase to two guest rooms, each with two single beds made ready, and said, "There you go, boys and girls, feel free to arrange yourselves how you please. I'll fetch you some hot water."

Oxana and Banno took one room, Roza and Jorxy the other, and the old farmer soon returned with a jug of hot water for each of their washstands. Roza laid Standley back on his feet, and he bowed his top hooks to her.

"Do you trust this old couple?" Jorxy asked.

"There's nothing to trust or distrust about them yet," Roza replied, "but I guess we're all happy enough to eat their breakfast and sleep in their beds. Their hospitality feels genuine, don't you think?"

Jorxy nodded. "Yes, I do. I keep looking for the trap or trick but can't see one yet. We ought to remain on our guard, though."

Roza nodded and started on her first good wash since the Thainsfoot Inn.

The smells of frying sausages and bacon soon lured them down from their rooms to a laden breakfast table in the farmhouse kitchen. There were also fried eggs, tomatoes, mushrooms, porridge, toast, honey, jams, pastries, and cakes. They tried everything, washed down with brews of tea, until they could take no more. Roza's Maximise and Rejuvenate spells had kept their food supplies ample and fresh, but nothing could replace the joys of excellent home-cooking.

Enoch and Celeste had already eaten but kept them company at the table with conversation about their farm while they replenished everyone's plates and cups.

As their eating finally slowed, Oxana said, "Please forgive our initial hesitation about testing your hospitality, but rest assured that our opinion of a Plains welcome has been fully restored."

"Aye, that's good to hear," Enoch replied, "but there's nothing to forgive. It's important to stay kind and generous, especially in evil times."

Roza and Jorxy exchanged a look, and then she said, "When you say 'evil times', do you mean the war? We've been away and haven't heard how things are in Gorge City now."

"Ah, yes, I do mean the war," Enoch sighed, shaking his head. "It's not too bad around here yet, south-west of the city, but I hear there's been fighting already to the north. Lord Vallance's men came round ordering us to take refuge in the city, but we refused, saying who would look after the farm? Aye, they still want our food for their soldiers, but don't think as to how we need to stay here to grow it for them."

Roza hesitated, then went on, "How do you think this war will go then, between Lord Vallance and the Emperor?"

The old man grimaced. "It's a bad business all round. Those two are as bad as each other, the Earl and the Emperor, and I don't care who hears me say it. The ones I feel sorry for are the young men signed up to fight it out and get injured or die in the process. Nope, it looks set to be a long business, and I can't say as I want either side to win."

"If you ask us to pick a side," Celeste joined in, "we wouldn't pick either the Earl or the Emperor. We say we're on the Warlock's side."

Roza choked and spluttered on her tea and had to make it look as though it simply went down the wrong way. While she recovered, Jorxy asked them, "What do you mean, you're on the Warlock's side?"

Enoch and Celeste stared at him. "You said you've been away," the old woman replied, "but surely you've heard about that young woman, the Warlock of Albany?"

Jorxy glanced at Roza and said, "Yeah, we've heard of her."

"That poor girl," Celeste went on. "We've heard nothing but good about her, how she can make people younger and won't even charge them for it. And yes, she weakened the Emperor, but we can't see how she wanted this to end up in civil war. Now she's been hounded from her home, in hiding and on the run, and everyone's hunting her either for the reward or to help them win this so-called war for immortality. She's a poor young lamb to be caught up in the middle of this, and if anyone needs us to be on their side, then it's her."

Roza's jaw dropped in the middle of this, and she stared at the old farmer woman. It felt surreal, but also deeply touching, to hear this old couple sympathising with her predicament so completely. She was conscious of Jorxy's, Oxana's and Banno's eyes on her as well. "Um … thank you," she said, before she could think of anything else.

Enoch's brow creased. "You're welcome, but why do you thank us?"

Too late Roza realised that her response sounded strange, and she was about to make it sound like gratitude for the hospitality. But a wave of intense weariness washed over her at all this hiding and deception. She longed to be honest and to trust people again, because it had turned out well with Oxana and Banno. And hadn't this old couple, without knowing who she was, already declared their sympathy and support for her? If magic and the Universe had given her a sign with their adopted names, then the least she could do was to trust them in return.

"Well … um … thank you for your hospitality and understanding. Because you see, I told you my name is Jacey, but it's actually Rozabella, and I'm the Warlock of Albany."

CHAPTER FIFTEEN

With a crash, the teapot Celeste had picked up fell back to the table and she only just caught it from tipping over. Roza looked around the table: Jorxy was glaring at her, Oxana's eyebrows were raised, Banno was chewing a cake, and Enoch and Celeste were open-mouthed.

Into the stunned silence, she added, "So, thank you for your support and for being on my side."

Celeste's voice was higher than usual. "You're … you're the Warlock of Albany, and you're sitting here at our table?"

Roza smiled at her. "As you say, I'm in hiding and on the run, and that led me to sneak into your hayloft for some sleep. But instead, you've offered us rooms and beds and a wonderful breakfast. So, thank you."

Enoch had regained his wits and voice. "Then I say again that you are very welcome indeed. But where are you going and how else can we help you?"

Roza reflected for an instant on how their response differed from that of the villagers of Thainsfoot, or Lord Vallance's trackers, and appreciated that there were still some good people in the world.

"We're going to Gorge City," Roza replied, "so I can try to hide myself among the crowds there. Any help you can offer us will be most welcome."

"Hmm, that sounds a brave move, young Miss Rozabella," Enoch mused, "one that we'll need to think about. Aren't you afraid of getting caught by Lord Vallance?"

Over the last few days of walking from Heismith Quarry, Roza had had time to think about her next move. This coming war for immortality pressed heavily upon her mind, that she'd caused it by weakening the Dragon Emperor. If she'd started it, was it also up to her to try and stop it? And if so, was she one of the few people in a position to do so? She hadn't mentioned this to the others, because of what they might think, but decided now was the time to explain.

"Am I afraid of getting caught? Well, yes, I am. But the way I see it, I need to talk with, or confront, either the Earl of the Plains, or the Dragon Emperor, or both, to end this war. If I can do anything to avoid this fighting and bloodshed, then I must. How do we get that to happen? I don't know. One of them to surrender, or to defeat the other and win the war, or to negotiate a peace, but it seems worthwhile to try. And I might be one of the few people able to achieve it."

Predictably, Jorxy, Oxana and Banno were staring at her, but Enoch was stroking his chin. "I think you may be correct, young lady, that you have the fame and influence to command the attention of both the Earl and the Emperor. But I caution you to be most careful in dealing with either of them, because they are both notoriously cunning and treacherous."

Banno gave a wide yawn, and Celeste said, "Enough of this talking, everyone. Can't you see that these young people are dropping to sleep over their plates? You need to rest, so off to your rooms and beds with you. We will clear up and ponder all these matters while you recover. See you later."

And with that she chivvied them from the table and up the stairs. Roza had much to think about, but having expressed her thoughts about the future out aloud eased her mind. The softness of the bedding, and the warmth of the welcome here, soon enabled her dreamless sleep.

When she woke in the afternoon, Jorxy's bed was empty, so she washed and went downstairs to find him in conversation with Enoch at the kitchen table.

"Ah, Warlock Rozabella," Enoch began, "we hope you slept well. I've mentioned an idea to young Jorxy here. I'm taking a load of grain to Gorge City in the morning, so if you like, the four of you could come along with me in the wagon. Being with me might help you get through the city gates without too many questions."

Roza nodded. "Thank you, because that would get us to the city sooner and avoid unwanted attention on the road. Do you need help loading up the grain?"

"Bless you, girl," the old farmer replied with a grin. "I appreciate your offer, but we have farm hands to help with such things. Most of the sacks are on the wagon by now, and they'll make sure the horses are ready too. Jorxy said you have a book of maps, and I'll be interested to see those."

Roza ran upstairs to retrieve her pack, and then amazed Enoch by Maximising Philoe's Maps of the World for him to look at. While she was in her box of books, Roza found, enlarged, and thumbed through her book of self-defensive magic. Ever since their experience at the Thainsfoot Inn, she'd been troubled by their inability to escape from a tight spot if they needed to. She remembered seeing at the back of this book a spell entitled Recall and read through it again.

It was described as advanced and powerful magic, which didn't encourage her much, but it enabled what she wanted: for warlocks to transport themselves out of a dangerous situation and back to a safe place. The power of general teleportation seemed way beyond her at present, but this seemed a more specific and limited version of it to start with.

Roza began to study it, and the essence was a strong connection with the place she wanted to return to. If she'd had a permanent home, such as her parents' cottage, or the cave on the Albany plateau, that would have been ideal, but she didn't want to return there. That was too far away by now and would only revert to her previous need to escape. If she got into trouble in Gorge City, she wanted to return here, to Enoch and Celeste's Sunrise Farmhouse.

A footnote at the bottom of the spell intrigued her: if a suitable place for the Recall cannot be identified, the spell can be set to Recall to a specific person instead. At first, she couldn't see how this might help, because Jorxy, Oxana and Banno would be coming with her into the city. And while Enoch and Celeste had been welcoming, the connection with them probably wasn't strong enough.

And then Roza hit on it. She ran back upstairs and found Standley watching out of her bedroom window at the wagon being loaded below. "Standley, I'm sorry we've had to hide you over the last few days, but would you come downstairs for something, please?"

Her coat stand nodded his hooks and followed her out of the bedroom. He managed the stairs with an amusing jumping movement, and then Roza went ahead of him into the kitchen, where Celeste, Oxana and Banno had now joined Enoch and Jorxy.

"Um, Enoch and Celeste," she began, "you said you wouldn't ask about my sentimental attachment to a piece of furniture, but I'd like to explain why I carry a coat stand around with me. This is Standley, and he can move and walk and understand us, and I've known him for the whole time I've been a warlock."

Roza beckoned her coat stand into the room, and Standley peered around the door frame, much to the amazement and delight of the old couple. Enoch and Celeste hurried over to him and chuckled in wonder as he shook hooks with them both.

"He's an enchanted coat stand, of course," Roza went on, "and I should tell you that he's amazingly strong, flexible and indestructible. We communicate by yes and no questions, which he answers by nodding or shaking his hooks at the top. He's saved me on a few different occasions by now."

Standley's eye knots crinkled, and he bowed his top.

"The thing is, Standley," she said, "we're planning to travel into Gorge City tomorrow, and I can't see how we're going to keep you hidden there. Do you understand?" She looked between Standley, Enoch and Celeste. "So, I was wondering whether we could leave you here safe at this farmhouse instead?"

The eye knots gazed at Roza, and she thought they looked sad, but he nodded.

"Yes, yes, of course," Enoch replied. "We can keep … er, Standley … safe and hidden here. It will be our pleasure."

Roza rested her hand on the coat stand's polished wooden pole. "If you're willing to stay here, Standley, then you can serve a vital purpose for me too. There's this spell called Recall, and if I'm in need, instead of returning to a safe place, I can set it to return me to a trusted person. So, if I'm in danger, Standley, would it be okay if I use the spell to Recall myself to wherever you are?"

If it were possible, Roza thought his eye knots filled with tears. As it was, he nodded vigorously, and then moved forward to give her a strong and firm embrace.

Roza laughed and then said, "Excellent, let's get started."

She and Standley left the others to study the maps and prepare the evening meal, while they went upstairs to learn the spell. The first part was to establish the spiritual connection between them that would enable this powerful magic to work. Roza had experienced a flow of magical energy a few times before, with Philoe, Kerenzi and the Dragon Emperor. But this was different and deeper, and when they touched and opened themselves up to each other, she was amazed at how vibrant and alive the coat stand's energy felt. It was both powerful and intimate to be this close with another living being, and Roza was relieved to do this with her coat stand rather than being this open with someone like Jorxy.

And for the first time, she received some impressions of feelings within Standley. They were not words or language, but distinct emotions – affection, loyalty, friendship, trust. Roza was delighted by how much her coat stand's feelings towards her mirrored how she felt about him.

Once their connection was made, Roza needed to learn

how to channel her magic into returning her body to her magical and spiritual partner. Unlike her other spells, this required no hand or arm movements, only the simple word, 'Recall'. They began on opposite sides of the bedroom from each other, but this didn't work, because Roza was distracted by seeing him in front of her. Their first success was when she went out onto the landing and teleported herself back into the bedroom next to him. They swapped places, and Roza Recalled herself from beside her washstand to join Standley at the top of the stairs.

They became more adventurous, knowing this needed to work across many miles to be effective from Gorge City to here. Roza went out to the barn and transported herself back to Standley in the bedroom. Next, Standley was in the barn, and Roza Recalled herself to him there. Finally, Standley went off to hide, so Roza had no idea where he was, and she still managed a successful teleport to his location.

The others were already eating their evening meal: a large joint of roast beef with potatoes, vegetables, gravy and all the trimmings, when Roza bounded in to report their success. She tucked in with relish, feeling more positive and encouraged than she had for a long while.

They talked late into the evening, and after the others had gone to bed, Roza sought out Enoch and Celeste where they sat by the fire in their living room. It was a cosy scene, and she felt she intruded on their warm, domestic companionship. She sat on a low stool between them while Celeste knitted, and Enoch kept adding logs to the flames.

"How long have you two been married?" Roza asked them at last.

"Ooh, it will be nearly fifty years now, won't it, dear?" Enoch replied, and Celeste nodded.

"And do you have children and grandchildren? Are any of them here?"

"Yes, two children and five grandchildren," Celeste told

her, "but they've all gone into the city. They don't consider farming an exciting enough life, and we don't begrudge them their choices. We employ what help and labour we need, and they visit us when they can."

"What will happen to this farm, then, when you die, and do you have any regrets about that?"

Enoch and Celeste looked at each other, and he said, "I suppose the place will be sold, and our children will get the money. But we've no regrets because we've made sure to enjoy our lives, haven't we, dear?"

Celeste smiled. "Yes, we have. I wouldn't change a thing about all our fifty years together."

Roza hesitated, but this was why she'd come to see them. "You've been so kind to me that I want to offer you something in return. You know I can make people physically younger, so would you like me to Rejuvenate the two of you so you can live here together for longer?"

Enoch and Celeste stared at her and then turned to each other. She asked, "How much younger can you make us?"

Roza shrugged. "As young as you like. To age fifty, thirty, middle aged, a young couple, or when you first met. Or just a few years younger than you are now, it's your choice."

"Could you take us back to our beginning, when we were newly married, and we can live out our whole fifty years of married life all over again?" Enoch asked, his eyes wide.

Roza nodded. "But that would be a big change, for you and your family, so I suggest you think about it for as long as you need to, before rushing into anything."

Enoch and Celeste looked at each other. "That's very wise," he said. "This would affect not just us, but our children, the farm and their inheritance, so we'll have a think, thank you."

Roza got up from the stool, said goodnight, and left them to think and talk.

After an early breakfast, Roza, Jorxy, Oxana and Banno said goodbye to Celeste and Standley and loaded themselves and their packs onto the back of Enoch's grain wagon. Since Standley was staying at the farmhouse, the miniature chest of gold, gems and jewellery had been moved into the bottom of Jorxy's pack, while Roza's still contained her box of Minimised magic books.

The old farmer sat up front guiding the pair of horses, while the rest of them sat or lay on the sacks of grain. The sun was rising as they set off from the farmyard along the bumpy lane to the road. As soon as they turned onto the main highway, their way was much smoother and faster, and Roza couldn't remember ever having travelled so fast. She gripped the wooden sides for fear of tumbling out the back.

The road was busy with other traffic: horse-drawn wagons and carts, lone riders on donkeys and groups of horsemen, marching soldiers, and pedestrians. The sun warmed them from a clear sky, and they stopped a couple of times to stretch their legs and take a drink. The land around them became increasingly well-cultivated and inhabited, from fields, farms, and hedges, to hamlets, villages, and small towns.

In the early afternoon, Oxana pointed out to Roza her first sight of the still-distant Gorge City: the most massive tower she'd ever seen or even imagined. On the hazy horizon, a round tower stretched skywards, and then a second one further away, each one topped with three horns.

"Those are the south and north watchtowers," Oxana explained, "built on the rims of the gorge to survey the Plains for many miles around. As the name suggests, our capital city is built around a deep canyon, and it is ancient, dating back to the heyday of the Sapiens themselves, the founders of our Empire. No one these days could construct those watchtowers, or the larger ones down in the gorge where the rich people live. We poorer folk live in the tunnels and caves around the gorge. But wait until you see the city's other wonders – the Earl's Palace on the canyon floor, and the Sapien Bridge that spans the narrowest gap between the north and south rims."

Roza and Jorxy were wide-eyed and dumbstruck about what sort of place they were coming to, so far above their humble Albany valley. As they drew nearer, Oxana told them about the fortified wall encircling the city and gorge, built along the rims, making the whole city much easier to defend.

They joined the queue of vehicles and people waiting to pass through the gatehouse in the city wall and took the chance to walk alongside the wagon while Enoch and the horses edged it slowly forwards. They ate and drank a late lunch and enjoyed the sunshine. Oxana and especially Banno were excited to be returning home, but Roza and Jorxy eyed the surrounding throngs suspiciously.

Had they made a mistake in choosing to come here? No, once they were inside and if they were careful, it would be much easier to lose and hide themselves among these crowds.

As their wagon neared the gatehouse, Enoch advised the four of them to clamber back on top of the grain in the back. They would arouse less suspicion as farm labourers having come along to unload the sacks rather than as individual newcomers to the city on foot.

There were soldiers at the gatehouse, armed with bows and swords and dressed in the blue uniform of the Plains Army, who stopped and questioned everyone entering the city through the gate. Roza supposed this was inevitable in time of war, that Lord Vallance needed to be vigilant against spies or saboteurs from the Imperial Army. It crossed her mind to use a Camouflage spell over the four of them but abandoned that thought because the afternoon sun was too high and bright to make that enchantment effective. But she raised her hood over her face to shelter from the heat of the sun.

When their turn came, an Army Sergeant halted them, and Enoch reined the horses to a stop. He explained he was a local farmer bringing grain to sell in the city to support the war effort, and the Sergeant nodded.

The man then turned to the others and said, "You four, out of the back."

Roza saw no option but to comply, and they scrambled down to the ground, assuming the Sergeant wanted to check the grain sacks. But instead, he faced the four of them and said, "Hoods down. I need your names, ages and where you're from."

With a sinking feeling in her stomach, Roza lowered her hood, as Oxana said, "I'm Oxana and I'm twenty-two, and this is my younger brother, Banno, who is fourteen. We're residents of Gorge City."

Jorxy followed that with, "I'm Charly and I'm sixteen, and this is my friend Jacey, who's seventeen. We're from Heismith Castle."

The Sergeant pointed at Banno and said, "You can go through, because you're still too young, but the other three of you are hereby conscripted into the service of the Plains Army."

CHAPTER SIXTEEN

No! Roza reeled in shock. They couldn't be in the Army. They needed to stay hidden and unknown.

What could she do? Any magic now would cause instant attention and uproar. She discounted the Recall spell because that would save only her. Even if Oxana was willing to fight to defend her home city, she couldn't abandon Jorxy to his fate. She needed to wait for a better opportunity to save them all.

Enoch had begun to argue with the Sergeant. "But I need these four as labourers to unload the grain and help me on my farm back at home." His eye was on Roza as he said this.

"Tough," barked the Sergeant. "We've a war to fight to protect your farm, and everyone must play their part. You can keep the fourteen-year-old to help you and manage the best you can. And don't push your luck any further, or I might forget your protected status as a farmer and conscript you, your wagon, and horses as well."

Roza caught Enoch's gaze and shook her head at him. She couldn't let him get into trouble over them and felt a sudden panic about her hidden box of magic books and treasure chest. "We'll be all right, Mister Enoch, sir, and can look after ourselves. But please take our two packs here back to Sunrise Farm. You should go home to your wife." She forced out a smile and hoped he didn't see the anguish in her eyes.

"When you get the chance," Oxana was saying to Banno, "go to our aunt and uncle and tell them what has happened." The boy looked terrified and tearful to be left on his own here, even though this was his home city. "Or Enoch will take you back to the farmhouse, if you prefer." But for Banno it was clear that no one could replace the protection and reassurance of his sister. Roza couldn't watch as they hugged each other with tears.

The Sergeant was barking at them to move: for Enoch and his wagon to go on through the gatehouse, and for Roza, Jorxy and Oxana to follow a soldier off to the barrack houses. They watched Banno enter the city perched alone on the back of Enoch's grain sacks, but before the boy was out of sight, they were ordered to move themselves.

Roza, Jorxy and Oxana followed a blue-uniformed soldier under the gatehouse arch, and the sight before her took Roza's breath away.

The highway into the city divided left and right to curve downwards following the natural rim of the gorge. Beyond the low wall at the far side of the road, the vast canyon stretched before them, dominated on each side by the massive towers for the rich people that Oxana had mentioned. Behind the towers leaped the span of the Sapien Bridge, joining the north and south rims of the gorge together. Dotted around the floor of the canyon were holes and fires in the tunnels and caves where the poorer people lived. Everywhere Roza looked were unnumbered dwellings – homes, inns, taverns, workshops, smithies, markets, and numerous others she couldn't guess at. Between them all were endless steps, lanes and alleyways, all teeming with people coming and going. She had never imagined anywhere so teeming, impressive or vast.

She had no time to stop or stare, because the soldier ordered the three of them to follow him to the left. On this side, the road sloped gently downwards, carved into the living rock of the gorge wall, leading to the upper tier of the north side of the city. Buildings perched wherever there was space on either side of the road, and this section of the city near the western gatehouse appeared to be reserved for the city guards and for the Army barracks and training grounds.

The soldier led Roza, Jorxy and Oxana through an arched gate into a dusty square, and then through a doorway into a cooler, shadowed building. He deposited them at the back of a queue, lining up to see a Sergeant seated at a desk, and then he disappeared back to the gatehouse.

While they waited in the queue, Oxana whispered to them, "Welcome to Gorge City. Given the imminent prospect of war, maybe we should have expected this to happen."

Jorxy turned to Roza. "What are we going to do? They can't find out who you are, or what you can do, so what happens if we end up in the middle of a battle against the Imperial Army?"

She laid a hand on his arm. "One thing at a time. Let's see what they intend to do with us. I have the Recall spell, but don't know if I can transport all three of us back to Standley. And that would leave Banno here on his own."

"I'm glad you asked Enoch to take our packs back to the farm and not bring them with us. We can't be sure they'd be safe here."

The queue had moved forward so they fell silent as they neared the seated Sergeant. When they reached the front, without looking up, he said in a bored voice, "Your names, and what you can do to help the Army."

Oxana spoke first. "I am Oxana, and I am a paladin. I'm a hunter, mercenary, adventurer."

He raised his eyes and looked her up and down, taking in her cloak, badge, chainmail, and sword. "Very good," he said, and repeated as he noted it down on a sheet of parchment, "Oxana, paladin. Next."

"I'm Charly, and I'm pretty good at throwing stones."

Roza marvelled again at Jorxy's ease with false names and believable lies.

The Sergeant looked less impressed than with Oxana. "Charly, missile weapons. And you?"

Roza shrugged, and said, "I'm Jacey, and I'm fairly good with herbs, so perhaps a healer?" The ironic thought came that she was particularly good with age-related ailments, such as deafness, blindness, heart disease, old age, or death, but decided not to mention these.

The Sergeant accepted her words and noted down, "Jacey, healer. Boys that way, girls this," and then turned to the next in his queue.

Roza didn't like being separated from Jorxy, and he seemed to like it even less, but there was nothing they could do. Jorxy headed off through a door on one side of the building, and Roza followed Oxana through an opposite one. Here they were issued with the blue uniforms, and Oxana made a fuss about wearing her chainmail over the blue. Her mail was of sufficient quality that this was allowed, but a bigger problem was finding a woman's uniform tall enough for Roza. In the end, she made do with one that was short at the ankles, but was short-sleeved and baggy enough for her to move in.

The rest of the afternoon was spent in physical exercise, and Roza and Oxana caught sight of scrawny Jorxy in his boy's uniform across the dusty yard. This was followed by a meagre evening meal of thin soup and stale bread. Roza wished she could Maximise and Rejuvenate it but didn't dare do so at the table with all the other new recruits. They were allocated a bed, and Roza and Oxana were separated because the fighters and healers slept in different dormitories.

As she prepared for sleep, Roza heard the girl on the next bed crying. The girl had been told off earlier, so Roza went over and sat by her. "I'm Jacey, what's your name?"

"Madison," the girl muttered.

She looked very young, with her dark brown ponytail, but Roza guessed she must be sixteen or so.

Roza laid a hand on the girl's shoulder, and said, "This is a bit of a shock, isn't it?"

Madison looked confused and said, "I'm sorry, I don't hear very well."

Roza frowned and tried to speak as clearly as she could. "Are you deaf?"

The girl nodded, wiping her eyes.

Roza sighed. Being conscripted into the army was bad enough, but this deaf girl had been punished for not hearing orders correctly. A risky idea occurred to her.

She turned to face the girl. "You can speak well enough. Could you hear when you were younger?"

Madison seemed to understand Roza's clear words and nodded.

Roza leaned closer and said, "If you can keep this secret, I can help you hear. Would you like that?"

The girl frowned, not understanding.

Roza put a finger to her lips to indicate the secret, then mimed opening the ears, and raised her eyebrows at the girl.

Madison still seemed confused but shrugged and seemed willing to let her try.

Roza looked around to check no one was watching them, then placed her hands over Madison's ears. She quickly ignited her magic, let it flow through her arms into Madison's ears, and made them younger.

When the girl's eyes widened, Roza stopped, put her finger back to her lips and breathed, "Shhh."

Madison gasped. "I heard that."

Roza nodded and whispered, "Please don't tell anyone I did this, but I thought it might help you through our time as Army healers together."

Madison's face cracked into a wide grin, and as she went back to her bed, Roza thought she might have made a new friend. She only hoped her impulse to help anyone who needed rejuvenation wouldn't get her into any more trouble.

Roza's thoughts were in too much of a whirl to let her sleep well, despite the barracks mattress being better than the outdoors. Breakfast was a watery porridge served at long tables where all the female recruits sat together, and she found herself longing for Celeste's farmhouse breakfast.

Afterwards, Roza and Madison were allocated to a training session for Army healers, which consisted of a very long morning of their group of recruits being talked at by a senior woman. The speaker was insisting that every healer must rush immediately to the aid of any wounded soldier, even if they were mid-battle, because this was their duty. The rolled eyes between Roza and Madison confirmed that neither of them would consider doing any such thing.

The speaker was interrupted by a soldier entering the room. "The Sergeant wants to see healer recruit Jacey."

Roza exchanged a puzzled look with Madison, shrugged and stood up. The training woman nodded, and Roza followed the soldier from the room. He led her to the entrance hall where the three of them had signed in yesterday, although the place was emptier now.

The same Sergeant was there again, but Roza was surprised to see the boy Banno among those waiting beside him. She thought he might have returned with Enoch to the safety of the farmhouse, but it seemed he'd followed his big sister's instructions and gone to his aunt and uncle here in the city instead.

Banno looked excited to see her. "Hello, Ro– … I mean, Jacey."

Roza glared at him for failing to use her false name.

But the boy didn't seem to notice. "I've brought a friend to see you. His name is Morton." He indicated a short, stocky man standing beside him, bald-headed and with a neat beard, dressed all in black, and holding a bag in his leather-gloved hands. "He says he can get the three of you out of needing to serve in the Army."

The Sergeant's head jerked up in annoyance. "What's this? Get you out of serving in the Army?"

Morton held up a placating gloved hand. "It's quite all right, Sergeant," he said in a smooth, persuasive voice, "I can explain." He stepped forward, opening his bag.

He spoke to Roza now. "I'm very pleased to meet you, Miss Jacey," he said, as he pulled a grey bundle out of his bag. "Very pleased indeed."

Before Roza realised what he was doing, Morton had thrown the grey bundle at her.

As though time itself slowed down, Roza saw with complete clarity as the bundle opened itself up into a network of grey ropes. The net hit her, wrapping itself around her bare arms, trapping her uniformed legs and stretching across her neck and face.

Her first thought was to get this Morton man away from her, and despite her resolve not to reveal her magic, started a Repulser spell. She reached down inside for the spark of magic and found that her arms were bound too tightly to complete the hand movements properly. She could still click her fingers though and switched to Enflame instead.

But her inner spark of magic refused to ignite.

For the first time since she'd rejuvenated her parents' eyes and heart outside the Albany stockade, Roza couldn't summon her magical energy to perform a spell. She kept trying to light the spark, but the power kept dissipating away into nothing.

And then the pain hit her.

Wherever the grey ropes touched the skin on her arms, neck, and face, they were burning. The ropes had vicious barbs along their lengths, which were digging into her flesh, and the more she struggled, the worse they tore. The barbs were penetrating the blue fabric of her uniform into her legs and chest and back, and the fire of her agony was building.

In horrified realisation, Roza knew what these ropes were.

Bindweed.

The one substance, known only to fellow warlocks, that could suppress the ability to use magic.

Roza lifted her gaze into the gloating, triumphant face of Morton, and knew she'd been captured by an enemy warlock.

Her next desperate thought was Recall, Recall, Recall, back to Standley and the farmhouse, to get her away from here, but the magic wouldn't come, and the spell wouldn't work.

She caught a glimpse of Banno's terrified, stricken face, and the Sergeant shouting orders, but then Morton commanded them all to Freeze, and none of them could move.

The searing fire in Roza's body grew, and overwhelmed her, and she panicked, and was falling, and she screamed and screamed and screamed.

CHAPTER SEVENTEEN

Roza returned to consciousness only because someone was shaking her. She far preferred oblivion to this reality of pain.

The fire in her torso and limbs was a steady burning now after the crescendo and furnace of her first capture. She screwed her eyes shut, and thrashed her limbs, but this only made the tearing barbs of the ropes cut deeper into her flesh. She tried to lie still and contain the agony into a controlled blaze, but the flames kept bursting out to torment her anew.

A man was shouting in her ear as he shook her. "Miss Jacey, Miss Jacey, wake up, wake up."

"Get off," Roza snapped. "Leave me alone. And get this Bindweed off me."

She forced her eyes open to see the loathsome face of Morton the warlock inches from her own.

"Ah, you're back with us, Miss Jacey," he gloated, "or should I say, Warlock Rozabella of Albany."

"Get these ropes off me," Roza hissed.

"I see you're familiar with the lovely Bindweed, are you?" Morton preened. "Very useful stuff, it is, yes, when we need to keep an errant warlock from using her magic. So no, we won't take these ropes off you, Miss Rozabella, because they're the only things keeping you here, aren't they? The only things stopping you from using your magic against us, and we couldn't allow you to cast spells now, could we?"

Roza couldn't bear the man's self-satisfied smugness any longer and looked about her. She was lying on a floor, but it wasn't the barracks any more. The floor was white marble and stretched away into the distance of a vast Hall, dotted with lines of similarly white pillars. The ceiling was so far above her she could hardly make it out, but it seemed highly decorated. Where was she?

"Ah yes," Morton was saying, "you must wonder what this lovely place is we've brought you to. Well, you should feel honoured, because this is nothing less than the Palace of the Earl of the Plains himself. But of course, a young woman of your fame and importance can expect nothing but the best of accommodations, eh?"

Roza frowned and gritted her teeth, trying to think back through her pain to her last memory. "I was in the barracks. How did I get here?"

Morton adopted the condescending tone of speaking to a stupid child. "Yes, you were up with the Army on the top tier of the city, just inside the walls. After you … er … collapsed, we loaded you onto a wagon and carried you down here to the floor of the Gorge. The Earl's Palace is on the lowest level of the city, set among the most beautiful gardens, right at the heart of his people."

Roza winced as she tried to twist herself around, to see if anyone else was here.

"But where are my manners?" Morton went on. "I should introduce myself as Morton, warlock of no fixed abode, and I offer my services to those who can provide me with appropriate recompense. As soon as the noble Lord Vallance heard of you and your remarkable gift, he enlisted me to his service, thinking he might need a warlock to catch a warlock. And so it has proved. You will find that he rewards most handsomely those who give him useful and faithful service."

Roza had located the blue-uniformed legs of some Plains Army soldiers standing near where Morton was tormenting her on the Hall floor.

"And now you need wait no longer." Morton clicked his fingers and got up from kneeling on the floor, as the soldiers marched up. "I know how excited you must be to meet Lord Vallance himself, and indeed he is keen to meet you too. So, let us move straight to the happy encounter."

Two of the soldiers were also wearing thick gloves and grabbed Roza under the armpits, hauling her upright. She cried out, because they were not gentle, and the burning ropes bit into her flesh.

"Gently, gently," Morton chided them. "Warlock Rozabella is an important person across the whole Empire and must be treated with consideration and respect, don't you think?" He gave a sarcastic chuckle, and the soldiers laughed as they dragged her across the marble floor.

Roza's legs were bound too tightly for walking, and they neglected to set her on her feet, so her hips, knees and ankles buckled and twisted as they pulled her towards a chair set in the middle of the floor. She ground her teeth against the pain, gasping and cringing at each yank and shove until they dumped her into the chair.

As she shifted and winced to sit herself upright, an ornate throne was carried in and placed opposite her. Roza stopped struggling and swallowed hard. Was she at last about to meet this horrible man who had planned to kidnap and exploit her, who had pursued her across the miles of the Empire?

When she heard boots clacking across the marble, she deliberately didn't look up but was determined to feign indifference until he was sitting directly in front of her. The corner of her eye saw someone sit on the throne, but she decided to make him wait even longer.

After a long pause came a soft voice, "Excuse me, Warlock Rozabella?"

The tone of the voice startled her into looking up, and a kind, gentle face regarded her steadily. He was a handsome, middle-aged man, dressed in smart clothes of deep blue, made from a rich fabric, with a subtle gold trim that wasn't ostentatious. His dark hair was greying and brushed back, and he watched her from warm, brown eyes.

Roza had already decided on her first words to this man. "Get this net of ropes off me now."

A pained expression crossed his concerned face. "I am

so sorry, Miss Rozabella, that we meet under these circumstances. Believe me, I wish we could have met in peaceful times, and nothing would make me happier than to release you from those vicious ropes. I apologise to you unreservedly, but I cannot remove your restraints."

The politeness and kindness of this man was unnerving Roza, and it crossed her mind that this might not be Lord Vallance after all, but an oily-spoken minister of his instead. "Apology not accepted," she snapped back. "So, are you that Lord Vallance, or not?"

"Oh, forgive me, Miss Rozabella," he bowed his head. "I have failed to introduce myself properly. Yes, Vallance is my name, Lord of Gorge City and Earl of the Plains, at your service."

"At my service, are you?" Roza retorted. "Then you can serve me right now by taking off this net and letting me leave your wretched palace and city, got it?"

"Alas, you ask the one thing I cannot do. You see, you need to be here, Warlock Rozabella, for your own protection."

Roza scoffed. "My own protection? What do you mean? I can defend myself well enough."

Lord Vallance nodded. "Yes, I'm sure you can, in your own way. But have you not already run into trouble with Thain Wicksteed of Heismith Castle, and in the village inn at Thainsfoot?"

Roza stared at him but should have expected him to know about those incidents.

"Ah, Miss Rozabella, you will find that I have many sources of information because I consider it my duty to keep abreast of any important matters that take place across the Plains. And of course, your personal safety and wellbeing are of the paramount importance."

She wasn't falling for his charm offensive one bit and decided to go on the attack. "Well, Mister Earl of the Plains, my personal wellbeing at present demands the removal of these agonising ropes. And is that why you galloped off to Albany to kidnap and imprison me – all for my personal wellbeing and safety?"

Lord Vallance's reply was unruffled. "I am sorry, but as you well know, I cannot remove those ropes because they are the only things preventing you from using your magic, and they stop you from rash and foolish things like disappearing off into the wilds. And yes, I rode to Albany with all speed, not to kidnap or imprison anyone, but to escort you here safely where your remarkable gift can be offered to everyone with decency and order."

Another of this man's crimes surfaced in Roza's mind. "You burned my plateau."

Again, the pained expression crossed his face. "Alas, it was the last thing I wanted to do, but it was necessary. I needed to ensure that your home on the plateau became less habitable so you wouldn't be tempted to return. As we have seen, we couldn't keep you safe there. I regretted very much setting flame to your fields and orchards, but already they will be recovering and regrowing. Nature has that way, you see, of beginning again when it needs to. It strikes me as very much like your rejuvenation gift, wouldn't you say?" He offered her a warm smile.

"No, I would never say that," she snapped back. "I don't burn anything down. And I suppose you slaughtered and feasted on my animals too?"

He looked genuinely hurt and shocked. "Miss Rozabella, I would never indulge in such butchery. You may rest assured that all your chickens and pigs, your sheep and cow, were moved to safety and cared for properly before the fires began. Now, if you will allow me, I must express my heartfelt thanks to you, and the gratitude of everyone on the Plains."

"Why?" Roza demanded. "What have I done?"

Vallance smiled again. "You faced down and overcame that tyrant and oppressor of an Emperor, of course. I have heard all about how you met and spoke with him at the gates of Albany and reduced him to a shadow of his former strength, opening up a unique opportunity for all the citizens of his Empire."

"The opportunity to declare independence, mobilise your army for war against him, and kill lots of your own citizens in the process, you mean. All to feed your selfish ambition to rule this part of the Empire by yourself."

"Now, now, Miss Rozabella, you misjudge me sorely. Perhaps you are too young to know the full extent of the Emperor's misrule of his subjects: the extortionate taxes, the threats of violence and destruction, the arbitrary and unfair use of his laws, the crimes committed by his Imperial Army. Even your small town of Albany lived under the constant threat of destruction because of the failure to bear unpayable taxes, until your heroic intervention saved them."

"I'm not here to debate the politics of the Empire," Roza replied. "I'm here to save lives by telling you to stop your war. I don't care how you do it: you can surrender to the Emperor or negotiate a peace treaty with him, but I won't have anyone being killed on my account as part of your so-called war for immortality."

"Ah, but the war for immortality is precisely what this is, Miss Warlock of Albany. Whoever has you on their side has access to practical immortality, and that alone is enough to turn the tide in this war towards the winning side."

"Listen to me, Vallance," Roza spat. "I am not on the Emperor's side. And I will never, ever be on your side. I am on my own side, and on the side of all the people out there who need my help. I am not doing anything to help you win your war."

Vallance sighed and then smiled at her again. "I hope you won't blame me if I keep up my efforts in trying to persuade you. In the meantime, let me bring in your friends to reassure you that they are also safe. I know you must be worried about their welfare too."

Roza's heart sank, but she should have realised that this evil man would capture her friends to keep them as hostages, or to use as leverage against her. Vallance clapped his hands once, and a soldier led in the boy, Banno.

Roza couldn't decide how she felt about Oxana's younger brother as she tried to piece together what had happened up at the Army barracks. Had the boy also been tricked and deceived by Lord Vallance and his accomplice, Warlock Morton?

"And here he is, the hero of the hour," Lord Vallance cried, and Banno looked decidedly nervous and uncomfortable. "This brave and resourceful young man came to us yesterday evening with information, he said, of the whereabouts of the Warlock of Albany." Vallance turned back to Roza. "Well, you'll understand that since we posted our reward for information about you, we've had a steady stream of would-be informants claiming to have relevant news, so we needed a way to test whether what they said had any shred of truth."

Roza was looking between Vallance and Banno and noticed that the boy wouldn't meet her eye. What had he told them?

"It so happens," Vallance went on, "that while I was in Albany, I gained a valuable piece of information that I could use to test the veracity of my reward-seekers. You see, on the night you went on the run from that charming town in the mountains, another member of the community also went missing. So, back here in Gorge City, I can ask those claiming to have found you, what is the name of the ugly boy travelling with Warlock Rozabella?"

Roza glared at Banno, the realisation dawning that the boy had betrayed them all to their current captors.

Vallance's voice was joyful in triumph. "This wonderful young hero could at last give me the correct answer – the ugly boy travelling with the Warlock is called Jorxy. And he could tell me more: the two of them were travelling under the false names of Jacey and Charly, and they were currently up in the first tier barracks having been conscripted into the Plains Army."

"You treacherous snake," Roza hissed at Banno. "You sold us out for that reward. You miserable, greedy coin-counter. I should never have trusted you, not since you were so keen about treasure back in that cave in the mountains."

"Now, now, Warlock Rozabella," Lord Vallance chided her, "don't be so uncharitable. The young man has done his patriotic duty as a good citizen of Gorge City and has fully earned the generous reward we offered. In fact, I am so pleased with him, I have offered to train him as one of my very own treasure assistants."

Banno spoke at last in a trembling voice. "I'm sorry, Warlock Roza. I didn't mean for it to turn out this way. I only wanted to rescue the three of you from being in the Army. I never thought they'd hurt you or tie you up. They only said how welcome you'd be here…"

His voice trailed away, and Roza saw he was wringing his hands. "Well, I hope you enjoy your reward, Banno," she said bitterly, "and being trained by this cruel and greedy Earl of the Plains. But in the future, you also need to learn some lessons about friendship and loyalty." She turned away from him, with nothing more to say.

"Come, come, Warlock Rozabella," Lord Vallance was saying, "you can't blame the boy for sensibly choosing the winning side in this coming war. Now, we have a few more small items to discuss." He clapped his hands twice more, and soldiers brought in Jorxy and Oxana. They were bound at the wrists but otherwise walking freely. They stared in shock at seeing her bound up in a chair facing Lord Vallance.

"What's going on here?" Jorxy demanded.

Roza decided to answer before Vallance could put his poisonous spin on the situation. "Banno betrayed us all to Lord Vallance to get the reward. I was captured by Warlock

Morton with this Bindweed net, which suppresses my magic and leaves me in agony. So, we're all now prisoners of this vicious Earl of the Plains."

"Prisoners?" Lord Vallance said in surprise. "Well, that depends very much on what you decide, Warlock Rozabella. You will find that many things now depend on how you respond to my generous invitation to work with me. Your accommodations, your food and drink, your treatment, your freedoms – while I keep all three of you safe, of course – will be determined–"

"You're blackmailing me," Roza protested. "You're going to keep all three of us prisoner unless I agree to whatever you say, aren't you?"

"Don't help him," Jorxy said at once, and Oxana nodded too. "We won't mind imprisonment or poor treatment if we know you're not helping this oily villain seize control of the Plains."

Roza turned back to Lord Vallance with a smug and satisfied smile on her face for the first time.

"Dear me, dear me," said the Earl, shaking his head. "You test my kindness and generosity to its limits. But never mind, because it was in case of such an eventuality that I took additional steps to persuade you to ally yourself with my winning side. The loyalty and self-sacrifice of your friends here does you great credit, my dear Rozabella, but will you contemplate the suffering of others if you still refuse to comply?"

At last, the soft and gentle voice of the Earl of the Plains took on an edge of steel, and it chilled Roza's heart to the core. What on earth did he mean by the suffering of others?

Lord Vallance clapped his hands three times and spoke again. "On my recent visit to Albany, I took the opportunity to locate the townsfolk there who held particular affection for you. I hope you understand why it was necessary to bring them to Gorge City, for their own protection, to keep them safe, you know."

The first to be led in by the soldiers, also with ropes on her wrists, was Amber-Jane, and she looked dreadful. Her pretty dark eyes were red-rimmed and puffy from crying, her black hair was dishevelled, and she looked gaunt and thin.

"No," Roza cried in indignation, "this isn't fair. Amber-Jane hasn't done anything against you. Her only crime is to have been our friend from the schoolroom, and that I rejuvenated her grandmother, and now you put her through all this?"

Lord Vallance opened his arms to answer her complaint. "As I say, their future treatment depends entirely on how you respond to my request that we work together to save the good people of the Plains."

Then soldiers led two other people into the Hall, and the last shreds of Roza's resistance crumbled. It was Helena and Arthur, her mother and father, cuffed and in ragged clothes, looking worse and older than she'd ever seen them. Their eyes, and Amber-Jane's, were dull with pain and weariness, with anguish and despair, pleading with Roza to save them from this torture.

And her spirit broke. She couldn't do this any more, to fight and resist, when it meant such pain for those she loved. "Stop, stop this," she cried. "All right, I'll do it, I'll work with you. Just leave them alone, don't hurt them, don't hurt any of them," and the burning pain of the Bindweed ropes surged to overwhelm her again as she sobbed and sobbed in her chair.

Lord Vallance leaned back in his throne and folded his hands in his lap.

CHAPTER EIGHTEEN

Roza barely noticed the journey out of the Hall. She was dimly aware that in order not to touch the dreaded Bindweed, the gloved soldiers picked up her chair and carried her out on that. It was better than being dragged across the white marble floor, but she could only sit and languish in pain and defeat.

At one point she looked around enough to register that the Earl's other prisoners were following: Jorxy, Oxana, Amber-Jane, Helena and Arthur, being marched along by a guard of soldiers. There were long, wide corridors, staircases to descend, and then they were finally admitted through a pair of bolted, barred and guarded double doors.

As the doors clanged shut behind them, the bars set in place and the bolts driven home, Roza understood that they were now in what Lord Vallance might have termed 'secure accommodation'. The corridor beyond was not as dingy as some dungeons she'd imagined, because flaming torches flickered along the walls, and the rows of doors on each side were heavy and set in strong frames.

Here they stopped, and the soldiers shoved their six prisoners into separate rooms. It seemed an unnecessary cruelty that Helena and Arthur could not be together, but clearly there were no cells for married couples, and it only added to their isolation and distress.

Roza was the last to be deposited, and the soldiers tipped her unceremoniously from the Hall chair onto the floor. She cried out in pain, and two of the men picked her up and dumped her on the single mattress that was the bed. They left, taking their precious chair with them, and bolted the door.

Roza lay there for a long time. There was no window, no lamp or torch, and the only light was filtering under the door. Her eyes accustomed to the dark eventually, but there was nothing else to see, nothing in the room except for the bed.

Her thoughts were consumed with the pain of the Bindweed, but there was nothing she could do to relieve or lessen it. It could only be endured. At last, she tried to think about something else, to see if diverting her mind away from the pain might help.

So, Banno had betrayed them all for Lord Vallance's reward as he'd said from the start. Roza had never asked how much the reward for her was, but she wondered whether the boy could be content with counting it, knowing he'd betrayed even his own sister. What did Oxana think of her little brother now? And had Jorxy been right, that they should never have trusted anyone else with Roza's true identity for as long as their journey and this war lasted? Or was she herself most to blame for deciding to come to Gorge City at all?

Mulling over who was to blame seemed easier than thinking about the future of what might happen now. From the outset back in Albany, she'd been determined not to work with Lord Vallance, and yet here she was, agreeing to just that. Did she have any choice? Could she countenance further torture for Jorxy, Oxana, Amber-Jane and her parents all because of her stubborn refusal to cooperate? No, she couldn't live with that thought.

But how would this work now? She was the famous Warlock of Albany but couldn't perform a single magic spell for as long as she remained trapped in the Bindweed net. She couldn't rejuvenate anyone either, so in order to exploit her gift, Lord Vallance would need to release her from the Bindweed.

So, when and how would he do that? Only when he felt safe enough to trust her not to use magic against him or to disappear off with a Recall or Teleport spell. But Vallance didn't trust her at all and wouldn't do so unless he still had his other five hostages behind bolted doors and under constant threat of torture. Whether Roza cooperated or refused, the fate of her parents and friends would remain the same: locked up under guard in these dark rooms.

If only she could get out of this Bindweed. Then she could cast that Recall spell and get herself out of here and back to Standley at Enoch and Celeste's Sunrise Farm. But no, that wouldn't be right, to save only herself and leave the others languishing in these dungeons at the mercy of the Earl of the Plains.

She made a resolution then, that she wouldn't escape alone, even if the others begged her to, but would get all of them out of here together, or else she would remain with them and share their fate.

Lord Vallance hadn't been as she expected. She hadn't anticipated the softly spoken, handsome, well-mannered man upstairs. Maybe those were the worst sort of beast, the men who hid their vicious cruelty behind kind-looking faces and gentle words.

Could she ever reconcile herself to being on that man's side? No, she couldn't, and she wouldn't. She and her parents and friends would resist and oppose that horrible man with the very last fibres of their beings.

So, that led to her next set of questions. She couldn't exactly fight him while they were all still his prisoners, not without an extreme risk of torture to the innocent Helena, Arthur, and Amber-Jane. She had to rescue them all, but how to achieve that while they were behind separate locked doors and with guards in the corridor outside?

She couldn't even walk around her cell, or move her arms, or roll off the bed, let alone escape out of a bolted door. It all had to begin with releasing herself from this Bindweed net. Quite apart from the pain of the ropes and their magic-suppression, she was trussed up like a turkey.

The phrase struck a chord in her memory. The old and former Warlock of Albany, Philoe, had described her as 'trussed up like a turkey' when she'd awoken as a bound and gagged prisoner in his cave on that plateau. Hers had been normal ropes then, because she'd had no apparent magical ability, and it was Kerenzi the spirit lord, her fellow prisoner, who was under the Bindweed. Now she felt for herself the constant agony from the ropes that he'd described, as well as the anguish of being deprived of her magic.

But Kerenzi had escaped from the Bindweed in the end. How did that happen? Roza hadn't been able to untie the knots because the magic in the ropes simply re-tied themselves. No, Kerenzi had only been released from the dreadful net when Philoe had at last consented to free him and ordered the Bindweed to untie. There was little chance here of either Lord Vallance or Warlock Morton agreeing to release her anytime soon.

What Roza needed more than anything was someone to help her.

And that was when the idea clicked.

She'd just been thinking about him. Why hadn't this solution occurred to her before?

Kerenzi. The spirit lord.

He visited her from time to time. He was able to become invisible or even adopt a spirit form. He'd come to Roza and Jorxy on the plateau and again in the forest up in the mountains. He'd been keeping track of events across the Plains and in Gorge City. Might he even be here, and would he hear if she called him? He'd promised before to keep a watchful eye on her and come if she was in need.

"Kerenzi," Roza breathed. "Can you hear me? Are you here? I'm in Gorge City, in Lord Vallance's Palace, in his dungeons, and I'm in desperate need of your help."

She waited, but the darkness was silent.

"Please, Kerenzi, my spirit lord, my friend, come and save me. I'm begging you. I've never pleaded with anyone so much in my life. I promise I'll do whatever you say if only you'll come and help me now. I'll be forever in your debt.

Just as I once saved your life from Warlock Philoe, I'm praying you'll now save mine from Lord Vallance. Please, Kerenzi, come."

Roza's whispers sounded quiet and forlorn in the dark stillness of her locked cell. She didn't dare to call or cry out, for fear of attracting the guards. Couldn't magical beings like spirit lords and Dragons hear if their name was spoken aloud, however far away?

She waited, and her hope of rescue faded, and then failed. It was wishful thinking, she decided, when she imagined that the dim light filtering into her room from under the door seemed to change. What difference would an invisible magical being in spirit form make to light under a door anyway?

Then she jumped out of her skin.

"I don't want to startle you – oops, too late," came an invisible whisper near her ear.

Roza stifled her cry because her jerk of movement had caused the Bindweed ropes to cut into her again. She was unspeakably relieved to hear him, but her pain smothered being reasonable. "Kerenzi," she hissed. "How many times have I told you never to sneak up on me invisibly?"

The spirit lord materialised into visibility inches from her nose, and the closeness of his bewitching face meant she almost forgot her annoyance with him. Almost.

"Well," Kerenzi breathed, "I was trying to decide whether speaking first, or appearing first, would startle you more. I concluded you'd probably jump either way, so what's the difference?"

"The difference is," Roza hissed again, "that I'm lying here in agony, with my magic suppressed, and you're the one wandering about free and invisible. Do you remember how annoyed you got, back in Philoe the Warlock's cave, when you were tied up in Bindweed, and I could walk about? So, stop talking and get me out of this net."

Kerenzi put on a wounded expression, and Roza was

momentarily distracted by breathing in his woody scent. "This is a fine welcome for your would-be rescuer. To think that only a few seconds ago I was hearing all these words of begging and pleading, and 'I promise I'll do whatever you say' and 'I'll be forever in your debt'. Alas, I fear the damsel in distress has changed her tune."

"Don't you dare call me a damsel," Roza retorted, forgetting for a moment to keep her voice down. She lowered it again. "All right. I'm very grateful. But I'm magic-less and in agony. Will you get me out of here or not?"

Kerenzi nodded. "Yes, my dear Roza, of course I'm here to save you. And I forgive your short temper because I know it's the Bindweed affecting you. Now, this will be tricky because these ropes won't give up easily. Normally, it needs to be Warlock Morton releasing you, so I must overpower his restraining spell."

"Please, quit the lecture and do it," Roza hissed.

Kerenzi stood up and Roza closed her eyes, repeating to herself that this agony would end soon. If she could bear it for a short while longer, she would be free of it. She regretted sounding ungrateful to him, but the pain made her unavoidably irritable. So, come on, Kerenzi, hurry up, she wanted to move and get her magic back.

The spirit lord was muttering in the darkness, and she felt ripples of magic wash over her, tugging at the ropes, which tightened and relaxed in turn.

"First part done," Kerenzi whispered. "I've stopped them re-tying automatically. Now I need the gloves." A pair of thick leather gloves materialised over his hands and forearms, and he stepped towards her cautiously. "None of these strands can touch me, or we'll both be trapped."

It seemed to take an eternity. He grasped each rope in turn, peeling it away from her skin, often pausing to untangle twists and knots, and many times Roza gave involuntary jerks of pain that alarmed them both. But Kerenzi worked methodically, and despite her desperate impatience, Roza appreciated the extreme care he took to ensure they both ended up free. The last few ropes were the worst, the ones around her legs, because the Bindweed seemed to know what was happening and staged a vicious last-ditch effort to hold her.

With a sigh from them both, the last strands came free, and Kerenzi dragged the net across the floor with his gloves, piling it in a corner, where it seemed to lie twitching and glaring at them with malice.

Roza stretched her muscles, and it felt so good to be free. She swung her legs over the side of her bed and sat up, while Kerenzi vanished his gloves. Her whole body ached, and she longed to scratch her itchy skin but that would only make it worse, so to distract herself, she stood up.

She wanted to thank Kerenzi properly but didn't know how to do it. She stepped towards him, flung her arms around his body, and hugged him tightly. "I know I'm sounding cranky," she whispered in his ear, "but I meant all I said about begging and pleading, and 'do whatever you say' and 'forever in your debt'. Thank you for saving me," and she kissed his cheek.

"My word," he breathed back. "A grateful hug and kiss from the mighty Warlock of Albany. I'm honoured and touched."

Roza let go of him at once and smacked his arm. "And so you should be." Their eyes met for a moment before she looked away. "Now, we have locked doors, guards in the corridor, and five other people to rescue. Suggestions?"

His eyebrows rose and he sighed. "I should have known you'd insist on playing the saviour for your parents and friends too. How is your magic?"

She frowned and closed her eyes. She reached deep inside and found the welcome spark of magic still glimmering there. But try as she might, she couldn't get it to ignite. "Hardly there at all."

Kerenzi nodded. "I suspected as much. It might return

quickly for you but will still take time to reach your full strength. Shall I knock out the guards in the corridor?"

Roza smiled at the offhand way he said this. "Please, if you would be so kind."

He vanished before her eyes, returning to invisible spirit, and filtered back under the door. She wondered how he would deal with the dozen or so guards on duty, and then a sound of rushing wind filled the corridor, followed by the dull thuds of men collapsing to the floor. Her bolt was drawn back, the lock turned, and after the gloom of her cell, the torchlight outside made her shield her eyes. Kerenzi stood in the open doorway, visible again, a bunch of keys in his hand.

"Let's find the others," she said, stepping over the unconscious guard and into the corridor. She tried to remember the doors where the others had been locked away, and together she and Kerenzi released Jorxy, Oxana, Amber-Jane, Helena and Arthur blinking into the torchlight.

Jorxy had met the spirit lord before, but the others stared at him in wonder and bewilderment. It was to Kerenzi's credit, Roza admitted to herself, that he remained visible for this, because he hated these mortals gawping at him.

"This is a friend of mine," she told them, as they untied the ropes binding their wrists. "A spirit lord named Kerenzi who I've known for a while. He's the one we need to thank for getting us all out of here."

The others all murmured their thanks, but Kerenzi said, "We're not out of here yet. How do you propose we arrange for all seven of us to leave the Palace without anyone noticing? And before anyone asks, no, I can't knock the whole city unconscious."

"Um, I learned the Recall spell," Roza offered, "to take me back to Standley at a farmhouse a day's ride away. But I only practised it with transporting myself, not anyone else as well. And I don't have my magic back yet."

Kerenzi rolled his eyes at her, but then said, "It's the start of a plan. I can provide the magical energy you need, like I did for you that day back in Albany when you first met the Emperor. Have you ever cast a group spell?"

"Camouflage," Jorxy said to Roza. "You started by hiding just yourself and then learned how to Camouflage a group of us while we travelled."

"That's good," Kerenzi replied. "Roza, you'll need to focus on sharing your Recall spell with the group while we all hold on to you."

She nodded slowly and nervously. This sounded like a complex and risky piece of magic, when she felt she'd struggle even to Maximise a book or rejuvenate a bread roll.

"But for any of this to work," Kerenzi went on, "we need to get your magic firing again. It's you who has the connection to Standley, not me, so I can provide the energy, but Roza, you need to cast the spell."

She sighed. How many minutes had it been since she'd escaped from the Bindweed ropes? How long did it normally take for magic to return? What was a simple spell she could manage most easily? And then an idea prompted itself.

"You know those Bindweed ropes?" she asked Kerenzi. "Do they burn?"

He stared at her. "Roza, what are you thinking? Yes, they burn, but Bindweed smoke is even worse than the rope. Ropes can't move on their own, but smoke can. One whiff of those fumes in our lungs would incapacitate us both."

"I wonder if starting with a spell where I have an overwhelming desire to see it work might kick my magic into action. Can I try an Enflame spell on that net?"

Kerenzi let out a nervous chuckle. "Risky, but I see your thinking. Yes, it might work. We'd need to get out of there fast and close the door behind us. And gather at the far end of the corridor for the Recall spell just in case. Let's do it, because I don't know how long these guards will stay out."

The two of them ushered the other five back towards the

double doors into the rest of the Earl's Palace. Roza and Kerenzi re-entered her cell, where the pile of Bindweed ropes lurked menacingly in the corner. She easily imagined the vile twists and knots on the floor glaring up at her, as though knowing her fatal plan for them, and she feared the end of a rope lashing out to catch her again.

She stepped as near to the pile as she dared, Kerenzi's warm hand resting on the small of her back. She reached inside for the spark again and focused all her effort on lighting it. All I need is a single flame, she thought. Because I want this dreadful net to be gone for ever. I won't let it hurt or remove the magic from anyone ever again. I'm free of it, but I need to save my parents and friends. I need to escape from here and use my magic to stop a war and help an Empire. Come on, magic, burn, burn.

And the spark ignited into a single flame.

Kerenzi's hand pressed on her back, that he'd felt it too. Roza drew the flame up inside her and down her arms to her hands. She clicked her fingers once, and the Enflame spell dropped a fire into the midst of the Bindweed ropes.

Kerenzi grabbed Roza around the waist, picked her up and ran. He dropped her onto her feet, slammed the cell door closed and bolted it. "Go," he ordered, and Roza leapt away.

Her foot caught the outstretched boot of an unconscious guard, and she went flying. She sprawled onto the floor, and Kerenzi, sprinting away close behind her, collided with her and fell over too.

Hurt and dazed for a moment, she heard a growing crackle of flame within her cell and stared in horror at a first wisp of grey smoke seeping under its door. She twisted away from it, scrambling on all fours along the corridor until she could regain her feet. Kerenzi had opted for his wings to lift him from the floor and was flying along behind her.

Roza had nearly reached the other five when she heard a cough and a groan behind her. She skidded to a halt and turned. It wasn't Kerenzi, but the guard she'd tripped over, who was waking up.

The man lying outside her door was stirring, and already a mist of grey smoke surrounded him. The Bindweed fumes were penetrating his lungs, and as Roza watched he began to choke and retch. The guard might not have any magic to suppress, but Roza was sure the dreadful smoke would sting and might even choke him to death.

"Focus, Roza," Kerenzi was saying. "The Recall spell."

Roza tore her mind away from the horrific scene in the corridor and tried to picture Standley. Her enchanted coat stand, the farmhouse of Enoch and Celeste, the happy time they'd shared there, how Standley had protected them against Thain Wicksteed and the Plains trackers, her strong, flexible, invincible bodyguard. She wanted to see him again, to be near and with him, to be safe and at home.

"Grab my arms," she shouted, and felt five pairs of hands clutch at her wrists and upper arms, while Kerenzi stood behind her, ready to send his magic into her shoulders. She reached for her own spark of magic, and it lit at once, fanning into a small fire.

The effect on the Bindweed smoke was instantaneous. It must have sensed her magic, for the tendrils wafting around her cell door gathered into a dense mass and came billowing along the corridor towards her.

Roza panicked. It was going to reach her before she could perform the Recall spell, especially before she could make sure it encompassed the whole group of seven.

"Let go," she yelled, because she needed her arms for something else first, and wrenched herself free from those who held her. As the smoke rolled up faster and faster to cover them all, she felt Kerenzi's magic surge into her body and thrust her hands forward, sending her strongest ever Repulser against it.

The smoke was blasted away back down the corridor, shredding into ragged trails as it went, and Roza dared to take a breath.

She stuck out her arms again, and called, "Hold on."

The coughing, choking guards on the floor were waking up. The air had cleared above them, they looked around, saw the group of prisoners at the far end of the corridor and gave a yell.

The Bindweed smoke was re-forming. At the far end of the corridor, Roza saw the boiling, churning grey mass gather its tendrils and lift its skirts for a final charge.

It was now or never.

Back to Standley, the farmhouse, home, safe.

The guards were running towards them and shouting.

All of us, the seven people here, all those holding me.

The thundercloud of Bindweed smoke raced closer, overtaking the slowest guards.

Kerenzi's magic flowed into her shoulders as Roza screamed, "Recall, Recall, Recall!"

CHAPTER NINETEEN

The corridor vanished.

Roza stumbled backwards to keep away from the Bindweed smoke and the guards … and collided with something.

Her knees buckled and she fell back, aware that everyone holding onto her was falling too. They collapsed in a heap on a mattress, and Roza, Jorxy and Oxana were the first to disentangle themselves and scramble to their feet.

Wherever they were, it was dark and quiet and still. Roza's heart thumped madly in her chest, the blood rushed in her ears, and she gasped down one lungful of clean air after another.

There was crying and sobbing behind her, and her eyes adjusted to a dim light filtering in through an un-curtained window at night. Standing beside the window was a polished wooden coat stand, and he was looking at her.

"Standley," Roza cried in relief. "We made it, everyone. We're back at the farmhouse. Jorxy, Oxana, can one of you fetch a lamp? Is everyone all right?"

"That depends on what you mean by all right," came Kerenzi's voice. "A last-second escape from prison guards and lethal Bindweed smoke may be all in a day's work for an adventurous warlock and her friends, but this poor Amber-Jane girl is a gibbering wreck."

Jorxy had fumbled his way out to the landing and brought back the oil lamp kept there. The flickering flame revealed the bedroom that Roza and Jorxy had slept in at Sunrise Farm. Fallen onto one of the beds, Amber-Jane was clutching hold of Kerenzi, sobbing uncontrollably on his shoulder. Near them on the floor, Roza's parents, Helena and Arthur, clung to each other, shaking, unable to speak.

Roza gulped, not knowing what to do. Her parents and

Amber-Jane were not used to this. They'd just been through the most terrifying moments of their lives, and what could she say?

"Um, Jorxy, Oxana, Standley, could you go and wake up Enoch and Celeste and get some help? We'll need blankets and beds, and hot baths, and food and hot drinks, and strong drinks, and I don't know what else."

They bustled off and Roza went to her parents first, kneeling beside them, hugging them. "Mum, Dad, I'm so sorry you had to go through this. And it's all my fault. We're safe now, it's over. Our friends here will look after us, and we can go home to Albany soon, I promise."

They found nothing more to say, as the tears streamed down their faces, and the anguish and horror of the recent days subsided under heaving breaths and tight embraces. For the time being, no one could persuade Amber-Jane to let go of Kerenzi, and the spirit lord was willing to let her stay where she was.

Enoch and Celeste had been awoken by their crashing arrival into the bedroom, and their cries of delight at welcoming their guests home turned into immediate concern for those so distressed. The old farmer returned at once with a bottle and glasses of brandy, which they gulped down, and Celeste and the others stoked fires for hot water and wrapped blankets around those still trembling.

Roza stopped Standley in the middle of fetching more blankets and gave him a squeeze of an embrace. "It's so good to see you again, my dear enchanted coat stand. Thank you for being here for me to come back to."

He bowed his top hooks to her, touched her shoulder and then hurried off to carry on helping.

At last, they were all coaxed downstairs to gather around the fireplace in the farmhouse kitchen, cupping mugs of hot tea in their hands. They went for hot baths in turn, ate as much of Celeste's delicious food as they could manage, and finally tucked themselves into beds for much-needed sleep.

Roza was exhausted enough to sleep late. As the morning sun filtered in through her bedroom window, a dread settled in her stomach about what on earth was she supposed to do next. She put off thinking about that by getting up and joining the others downstairs for breakfast.

She was the last to get up and the kitchen felt crowded as she looked around the seven at the table: Enoch and Celeste, Jorxy, Oxana, Amber-Jane, Helena and Arthur. Kerenzi hadn't been seen since the previous night and none of them knew where he was.

Roza accepted some tea from Celeste and the table fell silent as though they were waiting for her to make some sort of speech. But she didn't know where to start, so she asked something that had been nagging at her. "Oxana, do you think your brother Banno will be all right? We couldn't bring him with us out of Gorge City, so I was wondering how you feel about him now."

Oxana frowned and shook her head. "That stupid boy. Yes, he'll do all right for himself, but he's chosen the wrong side. He can stay with our aunt and uncle if he's not still at the Earl's Palace. And remember, he's won that reward money for getting you there, so I guess it's up to him what he does with it. But he has dishonoured our family, both himself and me, by breaking his promise and betraying you. He will answer to me when I next see him." There was a hardness in Oxana's voice Roza hadn't heard before, revealing the paladin's steel beneath her wisdom.

Roza nodded and turned to the others. "Mum, Dad, Amber-Jane, the safest thing is to get the three of you out of the way and back to Albany. If there's a war coming, we don't want you anywhere near it. Given the success of last night's Recall spell, I'll get out my magic books and try to learn to Teleport. It isn't safe to travel overland, and it would take too long. I want to get the three of you back home as soon as I can."

Helena, Arthur and Amber-Jane were staring at her as

though travelling by Teleport was the craziest thing they'd ever heard but seemed relieved at the prospect of returning to Albany.

"But what about you?" Jorxy asked quietly. "What are you and me going to do with ourselves after that?"

Roza turned to her best friend, with his oh-so-familiar lopsided face, and felt a surge of gratitude that he'd said, 'you and me' and 'ourselves'. Here was one person who still wanted to be by her side, who hadn't been scared to death by all they'd been through, who wasn't put off by the prospect of being captured and tortured in the future. This was what best friends were for. But she didn't dare to say any of that to him, obviously.

"To be completely honest," she replied, "I don't have much idea about that. Although there is one thing I've decided on." They all looked up at this. "I would like it very much if I never see that Lord Vallance again. He gave me the creeps."

They all nodded and murmured at this but didn't say anything.

Roza was thinking this through in front of them, which probably wasn't the best idea, but they were all her friends.

"So, I think that means," she went on, "that after he's kidnapped, imprisoned, and mistreated myself, my parents, and my friends to force my cooperation with him, I vow never to work with him in the future. I'd go so far as to say that I am against him, I oppose him and want him to lose his position and power. Since he's fighting a war, I want him to lose this war."

The others all murmured their agreement again. Roza hesitated. This next bit in her thinking, this thought she'd had, would not go down so well. But she needed to share what was on her mind and get their help and advice if she could.

"Which leaves me thinking that in this civil war I've become a natural ally, and on the side, of the Dragon

Emperor."

There were predictable sharp intakes of breath and shaking of heads around the table, especially from Enoch and Celeste, Helena and Arthur.

"But the Emperor is as bad as Lord Vallance," Celeste told her, "if not worse. He's been at this cruelty and tyranny for longer and has learned more of its tricks. He's worse because he's even more powerful."

"Not any more," Roza contradicted her, "not since I weakened him. He's vulnerable and afraid, and I hope that's taught him a thing or two. But answer me this: are the two sides evenly matched in this civil war, the Plains Army, and the Imperial Army around Gorge City?"

There were a few shrugs and nods.

"In which case," Roza went on, "the war risks becoming a stalemate. Lord Vallance can't fight off the Imperial Army for good, and the Emperor can't conquer and defeat Gorge City either. It becomes a stand-off, a siege, a war of attrition, with death, famine, atrocities, and suffering all round. So, my next question is this: can you see either of these two, Lord Vallance or the Dragon Emperor, surrendering or admitting defeat? Will they concede they've lost and let the other one get their way?"

Again, shrugs and shakes of heads.

Roza sighed. "In other words, this war for immortality risks going on and on, with more and more hardship and slaughter. They're both fighting over me, so it's all my fault, and I can't see any way to stop it."

These words came out sounding upset, which didn't surprise Roza because that was how she felt, but her tone seemed to startle the others. She got up from the table, left the kitchen and went out into the farmyard. She half expected some of them to troop out after her, wanting to keep talking or comforting her, but in a way, she was glad they didn't. She needed some space and solitude, and a chance to think.

Now she appreciated why this place was called Sunrise Farm. It was situated on a low rise in the plains, with an open aspect to the east, where the fields sloped gently away. Every morning, all year round, Enoch and Celeste could watch the daylight grow, and on clear mornings, see the sun come up.

The morning sun was warm on her face now, and in the distance, farm labourers worked in the fields. Nearer to hand, chickens pecked up grain in the yard, and Roza wandered over towards the paddock where the horses grazed. She leaned on the wooden fence and watched the animals.

She remembered the animals on the plateau, and the funny names Warlock Philoe had given them: Dairy the Cow, Shearer the Sheep, Torrence the Waterfall, the Chickens Boil, Scramble, Poach and Fry, and the Pigs Ham, Pork, Gammon and Bacon. Even though her captivity there was a difficult time, it hadn't been as complicated as this, and it had turned out well.

Then further back, she remembered the animals at her parents' Meadow Cottage, and how she'd looked after them because her parents couldn't. She'd resented it at the time, wanting more freedom and to make her own choices, but now that seemed a simple, peaceful, idyllic life.

When did her life become difficult? When Philoe captured her, and she'd had no say about that. But then he'd discovered her rejuvenation gift, and she'd had her first experience of magic, and this whole new world had opened up for her. Not this life of being in demand so much, or on the run, she thought wryly. No, she'd done that herself by rejuvenating the Dragon Emperor to save her hometown of Albany. It had seemed like her only choice, and the right thing to do at the time, so she might as well live with that.

But what about now? Had she lost her exhilaration and delight at the power of magic? Yes, it seemed she had. She'd given young healer recruit Madison her hearing back and then transported seven people from the dungeons of Gorge City to a safe farmhouse in the country. Wasn't that suitably amazing? Who would have thought that plain, tall Rozabella from little old Albany could do things like that?

So now, what was her aim, her desire? To restore peace to the Empire if she possibly could by stopping anyone fighting over her. To find a way of letting people be rejuvenated, in fairness and order, free of charge to those who couldn't afford to pay, without causing a mass rush and stampede to get to her, to control or exploit her. Was this too much to ask? Maybe so, but she had to try.

She stirred herself from watching the peaceful horses over the fence. In the meantime, she needed to get back to work, and the first job was to get Amber-Jane, Helena and Arthur back to Albany, and that meant learning the Teleport spell. She turned and walked back into the farmhouse and up to her bedroom where Standley still guarded the box with her Minimised magic books.

Having mastered Recall, Teleport was another step up in difficulty but didn't look impossible. Instead of a magical link to return to a person or place, Teleport required a visualisation of where the warlock wanted to go. The book suggested starting with somewhere within visible sight, and so Roza practised sending herself into the barn and back.

One of her anxieties had been about materialising within a pillar or a wall of her destination, but she was reassured by a sentence in her spell book which read: 'Trust the magic – it will guide you to a safe place to stand'. These trial exercises worked surprisingly well, and she appreciated how quickly her powers had recovered after the Bindweed suppression. Was this another sign of how gifted and magical she was?

The next step was to Teleport to somewhere she knew well, no matter how far away. Her obvious thought was the plateau above Albany, but she wondered whether she dared. The others had left her alone to learn her spell, so she could do this without anyone knowing, but what if someone saw her appear at the other end? That was always going to be a risk, and she needed to take Amber-Jane and her parents to Albany soon anyway, so this could be her trial run.

She chose to Teleport from the farmhouse barn, where old Enoch had first discovered them hiding. She closed her eyes and visualised her plateau above Albany, picturing herself among the trees of her orchard, near the wooden bench and Philoe's grave. She summoned her magic and performed the required movement of throwing her arms upwards.

Roza knew it had worked even before she opened her eyes because the smell in her nostrils changed from the wood and hay of the barn ... into smoke and ash. It broke her heart, but she had to see it.

Her fruit trees were charred stumps, the grass was a waste of scorched earth and ash, and the bench had crumbled into charcoal fragments. But new blades of grass were peeking through the soil. Lord Vallance had been right about one thing, that nature here would renew itself.

Roza turned around to check that no one else was here, but the plateau was deserted and lifeless. The cave mouth was also blackened, and she didn't have the heart to look in there. Instead, she walked towards Torrence, the waterfall, pool and stream which tumbled down from the cliff faces above and still ran fresh and clean. She stooped, dipped her hands into the cool water and drew out a drink of the refreshing liquid. It tasted as beautiful as ever and symbolised something that the Earl of the Plains couldn't spoil or destroy.

She followed the path beside the stream across the plateau until it came to the boulder on its edge, where she looked out over the whole town and valley. There lay Albany below her, as familiar and unchanged as ever, which comforted her. Lifting her gaze, the surrounding mountain tops were as breathtakingly beautiful as they'd always been.

But enough of this sightseeing and reminiscing; she had

work to do. The Teleport spell had succeeded, and the return journey to the farmhouse was easier because she could use Recall to get her back to Standley. Her coat stand was keeping watch from her bedroom window again, and he crinkled his knot eyes to see her appear there.

"Hello, Standley. I've just visited our plateau to see if my Teleport works, and I'm sorry to report how burnt it all looks. But the grass is starting to grow back again. I'm taking Amber-Jane and my parents back home to Albany now."

He nodded his hooks and returned to gazing up the lane that led to the farmhouse. Roza found Amber-Jane downstairs and asked if she was ready to return home.

The girl's face brightened with relief. "They'll be so worried about me, because they've had no news since the Plains soldiers came and took me from our house."

Amber-Jane said goodbye to the others, and they all came out into the farmyard to watch her go. Roza wished they hadn't, because it was distracting, but she had to get on with it. She instructed the girl to stand behind her and wrap her arms around Roza's waist because the spell required the use of the warlock's arms.

This time, Roza pictured a spot halfway down the track from the plateau to the valley, because there was no need for Amber-Jane to see the devastation up there. She ignited her magic, remembered to include the girl behind her in the spell and threw up her arms.

Roza kept her eyes open this time to see the flash of speed as she travelled, landing neatly in the middle of the dusty path beside the rocky cliff face. "You can let go now," Roza said, patting Amber-Jane's hands, because the girl's arms were threatening to squeeze her in half.

Amber-Jane opened her eyes slowly and stared around, holding onto Roza's arm as though afraid of falling over.

"Welcome back to Albany valley," Roza said, starting to guide her down the path. "I didn't want to appear in town for fear of alarming people, and it's probably safer if no one knows I was here. You'll be all right to find your way to your home and family from here. I don't want anyone from town to see me."

Amber-Jane nodded and embraced her. "I couldn't do what you're doing. Thank you for rescuing me and bringing me home."

Roza smiled. "It was the least I could do, because it was my fault you were picked on to be kidnapped."

"And that was only because you saved my Grandma Lily's life, so I'm still in debt to you."

They laughed, and Roza said, "Take care of yourself, give my love to your family, and I hope to see you all again soon."

Amber-Jane stepped back, and Roza cast the Recall spell to return herself to the farmhouse.

Her next trip was to take her parents back home to their Meadow Cottage. She Teleported into their downstairs living room, one holding onto each side of her. The room was exactly as Roza remembered it, with their kitchen on one side, and the armchair where Arthur used to sleep before she'd healed him of his blindness.

Now they were alone, her dad rested a hand on her shoulder. "Our dear Roza, before you go, you need to understand that this war is not your fault."

The upset welled inside her again. "Yes, it is, because I weakened the Emperor—"

"No," her mum interrupted. "What you did was to strike a deal with the Emperor that saved this whole valley from destruction. It was others who did the rest: pushing his rejuvenation too far, taking advantage of the Emperor's weakness to claim independence, and all the rest. You are innocent of all that came after and shouldn't carry around this guilt."

Roza sagged onto the settee. "Thanks, Mum, Dad," she breathed. "But what matters is what I do now, and I still feel responsible for sorting this out. Everyone knows me and will take notice of what I do or say."

Helena sat beside her. "We agree that you have the fame and influence to affect the outcome of events for the better. We can't advise you about civil wars or dealing with the Emperor, but we've brought you up to know right from wrong, and you have a good heart. Trust your instincts, because you genuinely care for everyone, and that might be your most precious and powerful gift of all."

Roza heaved a breath and stood up. "Thanks. I'd better go, and before you say it, yes, I'll be careful and look after myself. Love you."

They hugged, and Roza Recalled herself to the farmhouse. Downstairs, she discovered that Kerenzi the spirit lord had reappeared, sitting at the kitchen table talking with Enoch, Celeste, Jorxy and Oxana.

"Ah, my dear Roza," he said casually, "all well with your Teleport duties to Albany?" When she nodded, he went on. "I was telling the others the news from the Plains. I didn't say this last night because I knew it would upset you."

Roza sat in a vacant chair and accepted a mug of tea from Celeste. "Tell me what?" she insisted but dreaded what she was about to hear.

"You remember that charming man, Lord Vallance?" Kerenzi began, forcing out a smile. "Well, as soon as he had you in his custody, he announced to the whole of Gorge City that the world-famous Rozabella, Warlock of Albany, had now arrived in his Palace. As you might imagine, this was followed by much general rejoicing."

Roza rolled her eyes at him. "And has that wretched villain gone on to announce that I've escaped from his miserable dungeons?"

"Ah, no, that sad fact has been omitted from his proclamations. He doesn't want to dampen the useful enthusiasm of his subjects."

"But what happens when the people of Gorge City ask to see me?"

"The official line is that you are resting from your journey there, but that you will be available for widespread rejuvenation and other miracles in due course." He gave her another infuriating smile. "But perhaps more important is that the Earl's announcements are now known to the spies of the Dragon Emperor, and therefore to the generals of the Imperial Army too."

A chill ran down Roza's spine at this. "So, everyone thinks I'm in Gorge City, but I'm not."

"Indeed," Kerenzi replied, "which is turning out to be most unfortunate for the people of Gorge City."

Roza stared at him, but Oxana was the one who slammed her fist onto the table. "Why? What is happening to my home city?" she demanded.

"I'm not sure whether it's the Dragon Emperor himself ordering this," Kerenzi said slowly, "or simply his generals acting on prior orders if this were to happen. Either way, the Imperial Army cannot let you remain in Lord Vallance's possession, and even now they are moving to try to take the capital of the Plains. I regret to inform you that a massive assault on Gorge City has begun."

CHAPTER TWENTY

Roza glared at Kerenzi, at the laid-back, nonchalant way he was announcing the imminent deaths of hundreds or thousands of mere mortals, but Oxana was the one who jumped up and started pacing about the kitchen.

"No, this cannot be happening," she fumed, punching her fist into her palm. "It's not fair for the Emperor to take out his anger with Lord Vallance on the ordinary soldiers of the Plains. I should be there. I should be helping to defend my city."

Jorxy looked up at her sharply. "You're not suggesting we all rush back there and take on the whole Imperial Army, fighting for the man who locked us up?"

Oxana stopped pacing. "What about you, Roza? What do you think we should do?"

Roza knew they were all looking at her but didn't know what to think. As the tense silence in the kitchen lengthened, she decided to do her thinking out loud again.

"I agree this is appalling. I can't stand the thought of two armies fighting each other over me. Kerenzi, what are the chances that the Imperial Army will succeed in taking the city?"

The spirit lord shrugged. "About even, I should guess, but it's hard to say. How well will the Plains soldiers fight to defend their Lord, their homes and families, thinking the Warlock of Albany is on their side? How strong are the Gorge City walls and towers compared with the Imperial Army siege weapons? How motivated are the Imperial soldiers by their fear of the Emperor, or by wanting to gain Albany's Warlock for themselves? But in any case, many attackers and defenders will be killed."

"How many?" Roza demanded. "Hundreds? Thousands?"

Kerenzi nodded and then shrugged. "Maybe tens of thousands. It depends how long the fighting continues and whether it drags on into a stalemate and a bitter end."

"These are my fellow-citizens," Oxana spat at him. "Not just numbers. I happen to care about what happens to my home."

Roza held up a hand to calm and placate her. "We all care about anyone who is forced to fight and die, Oxana."

Well, maybe Kerenzi doesn't, she added to herself, because we're all just limited mortals to him.

She went on. "But even if we all rushed there to help, the few of us here wouldn't make much difference on the battlefield, or to the outcome of the assault."

Oxana was glaring at her. "So, I ask again, Roza, what about you? What are you going to do?"

She sighed. "We agree that our aim is to stop the fighting, to avoid as much bloodshed, injury, and death as possible. On all sides. So, we come back to the question of how to do that. Negotiating with Lord Vallance isn't going to help, because he won't surrender to the Emperor, or give up his hopes for freedom and independence. Which leaves us, I reckon, with only one choice." Roza braced herself for the reaction to this. "I think I need to go to see the Emperor."

The stunned silence was followed by a chorus of, "What? No! Are you mad?" from Jorxy, Oxana, Enoch and Celeste. Only Kerenzi sat there calmly, a slow smile spreading across his face.

When Roza didn't say more, but watched the spirit lord, and the others fell silent, Kerenzi said, "Are you sure, Roza? He blames you for weakening him, you know, and for all this trouble. He'll try to kill you on sight."

"Yes, I know, it's risky," Roza sighed again. "But at least I can defend myself now. If I prove to him that I'm not in Gorge City, by standing there before him, then he'll call off the attack, won't he? He won't waste his Imperial troops assaulting a heavily defended city to capture me when I'm not there any more. There's a logic to that, isn't there?"

Kerenzi gave a slow nod. "Yes, you have a certain brave logic. The Emperor has the authority to order his generals as he wishes, so if you can persuade him to desist, then good luck to you. But he still might see this as his chance to crush Lord Vallance once and for all."

"That might be no bad thing," Roza muttered, "if it were only him who suffered, but not if everyone in Gorge City needs to suffer or die in the process."

"But wait a minute, Roza," Jorxy interrupted. "Won't our newly younger and feeble Emperor decide to capture you and keep you in his dungeons too, just like Lord Vallance did? How would that be any better?"

Roza shrugged. "It might not be any better. But I doubt the Emperor employs wandering warlocks with Bindweed nets, does he? So that would be an improvement."

"How on earth do you hope to meet the Emperor?" Oxana asked.

"All I can think of is to Teleport myself to near his fortress and surrender myself to one of his officers. I can cast Enflame spells to prove I'm a warlock, and I'm sure Imperial soldiers would love the credit for delivering me to their Emperor. But I'll need to persuade him to talk with me, to convince him that I'm more use as an ally and friend than as an enemy or prisoner."

Roza already had an idea of what she could offer to the Dragon Emperor but didn't want to say it in front of them all. It involved something that only Jorxy knew about.

She stood up from the kitchen table. "I'd like to go for a walk. Jorx, want to come with me?" The way she caught his eye made him jump up at once.

"Yep, coming."

Before they left the kitchen, Kerenzi called, "Um, Roza."

She stopped and turned to him.

"I think you should know," the spirit lord said, "that our kindly Dragon Emperor remembers only too well the part I played in his weakening at the gates of Albany. So, I'm as unwelcome a guest at his fortress as you are. Therefore, if you go ahead with your plan to visit him, I'm sorry but I won't risk my neck to rescue you. If you enter the Emperor's fortress, you'll be on your own."

Roza swallowed hard, disappointed that the spirit lord wouldn't always be willing to rescue her if it came to the worst. But it appeared she couldn't presume on his goodwill if it involved risking his own safety again. Maybe the brush with the Bindweed smoke had been too close a call for him.

Roza nodded to him, he smiled back and then vanished into invisibility. The others gasped, but Roza turned to leave the kitchen again.

"But wait," Oxana said. "If you're going to the Emperor, will you go alone, or do you expect others to go with you? I'm torn now between helping you and trying to save Gorge City."

"I can't ask anyone to come with me," Roza replied. "Feel free to return to your city, Oxana, since that's where your heart is."

"I'm coming with you, Roza," Jorxy volunteered, "and I'm sure Standley will as well."

"Thank you," Roza said, "but I'll worry about you being captured and tortured again to force me to comply with something. Now that I can Teleport properly, I don't need Standley here as the focus for my Recall spell, so he could accompany me—"

"Don't be ridiculous," Jorxy snapped. "If you're going somewhere dangerous, then of course you need Standley and me along to watch your back. We didn't come all this way, and go through all we have done, to abandon you at the final showdown. Wherever you're going, we're coming."

Roza still hesitated at the unknown risks they were letting themselves in for but was touched at his declaration of loyalty and resilience. A sly smile crept onto her face as she tilted her head at him. "I could always Teleport away while you're not watching…"

Jorxy pointed a finger at her. "Don't you dare. You need to promise not to go without us. Promise me you won't."

Roza laughed. "All right, I promise. Come on, let's go for this walk."

The others let Roza and Jorxy leave the kitchen at last, and they wandered across the farmyard to a grass track Roza had chosen at random. It led nowhere except for out into the fields which suited her for not being overheard.

Jorxy bounced along beside her, seeming happier than he'd been for a while. After their separation in Gorge City, and with the crowds of others in the farmhouse kitchen, maybe the boy felt neglected in his cherished role as her best friend. Now he'd been singled out again as her most trusted adviser, and the honour of it clearly delighted him.

As soon as they were well out of earshot, Jorxy looked at Roza sideways. "You're thinking about something," he said. "You've had an idea and want to run it past me. Something you don't want to share with the others yet."

Roza nodded. "You know me too well." They walked in silence until she said, "So, if I've ended up on the Emperor's side, I need him to forgive me for weakening him. What can I offer him that makes me more valuable to him alive, rather than him destroying me?"

Jorxy scratched his ear as he walked. "Well, everyone wants you for your rejuvenation skill. He doesn't want that for himself, but it could earn him a fortune to control your use of it."

"For that matter," Roza chuckled, "I could simply make more treasure for him anyway. Why bother with the rejuvenation when I can enlarge his gold, gems, and jewellery with my Maximise spell? Dragons value treasure, don't they, so that might persuade him."

"I know next to nothing about Dragons, but from all I've heard, that's true."

"But if our aim is for him to stop this war, then it needs

to be something compelling, doesn't it? It must be worth more to him than crushing the rebel Lord Vallance and destroying Gorge City's independence. In fact, I doubt that persuading him to enter a peace treaty is going to work. I think he needs to win this war quickly and decisively so the fighting will stop at once, with his victory."

Jorxy stared at her as they walked along the edge of a field. "What are you thinking? Going to assassinate Lord Vallance or something?"

"No." She hesitated, for this was the bit she needed to discuss with him. "Do you remember our first days after we left the plateau, while up in the mountains, before Oxana and Banno found us? One morning, you got me to rejuvenate a loaf of bread, so it was soft and fresh again."

"Yeah, I remember those days. When Standley fought with those Plains trackers, and you sent their leader flying off a cliff."

"No, I wasn't meaning that," Roza said tersely. "Do you remember how I sent a piece of bread back to being dough, then flour, then seeds of grain again? And then we tried to reverse it, to make it bread again, but instead the seeds grew into stalks of wheat and then withered and died?"

"Yeah, I remember you got upset about that."

She heaved a breath because this was difficult. "Well, I keep thinking about that reverse rejuvenation power, the ability to age things, make them older. What if I offer to use that on the Dragon Emperor?"

Jorxy frowned. "What? To make him wither and shrivel and die? For one thing, he will never agree to that, and for another, that will let Lord Vallance win and the whole Empire will fall apart."

"No, I don't mean to take it that far. What if I reverse the effects of last time, when I made him younger and weaker? This time I could make him older and more powerful, make him huge, ancient, and invincible again."

He stopped walking and stared at her. "I can't believe

I'm hearing this. You want to make that Dragon so powerful that he can terrorise the Empire again, threaten everyone, extort money, burn down towns and villages, with no one to harm or stop him? You want to go back to that, do you?"

Roza wrung her hands. "No, of course I don't want to go back to that. But if the Dragon is huge and invulnerable again, then Lord Vallance and Gorge City will have to surrender at once, or risk being reduced to ash. That will stop the fighting, and the Emperor will win quickly."

"Yeah, that might stop the fighting pretty smartish, but it won't exactly be peace afterwards, will it? Not unless you count constant horror and fear as peace."

"Stop it," Roza snapped. "I'm trying to think and talk this through." They started walking again. "So, we can agree that my offer to make our Dragon Emperor older again – assuming I can do it – will grab his attention and stop him from killing us immediately. It's something I alone can do for him, and he wants it very much."

"Yeah, for the Emperor, that's a case of nothing to lose and everything to gain. If he's old and powerful again, he can crush Lord Vallance and Gorge City in a trice and bring the rest of the Empire to heel. He'd go for that like a shot."

"Exactly," Roza enthused, "it would be irresistible to him, wouldn't it? I could save him from his current fear and hiding in his fortress and restore him to power and authority again. So, I could dangle this unmissable prospect before his eyes and then hit him with my conditions for doing it."

Jorxy chuckled. "You're good at this, aren't you? Remind me never to negotiate with you."

She smiled at him. "What are my conditions, then? That I'll only age him back to full size and power if he promises not to be an oppressive tyrant afterwards? That's a bit weak, isn't it?"

Jorxy gave her a look. "Yeah, you need to be more definite and specific than that. Because what's to stop the wily old lizard saying he'll be a good boy afterwards, so you age him back to huge and ancient, and then he's powerful enough to ignore you completely."

"Yeah, that's the problem, isn't it? I need some ongoing hold over him, to keep him being good. It must be worth his while to work with me as a friend and ally into the future, so we can trust each other, and see the benefits of a kind and just rule for the whole Sapien Empire."

"You think you can do that? Get him to change his ways that much? Become a gentle, loving, father-figure for all his adoring subjects, because he's such a good, kind, and wise Emperor after all?"

Roza gave a chuckle. "Well, I can dream, can't I? Yes, that would be nice, and what I would call peace. It must be worth a try, and maybe I'm the only one with the influence and ability to pull it off. You didn't know old warlock Philoe, but he ended up changing his ways under my benevolent influence."

Jorxy smacked her arm. "You want to change the world, you do."

"And why not?" She grinned at him. "Maybe the Universe gave me this Rejuvenate gift so I can change the Empire for the better. No harm in trying anyway. Now, there are two things I want to do before we leave for the Emperor's fortress. First, I'd like to perfect that Barrier spell, because I haven't got it right yet, and I want that as an option. And second, some of my magic books will have information about Dragons. Can you and Oxana have a quick read of those while I perfect my spellcasting?"

They turned around on the grass path and headed back to the farmhouse. When they arrived, they said nothing to the others about what they'd discussed, but Roza fished out the books on Dragons, Maximised them, and gave them to Oxana and Jorxy. She then set to work on producing – with Standley to test it for her – a perfectly impenetrable Barrier.

When Roza asked Jorxy and Oxana later whether they'd found anything useful in the Dragon books, he shook his head. "The main message is to have as little to do with Dragons as you can. Sounds good to me, but since we need to face one, that doesn't help us much."

"One paragraph surprised me," Oxana chipped in. "Legend has it that all Dragons have a 'true name' known only to themselves, and if you can discover it, that will give you power over that Dragon – to summon them, command them, and so on. But the book added that since sharing their 'true name' will make that Dragon vulnerable, none of them will ever do it, so don't even bother trying."

"Well, that was helpful," Jorxy scoffed. "Why write that in a book if no one can ever make use of it?"

Oxana shrugged. "Mine wasn't much of a practical book. It was trying to gather in one place all the known lore and legends about Dragons."

Enoch and Celeste found Roza and called her into their sitting room. The old farmer cleared his throat. "We've been thinking about your kind offer to rejuvenate us, and we'd like to take you up on it. Neither of us can stand the thought of losing the other, so we'd like to go back to when we were first married, please."

"Can you even remember what we looked like back then?" Celeste teased her elderly husband.

"No need to remember," Roza replied. "You'll see it in a minute. So, if you're sure, I'll need to hold your hands."

The old couple perched facing each other on their armchairs, and Roza knelt between them, her hands on theirs.

She reached down inside for her spark of magic, fanned it into flame, letting it grow and course its warmth down her arms and into their bodies. It felt so good to be doing this again: using her gift and rejuvenating those who dearly wanted it. She found it meant more this time, because she knew the couple before her, more than all those strangers in the Albany marketplace. She concentrated on what she was doing, taking their bodies back to their early twenties, as they'd asked.

Roza finished and opened her eyes. Enoch was on her left, his straight blond hair neatly parted, sitting erect with muscular arms; Celeste on her right was slimmer and curly-haired, their faces smoothed free of wrinkles and lines.

The young couple opened their eyes, stared, giggled, and touched each other's faces. Roza got up quickly and left them to it, as the newly-weds re-discovered their first romance.

Later that afternoon, Jorxy and Oxana exclaimed in astonishment at the youthful transformation of the old farming couple. Roza shrugged and explained she'd offered it as a thank you for the hospitality.

Young Celeste was impressing upon them to stay for an evening meal and get a night's sleep before heading off. Oxana had decided to return to Gorge City the next morning, with riding in Enoch's wagon as the fastest way to get there, so she agreed to stay the night. Roza knew the paladin was anxious about the assault on Gorge City and needed to play her part in the fate of the Plains as it was decided through vicious battle and many deaths.

Roza too felt an urgency to get on with her plan, and to Teleport to the Emperor's fortress before it became fully dark. She'd never been there and so couldn't visualise it to Teleport straight there. She needed to resort to the alternative: limiting herself to a line-of-sight destination and trusting the magic to find them a safe place to stand each time. Jorxy consulted Philoe's Maps of the World to discover where in the whole Sapien Empire the Emperor's fortress lay, and found it marked among forested hills far to the north of Gorge City.

Since Standley was leaving the farmhouse as well this time, they all loaded up their packs, including Roza's box of Minimised magic books and the chest of donated treasure they'd brought with them from Albany. They said goodbye to Enoch and Celeste in the farmyard, thanking them for all their generosity and kindness. The newly younger couple replied that these last few days with the Warlock of Albany would be related to their children and grandchildren for many generations to come.

Oxana embraced first Jorxy, and then Roza, and said, "Good fortune to you both, Jorxy and Warlock Rozabella of Albany. May your mission with the Dragon Emperor succeed, for all our sakes. I will do what I can at Gorge City, and I'll find my little brother, Banno. He has wronged us, but he's the only close family I have, so I need to make sure he's all right."

Roza nodded, and finally they were ready. Standley stood on Roza's right, his hooks clipped firmly onto her shoulder and hip. Jorxy stood on Roza's left, his arm hooked around her waist.

In the far distance to the north-west, the snow-capped peaks of the mountain ranges north of Albany were visible, so Roza chose to make for those, rather than anywhere on the Plains. She selected a large ridge and ignited her magic, trusting it to find them a safe place to stand.

"Hold on," she called, expanding the spell to include all three of them, and threw her arms upwards. In a flash of speed, their boots sank into snow. It was less than a foot deep, and they steadied themselves against a strong east wind blowing into their faces. They looked about, and saw how high up they were, with a panoramic view north and south along the mountains, and eastward over the Plains. Roza imagined she could see armies marching over the country like unnumbered ants on the warpath, but the distances were too great to make anything out.

"Ready to move again?" Roza shouted over the wind, and they both nodded. She scanned the slopes further north and spotted some cliffs lower down than their current elevation. They held on tightly and Roza Teleported them to stand on top of those cliffs. The wind was almost as intense here, but the ground underfoot was dry.

They made two more Teleportations northwards until they stood on the buttressed shoulder of an icy mountain, shivering from a bitter north wind. This time when they peered to the north-east, Roza thought she could see forested hills in the distance.

"Have we come far enough north yet?" Roza asked.

"How should I know?" Jorxy shrugged in return. "How many miles has each of your Teleport spells brought us?"

"Um, as far as our eyes could see, so a good number of miles each time. Shall we aim for those hills and see what we find?"

"They're in the right direction," Jorxy agreed, so they settled on that.

Again, Roza trusted the magic not to bring them down inside the trunks of trees as she picked out a forested slope near the summit of one of the highest hills. She held her breath and transported them instantly from the mountain shoulder to among the trees.

It was darker under the branches, and they all stumbled on the uneven ground. They were not in a clearing but had materialised on a narrow animal track through the undergrowth, and the ground sloped.

"Are you both all right?" Roza called, as they each let go of her and regained their balance against branches and trunks. They peered around but saw nothing but gloomy forest in all directions.

"We should go up," Jorxy suggested, "because there might be an open space with a view at the top, or one of us could climb a tree to see where we are."

It was no easy task to fight their way through the branches and leaves, twigs and needles, bracken, brambles, and undergrowth. Standley had the easiest job of it, being so much thinner than the humans, and using his hooks and clawed feet to manoeuvre his way over the rough ground. He led the way, and the other two hacked, panted, and forced their way upwards in his wake.

At last, as the daylight faded around them, they fought their way onto a rocky outcrop which looked northwards from the western shoulder of the hill. The treetops fell away below them, and the view beyond took their breath away.

A stone wall with towers, ramparts and battlements encircled the largest of the hills in this range. Beyond this outer wall stood circle upon circle of buildings, turreted walls, and other fortifications. It dwarfed tenfold anything Roza had seen at Gorge City, and across the hilltop was a vast – she didn't know what to call it – castle, palace, fortress? She gaped at it, and there could be no mistake: this was where their Dragon Emperor was hiding.

She wondered what madness had possessed her to come and visit the one creature in the whole Sapien Empire who most wanted to avenge himself on her. Was it too late to return to Albany and hide in the back of her cave on the burned-out plateau? But even there, these people would seek her out – the Earl of the Plains, the Dragon Emperor, and everyone else – to control and exploit her powers for their own ends.

No, here was where she needed to confront them and carve out her destiny on her own terms.

CHAPTER TWENTY-ONE

Anyone want to go home?" Roza asked quietly. "I won't blame you if you don't want to come with me into there." She nodded at the fortress in front of them, unable to tear her eyes away from it. "This venture may end in death, but I want to try to make everything right if I can."

Something touched her arm, and Roza looked down to see a polished wooden hook on her elbow. She laid her other hand on top of it and asked, "Are you willing to come with me, Standley?"

The coat stand's knots looked straight into her eyes, gave her a slow, definite nod, and then squeezed her elbow.

Roza looked at Jorxy, who'd gone white and kept swallowing. "You sure you've got that Barrier spell working properly?" he whispered. "And it will keep everything away from us?"

"Yes, it worked against whatever Standley could throw at me. And the magic books say it's effective against all but the hottest Dragon-fire. But you can stay here if you prefer, or I could still take you home."

"Nah," Jorxy shook his head. "We've come this far so we might as well finish the rest of the way. For Albany and Gorge City and the whole Sapien Empire, eh?"

"Yes, for our home and town and Empire," Roza said.

Jorxy gave an unexpected chuckle. "I remember when the three of us set off from that cave on the Albany plateau, all in a rush because Lord Vallance had galloped into the valley. We said it might be an exciting adventure to run away together, but I don't think I'd call it that now."

"No, I'm not sure what to call this either," Roza sighed. "But whatever it is, I'm glad I've got the two of you for company." She squeezed Jorxy's shoulder and Standley's hooks. "Now, I think we should Teleport onto one of those outer walls we can see from here. That will get us noticed, which is the whole point – to find someone to escort us to the Emperor. As soon as we land, you must let go of me at once, because I'll need my arms free to cast the Barrier spell. Understand?"

They nodded and got into position around her on the rocky outcrop. The sun had set behind the western mountains casting a gloomy shadow across these hills, but watch-fires burned at intervals along the fortress walls. Roza picked one of these where she could see no guards patrolling, made sure her magic was alight and heaved a deep breath in and out.

"Right, here we go, three, two, one," and she threw up her arms.

They landed in the middle of a wide, stone-flagged wall with parapets on either side, watch-fires burning some distance in front and behind them. As instructed, Standley and Jorxy let go and moved to the side. Roza lifted her hands and spun on the spot, erecting a magical Barrier around them.

Even as she did so, cries came from both ends of the wall. Soldiers in the dark red uniforms of the Imperial Army were pointing and shouting, already running towards them.

"Stay back," Roza called. "We mean you no harm."

"Drop your weapons," a soldier ordered, because Jorxy was twirling his stick, looking in turn to front and back. "We have archers trained on you."

As he spoke, Roza saw soldiers nocking arrows to their bowstrings, aiming at each of them. "Hold your fire," she shouted. "We come in peace." She raised her open palms to show she was unarmed.

"Three seconds to drop that stick," the soldier shouted back, "or we shoot."

That was long enough for Roza to look at Jorxy, who shook his head, and then the bowstrings twanged. To front and back, several arrows crashed into the magical Barrier, which flashed and crackled, and the missiles bounced away upwards or to the side.

"I said hold your fire," Roza yelled. "Your arrows can't reach us so stop wasting your time."

"Again," the soldier ordered, and the bows twanged a second time, the arrows deflecting off the Barrier.

Roza decided she needed to do something more. Picking out the archers, she sent Repulser spells against them, knocking each of them backwards onto the flagstones. "Stop firing arrows at us," she shouted, "or I'll throw your archers over the side of this wall."

By now a Sergeant had come up, and he'd seen what had happened to the arrows and archers.

"We don't want to fight you," Roza called to him. "We need to talk to you."

"What are you waiting for?" the Sergeant ordered. "Grab them!"

"Don't," Roza yelled, "the Barrier will hurt–"

But it was too late. On all sides soldiers rushed forward to charge the Barrier and were thrown back with flashes, crackles, and yells of pain.

"Listen to me," Roza screamed. "I will throw all of you off this wall if I have to, until you let me tell you who I am and why I'm here."

"How are you stopping the arrows and my men?" the Sergeant demanded.

Good, Roza thought, he's asking questions at last instead of trying to start a fight. "This is a magical Barrier," she called, "which I have created to protect my friends and me. Nothing can get through it, and it will continue to hurt you if you try."

"No such thing as magic," the Sergeant scoffed. "It's just some trick. I bet I can get through it." With that, he drew his sword and charged at them. To his credit, he bore the pain of the impact better than the others but was still thrown back. Roza wondered how much more stupid this Sergeant could get.

"All right," he said next. "You threatened to throw us off this wall. I'd like to see you try." He grinned at the soldiers around him, who all nodded back.

Quite a lot more stupid, apparently. "Shall I start with you, then?" Roza asked.

"Yeah, go on, if you can," the Sergeant taunted.

Roza spotted a bank of thick bushes on a slope inside the wall, and with a flick of her wrist she Repulsed the Sergeant high into the air and then he fell, flailing and shouting, towards those. If the situation hadn't been so serious, she'd have found it comical to watch the gaze of every soldier following their Sergeant's flight up and then down again out of sight.

"I need to speak with someone more senior than him," Roza stated.

"Send for the Captain," the first soldier ordered, only for the reply to come, "She's on her way."

Roza glanced at Jorxy and Standley, who both looked tense, as ready for whatever came next as they could be. She wondered whether she looked more confident than she felt. She hoped so.

Roza turned back to a sound of marching boots and a tall middle-aged woman striding towards her. "Captain, I need to speak with you."

"What's all this? Who are you?" the Captain demanded.

The time had come to reveal her identity, and she braced herself for the reaction to her next words. She lifted her chin and declared, "My name is Rozabella, and I am the Warlock of Albany."

Whatever reaction she expected, it wasn't what followed. "I don't believe you," the Captain stated flatly. "You think you're the first girl to come here and claim to be that wretched warlock? Hardly a day goes by when we don't catch some imposter saying they're her."

Roza was staggered. How could she prove herself? "But

… but I Teleported us here onto this wall. I cast a Barrier spell around us to protect us from arrows and soldiers. I used the Repulser spell to throw the Sergeant off the wall and into those bushes."

The Captain was shaking her head. "I didn't see any of that. Go on then, perform some magic."

What else could she do – Enflame? Roza walked around inside the Barrier circle, clicking her fingers as she went, dropping fires onto the smooth flagstones. The watching soldiers murmured, but the Captain looked less impressed.

"All right, so you appear capable of doing a little magic. But you might be any old warlock disguised to look like a girl. Prove you're her."

"How can I?" Roza demanded, getting annoyed. "Do you want me to Rejuvenate you? Or what about my companions? This is Jorxy, my school friend from Albany, and my enchanted coat stand, Standley."

The Captain still looked uninterested. "No, you certainly won't touch me to perform any of your supposed magic. We've had no instructions about companions," – she eyed Standley for a moment – "although I grant you the coat stand looks … different. Can it move?"

In answer, Standley scuttled forward, flexed his hooks, and bent his pole as deeply as he could towards her.

The Captain shrugged. "Could be an illusion." She paused, regarding Roza keenly. "All right. We've been given a final question to ask anyone claiming to be Albany's warlock. But I warn you, answer this incorrectly and you're all straight to our dungeons, magic or no."

Roza wondered whether to alert the others to be ready for an immediate Teleport out of there if this went wrong, but as calmly as she could said, "Ask your question."

"When our noble Emperor visited Albany recently, he met the real Warlock Rozabella outside the town gates. The girl claimed she had someone else there helping her. Who was that?"

Roza sighed in relief. A question she could answer, and one that only she would know. She looked the Captain in the eye and declared, "I am the real Warlock Rozabella of Albany, and when I met the Dragon Emperor outside our gates, the person helping me was a spirit lord from the forests in the valley by the name of Kerenzi."

For the first time, the Captain looked surprised as her eyebrows shot up. "Well, well, so you might be the real girl after all. Next question, we heard you were in Gorge City. How come you're here?"

"Yes, I was in Gorge City. Lord Vallance captured and imprisoned me and my friends, but we managed to escape. I have Teleported us all here this evening."

The Captain scrutinised her. "Therefore, the Earl of the Plains might have sent you here as a spy. Otherwise, why else are you here? The Emperor has given clear orders for you to be killed on sight."

"We are not spies," Roza countered. "Lord Vallance bound me with Bindweed and threatened to torture those I love. After that experience, I will never do anything for him. In fact, I now want that wretched man to lose this war. Yes, I know that the Emperor blames me for what happened at Albany, but I bore him no malicious intent then, and I don't now. I am here to make amends for what I did. I find myself on the same side as the Dragon Emperor in this war and have come to seek alliance with him to help him win it."

The Captain studied Roza for what felt like a long time and then she nodded. "Very well. You have given reasonable proof of who you are and have made an offer that the Emperor might be willing to hear. Follow me." She turned and strode away along the top of the wall.

Roza gave Jorxy a nervous but hopeful smile. "I need to draw in the Barrier while we move, so we'd better gather closer." With Standley, they formed a tighter group and passed between the soldiers who retreated out of their way and lined the battlements. When they came to the door of a tower, however, Roza had to lift the Barrier altogether, hoping that no soldiers tried anything stupid. With this Captain in command, the fortress guards seemed content to march along in front and behind and give them no further trouble.

Roza took in little of the walk from the outer walls towards the Emperor's main fortress. They descended tower steps, crossed courtyards and gardens, passed through great doors and gatehouses, and finally climbed a wide tree-lined drive towards the top of the central hill.

As they approached this, Roza saw that the entire fortress was carved out of the hilltop, with walls and pillars of living rock and the hill summit as a roof. Access to the vast excavated space inside was through wide iron gates. She remembered the mountainous size of the Dragon lying across the highway outside Albany, blocking all escape from the valley, and noted how these access gates were of a size to accommodate even him.

Before they entered under the shadow of the hill, Roza turned a wistful gaze back westwards to the beautiful sunset colours over the mountains, hoping this wasn't the last glimpse of daylight she would ever see. As they trudged inside the hilltop, along torchlit passages too broad and high to see their ceiling or walls, her insides began to tremble uncontrollably.

She'd met this Dragon before, she told herself, and now he was less massive, powerful and intimidating than he'd been then. But her fears answered that last time he'd thought her of no consequence, whereas now he regarded her with implacable hatred. How could anyone negotiate with a Dragon who was furious with you and determined to kill you whatever chance he got? Was a Teleport spell out of here, even now, the wisest choice? No, this was her chance to solve all her problems at once, if only she could win over this Dragon, and she was determined to try.

The Captain stopped in front of large double doors, but

these were human-sized and not scaled for an ancient Dragon to pass. "Wait here," she said. "I will inform the Emperor who you are and what you've said about why you're here. I caution you that all of us enter here at our own risk." For the first time, Roza thought the Captain looked nervous, and when a door opened, the Imperial Army officer stepped through it. Roza hastily recast the Barrier spell around the three of them.

They waited. The interior of the hillside seemed to wait with them, with drips of water and cracks of stone, as though the hilltop fortress itself listened in to what the Captain was saying to the Emperor.

They all jumped as a booming voice echoed throughout the vast caverns and passages. This was not the deep, ancient roar that had split the rocks and shaken the mountains around Albany, but it was unmistakably a Dragon voice, enough to strike terror into all who heard it, even when uttering only a single word.

"Enter."

CHAPTER TWENTY-TWO

The door wardens pulled back the double doors to reveal a vast and gloomy cavern. Roza renewed her casting of the Barrier spell, glanced left and right to Jorxy and Standley, and edged shakily forward. As soon as they'd all crossed the threshold, the doors closed behind them with an echoing crash.

The cavern was dark, lit only by the flicker of fire-pits at intervals across the stone floor. The walls were black and polished smooth, reflecting the dancing shadows of the flames, but the roof was too high to see. As her eyes accustomed to the gloom, Roza made out the figure of the Captain some way across the floor, tiny in front of the huge shadow behind her. With shaking limbs and a thrill of terror, she realised this was the Dragon himself.

Without warning, the cavern filled with fire. Roza ducked as the light and heat blasted into her, but the Barrier spell held. The flames licked upwards where they met the circle around them, but Jorxy was curled on the floor, singed but not burned. Standley stood firm on her right.

The fire faded into flying embers and trailing smoke, and Roza hastily re-cast the Barrier as Jorxy picked himself up. She peered across the cavern through the heat haze and drifting ash to see the charred and smoking body of the Captain lying on the stone floor. Above her corpse gleamed the fiery eyes and nostrils of the Emperor.

A deep rumble reverberated around the cavern as the Dragon spoke again. "So, your Barrier can deflect my fire. But can it stop my tooth and claw?"

In horror, Roza saw that the Emperor had risen into the air, his mighty wings beating powerful downdrafts that dimmed the fires. With claws outstretched and jaws agape, he meant to land on top of them and crush them utterly.

She doubted the power of her Barrier to withstand the huge weight of a diving Dragon and did the only thing she could think of. Summoning all her magic into a raging inferno, she channelled it into the hardest shove of a Repulser spell she'd ever imagined.

The Emperor swerved.

Even Roza's fiercest spell couldn't stop him in his tracks, let alone push him backwards, but it diverted his dive to crush them. His massive bulk landed with a ground-shaking crash to Roza's right and she prepared another Repulser to try to fend him off. Standley stood between them now, tense and ready, as the Dragon snarled and turned his jaws towards them.

The Emperor reared onto his hind legs, his vast wings overshadowing them, the fire in his eyes and throat like a piercing lance to lunge at them. Roza braced herself to Repulse him or die, as the Dragon's claws and teeth bared for a final pounce to seize and rend them.

Then the Emperor did the last thing Roza expected.

He froze in mid-air, in mid-pounce, his fierce eyes glaring down at them … and then he dropped. He fell back onto his front claws, staring intently at them. The deep voice came again, but although closer, it was now softer.

"Standley?" he said. "Is that you?"

Roza's mind reeled, failing to understand. Her enchanted coat stand tottered a few steps forward and then gave the Emperor the deepest bow he could manage.

"It is you," the Dragon exclaimed, and the cavern echoed with an incredulous laugh. "But how come you're here, after all these centuries?"

"Wait," Roza called. "You know my coat stand? The two of you recognise each other?"

"Ah, Miss Rozabella, Warlock of Albany," the Dragon said, swinging his head to gaze directly at her, such that she wilted, "do you not know who you have here? Standley, your enchanted coat stand, has walked this earth for many thousands of years before even I was born. He is one of the Sapiens, the Wise Ones, the Founders, after whom this whole Empire is named."

Roza's jaw dropped. Standley is a *what?*

"But I ask again," the Emperor went on, "how can this be? Your predecessor, that wily old Philoe, never mentioned he had Standley in his possession."

"N-No," Roza stammered, "Philoe didn't think much of his coat stand, or treat him very well, but I seem to have inherited him. He's been my faithful bodyguard ever since."

"Has he now?" The Dragon's gaze shifted back to Standley. "So, tell me, my old friend, what do you make of your new mistress, Miss Rozabella? What sort of person is she?"

The Emperor paused, as though waiting or listening, so Roza felt she had to explain. "Um, Your Majesty, Standley can't speak, so we communicate by 'yes' or 'no' questions, and he nods or shakes his hooks."

"Silence," the Dragon snarled at her. "It's rude to talk over someone while they are speaking."

"Wait," Roza said again. "He can speak to you? You can hear him?"

The Emperor's gaze slid back to her. "I will forgive your foolish ignorance because you are a young and new warlock. Some day you may learn to tune your thoughts to hear what Standley wants to say to you, but in the meantime be silent."

Roza shut up, staring at her coat stand in disbelief. Standley could talk? All this time, she could have tuned her thoughts to hear him, instead of using yes or no questions? She looked at Jorxy, who seemed as dumbfounded as she was, and they shrugged.

"Hmm," the Emperor said at last. "Standley speaks very highly of you, Miss Rozabella, so for his sake I will not kill you immediately."

"Um, thank you, sire," she ventured, not sure how grateful to be about that. She couldn't help asking, "But you killed your own Army Captain. What did she do wrong?"

The Emperor didn't even glance towards the still-smoking corpse. "She got in the way. She forgot the rule to stand clear of a Dragon who might want to breathe fire. Besides, she angered me by saying you were here on some misguided mission of peace and friendship."

Roza swallowed hard. Now she was here, while the Emperor was listening, it was time to state her case. "Your Majesty, I regret very much that our meeting at Albany resulted in war in your Empire. I and my friends have been badly mistreated by Lord Vallance, and so we wish to join your cause and see him defeated. I offer to make amends for the past by helping you win this war."

The Emperor's voice rose to a bellow. "And how can you possibly help my Imperial Army to capture Gorge City?"

Roza hesitated. She remembered vowing up in the mountains, when she discovered she could make things older, that she would never use this reverse side of her gift. It was too frightening and deadly, and once mentioned, she could never take it back. But her whole plan depended on using it on the Emperor. This was what she could offer, and it would end the war and save countless lives. She had to say this and get it over quickly.

"Your Majesty, I have discovered that my gift of Rejuvenate can also be used in reverse, to make things or people older. I could therefore return you to being ancient, huge and invincible again."

The Dragon's head swung closer, fixing her with his searching gaze. "Is this some trick or lie? Reverse Rejuvenation? Making things older again? I've never heard of such a thing."

"It's true," Roza spluttered. "I've done it before, with wheat seeds, trying to turn them back into bread, but they grew into healthy grain plants instead." She thought she'd omit the wither, shrivel, and die part. "Jorxy saw it, and

Standley was watching too." She prayed her coat stand had paid attention at the time and could back up her story.

"Standley, is this true?" the Emperor demanded.

Roza didn't know whether her coat stand said or thought anything in reply, but he certainly nodded.

The Dragon's piercing gaze fixed on her again. "Explain this to me in full and complete detail."

Roza realised she was wringing her hands and stopped it, to avoid looking as nervous as she felt. "Well, sire, I've only tried it once before, because not many things or people want to get older, and like with Rejuvenation, it requires the consent of the subject. My gift works with a person's lifecycle, sending it backwards, making them younger. But it occurs to me, Your Majesty, after the unfortunate events in Albany valley, that you might want your lifecycle to advance forwards quickly, aging magically, since your size, strength and armour depend on your age. Therefore, I could return you to your former Imperial authority, with no one daring to challenge you, for fear of being destroyed by your invincible might." Roza bit her lip, hoping she'd succeeded in selling this proposal to a power-hungry Emperor.

"I could venture forth again," the Dragon murmured. "No more keeping myself safe in here. I could lead my Army into battle, and who would dare to oppose us? I wouldn't even need the Army, because the mere sight of me, restored to my former size and power, would strike terror into my enemies. They would crumble and flee, they would surrender and fall, they would beg for mercy, before the invincible might of the true Emperor of the Sapien Empire!"

The Dragon's voice had risen into a ringing trumpet call and Roza gulped. The Emperor had clearly grasped the gist of the plan, but now she needed to raise the awkward subject of the conditions she wanted to attach to this.

"So, am I clear, sire," Roza ventured, "that you might be interested in my doing this for you?"

"Yes, indeed," the Emperor boomed, "as long as there are no tricks or unfortunate side effects this time."

"No, of course not, I promise to deal with you honestly." Roza looked around to where Jorxy was shifting uncomfortably on his feet. "We might have other ways of working together to benefit you and your Empire, so rather than standing near an entrance to your cavern, could we sit somewhere more comfortable to discuss this?"

The Dragon's gaze flicked over them, as though sizing up any possible threat, and then he nodded. "My manners have deserted me. Come to my treasure mound where I hold Council."

With a downdraft from his wings, the Emperor rose into the air, and the three of them hurried across the smooth stone floor after him. They reached a circle of fire-pits around a glittering mound of treasure with some bronze thrones in front of it. The Dragon coiled himself around the top of his pile of gold, silver, gems, and jewellery, and Roza took the seat nearest to the Emperor's head. She purposefully sat back in the throne, despite her inclination to perch on the edge in readiness to flee at any moment. Jorxy also sat, more perched than lounging, and Standley remained upright beside Roza.

She'd thought hard about raising with the Emperor the issue of his previously oppressive tyranny, and the best she'd come up with was this. "Your Majesty, if we are to work together in alliance, I hope you'll forgive my boldness in suggesting ways I consider might benefit you and your Empire. Isn't it in all our interests for your reign to be prosperous and successful?" She offered him what she hoped was a friendly and persuasive smile.

The Dragon's eyes narrowed with suspicion, but his words remained polite. "Indeed, Miss Rozabella, I insist that all my counsellors offer me their very best ideas and advice, otherwise what use are they to me?"

She drew a deep breath. "Very well, sire, I will come

straight to my point. It concerns me that as soon as Your Majesty was weakened, your vassal in Gorge City betrayed his allegiance to you and declared independence. I conclude that he, and perhaps others, were only loyal to you for as long as they were afraid of you. The cohesion and functioning of the Empire rested on their terror of your retribution if they stepped out of line."

"Which means I should make them all petrified of me again," the Dragon interrupted. "And your aging ability will achieve that for me admirably."

"Quite so, sire." Roza swallowed hard. "Or perhaps – if Your Majesty will forgive my youthful naivety – might I suggest that if you were … well, frankly … nicer to your subjects, they might love you instead?" There, she had said it, and she waited for the Emperor's reaction.

The Dragon's expression was impossible to read, whether he was furious, baffled, or amused. "But I'm always nice to them. I do lots of things for them, such as providing security and strong leadership."

"Ah, yes, strong indeed," Roza agreed, "and about to become stronger still when our plan goes ahead." She thought it wise to remind him of her existing offer. "But my point is that your subjects probably feel they pay for your protection and leadership through their taxes. It's a relationship of obligation and duty, rather than kindness, generosity and love."

The Dragon made a noise in his throat that sounded like a splutter of disbelief, which caused a billow of smoke to erupt from his nostrils. "You think I should govern my Empire on woolly notions of kindness, generosity and love, rather than the strength of a well-resourced army? Go on then, tell me what I could do to make my subjects love me."

It was time for Roza to make her next offer. "I was thinking, sire, that your subjects would love you very much if you cancel all the taxes they owe you."

There was a moment of silence followed by a cacophony

of thunder that made them all cower in alarm. It soon became clear, however, that the mighty din was caused by the Dragon bursting out laughing. Roza had expected this reaction and was ready to follow it through.

At length, the Emperor controlled himself. "You asked me to forgive your youthful naivety, and I am willing to do so. I fear you are unaware of the vast expense of running an Empire, of paying my soldiers, ministers and officials, maintaining the institutions of government in every place, not to mention my own needs. If I were to cancel all my taxes, as you suggest, how would we pay for all this?"

"That is where I come in, Your Majesty," Roza declared. "If we work together in alliance, then I would provide all the treasure you could possibly need."

She had the Emperor's attention now, and he seemed to be thinking fast. "Ah, I see your proposal. If you come and work for me, then we can charge the citizens of the Empire for the benefit of your Rejuvenate gift. That would bring in a steady and handsome income because it would always be in demand. But I heard that you offer your rejuvenation for nothing, accepting only donations in return. Have you changed your mind, and seen the wisdom in gathering a substantial income from the use of your remarkable ability?"

"No, sire," Roza replied calmly. "My unique gift came to me freely, so I offer it to everyone freely in return. If people offer a grateful donation, that is up to them. I don't insist on it now, and I won't in the future either. You see, Your Majesty, that is the kind, generous and loving thing to do." She smiled, wondering whether she was getting anywhere in winning him over.

Instead, the Dragon shook his head. "Young Miss Rozabella, you pass over a priceless opportunity to gather vast treasure for yourself. It breaks my heart to think what riches you are rejecting. But now tell me, if you will not charge to Rejuvenate, how do you propose to meet the Empire's financial needs?"

Having offered invincible strength to a power-hungry Emperor, it was time now to offer limitless gold to a treasure-hungry Dragon. "Well, there's this simple warlock spell called Maximise," Roza began.

"Stop," the Emperor commanded, raising a clawed foreleg to interrupt her. "Do not insult my intelligence, young Miss Warlock, or attempt to trick me, by pretending that the Maximise spell works on treasure. All warlocks, and everyone who uses magic, know that gold, silver, gems, and jewellery are the exceptions to being enlarged by magic."

Roza's jaw dropped open. "What? You're telling me that warlocks can't use the Maximise spell to increase their treasure?"

"No, of course they can't," the Dragon snapped. "Otherwise, the whole financial system of the Empire would be in chaos. There would be more treasure swilling about than anyone would know what to do with, and it would lose all its value. So, if you were about to suggest you can Maximise the treasure we need to run my Empire, then I know that you are lying and trying to trick me."

Roza thought it best to say nothing. He needed to be shown, or he would never believe her. It hadn't been a dream that she could do this, had it?

She stood up from her throne and stepped across to Jorxy, who was wearing his backpack. He unslung it, and together they lifted from the bottom of it the Minimised chest of all her donations.

Opening it, she picked out the small ruby-embedded chain of office that Grandma Lily and Amber-Jane had given to Jorxy. She held it up for the Dragon Emperor to see, who watched this with suspicion and scorn, and laid it on the stone floor. Lighting up her magic, she cast the Maximise spell over it, tapping its bottom left and top right, and was relieved to see it enlarge to normal size.

She held it up and saw the Dragon blinking and peering at it. For good measure, she laid it down again and enlarged it to double size, making it too heavy for anyone to wear. When she struggled to lift it up, she indicated for the Dragon to pick it up and inspect if he wished.

"This is some trick or illusion," the Emperor rumbled. "No one can enlarge treasure. It's one of the rules of magic. How have you done this?"

Roza shrugged. "Your Majesty, I don't know how to cast tricks or illusions. I don't know why I can do this, but I can. Until you said it a moment ago, I didn't know no one else could do it. And I can shrink it. I expect I can enlarge your treasure as well, if you want me to prove it."

While the Emperor watched, Roza Minimised the chain of office back to normal, and then small size, to return it to the chest. She took out a miniature gold coin, almost too small for the Dragon to see, and enlarged it to normal size, then larger to cover her palm, then larger again to plate size. With an effort, she lifted this heavy gold disc and laid it by the Dragon's front claw.

"Pick it up, weigh it, bite it, whatever you need to do. It's normal gold, and there's simply more of it. This is what I could do to finance your Empire, instead of taxes, Your Majesty."

The Dragon picked up the enlarged coin in his claws. He weighed it in his palm, scrutinised it, bit it, licked it and laid it down again. Next, he picked up a silver coin from his own treasure hoard and handed it to Roza. Assuming he wanted it larger rather than smaller, Roza set about Maximising it until it was too heavy for her to lift. The Dragon inspected it again.

"I assume you have your own furnaces for melting gold and silver," Roza said, "and coin presses for minting the Imperial currency. So, if I provide the raw metal, in whatever quantities you need, you can make it into the coins to pay your soldiers, ministers, officials, and whoever. And if, as you say, I'm the only one who can do this, then that shouldn't cause chaos to the Empire's economy. I can also

Maximise other natural resources for you, such as food, iron, wood, stone, and so on. You can simply cancel all taxes, and everyone will become more prosperous and love you for it."

"But how can you do it?" the Emperor demanded. "It's impossible. No one has ever been able to do it before."

Roza shrugged again. "Maybe it's like my Rejuvenate gift. No one can do that either, so perhaps this is something that goes with it."

Standley's clawed feet scraped on the stone floor as he moved to stand in front of the Dragon Emperor's face. Nothing happened, so Roza wondered what he was doing, and then remembered the two of them could be talking with each other in thought. Jorxy looked as puzzled as she was, until the Emperor and Standley looked at her again.

"Miss Rozabella, Standley is wise and experienced in the ways of magic and the Universe. Since he met you, he has watched and pondered. He suggests it may be a principle of the Universe that a warlock over whom treasure has no hold can multiply it. Since you offer your rejuvenation for free, that is a kind, generous and beautiful thing to do. And magic flows from beauty, so the Universe has allowed you to multiply treasure as well. It's a sign of a heart that isn't greedy, and since we can think of no other explanations, what do you say to that?"

Roza thought back to sitting on the boulder overlooking Albany valley when Kerenzi the spirit lord told her she was supremely beautiful in the way that really mattered. Was this what he meant? "Um, well, I don't know how un-greedy I am, but it seems the right thing to do, that my rejuvenation is available to all, rich and poor alike. I've never been interested in gaining lots of treasure, just enough to live on and be content. So, if this means I'm kinder and more generous than most, how I can argue with that?"

"So, let me get this straight." The Dragon Emperor fixed Roza with his withering stare. "You walk in here and offer me invincible power as the huge and ancient Dragon I used to be, to defeat my enemies, end this war, and bring peace to my Empire. You also offer me your unique ability to Maximise treasure, so I can have limitless wealth, cancel all Imperial taxes, and still have more than enough to run my Empire. And in return, all you ask is that I be 'a bit nicer' to my subjects?"

And he erupted into a deafening cascade of laughter that made them both shove fingers in their ears.

CHAPTER TWENTY-THREE

Roza was relieved that the Dragon Emperor was now in a good mood, because her next move would either anger, challenge or upset him, and probably all three. How could she address this and still make the deal happen?

When the echoes of the Emperor's laughter finally died away into the recesses of the cavern, Roza returned to sit on her bronze throne and said, "I am delighted that you see the full value of my offer, Your Majesty, and that this agreement can begin a firm and lasting friendship between us. The Sapien Empire will benefit greatly from our cooperation – your strong and fatherly leadership, my rejuvenation ability, and all based on the sound finances of cancelled taxes and my enlarging of your treasure."

The near-constant suspicion in the Dragon's eyes burned again. "Yes indeed, Miss Rozabella, I see that you have much to offer me and my Empire. But I sense in your tone a catch or condition approaching. You speak of friendship, cooperation, and fatherly leadership, and I need to understand what you mean by these terms."

Roza forced out a laugh. "I knew I could rely on Your Majesty's perceptiveness, and agree that we should be clear what we mean by 'being a bit nicer to your subjects'. What gestures of goodwill and trust could we share?"

"Hmm, I understand what you are saying, that our deal requires assurances and guarantees on each side, to ensure we fulfil our promises. Do you have something in mind?"

"An accomplished negotiator such as yourself understands my situation, sire. For example, when I use my reverse Rejuvenation gift to age you back to huge and ancient, you could return to however you ruled your Empire before, ignoring my desire for you to be kinder, more generous, or fatherly. I would have no further bargaining power over you."

"What about your ability to enlarge treasure? You could withhold that from me to encourage my compliance."

"Yes, I could, but then you could return to collecting your previous taxes from the Empire and nothing would have changed. Please understand, Your Majesty, that I am determined and in earnest that the running of this Empire should change because of what I offer you today."

"You are a wily negotiator yourself, young Miss Warlock, and I suppose I could learn from you about compassion and concern for the peoples of my Empire. But do you really want me to become like a father to them all? I never desired to be responsible for so many children."

"I would imagine that being a father to so many could be a wonderful thing, especially when they love you in return, are concerned for your welfare, and delight to live out their lives alongside you. Isn't that what families and friendships are about?"

"Humph," snorted the Dragon. "I never had the time or inclination for a family or friends, but I see you're determined that I should have both. I sense you have something in mind to suggest, so go ahead and spit it out."

Roza wondered whether she needed to defend herself when she said these next words, in case an angry or upset Dragon breathed fire. So, she got up from her bronze throne, and paced around the centre of the throne circle, as though thinking, choosing her words carefully, but at the same time igniting her magic and preparing her Barrier spell to protect the three of them.

"Very well, Your Majesty, since you insist that I speak about this, and please forgive me if I mention something which angers or offends you. I know very little about this, but I read somewhere that Dragons are rumoured to have something called a 'true name'…"

Roza was careful to watch the Dragon Emperor as she said this and saw his face contort in anger as he drew breath.

She had already spun the Barrier spell before the first flames blasted into it. But this time they were nearer to the Dragon's mouth than when they'd entered the cavern. The heat and force of the blast knocked them all flat, toppling the bronze thrones, but the Barrier was strong enough to prevent them being incinerated.

They could only curl on the floor and endure the scorching, singeing fire until the Dragon's breath was spent and Roza could scramble to her feet again. Standley was also up and beside her, as Roza sent her strongest Repulser spell straight at the Emperor's head.

The Dragon's skull was punched sideways, and his furious glare bore down on them as he drew another breath. But the sight of Standley and Warlock Rozabella side by side caused him the moment's hesitation for Roza to Repulse his head upwards.

The fire-breath missed them, roaring over the top of the Barrier spell and stretching across the width of the cavern to lick the opposite wall. The Dragon let out an ear-splitting bellow and launched himself into the air from the top of his treasure mound.

Roza, Standley and Jorxy scrambled together against the wind of his wings and into the middle of the blasted circle of bronze thrones. Roza re-cast the Barrier, but they cringed and waited for the full weight of the Emperor to land and crush them to death.

It didn't come. No crushing weight fell, no claws rent them apart and no razor-sharp jaws bit into them. In tense silence they heard the beating of great wings recede and fade until the cavern became quiet.

They gasped and panted for breath in the gloomy stillness.

"Well, that went well," muttered Jorxy. "All up until the last bit."

Roza sighed. "I thought we were doing well too, but the mention of a Dragon's true name is clearly more upsetting than we realised."

Standley touched Roza's arm with one of his hooks. "Oh, thank you, Standley," she breathed, "you were amazing. Having you here saved us, both when the Emperor first recognised you, and when you could speak to him on our behalf."

But Standley still nudged her upper arm, clearly wanting to communicate with her. "What is it? I'm sorry I can't hear your thoughts, so you'll need to help me with what you want to say."

Her coat stand pointed with his hooks towards the treasure pile and then out across the cavern in the direction the Dragon had gone.

"Um …," Roza guessed, "do you want to go and check where the Emperor has gone?"

Standley nodded and then did a slow rotation movement with his flexible hooks.

"What is that, then? That rotating motion?" She peered into his topknots that she'd always taken to be his eyes. "Does it mean something like thinking?"

His top hooks nodded vigorously, and his eye knots smiled. He pointed again where the Dragon had gone and repeated the thinking motion.

"Do you mean…," Roza said slowly, "that we need to think about the Dragon?" Standley shook his hooks. "That the Emperor has gone away to do some thinking?"

Her enchanted coat stand gave his delighted nodding and then hurried away to check whether the Dragon had indeed left the cavern.

"Phew," Jorxy said. "Should we learn some sort of language with signs to communicate with him, then?"

Roza chuckled. "Yes, maybe so, as well as spending time trying to hear what he's thinking."

"But wow," Jorxy added. "I was always impressed with that furniture of yours, but to see how the Emperor himself recognised and respected him, and that he's one of these

Sapiens, whoever they were, who established this Empire at the start."

"I know," said Roza. "There's so much I want to learn from Standley that I'm definitely going to study that trick of tuning my thoughts into his."

After the effort of getting here and the nervous energy of talking with the Emperor, a wave of tiredness swept over her. Before she fell over, she sat down on the floor and crossed her legs. "Come on, if we've nothing better to do, let's eat and drink and get some rest. I'm thirsty and starving and Standley will keep watch for us."

It was a bizarre setting to camp for a meal, beside the Dragon Emperor's treasure mound, in the middle of toppled bronze thrones, between flickering fire-pits. Jorxy got out the bread, butter, cold meat, cheese, fruit, and milk that Celeste had pressed on them earlier, and they munched in the quiet darkness. The cavern felt vast enough for them to be under the night sky outside, with clouds covering the stars and a cold breeze blowing through unseen openings.

In time, Standley returned, confirming that the Dragon had left the cavern. He nodded that he would keep watch while the two of them curled up in their blankets on the stone floor and tried to sleep.

But before she slept, Roza couldn't resist a couple of questions for her coat stand. "Hey, Standley, are you really one of these Sapiens then, the Founders of this whole Empire, and thousands of years older than even the Emperor?"

He seemed delighted that she finally knew about his famous heritage as he nodded and bowed.

"One other question then. Will you teach me to hear your thoughts, and then answer the million questions I have for you? Like who the other Sapiens were, how this Empire was founded, what happened to all the others, how you became a coat stand, and everything else?"

Standley seemed to chuckle, then nodded again.

Roza turned over under her blanket, and the next thing she knew was Standley nudging her awake. A dim half-light of morning was filtering into the cavern through far-off entrances, a cold northerly air blew in and the fire-pits had burned out.

Roza threw off her blanket and leapt to her feet because the Emperor was returning. She lit up her magic and cast Barrier around them as Standley woke up Jorxy. Instead of flying, the Dragon was walking, slowly and calmly, across the cavern floor towards them.

"Have no fear, I mean you no harm," the Dragon called.

But as Jorxy got up, he readied his stick and slung on his backpack in case they needed to go. Roza rubbed her face and stretched her limbs to be fully awake, ready for more magic – Repulser or Teleport – as soon as they might need it.

They watched the Emperor closely, but he made no threatening move and coiled himself around the top of his treasure mound as before.

"Warlock Rozabella, Standley, and your friend," said the Dragon, "I sincerely regret my fit of temper last night. What you said took me by surprise, and I apologise that I responded with such rage. The truth is that … what you mentioned … is so personal and dangerous that we never speak of it."

"I understand," Roza replied. "Apology accepted, and no lasting damage was done. I also regret that I inadvertently angered and upset you so much." She shivered. "I'm cold. May I light the fires?"

The Emperor seemed to smile at her and nodded. Roza prepared her Enflame magic and went around clicking fireballs into the flame-pits, and soon the coals inside were burning merrily to warm them.

When she stood in front of the Emperor again, Roza said, "Your Majesty, our business here is urgent. While we slept, the soldiers on both sides have been fighting and dying at Gorge City. With your permission, may we continue our discussion of last night? Have you had the chance to consider my proposal?"

The Emperor's words were slow and careful. "I have indeed thought long and hard about your offer. The cold night air cleared my mind, and I cannot deny that I am keen to return to my original age, to my former size and strength. I am also amazed and intrigued by your ability to enlarge treasure. Your proposal of friendship holds great appeal because I have developed a healthy respect for you, Miss Rozabella. I am sorry that my fit of anger interrupted our negotiations, because I wish to understand more clearly what you ask of me in return."

Roza glanced at Jorxy, who nodded, and she swallowed hard before speaking. This was perhaps her one chance to lay out all she wished to gain from the Emperor. "As you know, sire, I offer to rejuvenate people free of charge. I can also make people older if they wish, although you may be one of the few who wants this. I am willing to use my unique ability to enlarge treasure if it is for the common good rather than for anyone's personal gain. But our experiences at the gates of Albany taught us that my abilities are so powerful that they come with consequences. Whether I intend it or not, my choices and actions seem to end up changing the world."

"They do indeed, Miss Warlock," rumbled the Dragon, "which is why we need to be as careful and as far-sighted as we can be in what we agree together."

"Exactly." Roza realised she was trembling inside and so paced back and forth to try to calm herself. "I travelled here yesterday, sire, in the hope of stopping a war. People are fighting and dying as we speak, and I can't stand the thought of anyone fighting over me, or of a war being waged to control me. I see only one way to end this civil war, this war for immortality, which is for you to win it quickly. I don't think Lord Vallance can win it, and I can't see the two of you negotiating a peace anytime soon."

The Emperor was shaking his head.

"But what concerns me just as much," Roza went on, "is what comes afterwards. As you said, sire, we need to be as far-sighted as we can be. Suppose your victory over the Earl of the Plains is a narrow and hard-fought one. That would leave your Imperial Army weakened and other Lords across your Empire might choose to rebel and claim independence. The danger of continuing civil war is too great, whereas a powerful Dragon Emperor would be sufficient to win this war quickly and deter others in the future."

The Dragon nodded. "I agree."

"But my desire is that a powerful Dragon Emperor should not rule through might and invincibility alone. A reign of oppression and fear is no solid basis for a lasting peace."

The Emperor's eyes widened at this and Roza forced out a nervous laugh. "I'm not suggesting that's how you've been ruling, Your Majesty, but simply that a reign of justice and respect encourages virtues that lead to prosperity and peace. Would you agree?"

"I begin to understand your point of view, Miss Rozabella, but I remain to be convinced of its effectiveness."

Roza heaved a relieved breath because this sounded like progress. "We agree, sire, that we need to be careful about the conclusions we come to today, and to act in the best interests of all the citizens of the Empire. That prevents me from aging you back to your former strength without some guarantees that you will rule us in a just, peaceable, and fatherly way. I refuse to have on my conscience that I allowed any reign of greed or fear."

"I refute, of course, the way you characterise my former rule, but accept that this encompasses what you mean by 'being nicer to my subjects'."

It was time to come to the point. "My price, therefore,"

Roza declared, "in return for using my reverse Rejuvenation on you, and for Maximising your treasure, is that you need to tell me your – forgive me – your true name."

She braced herself for the reaction, ready with Barrier, Repulser and Teleport if needed, but although a fire lit up the Dragon's eyes, there was no attack. This time, he was expecting it.

Again, the Emperor's words were slow and careful, hissed through clenched teeth. "Young Miss Warlock, you do not understand what you are asking. The reason why we Dragons do not speak of what you mentioned is because letting anyone know our … our true name … renders us completely vulnerable. We can be summoned and commanded at will. We surrender our autonomy and identity. We lay ourselves entirely at the disposal of the master we serve. No self-respecting Dragon could ever willingly put themselves in that position."

Roza knew she needed to hold her nerve. "I understand that I am asking a lot of you, but I am also offering much. You will be unrivalled in power, ruling an Empire at peace. You can also be immortal, maintaining whatever age in life you wish. You will have wealth surpassing the combined treasures of all the Dragons who have ever lived. These benefits are worth some compromise of dignity and pride, are they not?"

"They are indeed worthy prizes to gain but you must understand, Miss Warlock, that it is against the nature of an Emperor to have anyone in command over them. If someone has authority and power over me, then I am no longer the Emperor. It is as simple as that. Even if I swear to be nicer to my subjects, I will not abdicate my Imperial authority to another."

Roza could feel any agreement to this deal slipping away through her fingers and she tried desperately to keep hold of it. "Your Majesty, if you will not tell me your true name, then I also refuse to use any of my gifts or abilities to help you, because that is my price."

The Dragon's expression hardened. "Then so be it. Because I vow and swear to you, Miss Rozabella, Warlock of Albany, that I will never, ever tell you my true name."

Roza's insides were stricken with grief. No, this couldn't be happening, that everything was now falling apart. They had come so far, survived so much, risked so much, and now all for nothing.

She sagged and turned away towards Jorxy. He held her arm, and said, "For any negotiation to work, we need to be willing to walk away. We can't allow him to get what he wants with no guarantees that he'll change. You did well, Roza. We almost got there, and it's not your fault there isn't a deal."

But Roza couldn't help feeling that this failure was all her responsibility. The war would continue, soldiers would fight and die, Lord Vallance and the Dragon Emperor would remain as selfish, greedy and power-hungry as each other, and the Empire would fall apart into ruin and death.

All because she'd messed up this one chance to bring peace and justice to the Empire.

CHAPTER TWENTY-FOUR

Roza walked away. She couldn't face any more of the talking, thinking or feeling. She wanted to be alone, but Jorxy came after her.

"Wait, Roza, where are you going?"

He caught up to her, but she tried to keep walking. He grabbed her into a hug and held her. She surrendered to the embrace and the tears came. She wept into his shoulder, shaking, clinging to him.

"It's over," she sobbed. "We've failed. I can't do this any more. It's too hard. I give up."

Jorxy didn't say anything but stroked her back until her tears and shaking eased.

Then Roza managed, "What can we do? Go away and hide somewhere, leaving them all to it until this war is over and everyone is dead? That is, if he'll let us escape from this place and not throw us in his dungeons or burn us to a crisp."

"My Roza," Jorxy breathed at last, "don't despair. You've always been the one with the hope. You've still got those gifts he wants so much. Okay, we haven't got there yet, but you came very close, and we might still work something out. Come back and sit down."

Roza straightened and wiped her face. "I'm sorry, I'm a mess."

Jorxy nodded. "A complete disgrace."

And the twitch of a smile in the corner of his lopsided mouth was enough. She let him take her hand and lead her back towards the toppled bronze thrones and treasure pile. Standley was still there, and Roza wondered whether he and the Emperor had said anything to each other.

"My friends," the Dragon Emperor boomed, "if I may still call you that, we have worked hard this morning. Let me do you the courtesy of offering you some refreshment and we can break our fast together."

He beat his tail twice on the stone floor of the cavern and it gave a shuddering thud. In answer to this signal, servants came hurrying in through the darkness bearing all manner of tables, implements, food and drink. The main item was a carcass of meat roasting on a spit, which they set up over one of the fire-pits. The servants righted the toppled bronze thrones and set tables before the seats for Roza and Jorxy. They didn't know what to make of Standley, and Jorxy informed them that their coat stand didn't need to eat or drink.

Roza slumped into her throne, but couldn't face even a sip of wine, or to nibble a corner of the roast meat they brought her. She was hungry but had no appetite for any of it. She watched the Dragon's claws and teeth tear into strips of meat from a large bone and wondered how she'd ever hoped that such different creatures could find common ground. Maybe Dragons were meant to rule Empires, and mortal humans were meant to be their slaves.

No, she wouldn't believe that. Unable to stay seated, she pushed her table away and got to her feet. Jorxy wouldn't let her walk away again, so not caring what she did any more, she clambered up the Dragon's treasure pile and threw herself down next to his right foreleg.

Jorxy had been eating but now stared in alarm as she perched next to the Dragon's lethal claws and teeth. Part of her hoped he might flex his claws, tear her in half and end her misery. She was raised up enough on the pile to gain a different view of the cavern, looking down on Jorxy and Standley, and level with the Emperor's head instead of looking up at him.

"I'm sorry we haven't managed to reach an agreement this morning," the Dragon Emperor rumbled beside her.

Roza didn't reply but absent-mindedly picked up some of the mound's gold and silver coins and flicked them to roll down the slope.

He spoke into her silence again. "It was very brave of you to come here and face me again, when I had declared you my enemy."

Roza sighed. "I hoped to make a real difference to the Empire."

The Dragon looked at her sideways. "You have made a difference already, Miss Roza. I begin to see why Sapien Standley thinks so highly of you, because you have given me much to think about. Your openness and honesty in our conversations, your desire for peace, kindness and generosity are all most refreshing."

Roza forced out a smile. "You mean we can at least agree not to be enemies?"

The Emperor definitely smiled back. "Agreed. Not enemies." He lifted a claw and Roza shook it as a deal. "But come now, Miss Roza, I'm curious about something else. That spirit lord creature, Kerenzi, who was with you at Albany's gates. Have you seen him since?"

She remembered that Kerenzi refused to come here because of the Dragon's grudge against him, so she needed to be careful about what she said. "Yes, he visited me on the plateau and during our travels, mostly to bring me news about what was happening on the Plains and across the wider Empire. You should know that he rescued me when I was trapped in Bindweed in Lord Vallance's dungeons, so we have him to thank for that."

The Emperor's eyes widened. "Did he really? Then he has gone up the slightest fraction in my estimation."

"Yes, it was a narrow escape for both of us. I was so determined not to get caught in a Bindweed net again that I set fire to it. Kerenzi had warned me that Bindweed smoke is equally as vicious as the ropes, and I Teleported us out of there with only a second to spare."

"So Kerenzi risked his own magic and safety to help you escape? I will mark that down to his credit."

"Does this mean you forgive him for his part in weakening you at Albany? I don't know what ill-will from the past he bore towards you, but I hope that our friendship can heal past hurts and grievances."

The Emperor turned away from attacking the meat and regarded her sideways again. "You have an instinct to heal and forgive and reconcile, which is most commendable, Miss Roza. So, for your sake, I promise I will not kill the spirit lord Kerenzi immediately on sight."

Roza managed a smile. "Well, I suppose that's progress anyway." She watched the Emperor and Jorxy eating and enjoyed the warmth rising from the fire-pits. After a while, she asked, "So, what happens now? The fighting at Gorge City continues until one side or the other gains the upper hand, and at the same time you try to keep control of the rest of your Empire?"

The Dragon let out a long, smoky breath. "It is very frustrating, you know, being cooped up in here, when there is so much need for my presence on the battlefield. But I dare not risk it."

"Because of Lord Vallance's ballistae, you mean? Could they really injure you?"

"Ah, you've heard about those, have you? Could they injure me? Yes, probably. I have felt the bite of iron arrows from those weapons in the past, and that was when my armour was stronger. I dare not risk a lucky strike from one of them penetrating between my scales and causing me serious injury."

Roza nodded, and after a pause started thinking out loud. "I wonder what I should do now. It seems that everyone in the Empire is still hunting for me, and my risk of being kidnapped and imprisoned remains as high as ever. Where can I go to be safe?"

The Emperor looked at her again. "You may stay here if you wish. That is, if you feel safe here. It is one of the best protected fortresses anywhere. Your friends can stay too, and I will be happy to provide for your needs."

Roza gave him another smile. "Thank you, that's very kind and hospitable of you. It seems my good influence must be rubbing off on you after all." And they both chuckled. "But look at us, the two most famous and powerful creatures in the whole Sapien Empire, and we're reduced to hiding away in a hilltop cavern for our own safety. How did it come to this, eh?"

The Dragon smiled again, and Roza was surprised at how companionable this felt. Here they were, the Dragon Emperor and the young warlock of immortality, sitting side by side on a mound of treasure and chatting away like old friends.

"So, tell me," she asked, "since I've got one of you old people to talk to, what was it like when you were young? I don't know how old Standley is, and the immortal Kerenzi told me he is tens of thousands of years old, but it sounds like you are younger than either of them."

"The history of this Empire is a very long tale, my girl, and I won't bore you with it now, but yes, I am younger than those two. I established my position over this Empire over a period of many centuries. The spirits of the forests, and their lords such as Kerenzi, always kept to themselves, not bothering much with the affairs of mortals and their Empires. But those we call the Sapiens, who founded this Empire and after whom it is named, are much older and wiser than any others alive today."

"And you recognised my enchanted coat stand, Standley, as one of those? An ancient and wise founder of this Empire?"

"Yes, indeed, and I could hardly believe it. I heard that many Sapiens died or were killed, went away or were driven out, or otherwise faded into obscurity like your Standley here. Who can say how many of them are left in the world today? But if you want to know more about the history of the Sapiens, then the person to ask is that Irvine, your

Master of the Warlocks."

They lapsed into silence, and Roza's thoughts wandered away into dreams of these ancient Sapiens travelling the world, founding their Empire that would endure for all time.

At length, Roza clambered back down the treasure pile and sat next to Jorxy.

"Were you and the Emperor having a nice little chat, then? Discover anything useful?"

Roza shrugged. "He says we can stay here if we want, but other than that, not really. We're still in the same place of having come this close and yet can't reach an agreement."

Jorxy scratched his neck. "Yeah, the sticking point is this true name thing. You insist on knowing it, and he won't share it."

"Come on then, Mister Ideas Man, how can we get round this one? What would you do in my place?"

Jorxy rested his chin on his hands. "It all comes down to the guarantees," he muttered. "Perhaps what you need is a middleman, a go-between, someone you both trust who can stand between your two sides."

"Yeah, well, I trust you, Jorx, but he doesn't know you at all. And who else is there?"

As she said this, both their heads turned towards their coat stand.

Roza froze, staring. A stupendous, wonderful idea had occurred, and she trembled inside at the hope of it. She jerked her head back to Jorxy's face, who was also looking between Standley and her, a slow grin spreading.

Could this possibly work? But she didn't want to betray her thoughts, and she needed to be careful.

She got up slowly and wandered over to where Standley stood to one side of the circle of bronze thrones. It seemed incredible that this simple piece of polished wooden furniture, whom she'd met as a lowly domestic servant in Warlock Philoe's cave, was some revered founder of the whole Sapien Empire.

"Um, Standley," Roza said, touching him, "I hope it's all right that we've been talking about you, but could you hear what we've been saying?"

He nodded slowly as he regarded her.

"You've helped us so much already," she went on, "but would you be willing to help us with something very important?"

At once Standley stepped forward with her towards the Dragon Emperor.

Roza drew in a deep breath. "Please don't be angry with me, sire, but I've had an idea that I hope might help us to reach an agreement. Please will you dismiss all the servants from the cavern, and let me explain it to you?"

"My dear Miss Roza," the Emperor replied, "I would be delighted if we can find a way to agree our deal. Leave us," he ordered the servants, and they scurried away.

When the last distant door closed and the cavern was silent again, Roza began, "I understand, sire, that you don't trust me enough to share your true name with me. But maybe someone we both respect could be an arbiter and intermediary between us. Would you be willing to share your true name with Standley here on the understanding that he keeps it absolutely secret except in uttermost need? I trust him enough, that if he knows your true name, I will age you and Maximise your treasure, and don't need to know your true name myself. So, could you trust Standley enough, a founder of our Sapien Empire, for him to keep this secret forever, and allow us to agree our deal and end this war?"

The Dragon Emperor raised his head and licked his lips. She'd piqued his interest and not provoked a fit of rage. This was good.

"Warlock Rozabella," he rumbled. "Let me be sure that I understand you. I would share my true name, in private, with the Sapien Standley, on the understanding that he would never tell it to anyone else. Or only under what circumstances?"

Roza was thinking fast. "Only if, for example, you tried to use violence against me to force me into something against my will. Or if you abandon all intention to rule the Empire justly and peaceably, and indulge in cruelty, greed or oppression. Only then would Standley be at liberty to share your true name with one other. But so long as you agree to work with me, to follow my suggestions of kindness, generosity and respect, then your true name will remain secret with him forever."

The Dragon narrowed his eyes. "Which would happen first? Me sharing my true name with Standley or you aging me back to my previous size?"

She tried to work this out. "You would need to give it to Standley first," she insisted, "otherwise you've already got what you want before we get any assurance or guarantee."

"But Standley is your servant," the Emperor objected. "You can order him to tell you whatever you want to know."

"Before you share anything with Standley, I will order him never to reveal his secret to me, or to anyone else, unless he thinks that your actions and the circumstances in the Empire warrant it."

There was a silence while Roza chewed her lip and the Dragon Emperor's gaze flitted between her and Standley and back again.

"Are you willing to do this, Standley?" the Emperor asked. "Do you understand the importance of what we're discussing here, and how crucial it is that we can all trust you to keep this secret, and act in due course only out of your deepest wisdom to safeguard our Sapien Empire from my possible future violence or oppression?"

The coat stand nodded gravely, and Roza wondered whether he added more reassurance by thought to persuade the Emperor. Roza trusted Standley completely, for he'd saved her life on various occasions, and she prayed that the respect between Standley and the Emperor was sufficient for this task also.

When she could bear the tense silence no longer, Roza ventured, "So, do we have a deal?"

The Dragon Emperor gave a deep rumble in his chest before saying, "Hmm, I do believe we find ourselves with an agreement."

Roza couldn't stop herself from jumping in the air, heedless of the serious moment. Jorxy punched her shoulder, and they hugged each other in celebration. Relief and happiness flooded through Roza, and she couldn't help grinning.

She turned to face the Emperor. "Thank you, Your Majesty. I pray this is our first step towards a growing trust between us, a bond of friendship and cooperation that no one and nothing will break."

"I hope so too, young Miss Rozabella, and I commend your determination and resourcefulness towards making our Empire a better place. Now, if I understand your intentions correctly, you wish to end the fighting at Gorge City as soon as we may. Let us then proceed to implement our plan at once."

She gave him a bow and went to Standley, touching his hooks. "My dear enchanted coat stand, I am in your debt, and the whole Sapien Empire owes you gratitude for what you accept today. But now, as your mistress, I command you to keep this secret for ever. Under no circumstances are you to reveal the Dragon Emperor's true name, either to me, or to anyone else, unless you consider that the actions of the Emperor, or the circumstances in the Empire, are so catastrophic that it is the only option left to you. Do you accept this charge and agree to its terms?"

Standley nodded solemnly and bowed as low as he could, and for the first time Roza heard in her mind the word, "Yes."

Her mouth dropped open, and she stared at him, grinning. "I heard you!" And his eye knots scrunched up, and he tottered forward to embrace her.

When they parted, Roza turned to face Jorxy. "The two of us also must promise never to reveal this agreement. What Standley holds in secret is highly dangerous information, for him, for the Emperor and for the Empire. So, we both say: I, Warlock Rozabella of Albany," – and Jorxy added his name – "promise never to reveal what I have witnessed here today. In the presence of the Dragon Emperor and the Sapien Standley, I vow that this secret will never be mentioned to anyone, or even discussed among ourselves, on pain of death, for as long as I live."

They bowed to each other, to Standley and the Emperor, and Roza felt relieved for the formalities to be over.

"Very good," said the Emperor. "Now, my old friend Standley, let me take you to the most private place I know to reveal to you what I must." The Dragon clambered down from his treasure mound, let the coat stand skitter up onto his back, and beat his wings to fly them out of the cavern and into the morning air outside.

Roza and Jorxy turned to each other and grinned at the light and hope in their faces. "Now," Roza said, "while we wait for those two to come back, I'm starving. Let me stuff myself with some breakfast. I deserve it."

While she ate, Roza wandered over to the Emperor's treasure pile, and absent-mindedly Maximised some gold coins, gems, and pieces of jewellery to giant size for him. It couldn't hurt, she reckoned, to reward his trust so far with this gesture of goodwill.

An hour or more later, when the Dragon Emperor and Standley flew back into the cavern, Roza was still finishing off extra helpings of the roast meat, bread, cheese, milk, wine, and everything else she could find, with Jorxy keeping her company. She jumped up to greet them and had never imagined seeing the Dragon Emperor looking so anxious or distressed. That alone confirmed that his true name had been shared, but she still felt it necessary to ask Standley,

"All done and checked?"

When her coat stand nodded and bowed, Roza went to stand before the Emperor. "Thank you, Your Majesty, and I understand how keen you are for me to fulfil my part of the bargain, so let us proceed to it at once."

The Dragon seemed incapable of speech but ran off to lie in the centre of the cavern's vast open space. Roza hurried after him, instructing Jorxy and Standley to remain by the treasure pile and bronze thrones.

As Roza approached the Dragon Emperor's prostrate form in the gloomy half-light of the cavern, she remembered touching this mountainous and legendary beast on a bright afternoon outside Albany. Then she'd hoped to save her hometown from destruction, but this time she had a civil war to stop, the lives of many soldiers to save, and the future of the whole Sapien Empire in her hands. And it all depended on her accelerating this Dragon's natural aging process through a magical spell she'd tried only once before on a handful of seeds.

Roza gulped and wiped her sweaty palms down her trousers. She'd better get this started before her shaking limbs and trembling inside made it impossible.

"We will need your own magic to help with this transformation, sire," she told him, "but not too much and not too quickly. We must work gradually and carefully, making no mistakes this time, because so much depends on its success. Please slow and stop the process as you approach the age and size you wish to be. And don't send any magic my way until you feel my magic flow into you."

The Dragon nodded dumbly, and Roza guessed his desperation to complete this as soon as possible. "Please don't worry, sire, because I'm sure we can achieve this together." She tried a smile up at him, but her own nerves made it feel like a grimace.

He rolled his head to reveal the softer underside of his neck, and she placed her hands on the cracks where his scales met, reaching her fingertips to touch the flesh beneath. She closed her eyes, reached inside her for the spark of magic and ignited the fire. When it was burning steadily, she began to channel it through her Rejuvenate gift, but the wrong way round, back-to-front, inside out, and upside-down, like with the grain seeds up in the mountains.

Again, the magic resisted her, feeling this to be wrong, but she persisted through the awkwardness because this was what the Emperor wanted. Don't send the lifecycle backwards towards youth, she told herself, but advancing, marching forwards with time, towards maturity, ripeness, seniority. She began to send her magic out through her hands and into the Dragon Emperor's body.

It was working. She felt the adolescent Dragon become a young adult, and suddenly the Dragon's magic joined with hers and it was a torrent and a flood she couldn't control. So desperate was the Emperor to be back to full strength that he was in danger of rushing it. It became a wild, reckless ride, threatening to overwhelm and de-rail her focus.

"Less, Your Majesty, slower, please," she gasped, but the Dragon was growing fast under her hands. The scales were hardening, the cracks widening, the vast bulk of his body expanding to become a mountainside before her.

Roza gritted her teeth and clenched her hands because she needed to control and slow this, otherwise the Emperor was careering towards the withering, shrivelling, dying end of the process. But what could she do? If she couldn't stem the Dragon's magic flowing into her body, it would overheat and burn her up from the inside. She needed to stop it coming.

She tried to wrench her hands away from the Dragon's scales, but found she couldn't, because the deluge of magical energy held them bonded there. And she couldn't cast Barrier or Repulser without using her hands.

But her desire to stop it caused a massive jolt in the flow, with the effect of a Repulser slapping him across the face and shoving him away. The magic backfired into the Dragon, and he yelped.

"You must stop it, sire," Roza yelled. "Calm down and let me manage this. I know what I'm doing, don't rush me."

The Dragon's magic stopped flowing into her and slowly Roza regained control, emptying the built-up fire through her arms and her reverse Rejuvenation gift into the Emperor's body. She probed with her magic throughout his massive bulk, trusting the magic to find what needed aging equally and evenly all over, his internal organs, his armour of scales, his bones, muscle and flesh to support his mountainous frame.

How old was he now? Was this the age he wanted? He'd passed quickly through adult and middle aged towards mature and old. Roza estimated this might be correct, so she slowed the process, let the fire inside her die down, and stopped.

She opened her eyes and gasped. The adolescent Dragon before her had risen to become a metal-hard wall of scales. The Emperor who had lain in the centre of an empty space of cavern now filled it. She removed her hands from his neck and looked around.

Roza couldn't see Jorxy or Standley, because she was surrounded by the Dragon Emperor's skull and neck, his muscular forearm, and the canopy of a wing as wide and high as the invisible roof. She stepped back, filling up with fear that she'd resurrected a monster. She edged around towards the Dragon's face and looked up, but his eyes were closed.

"Your Majesty?" she called. "I'm sorry I had to stop and send your magic back, but you were in danger of aging too far and too fast. You needed to trust me to do this carefully and properly, and I think we've succeeded. Sire?"

For a terrible moment Roza feared something had gone horribly wrong, that she'd killed the Emperor, for his mountain of a body remained quiet and still. Then he drew in a massive breath, a gale of wind filling the cavern, and the wall of scales down his side expanded towards her. She stepped further back and breathed out in relief.

A deep boom echoed around the cavern as the now mature Dragon spoke. "You know, I'd forgotten how this felt. To be so … large. The twinges and stiffness here and there. No longer the sprightly energy of a youngster. But still, such is the price I pay to be invulnerable and fearsome again. Warlock Rozabella, I thank you."

"In the end, I guessed what age you wanted to be. Not as ancient as you were, but still old enough, I think. Do you agree?"

The Emperor stirred, flexing his muscles, and Roza retreated towards the cavern wall as the Dragon stood up. Looking up, she thought the spikes on the ridge down his back must nearly scrape the roof, and the span of his unfolding wings reach from wall to wall.

"Yes, Miss Rozabella, I think this will do fine. Now, where are your friends?"

Roza called them, and before long, Jorxy and Standley trotted towards her around the Emperor's hind leg, which now resembled a hillside. They carried the packs, and Jorxy gazed up in trepidation at this creature who now shared the cavern with them.

Roza had a nagging doubt that the Emperor – having received what he wanted most – might decide to amend their agreement, so she said, "We are doing well, Your Majesty. You have trusted us with something precious to you, and we have trusted you by giving you what you need. What steps should we take next? I've already enlarged some of your treasure, so I suggest ending this civil war is our most urgent matter now."

To her relief, the Emperor answered, "Quite so, Miss Roza. I must go to Gorge City at once, and it is only right that you all come with me. I will order my Imperial Army to stop their attack and withdraw from assaulting the city."

"But how on earth can we come with you?" Jorxy asked. "Will you grab us in your claws and carry us there?"

The Emperor rumbled a chuckle. "Not unless you want to travel that way, Master Jorxy, because I imagine it would be uncomfortable. I invite the three of you to ride on my back, as Standley did, holding on between the spikes down my spine, as the proper way for a Dragon to transport his friends."

CHAPTER TWENTY-FIVE

The Dragon Emperor had to learn how to manoeuvre within his cavern again, because he kept scraping his wings or lashing his tail against the walls. Only one of the cavern openings was large enough to allow his ancient body to pass through, so to reach this he needed to turn completely around.

As he shifted his massive bulk, Roza kept pace with his head and talked to him. "How do you feel now, sire? Before I aged you, there was a period when you seemed most anxious and distressed. I'm sorry we stretched your trust in us to the limit."

"You are perceptive, Miss Roza. It was the most unnerving experience of my long life. I had made myself vulnerable and not yet received your side of the bargain as you'd promised. It was a humbling feeling – and no doubt you'll say that was beneficial for me – to place myself at the mercy of your goodness and trustworthiness. And you have not disappointed me, which leads me to trust you more."

Roza beamed. "I see you grasp the main point, Your Majesty. Trust is not grabbed or given away; it needs to be earned. We are earning each other's friendship, and I look forward to when that grows further."

Instead of making his passengers climb up the side of his vast body, the Emperor consented to roll on his side. With their packs on their backs, Roza, Jorxy and Standley each took hold of a spine spike and clung on for dear life as he rolled back upright. Neither Roza nor Jorxy considered themselves safe or comfortable at this height near the cavern roof, but Standley looked to be enjoying himself, wandering along the Dragon's back, holding on with only a hook or two.

At last, it was time to take flight, and they braced

themselves for the hurricane-force wind of the Dragon's wings and the soaring power of his muscles in launching them skywards. The Emperor crouched his way through the arch of the opening and then catapulted himself away from the hilltop, and Roza felt the beating of his mighty wings.

Her eyes were firmly closed, and her arm and leg muscles ached from holding on as tightly as she could. The wind blew cold in her face from the speed of their flight, and she tried to grip the Dragon's scaled back with her boots and knees. When they had not fallen or crashed yet, Roza cracked open her eyelids and gasped.

The land had fallen away below them, and heavy clouds seemed close above. A panorama of hills and forests passed underneath, small and distant as though viewed from a mountain summit. A momentary panic gripped her about the lack of any clear landing ground if they needed one, but the Dragon's flight was smooth and confident enough to need no landing.

Her eyes watered from the fierce wind, so she turned her head to look sideways. The corner of her eye caught Jorxy looking as sick and fearful as she felt, but he was cursing and swearing with this ordeal. Standley, by contrast, was standing aloft, holding on at the rear with no more than a few hooks despite the wind, peering down the Emperor's sides at the land passing below. He appeared to be enjoying himself immensely, relishing the flight as though he was one of the fabled Dragon Riders of old.

Roza cautiously relaxed her taut and aching muscles and discovered that she didn't fall or get blown away. It occurred to her to fix this in her memory, a moment in her life which might never come again, riding on the Dragon Emperor's back from his northern fortress across the Plains of the Sapien Empire to try to halt a war. Was this the day when the Imperial Army and the Gorge City defenders would behold their Emperor in his former strength and lay down their weapons so the war for immortality could end?

The hills and forests below had petered out and been replaced by bare and undulating plains. The Emperor angled his head and neck downwards and they began to descend, so Roza gripped tighter again. She saw occasional farms, fields and villages pass below, and then an Imperial Army camp came into view.

The Emperor had been heading for this spot, for he let out a roar as he approached, making Roza jump. Having gained the attention of everyone below, he called down his orders, "Hold your positions. The war is ending. Await further instructions."

He made an impressive swoop low over the camp, angling his wings in a controlled glide, and Roza caught the shouts and cheers from the troops below. The Dragon beat his wings to gain more height, and she felt the first spots of rain on her arms and face. Looking ahead, the heavy clouds were dropping their rain, and they would all get soaked. It had to be near midday, but there was no glimpse of the sun.

The Dragon Emperor passed low over other Imperial Army camps, giving his instructions, and then through the rain Roza saw a fortified town on a hilltop. The Dragon swerved downwards in their approach, for the town looked under siege from encampments of Imperial soldiers.

This time the Emperor called down different orders. "Return to your camp. Abandon your siege and assault on this town. The war will end soon and there will be peace."

And then to the defenders: "Soldiers of the Plains Army and citizens of the Empire, return to your homes and put away your weapons. We have no further cause to fight each other. Let there be no more bloodshed. I fly now to Gorge City to meet with your Earl of the Plains, so await the instructions of his officials, for peace is coming."

They made a couple of low circuits around the town, repeating the message, and Roza saw astonished and fearful faces staring up at them, with a first few cheers from those who believed the war might really be over.

As they rose in the sky and continued southwards, there were unmistakeable signs of battle and destruction below. Smoke rose through the rain from burned out buildings, and there were piles of bodies. The roads and lanes were littered with broken carts, abandoned catapults, dead horses, discarded weapons and armour, blood-soaked mud, and more corpses.

Roza's stomach clenched. They hadn't acted in time to prevent all the fighting and death, but at least – she told herself – it should stop now. The land passing beneath them had frequent battlefields scarring it, with a few buildings, trees, and haystacks still in flames under the rain. The red of the fires caught the Dragon Emperor's glistening scales as his wings kept on beating their way to Gorge City.

The Emperor repeated his messages to settlements and companies of soldiers below, but Roza's nerves were rising over how this flight might end. What would happen when they arrived at Gorge City?

It was too much to hope that Lord Vallance would take one look at the newly enlarged Emperor and capitulate. The sight of the Dragon would send the Plains soldiers scurrying away to their homes and families, but the Earl of the Plains wasn't the sort to admit defeat easily. Would there be a final battle between these two leaders, a last stand, when the hardness of Dragon scales would be tested against the spears of the Gorge City ballistae?

At last, the towers and walls of the capital of the Plains came into view. The Emperor began to climb, flying higher and wider around the city, circling above his own troops first. He called down his orders, "Withdraw to your camps, cease your attacks on the city, for I come to bring peace. To my generals, await further instructions from me."

Roza peered down through the rain and tried to make out the deep red of the Imperial Army uniforms moving back from the city, and the longer she watched, the clearer that became.

Then she turned her attention to the towers, walls and gates of Gorge City, where there was much shouting, pointing and confusion. The first sight of the Dragon might have led the defenders to prepare their chance to stick a ballista arrow through their weakened and vulnerable enemy. But the closer the Emperor flew, his restored size must have become clearer.

Steadily, the Dragon circled lower and closer to the towers and ramparts of Gorge City until one by one those who manned the ballistae tried their luck at spearing him. These all fell short, but before he came any closer, the Emperor called out to the whole city and those who defended it.

"Hold your fire, Soldiers of the Plains," he bellowed. "Save your ballista arrows, for they cannot pierce my armour. My Imperial Army is withdrawing from your gates and walls because I wish to end this war. Let there be no more fighting or bloodshed because I come to parley with your Lord Vallance, the Earl of this city. Let him meet me at the city's West Gate."

This prompted another volley of ballista arrows, so the Dragon veered away further out of range. The Emperor turned his head towards Roza on his back, and said, "I need to appeal to the soldiers themselves and offer them more. May I tell them I have you with me?"

"Go ahead," Roza called back.

The next time the Dragon circled back over the city, he called down again, "Citizens of Gorge City, I have no wish to fight you. Please return to your homes, put away your weapons and let there be peace between us. My only quarrel is with the Earl of the Plains, and I seek to come to terms with him. As a token of goodwill, I bring to you, riding on my back, young Rozabella, the Warlock of Albany. Together, she and I offer you a new era of peace, prosperity, and immortality. Let today be the day this war ends."

On their next pass, Roza peered down on the city walls,

where there looked to be confusion. Some commanders seemed to be ordering their soldiers to issue from the gates and pursue the retreating Imperial Army. Others were still at their posts, but it was unclear whether any were following the Emperor's invitation to disarm and stand down.

Ballista arrows were still being launched skywards, and one even bounced off the Dragon's scales. Hearing the tone of the Emperor's next message, Roza couldn't blame him for his patience wearing thin.

"Let me repeat," he boomed, "your arrows cannot hurt me. I do not wish to breathe fire over any of you but be assured that I can now reduce this entire city to smoke and ashes if you refuse to come to a parley. Let Lord Vallance meet me at the West Gate."

To underline his point, the Dragon breathed a jet of flame into the air over the gorge, vaporising the rain in front of them, and sending a flurry of sparks and cinders over the city in a cloud of smoke and steam.

As they wheeled away, the Emperor turned his head again, calling, "Miss Rozabella, is there something you can do to show them who you are? To prove you're a warlock?"

"Um … fireballs?" Roza suggested.

The Dragon nodded as he beat his wings and banked around again. Roza prepared her Enflame spell and clicked her fingers to send balls of fire alternately left and right down the Emperor's sides as they flew over the city. The fires made an impressive stream of descending lights behind and below them but were quenched by the rain before landing on any roofs.

"Behold," the Dragon Emperor called again. "Here is Warlock Rozabella of Albany, riding on my back, showing herself by her Enflame spell. But neither of us wish to rain fire on you, only peace, prosperity and immortality. Please, my people, let this war end."

On their next flight over the city, the Dragon's keen eyes spotted something, which he relayed to his passengers. "Ah,

I see Lord Vallance's bodyguard heading for the West Gate. Perhaps he is among them. Come, let us find somewhere to land west of the city."

The rain was easing as they headed away towards the mountains and began to descend. They were well out of ballista range of the walls and towers when the Emperor touched down in a field. His landing caused farm workers and soldiers to run away as fast as they could – not to mention the panicked grazing animals – but no one dared to approach or attack them.

"Miss Rozabella," the Dragon called over his shoulder, "I advise you to stay on my back and cast whatever protective spells you know."

"Of course," Roza replied, and heard a groan from Jorxy behind her.

"I want to get off!" he shouted.

She turned and was shocked by how ill he looked. There was vomit down both the Dragon's sides below his perch, which was only gradually being washed clean by the rain.

"Oh, Jorx, I'm sorry," she called. "We'll be safer up here, and we'll dismount as soon as we can, I promise."

Standley behind him looked healthier, his polished wood glistening with rain.

Before the Dragon Emperor moved nearer, Roza stood up on his back and twirled to cast Barrier around the three of them. She sat down as he stepped steadily closer to Gorge City's West Gate and got ready to follow up with Repulser if necessary. From her high seat between the ridge spines on the Dragon's back, she was level with the top of the Gorge City guard towers.

With a jolt, she recognised this as the same gatehouse where they'd entered the city some days before on their way in from Enoch and Celeste's farmhouse. The contrast now with their arrival in secret anonymity, sitting on sacks of grain in the back of a farmer's wagon, was stark.

Roza scanned the turrets and battlements, and her

uneasiness grew as she spotted eight or ten ballistae trained on them. These were as large as catapults but resembled giant crossbows with deadly metal arrows up to five or six feet in length. Their missiles were loaded, their firing wires drawn back, and all aimed at the approaching Dragon. Could the Emperor's metal-hard scales really withstand a well-aimed, short range shot from one of these? Now Roza understood why the Emperor had kept to his northern hilltop refuge until now.

The Dragon stopped well back from the gatehouse and swung his head to left and right in an obvious survey of the scene before him. "I have come to parley with the Earl of the Plains. Is Lord Vallance here?"

A figure in dark blue robes stepped forward to the parapet atop the tower to the left of the gate. "Your Majesty, our noble Dragon Emperor," he called, "welcome to Gorge City. I am your humble servant, the Earl of the Plains."

The Dragon snorted, and a puff of smoke and sparks issued from his nostrils. "Lord Vallance, save your oily flattery and insincere words for those who believe them. I am here to speak plainly with you. Your declaration that the Plains shall be independent of our Sapien Empire has brought unnecessary war to your lands, towns, and cities. Will you withdraw that stance and re-join our family of territories and peoples united under my benevolent leadership?"

"Ah, Your Majesty, I fear it is you who does not speak plainly. For your words describe a family united under your benevolent leadership when your actions speak otherwise. Your taxes place a heavy burden on the meagre purses of your cities and people. It became impossible for the people of this noble city to eat or survive, so I had to act to save their lives."

"Lord Vallance, I call your bluff," the Emperor declared. "You describe my taxes as unbearable, so I make you this offer. I will cancel all your city's taxes due to me from this day forwards, provided you return your allegiance to me and remain within the Empire. What do you say to that?"

Roza saw Lord Vallance lean forward and grip the parapet. "You will cancel all your taxes, you say? But sire, how will you pay for the security and functioning of the Empire without your usual revenues? I am sorry, but this cannot be a genuine offer, but rather some trick or lie to deceive us into further servitude under your oppressive rule."

"How I pay for the running of my Empire is my own concern, Lord Vallance. So, you disbelieve and reject my generous offer? For your words are no more than a veneer, a cover for your desire to be free of any master. Therefore, I make you a further offer. I have been persuaded that my rule from henceforth should be kinder, gentler, more tolerant, more generous, and I have made assurances to that effect. If you remain within my Empire, you will find your lives more peaceful and prosperous."

"You have made assurances, you say, to reform your manner of ruling?" Lord Vallance scoffed. "But these assurances have not been made to me. How can I lend any credence to them until I see the fruit of your words?"

"As evidence of my good faith, I have ceased all attacks on your city and towns and have withdrawn my Imperial Army to their camps. I have come here in person to meet with you despite your ballistae trained on me as we speak. And as for the assurances, they were made to Warlock Rozabella of Albany, who rides upon my back."

"Ah, yes, the slippery warlock girl who escapes from Bindweed nets and locked dungeons in the dead of night and disappears into thin air. Why should I take notice of one who spurns and abuses my hospitality so?"

Roza couldn't restrain herself. "If you call that hospitality, mister Earl of the Plains, then you have much to learn. And the assurances from the Emperor that he will change his ways are more than adequate, otherwise I would not have allied myself with him."

"You are a traitor then to all the Empire's people who long to be free," Lord Vallance snarled, his composure of politeness slipping at last. "For you have allied yourself with a cruel and oppressive tyrant who will enslave and extort from everyone. You should be ashamed of yourself, little girl, and go back home and leave the big boys to deal with the Empire's important matters."

Roza's indignation burned, especially remembering the torture of the Bindweed net, and how this man had treated her parents and friends. "One of the big boys, are you? You don't look so impressive now, without a hired warlock by your side to do your dirty business for you. Where is he, that wretched man you bribed into helping you catch me?"

As she said this, she noticed a man with black robes and a neat beard hovering behind Lord Vallance's shoulder.

"Ah, there he is," she cried. "Hello again, Warlock Morton, how pleasant to see you. What's the matter, no Bindweed net to throw at me this time? No, silly me, of course not, because I burned it, didn't I?"

The Dragon Emperor intervened in their taunts. "Warlock Morton," he rumbled, "if I were you, I would leave this city before you find yourself on the losing side."

Roza saw him look from the Dragon to Lord Vallance and back again before throwing his arms straight up in the air and vanishing, the movements for the Teleport spell. She hoped it was the last time she'd ever meet him.

The Emperor spoke again. "Lord Vallance, your rats are scurrying away from your defeated city. I give you one last chance. Surrender to me now, order your men to stand down and hand over control of this city."

"Never," the Earl of the Plains screamed. "And if I can't possess her, then no one will!"

With that, he ran to a ballista and shoved its soldiers aside. "Open fire!"

Before Roza or the Emperor could react, the ballistae

shot their arrows. Most headed for the Dragon, but Lord Vallance raised his ballista's aim, and his missile shot straight for Roza's chest.

She screamed and threw herself sideways on the Dragon's back. The ballista arrow collided with her Barrier spell and deflected away. Roza reacted on instinct, casting a Repulser spell and sending it straight at Lord Vallance to stop him from firing again.

The magic left her fingertips, and the Earl of the Plains catapulted high into the sky above the gatehouse battlements. He hung there, flailing for a second, until a blast of Dragon-fire roared up from below and consumed him.

When the torrent of flames ceased, only a few tatters of burning blue robes, ashes and smoke wafted down towards the city.

CHAPTER TWENTY-SIX

Roza's seat on the Dragon's back shook as he roared. And this was the voice that had split the rocks and shaken the mountains around Albany valley.

"Step away from those infernal weapons," he bellowed. "Otherwise, I will turn both you and them into smoke and ashes as well."

Before he finished speaking, the Plains soldiers were scrambling to abandon their ballistae and get themselves down from the battlements. At the gatehouse and along the walls, it seemed that the death of the Earl in a single burst of Dragon-fire had ended the war. The city defenders were hurrying to their homes and putting away their weapons, as their Emperor had commanded.

Roza swivelled round to check that Jorxy was all right and saw that he looked down towards the Dragon's neck. She followed his gaze and gasped.

Nearly all the Gorge City ballista arrows had bounced harmlessly off the Dragon's scales, but one lucky strike remained embedded in his neck.

"Your Majesty, you're wounded," Roza cried.

"Yes, I am," he complained. "It hasn't hit anything vital, so I won't bleed to death, but it's in my flesh, so it hurts. That's why I breathed fire, to stop any more lucky close-range strikes like this one. Come on, let's get down to the Palace."

Before they could reply, the Dragon Emperor launched himself into the air with a mighty leap and a beat of his wings, so they all lurched and grabbed his back spikes to hold on. With a graceful glide, he soared over the gatehouse and on towards the Sapien Bridge that spanned the midst of the gorge. Passing above that, they descended in wide spirals towards a vast expanse of grass and flagstones across the canyon floor.

Roza hadn't seen the Earl's Palace from the outside, only woken up in Lord Vallance's hall and then Recalled them all from the dungeons. It was easily the largest building she'd ever seen.

They landed on the only flat space large enough to accommodate the Dragon, which fronted a palatial mansion. Roza had never imagined a building with so many floors, or windows, or such vast lengths of marble, stone and brickwork, extending in all directions into wings and outbuildings, with roofs and chimneys, and surrounded by rows of columns.

But as soon as they landed the priority was to attend to the Dragon. He folded his wings and rolled onto his side so they each tumbled onto the grass instead of sliding down his scales. Roza released the spike gratefully, flexing her aching muscles and limbs from the flight. Jorxy collapsed on the lawn and vomited again. Standley jumped down with no apparent ill effects and scuttled off to attend to the Dragon's neck.

By the time Roza reached the wound, Standley had gripped the long metal ballista spear in his hooks and was easing it out from between the Dragon's scales. They needed bandages to stem the bleeding, but where could they find so much fabric quickly?

She spun towards the building and saw huddles of the Palace servants gathered in clumps around the doors. Among them were butlers, maids, cooks and cleaners, so she ran towards them, shouting, "Can you help us, please? We need old or spare sheets, blankets, curtains, or long strips of fabric to use as bandages. As quickly as you can, thank you."

The servants bustled back into the building and soon returned with armfuls of linen, which Roza ferried over to the Dragon's neck. None of the servants would venture near the vast creature, and Standley soon revealed his expertise with bandaging. He held the sheets or blankets in his top hooks and clambered up and down the Dragon's neck using his clawed feet to grip the edges of the scales. He'd removed the arrow, staunched the flow of the Emperor's purple blood with a wad of blankets, and now secured this with circuits of sheeting around his neck.

Once this was done, a pale Jorxy reappeared, wiping his mouth, saying, "I am never climbing onto his back again. What are we supposed to do now?"

The Dragon Emperor replied, "Roza, Jorxy, Standley, you can accommodate yourselves within this Palace. I will stay here tonight to keep order, and to arrange an assembly of the people tomorrow. Everyone in Gorge City needs to hear from us directly about our plans, so go and let them look after you for the evening."

The Emperor turned to address the waiting Palace servants. "These are my guests. Look after them all in the best way you can."

Roza and Jorxy turned to each other and shrugged. "Time to find out how the Earl of the Plains lives for a change?" Jorxy said with a grin.

An elderly man introduced himself as the Chamberlain and invited them to follow him. Roza and Jorxy felt self-consciously out of place in their rough and dirty clothes as they were ushered between lines of waiting servants into a white marble colonnade. Jorxy had vomit on his trousers, and they both bore the marks of mud, sleeping rough and being singed by fire. Standley pottered along behind, looking around at everything, with the servants throwing him amazed and nervous glances.

They were shown into adjoining rooms which were nothing short of palatial. They'd never imagined bedrooms so large, with wide spreads of soft carpets between four-poster beds, plush armchairs and sofas, ornate mirrors and pictures on the walls, embroidered curtains and hangings, and polished wooden dressing tables. Side doors led off to closets filled with clothes, hats, boots and shoes, and to their own personal bathrooms, where hot baths would be ready for them in minutes.

Roza and Jorxy stood in the middle of all this, laughing, and then picked out for themselves the fanciest clothes they could find in the closets. As soon as the baths were ready, they went to their separate bathrooms to strip off their travel-stained clothes and soak in the hot, soapy water.

Once they were dried and dressed, they were conducted to an ornate oak-panelled dining room for the best-tasting meal they'd ever eaten, served to them on the finest bone china, at either side of a polished mahogany table. Gorge City had been at war, but Lord Vallance had kept the best of everything for himself. They filled themselves to bursting, washing it down with delicious wines that went to their heads. They were sure the servants disapproved of their raucous toasts, "To the Gorge City Palace, To the Earl's Kitchens, To the Dragon Emperor!"

As she curled up on a featherdown mattress between silk sheets, Roza reflected she could get used to this for a night or two, after all her efforts and labours for the Empire, before she returned home to Albany.

The following morning, Roza found Standley busy investigating the Palace's maze of corridors and asked whether he'd like another treatment of Gymbo's Furniture Polish that they'd brought all the way from the cave on the plateau. He nodded enthusiastically, and Roza applied this to his wood in her room, as a thank you for all the help he'd been on their journeys.

When she and Jorxy were finally hungry enough for some breakfast, they had this in the dining room from the night before. Halfway through it, the Chamberlain approached them. "My apologies for disturbing you, Miss Warlock Rozabella, but there is someone at the Palace gates who insists that you know her. She is a paladin and goes by the name of Oxana."

Roza spluttered, and she and Jorxy shared a grin. "Of course. Show her in."

The Chamberlain returned a short time later, followed by Oxana, who was leading her younger brother, Banno, to stand before them.

Roza and Jorxy laid down their cutlery and faced their former companions.

Standing behind her brother, Oxana's hands gripped his shoulders. "My brother has something to say to you."

Banno swallowed hard, pale and trembling, as though in terror of being condemned to death. "Warlock R–Rozabella, and M–Mister J–Jorxy," he stuttered, "I'm s-sorry I betrayed you. I never meant you any pain or trouble. I only wanted to rescue you from the Plains Army, and I'd no idea that Morton man was a warlock. So, I'm sorry, and I ask you to forgive me."

Roza beckoned for Banno to come closer, and he did so. "Have you learned some lessons from this, young man? About who you can trust, and the consequences of your choices and actions?"

Banno nodded dumbly, looking down.

"Then we forgive you. We accept you had no malicious intent and were blinded by your desire for the reward. Do you still want to be a coin counter – no, what was it? – a treasure assistant?"

Banno looked up. "Yes, I do. And Lord Vallance said I have the potential to become a very good treasure official."

Roza let out a deep breath. "Well, you won't be working for Lord Vallance any more, but I guess the Dragon Emperor and I will still need some treasure assistants, if you're interested and your sister can spare you?"

Banno whirled around in glee to look at his sister, who answered for them both. "You are very forgiving, Warlock Rozabella, and we would both be delighted to help you in any way we can, if you can find use for us."

"Agreed. Welcome back on board for whatever comes

next. And if you're going to work for us, I'd better show you something."

She sent a servant for Standley to bring the backpack he'd carried on their journeys, the one with the Minimised chest of donations they'd received for her rejuvenations in Albany. That all seemed such a long time ago now.

"Banno, do you remember what I could do with the books up in the cave in the mountains?"

"Yeah, you could shrink them to fit in your pack and then grow them to read them."

"Well, this is our treasure chest," she said, resting a hand on its closed lid.

Banno surveyed it. "That's your chest full of treasure? It's a bit small. I thought you had more treasure than that."

"Yes, we do. But I Minimised it so we could fit it into Standley's pack and carry it around. Have a look." She opened the lid and revealed the miniature coins and the tiny gems and jewellery.

"They're all so small," Banno muttered, "they're not worth much."

"Watch," Roza said, and she lifted out Jorxy's Minimised ruby-encrusted chain of office that he'd received from Amber-Jane's Grandma Lily. When she began to Maximise it, Banno gasped beside her.

"Wait, you can enlarge treasure?" The boy couldn't believe what he was seeing.

"Yes, I can," Roza replied. "The coins too." And to prove her point, she pinched half a dozen miniature coins onto her palm and Maximised them to full size too.

"But this is amazing," Banno spluttered. "You can create as much treasure as you like."

"And I can make it giant size too," she said, and enlarged a gold coin up to the size of her whole hand. She gave it to Banno, who stared at it, heavy in his two hands. "Now then, young mister treasure assistant, how would you go about valuing that?"

The boy's lips moved soundlessly, then, "Umm … well … it would be worth a lot. There's so much gold here."

"Exactly." Roza took the giant gold coin back, Minimised it to normal size, and then reduced all the coins and Jorxy's chain of office to miniature again to fit inside her small chest. Banno was reluctant to hand back his heavy gold coin and looked dismayed when it all shrank and disappeared away.

"I remember you saying, Banno, that treasure is the most important thing in the world. But when I can do this to treasure, it's not that important to me. Since I can make more or less of it as I wish, a warlock's power to use magic becomes the most important thing in the world."

The boy was staring at her, nodding. "Yes, I can see that."

"And whatever we have, whether it's lots of treasure or lots of magic, what we do with it is more important than how much we have. In other words, what makes a difference to the people around us is whether we're greedy and selfish, or kind and generous. I have lots of magic, and can rejuvenate people from old age to youth, so I decided to share that with everyone I can. Whether you end up as a brilliant treasure official, or maybe learn some magic of your own, I hope you'll think about what I've said." She finished with a wink and a grin at the open-mouthed boy.

Their next duty was the public assembly of Gorge City's people, for which the Chamberlain came and summoned them. Roza, Jorxy, Oxana, Banno and Standley were led out to the courtyard and lawns in front of the Earl's Palace, where the Dragon Emperor lay in front of as many of the population who could fit into the space.

Roza looked up and gasped to see the streets and alleyways leading upwards, the gardens, balconies, windows, doorways and even rooftops as far as her eyes could see, all thronged with more people than she'd ever imagined. The whole city seemed determined to witness this, and when the

Emperor spoke, his voice reverberated around the gorge for everyone to hear him.

"Good people of Gorge City, I greet you with peaceful intentions and hope we can lay aside the quarrels of the past and begin a new age of prosperity and harmony for your city, for the Plains, and for the whole Sapien Empire. I regret that blood has been spilt between us, and I pay tribute to the fortitude of the Plains Army in defending your homes and freedom. But in truth, my dispute was not with you, my brave people, but with the last Earl of the Plains, the late Lord Vallance. As you may have heard, he died yesterday afternoon at your Western Gate, and so we pause in silence and respect, to remember the fallen on both sides, and to mark the end of his long and illustrious reign over your city and lands."

As the Emperor's words echoed away, a quiet fell across the multitudes gathered around the gorge, and Roza reflected that although she'd detested Lord Vallance, perhaps some here had trusted and respected him.

"But now, what of the future?" the Emperor went on. "I wish to make amends for the war that has been fought, to pay reparations to those who have lost loved ones. I long for a new era of prosperity for you, my people, and so I bring peace offerings for you today."

Roza sensed an uneasy expectancy among the people. Some might hope for a genuine fresh start in their relations with the Empire, but many more were probably suspicious of fine-sounding words that masked the same old oppressive regime.

"First of all," the Emperor declared, "you know that I have a very long list of all the duties, excise, fees, tariffs, taxes, tithes and tolls due to me from the people of the Plains. From today and for the foreseeable future, I hereby cancel them all, and you may keep the entirety of your hard-earned income and pay nothing of it to the Empire."

There was a stunned silence at this, followed by an

outbreak of murmuring. Some were no doubt trying to understand what the Emperor had just said, while others were waiting for the catch that went with it.

The Dragon Emperor interrupted their discussions. "You may wonder how I propose to fund the running of my Empire from now on without your taxes. Allow me to furnish you with an explanation. I have recently got to know the most remarkable young woman to have been born in the Empire throughout my long life."

A chill washed over Roza's skin that he was about to talk about her, and she would need to do or say something in response.

"I know you have heard about her already," the Emperor continued, "and yesterday I had the pleasure of bringing her with me. People of Gorge City, I present to you the uniquely gifted Warlock Rozabella of Albany."

Yep, sure enough, and Roza's limbs were trembling.

The Emperor turned his head towards her and murmured, "Miss Roza, feel free to identify yourself."

She felt utterly foolish but moved forward a few paces from where the others stood on the flagstones and lifted an arm in the air. For the first time, there was scattered clapping, a few cheers, and an audible sigh of wonder and excitement. Roza was bowled over at this reaction, that these former enemies might be craning their necks to catch their first glimpse of her, this world-famous young woman.

The Emperor was speaking again. "You may have heard rumours and reports that Warlock Rozabella has a wonderful magical gift, and I can confirm that all you have heard is true. She possesses the ability to Rejuvenate, to make people physically younger. Miss Rozabella, would you like to say anything about your offer of your gift, and since your voice won't carry, please say what you wish to me, and I will repeat it for everyone to hear."

Roza gulped. She should have prepared a speech. At least she had a few moments to think of what to say next while the Dragon repeated each sentence to the expectant throngs.

"Yes, thank you, Your Majesty. People of Gorge City and the Plains, I have always wanted to offer my gift of Rejuvenate to as many people as possible. While I was in Albany, crowds flocked there to receive my help, but they soon became too many for my small hometown to cope with. When civil war broke out between Lord Vallance and the Emperor, my first thought was to try to restore peace as quickly as possible. For this reason, I sought out our Dragon Emperor and have come here with him to establish that peace if I possibly can. The Emperor and I have agreed that I can Rejuvenate anyone here who wishes it, in a calm and orderly way, as soon as we arrange how to manage this. I emphasise that my gift will be available to everyone with no expectation that anyone pays me anything in return for it."

While the Dragon repeated Roza's last sentence, she glanced at Jorxy who rolled his eyes and grinned at her. She was relieved that the Emperor then continued himself, saving her the need to say more.

"Yes, I wish to stress also," said the Dragon, "that I will not seek to fund the running of my Empire through charging you for the use of Warlock Rozabella's gift, in case any of you were thinking that. She is a generous, caring, and public-spirited young woman who only wishes to serve and heal the people of the Empire."

This was met with the crowd's first genuine applause, and Roza felt she ought to acknowledge this with a visible sign, so she bowed towards the different sections of the people. This elicited some cheers and whistles, making her wonder whether she might even be winning them over.

"I ought to add," the Emperor went on, "that as part of my agreement with her, this impressive young woman insists that I act in a more generous, kind and respectful way towards my subjects. Hence why I began today by cancelling all my taxes. She has persuaded me that fear is no solid basis for a lasting peace, and that henceforth my relationship with you should be one of fairness, trust, and dare I say it, fatherly concern. She will hold me to account for how I act towards you, so feel free to complain to her if you think I am being unjust or oppressive, and no doubt she will proceed to tell me off."

As he said this, the Dragon managed to sound like a grumpy old man being teased by a beloved granddaughter, such that many in the crowd laughed. Roza couldn't believe how well this was going and decided to play her part by wagging a scolding finger at the Emperor, which prompted further laughs.

When the multitudes became quiet, the Dragon Emperor spoke again. "Which brings me to my second peace offering. Alas, we find ourselves today with no Lord of Gorge City or Earl of the Plains. Therefore, I have pleasure in announcing today that the successor to Lord Vallance in both these roles will be none other than Warlock Rozabella of Albany."

It took Roza some seconds to register what the Emperor had just announced. And then she froze in shock.

What?

No, she didn't want to be Earl of the Plains or ruler of the city. What was he talking about? She wanted to go home to Albany and come here from time to time to do some rejuvenating. She was also annoyed that the Emperor hadn't mentioned anything about this before announcing it.

But the crowds had erupted into ecstasy. A wild roar of cheering, clapping and whistling crashed into Roza and rolled around and around the Gorge. She saw people jumping up and down and hugging each other in excitement and delight at the news. That she would stay with them. That she would look after them.

Tears stung the backs of Roza's eyes at this welcome and embrace from complete strangers. She wiped her eyes and turned to glare at the Dragon Emperor, who had a mischievous glint in his eyes that revealed he'd enjoyed springing this surprise on her.

She whirled away from the Dragon and marched over to Jorxy instead. His mouth had dropped open, suggesting he hadn't known about it either.

Then he grinned at her. "Well, look at you, Earl of the Plains and all."

"Don't be ridiculous," she snapped. "I don't want to be Earl of the Plains or ruler of any city."

Jorxy gawped at her, waving an arm towards the Palace. "What? Didn't you enjoy those rather nice bedrooms and hot baths and delicious waiter-served dinners? Because I could get used to them."

"Shut up, because that's not the point. Of course I enjoyed them, but I don't know anything about being an Earl or how to rule a city. What am I supposed to do?"

He shrugged. "Well, you said you wanted to change the world, to make a difference to the Empire and improve people's lives. So, here's your chance to do that."

She stared at him, because that was what she'd said. "Oh, yeah." Could she give this a try?

"Listen, just say yes," he went on, "and then we'll sort out how to make it work. You'll have ministers and advisers to help you run the place, and we'll all help you, won't we?" He indicated Oxana, Banno and Standley, who were all nodding.

"But ..." Roza hesitated, "... but I'll miss Albany, and the plateau and cave, and my parents, if I stay here."

Jorxy chuckled. "You know, Roza, for a clever person, you're a bit dim sometimes. Have you forgotten you've got this little thing called the Teleport spell? You can disappear off to visit your mum and dad, say hello to the plateau whenever you want, and be back here with a flick of your arms. So, what's the harm in having a rather nice base for while you're in Gorge City?"

A slow smile spread across Roza's face and then she

laughed too. "Oh, yeah. Teleport. I'd forgotten about that. Warlock, that's me. Kind of handy, eh? Can live where I like and visit whoever I want. Great."

She clapped her hands together and turned back to the Dragon. The people of Gorge City were at last calming down from their joy at the announcement that she was their next Earl.

Roza said to the Emperor in a sarcastic tone, "Thank you so much for giving me advance warning of your little surprise. Why didn't you mention this minor detail before?"

"If I'd offered you the role, and you hadn't seen the overwhelmingly positive reaction of the people, would you have accepted it?"

Roza thought about that. "No, probably not. Would you now be kind enough to repeat my words for the crowds?"

The Emperor smiled and passed on Roza's message.

"People of Gorge City, or – dare I say it? – my people." This prompted another cheer. "Thank you for your enthusiasm. I apologise in advance that I am inexperienced at being an Earl or ruling a city, so please forgive me when I get things wrong. But I promise that I will do my best to serve you. As I said, my rejuvenation gift is at your disposal, and I wish to announce something else today. Following the excellent example of our Emperor, I am also hereby cancelling any and all taxes that are due to me as Earl."

The crowds erupted again, finishing up with a new chant of "Roza, Roza, Roza," and she couldn't help but laugh and bow to them. Before the people became quiet, she checked whether the Emperor, or anyone else, had anything further to say. When they shook their heads, Roza held up her hands and the Dragon repeated for her.

"My good people, one last thing before we all return to our homes. We have all suffered much in recent days, but this is a day of happiness and relief. Feel free to take the rest of the day off. No, on second thoughts, let's make it a week. Give yourselves a week of holiday, to celebrate with your families and friends, and please present the costs for it all here at the Palace, because I wish to pay for the whole party myself."

The people went wild with celebration, and Roza grinned at Jorxy, saying, "I think I like this ruling a city thing."

They turned and went back into the Palace with the chants of "Roza, Roza, Roza," still ringing in their ears.

CHAPTER TWENTY-SEVEN

The following morning, the wound on the Dragon's neck was sufficiently scabbed over for Standley to remove the bandage of sheets around it. The Emperor considered the situation to be safe and settled enough in Gorge City for him to fly away and attend to matters in the rest of his Empire.

Roza and Jorxy were sitting together after breakfast enjoying the morning sunshine on a veranda overlooking the Palace gardens when Kerenzi the spirit lord appeared out of thin air next to them. They both jumped and Roza told him off again for sneaking up on her invisibly.

Kerenzi helped himself to a comfortable chair and said, "You'll forgive that I've kept a low profile in recent days, but I thought I'd wait until that Dragon was out of the way. The Emperor doesn't like me, remember, so I steer well clear of those who hold grudges against me."

"I'm pleased to say you were completely wrong, Kerenzi," Roza snapped. "We've been perfectly safe throughout our dealings with the Emperor, and he has promised to change his ways and rule in a just and generous manner."

Kerenzi's eyebrows rose. "Perfectly safe, were you? Like when he breathed fire on you and tried to crush you? Don't lie to me, Roza, because I was there, and I saw it all."

She gaped at him. "You were there in the Emperor's fortress, invisible, in spirit form, and you didn't help us or reveal yourself at all?"

"Correct," Kerenzi replied. "I only said I wouldn't rescue you from him, not that I wouldn't come with you. I keep in touch with what's going on around the Empire, and your expedition to see the Dragon was far more interesting than mortals killing each other in battle around Gorge City. I've never taken much notice of your enchanted coat stand, Standley, but now I think I'll pay him a bit closer attention."

Roza stared at him in alarm. "Kerenzi, don't you dare do anything to sabotage our agreement with the Emperor."

Kerenzi held up a hand. "Relax, Miss Rozabella, all your secrets are safe with me. Besides, Standley is far too loyal to betray what you've commanded him, and far too noble-spirited to take advantage of the knowledge he possesses. Still, I'm sure you understand why I'll keep an eye on him, just as I'm sure you and the Emperor will too."

He gave her a wink, but Roza glared back.

"So, you've offered free rejuvenation to everyone in Gorge City," Kerenzi went on. "How will you avoid getting swamped like you did in Albany?"

"Actually," Jorxy butted in, "I've been thinking about that and come up with a plan."

Roza looked at him in surprise. "When were you going to tell me?"

"As soon as I had the chance. I am your Ideas Man, you know. We should use the Plains Army to organise the whole thing, because they've got less to do now they're not at war with the Emperor. We should rejuvenate the oldest first, because they need it most. We announce that anyone over the age of, say, eighty, can come down to the Palace first. Once they've been done, we invite anyone aged seventy-five to eighty, and so on, down the age groups. What do you reckon?"

Roza nodded. "Yes, that sounds good. And the Army keeps order with the queues and checks that everyone tells the truth with their ages."

"That's right," said Jorxy. "Plus, we say that anyone who has an age-related condition, such as blindness, deafness, heart, or whatever, can apply to the Army to be seen earlier than their age groups."

"Brilliant," said Roza. "And the Army healers can check those people, can't they? Which reminds me, I met a deaf girl, Madison, when I was a trainee healer for an evening up in those barracks. I could invite her to help us with all this."

Jorxy looked thrilled that she liked his ideas, but Kerenzi was rolling his eyes. "So, this is it, your grand plan, is it?" mocked the spirit lord. "You sit here for the rest of your very long lives and keep rejuvenating everyone again and again for as long as they want it? It's not proper immortality, is it?"

Roza glared at him again, affronted. "What do you mean?"

Kerenzi leaned forward in his chair. "What I mean, young Miss Roza, is that what you offer is endless mortality. If you stop what you're doing, everyone dies. That incoming tide of death is still coming for you all, and all you can do is stave it off for a while. My immortality goes on forever, whatever I do. You're just holding off an inevitable defeat for as long as you can, until eventually you become weary of the effort involved in your losing struggle."

The spirit lord's words cut Roza to the heart because they were true, but she wouldn't let him gloat about his own immortality. "Well, I'm very sorry we can't all enjoy your sort of immortality, Mister Kerenzi, but it's the best we mortals can manage, all right? So yes, I'll keep on rejuvenating everyone for as long as I can, because life is better than death, and youth and health are better than old age and frailty. So there."

Kerenzi held up a finger. "Are you implying that being young and beautiful is more important than being old and wise? Those of us who are wise and mature might question your youthful assumption that a beautiful appearance matters above everything else."

Roza shook her head, furious. He was playing his games and mocking her. "I'm not having this argument with you, Kerenzi. What I'm doing for people is both important and worthwhile, and I won't let you suggest otherwise." But his assertion that she couldn't offer true immortality niggled.

"As you wish," Kerenzi replied, and there was an awkward silence. Then he went on, "There's something else I've been pondering. Did old Warlock Philoe ever explain to you that longevity must be paid for?"

Roza racked her brains but couldn't remember that.

"He may not have mentioned it, but as I understand it there's this principle among mortals of a death for a life. There's a cost or a sacrifice required in order to cheat Death. So, with Philoe's longevity potions, he made others pay with their lives for his longer life."

Roza glared at Kerenzi, because she'd never told Jorxy that whole story.

"But with your gift," the spirit lord went on smoothly, "there doesn't seem to be a cost, does there? You've rejuvenated lots of people, and their longevity appears to have come for free. I don't get it. You should watch out for that, any cost, sacrifice or reckoning for all those beautiful, generous things you're doing. Because Death is not the sort to let anyone get away with anything."

Roza threw him an irritated grimace. "Thanks for the warning. And thanks for insisting on spoiling my happiness."

Kerenzi smiled back, seeming unconcerned about upsetting her. "So, you're the Earl of the Plains now. Did you know that the proper name for a female Earl is a Countess? How do you fancy being the Countess Rozabella of Gorge City and the Plains?"

Roza snorted. "I am not being a Countess. It makes me sound like a hundred years old. No, I am a female Warlock, so I can be a female Earl too. Why do we need different titles just because we're male or female anyway?"

"Whatever you say, Countess," Kerenzi replied, smirking, and Roza fumed. "And you've this fine city to run. Are you sure you know what you're doing?"

"Why?" Roza demanded. "Are you offering to help me?"

"Not really." He was still giving her that annoying smile.

"As I said, I need to be careful around that Dragon Emperor of yours."

"Listen, Kerenzi," Roza snapped. "Why don't you try to make your own peace with the Emperor? You probably heard that he's grateful you rescued me from Lord Vallance's dungeons so he's not going to kill you on sight. There are benefits in having friendly, trusting, peaceful relationships with people, you know."

"Hmm," mused Kerenzi. "You mortals have such short lives and memories that you forgive so quickly and easily. I, on the other hand, have much to remember, much to ponder and much to forgive. I choose not to be hasty in mercy until I see the fruit of the other's repentance. I will watch and judge the Emperor's actions for a while before I consider being reconciled with him."

Roza shrugged. "It's your loss. A friendship with him has proved beneficial for me. As you can see." She spread her arms to encompass the Palace buildings and grounds.

The spirit lord fixed his gaze on her. "Such trivial rewards for giving away your loyalty and trust. So, does your friendship with him imply that you won't be bleating for my help the next time you find yourself in a sticky situation?"

She sighed. This gorgeous, immortal spirit lord was being irritating again. He was still bewitchingly handsome, and they'd been through a lot together. She remembered the times they'd saved each other, and wished their relationship could return to that, instead of this mocking and teasing.

"Kerenzi," Roza said, "there was a time when you and I were on the same side. We were friends, we respected and helped each other. You used to find me interesting, or intriguing, or entertaining. Are you bored with me now?"

He looked at her, and when he smiled, it was genuine. "Not at all, my dear Miss Roza. I still find you one of the most delightful people alive in the Empire today. But you've changed and grown so quickly, and we immortals are slow to adapt to change. Forgive me when I treat you like the helpless seventeen-year-old girl chopping firewood in the forest or the captive in Warlock Philoe's cave. You are an impressive young woman now, influential, making a difference in the world, and somehow, I can't help feeling you've left me behind."

Roza smiled back. This was more like the old Kerenzi again. "Thank you, my old ally and friend. Yes, we've come a long way, haven't we? From unknown girl to Warlock of Albany, and now to Earl of Gorge City and the Plains and friend of the Emperor. But underneath all that, I'm still just Roza. You remember, Roza with a 'z'."

Kerenzi beamed and stood up. He stepped across and kissed her on the cheek. "Yes, I remember, Roza with a 'z'. And I'm honoured if I might still be your friend." He reached and shook Jorxy's hand. "And you too, Master Jorxy. Take care of yourselves, both of you. Feel free to call if you need anything because I'll be around." With that, he vanished back into invisibility.

They sat in silence for a while, and Roza soaked up the morning sun. She sensed Jorxy's gaze on her, so she turned to him. She didn't want to talk about Kerenzi, what he'd said, or his kiss, so she said, "And thank you too. You've been with me through all this."

His ugly, lopsided face broke into a grin. "No problem, my pleasure. We said it might be an adventure when we left Albany plateau, didn't we? And it hasn't been too bad, has it? Well, apart from throwing up the whole time that Dragon was flying us here."

Roza laughed. "And that time I was tied up in Bindweed." She shivered. "Anyway, we survived, and we're here. But Kerenzi was right about one thing. We've a lot of work to do, and much to learn about ruling a city. How about if we spend the next few days of holiday looking around this place? We could make an appearance at some of the celebrations – I'm sure they'd love that. We should explore this Palace and city and get to know people. What do you think?"

Jorxy nodded. "Sounds good to me. Take me to the party, Lady Roza."

She laughed again and stood up. She liked the sound of that.

Roza held out her arm and Jorxy hooked his through hers. Then together they re-entered the Palace and set off for the streets up into the city.

Roza's story continues in Book Three of the Immortality series,
End of Immortality.

Roza's journey began with the first book in the
Immortality series, *Cave of Immortality:*

What price for eternal youth?

Seventeen-year-old Roza doesn't know
she has a secret power.

When an ancient warlock kidnaps her because he needs
her for a potion he is brewing,
he discovers her unique and powerful gift.
But revealing her ability would plunge the whole Sapien
Empire into civil war to possess and control it.

Roza's valley is threatened with destruction,
and if her power is the only way to save it,
how can she keep it secret?

If you enjoyed this story,
you might also enjoy the *Destiny's Rebel* trilogy:

Can you escape who you're meant to be?

Kat never asked to be in line to be Queen.
Eleven days until she comes of age, and she feels
suffocated. Bullied by her guardians and oppressed by
expectation, Kat dreads the Coronation Day that will end
her dreams of freedom and adventure. She refuses to
surrender to her fate and runs away – straight into a
different kind of trap.
Will Kat get back to Anestra in time to save her Kingdom
from their enemies' schemes? Can she accept the fate from
which she flees? Can she, on this last quest, restore the lost
and broken Crown of Anestra with its sacred powers as a
relic of the Divine?
Kat's adventure weaves through treachery and intrigue to
discover the truth about herself, her friends and her place
in history.

ACKNOWLEDGEMENTS

The ideas behind this *Immortality* series grew out of realising that I am getting older. An essential part of our human existence is that we all age and must face the truth of our own mortality. But this prompted the simple story premise: what if someone could make people physically younger?

Whenever I have voiced this idea, the reactions have varied from wonder and excitement (Yes, please!), to an uncertainty about whether we'd want to live for ever in such a divided and troubled world. So, my first thanks are to all of you who have helped me to ponder about aging, mortality, death, eternal youth, living forever, rejuvenation, and an immortal life.

Thanks also to the young people in the schools I visit, for your constant encouragement and inspiration, and to my amazing cover artist James Hayball and cover designer Liz Carter. A special thank you to those who have read, commented, critiqued and made suggestions on the draft and proof copies of this story, especially Fran, Sheila, Rae, Paul, Jamie, Ellie, Daisy, Leo, Heidi and Savanna.

And my everlasting gratitude to my ever-patient family: to my wife Ann, our son Mark and his wife Nell, and our daughter Rachel, who forgive me (I hope) when I disappear off into my study, close the door, and revel in my imaginary worlds.

Philip S Davies, 2025.

ABOUT THE AUTHOR

Philip S Davies has been a full-time author since 2012, and the highlight of every week in term-time is to run Creative Writing Clubs in four local secondary schools.

His first books, the *Destiny's Rebel* trilogy, were bestsellers in Teenage and Young Adult Fiction at Blackwell's Bookshop in Oxford, and were Shortlisted as Finalists for the Crystal Kite Award from the international Society of Children's Book Writers and Illustrators in Los Angeles.

He spends too much of his time enjoying the beautiful view of an Oxfordshire valley outside his study window, while also wishing there could be mountains out there like those surrounding Albany.

You can find out more about Philip at:
www.philipsdavies.com

www.ingramcontent.com/pod-product-compliance
Lightning Source LLC
Chambersburg PA
CBHW030607170726
48283CB00002B/499